W9-CCK-145

LET'S MAKE A DEAL!

Gordon's eyes sharpened. "Yes, sir. I've made a discovery that I think will really interest you. I'm proposing that you and I create an expedition to explore it, creating a business deal to share resulting profits."

Sloan didn't change expression, despite Gordon's incredible effrontery. Why had Sophia admitted him? Sloan did not see people like this. He was, after all, Director of Peregoy Corporation and governor of the corporation's three planets, all of which were run both benevolently and with the tight control necessary to ensure that none of them would ever suffer Earth's fate. Most important, the stargates between worlds, those precious portals that made everything else possible, were so well guarded by the Peregoy Corporation Space Service that not even the Landry fleet could get through. And this arrogant puppy from a world with no central government, no ruling family, not even a common language—from a planet rife with constant "international" tensions and wasted resources—this unmannerly scrap of space jetsam wanted to make a deal with Sloan Peregoy?

He said frostily, "I am not interested in acquiring another mining asteroid."

"It's not an asteroid. It's another gate."

Sloan stared at him, for once unable to control his expression. But only for a moment. "There are no more gates. Everyone has looked."

"Not where I did. I'm the only one who knows where it is..."

BOOKS by NANCY KRESS

Sleepless: *Beggars in Spain • Beggars and Choosers • Beggars Ride • Sleeping Dogs*

Probability: *The Flowers of Aulit Prison • Probability Moon • Probability Sun • Probability Space*

Yesterday's Kin: *Tomorrow's Kin • If Tomorrow Comes • Terran Tomorrow*

Crossfire: *Crossfire • Crucible*

Oaths and Miracles: *Oaths and Miracles • Stinger*

The Soulvine Moor Chronicles (writing as Anna Kendall, YA): *Crossing Over • Dark Mist Rising • A Bright and Terrible Sword*

Yanked • Flash Point (YA) *• Steal Across the Sky • Dogs • Nothing Human • Maximum Light • Brain Rose • An Alien Light • The White Pipes • The Golden Grove • The Prince of Morning Bells*

Fiction Collections: *Trinity and Other Stories • The Aliens of Earth • Beaker's Dozen • Nano Comes to Clifford Falls and Other Stories • Future Perfect: Six Stories of Genetic Engineering • The Body Human: Three Stories of Future Medicine • AI Unbound: Two Stories of Artificial Intelligence • Fountain of Age: Stories • The Best of Nancy Kress*

To purchase Baen titles in e-book form, please go to www.baen.com.

THE ELEVENTH GATE

NANCY KRESS

PAPL
DISCARDED

BAEN

THE ELEVENTH GATE

This is a work of fiction. All the characters and events portrayed in this book are fictional, and any resemblance to real people or incidents is purely coincidental.

Copyright © 2020 by Nancy Kress

All rights reserved, including the right to reproduce this book or portions thereof in any form.

A Baen Books Original

Baen Publishing Enterprises
P.O. Box 1403
Riverdale, NY 10471
www.baen.com

ISBN: 978-1-9821-2526-4

Cover art by Bob Eggleton

First printing, May 2020
First mass market printing, March 2021

Distributed by Simon & Schuster
1230 Avenue of the Americas
New York, NY 10020

Library of Congress Control Number: 2020000512

Pages by Joy Freeman (www.pagesbyjoy.com)
Printed in the United States of America
10 9 8 7 6 5 4 3 2 1

For Jack

Thanks to my hard-working and efficient agent, Eleanor Wood; to Dr. Maura Glynn-Thami and Jack Skillingstead, my trusted beta readers, for their advice and support; and to my sister Kate, for her continuing cheer-leading throughout my long career.

MAJOR CHARACTERS

ON NEW CALIFORNIA

Sloan Peregoy, CEO of Peregoy Corporation

Sophia Peregoy, Sloan's older daughter and chief advisor, heir to all Peregoy holdings

Candace Peregoy, Sloan's younger daughter

SueLin Peregoy, Candace's daughter and Sloan's granddaughter, heir after Sophia

Captain Luis Martinez, captain of the *Skyhawk*, Peregoy Corporation Space Service

Scott Berman, leader of the Movement

ON GALT

Rachel Landry, CEO of Freedom Enterprises, head of the Landry Libertarian Alliance

Annelise Landry, Rachel's oldest granddaughter, Freedom Enterprises

Celia Landry, Rachel's granddaughter, Freedom Enterprises Vice-President of Mining Operations on New Hell

Jane Landry, Rachel's granddaughter, Freedom Enterprises Vice-President of Security

Caitlin Landry, Rachel's granddaughter, president of Galt University

Tara Landry, Rachel's youngest granddaughter

ON POLYGLOT

Philip Anderson, biologist, Polyglot International Environmental Service

PART I

"The elementary particles are certainly not eternal and indestructible units of matter; they can actually be transformed into each other. The world thus appears as a complicated tissue of events, in which connections of different kinds alternate or overlap or combine and thereby determine the texture of the whole."

—Werner Heisenberg

1

NEW CALIFORNIA

The wolves needed dusting again.

Sloan Peregoy rose from his massive karthwood desk and ran a finger over the film on the animals' gray pelts and yellow glass eyes. The cleaning bot should be able to do better than this. He said to the wallscreen, "Note to Morris: reprogram J84. Dusting."

Sophia entered Sloan's office. "Father, two more appointments."

Sloan glanced appreciatively at his daughter. His dead wife had chosen for Sophia the genetic template of a Mayan princess rather than Yvette's's own watery Nordic beauty, and the choice suited Sophia. Tall and strong-featured, she had inherited her father's drive, competency, and preference for formality. You couldn't engineer personality, but Sloan's famous luck had held with Sophia. She ran as much of Peregoy Corporation and its three worlds—four if you counted Prometheus, not technically a Peregoy planet but no one else was on it—as Sloan did, and Sophia was his sole heir. He'd made sure of that. Neither her sister nor Sloan's son, dead in the same plague that had killed Yvette, had possessed ability or inclination to govern.

But in line after Sophia—

Sloan didn't choose to ponder that long-term problem right now. He was tired. It had been a long day; beyond the window, two moons gleamed above his corporate headquarters' soaring towers. Sloan wanted his dinner, whiskey, and bed. The rejuv treatments could do only so much for someone as old as he was, and it was unlike Sophia to allow appointments this late. In fact, Sophia rarely facilitated appointments at all—that was Morris's job—so these must be important.

"Who are they?" He'd had his biweekly meeting with the full Board of Directors just this afternoon; it was unusual for something urgent to arise since then.

"SueLin," Sophia said. "I'm sorry, Father. She insisted."

Of course she did. Still, Sophia could have denied SueLin if she'd wanted to. That SueLin was here was testament to the one thing Sloan and Sophia disagreed on, which it looked like he couldn't avoid after all. Some distant day, SueLin, as Sloan's oldest grandchild, would inherit Peregoy Corporation. Sophia wanted her trained for that, which was why she maximized SueLin's time with her grandfather. Sloan, however, had other plans that he did not yet choose to share with Sophia. Too vague, still.

"Who's the other appointment?"

The sharply angled planes of Sophia's beautiful face hardened, which meant that she considered something important. "A spacer from Polyglot, who—"

"Why would I see a spacer from Polyglot?"

"—claims to have discovered something important. He's been vetted, and I think you should hear his story."

"You've already heard it?"

"I have."

Sophia said no more, and it wasn't like her to be so mysterious. Sloan didn't like it, but he trusted her judgement, even though Polyglot wasn't to be trusted. The planet was weak because it was not unified, a patchwork of individual nations. Nations, that outmoded concept, could never equal the efficiency and strength of a corporate state. It was amazing that once, on Terra, they ever had. Or so Luis Martinez informed Sloan.

He said, "Show in the spacer. What's his name?"

"David M. Gordon."

At least he wasn't a Landry. But then, no amount of vetting would have admitted a Landry.

"I know how busy you are—I'll see Gordon alone." They both knew that "alone" actually meant with Carl Chavez, Sloan's augmented and superbly trained bodyguard.

But Sophia said, "Without Chavez."

Sloan raised an eyebrow, but he trusted Sophia's judgment. She and Chavez left as David Gordon entered. He spotted the wolves and stopped cold. The taxidermist had captured well the animals' fierce, vanished vitality. "Wolves?"

So he recognized them. Most people did not; neither wolves nor anything like them had ever existed on any of the Eight Worlds. Gordon was short enough to suggest no genetic augments, more muscled than most spacers, younger than Sloan had expected. Handsome, with an unpleasant swagger. His eyes, deep brown, studied the wolves. "You had them gene-made? Of course."

Of course indeed. Wolves not only didn't exist on the Eight Worlds—they didn't exist on Earth. Almost nothing existed on the ruin that Earth had become. Had been allowed to become. Gordon might be intelligent, but he had the bad manners that flourished on Polyglot, the first-settled world, neither Peregoy nor Landry.

Sloan said deliberately, "Hello, Mr. Gordon. I'm Sloan Peregoy."

Gordon ignored the rebuke. "Why did you have the wolves made? And then kill them?"

"I didn't kill them," Sloan said, irritated. Further rebuke was necessary; Gordon didn't know as much as he thought he did. "They died of natural causes."

"Without breeding first?"

"Please state your business, Mr. Gordon. My time is limited." Sloan had no intention of explaining to this rude outsider that geneticists had been able to reconstruct the wolves from Terran DNA, but had not been able to create a female that could carry to term. Seven miscarriages had weakened the female; the last had killed her. The male had died alone and defeated, unwilling even to hunt in the preserve Sloan had created for him. Sloan kept them as a powerful reminder of what happened to a family that did not expand, did not breed strong heirs, did not continuously master its environment.

Gordon's eyes sharpened. "Yes, sir. I've made a discovery that I think will really interest you. I'm proposing that you and I create an expedition to explore it, creating a business deal to share resulting profits."

Sloan didn't change expression, despite Gordon's incredible effrontery. Why had Sophia admitted him? Sloan did not see people like this. He was, after all, Director of Peregoy Corporation and governor of the corporation's three planets, all of which were run both benevolently and with the tight control necessary to ensure that none of them would ever suffer Earth's fate. On Peregoy planets, everyone worked, everyone ate, everyone had medical care, everyone was educated. The small land masses on each planet were environmentally protected, the population kept optimal. Most important, the stargates between worlds, those precious portals that made everything else possible, were so well guarded by the Peregoy Corporation Space Service that not even the Landry fleet could get through. And this arrogant puppy from a world with no central government, no ruling family, not even a common language—from a planet rife with constant "international" tensions and wasted resources—this unmannerly scrap of space jetsam wanted to make a deal with Sloan Peregoy?

He said frostily, "I am not interested in acquiring another mining asteroid."

"It's not an asteroid."

"Or a drifting renegade moon."

"It's not a moon."

"I don't—"

Gordon said, "It's another gate."

Sloan stared at him, for once unable to control his expression. But only for a moment. "There are no more gates. Everyone has looked."

"Not where I did. I'm the only one who knows where it is, Director Peregoy. I—are you all right? Should I call your aide?"

"Certainly not," Sloan snapped, although he put one hand on his desk. Another gate . . . *not possible*.

But Sophia had vetted Gordon. If he was a habitual liar, or crazy, or in the pay of the Landrys, she would know. Sloan's intel network, both overt and covert, was superb.

He said, "Did you take your vessel through this alleged gate?"

"No. I don't know what's on the other side, but since the gates are always near a planet—or pretty near, anyway—and there isn't a planet on this side of the gate, I want a big ship under me before I confront whatever's beyond the gate."

"Why didn't you take this to the Landrys? Why me?"

Gordon made a face. "Libertarians—they don't agree on how to act, and with everybody doing their own thing, you're never sure that one Landry's thing won't derail another Landry's thing. I don't want to be derailed or delayed by endless discussion because everybody is equal."

"They do have a military organization." Although Sloan always wondered how Landry men and women, raised with doctrines of individuality and self-reliance as their supreme values, could become soldiers who had to take orders. But somehow they did, despite the fact that their independent businesses often ignored their home planet's best interests if it would make individual corporations more money.

Gordon said, "Yes, they have a military. But you have totalitarian control of Peregoy resources."

"That isn't accurate. I am a CEO, not a dictator."

"Is there any difference when the corporation *is* the state?"

Sloan scowled but wasn't about to digress into a discussion of political philosophy. *Another gate* . . .

There had always been only ten gates. Physicists said they were a natural phenomenon, inexplicably stable children of the unstable quantum flux. No one understood the gates' origins, not even after a hundred fifty years of trying. The gates were inexplicable, permanent, and immovable, not unlike the enmity between Landrys and Peregoys. Both families had been among the first to escape the dying Earth, and both had claimed planets connected by the newly discovered gates orbiting Earth's Moon. Both had defended their claims. In a bewildering new environment, facing unknown challenges, family was all the settlers had had, and they had built civilizations on it.

Polyglot, however, had been discovered by an eccentric without family, multi-billionaire Patrick Fenton. He had opened the planet to everyone who could somehow arrive there, resulting in a patchwork of remnants of Terran nations. That was possible only because, of all the Eight Worlds, Polyglot possessed the most land mass, the best climate, the most resources. Fortunately, each city-state was too small and uncohesive to mount any sort of challenge to the Peregoys. Branching off from Polyglot, Kezia Landry had managed to claim three worlds. Samuel Peregoy, Sloan's great-great-grandfather, claimed three more.

As space expansion continued, it was discovered that each new gate led to a different planet, hundreds of light-years apart but all—except for Prometheus—habitable by humans. The other seven were in the Goldilocks zone, each with breathable atmosphere and gravity close to Terra's, and no one understood that, either. The odds were infinitesimally small. Religions, theories, and demagogues had sprung up around this habitability, especially during the years of discovery. The map of the Eight Worlds became to every schoolchild everywhere as familiar as his own family's allegiances: the Landry Libertarian Alliance of Galt, Rand, and New Hell. The Peregoy worlds, all named for the lost nation Samuel Peregoy had hoped to recreate:

THE EIGHT WORLDS

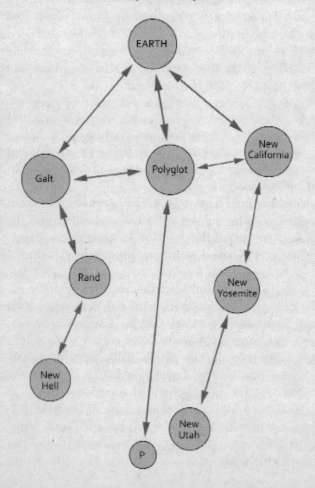

Sloan was not interested in where the gates came from or why they orbited only habitable worlds. All that was as abstract and pointless as Earth's ancient history. What mattered was the fact of the gates' existence, not their cause. What mattered was Peregoy Corporation's obligations to its citizens.

What resources or opportunities might lie behind an eleventh gate?

"Have you proof of this gate, Mr. Gordon?"

"I have. Spectrum readings and other scientific evidence."

Sloan said to his implant, "Sophia, I want three physicists from the university here immediately."

She said, "I already have them waiting."

Sloan moved toward a conference room, saying over his shoulder, "This way, Mr. Gordon." Gordon followed him.

SueLin would have to wait. Let her pout. She never wanted anything substantial, anyway. *Another gate . . .*

As Sloan passed the dead wolves, their dusty, glassy, yellow eyes gleamed at him in the overhead light.

David Gordon blinked at the size and opulence of the conference room. Well, what did he expect—this was *Sloan Peregoy*. Certainly no Landry had ever seen this gorgeous room with its curved walls softly programmed in shifting pastels—although if it hadn't been for Tara Landry, David wouldn't be here, either.

Not that the Peregoys would ever know that.

He'd been half afraid that somehow Sloan or his daughter would discover what he and Tara were up to. Weren't the Peregoys famous for their spy network? David must have passed initial vetting, but what about truth drugs or even torture? He'd heard stories…

Apparently the stories weren't true. Landry disinformation, maybe. Nobody seemed eager to drug or torture him. He and Tara might—could it happen?—actually get away with this desperate, necessary deception.

That would be worth the personal risk. David would be a hero, a man who had singlehandedly (well, almost) united worlds, maybe even averting a war. And, not incidentally, for the first time in his ramshackle life, he would be rich.

He sat down at the conference table, polished karthwood with inset holoscreens, and watched the scientists file in.

2

POLYGLOT

Near the sparsely settled northern pole of Polyglot, Philip Anderson walked across the savannah away from the jeebee nest, stripping off his protective gear. He glimpsed Tara Landry coming toward him and immediately turned around, jamming the helmet back onto his head. But putting on all the gear took too long and she was between him and the temple, so he resigned himself.

"Hello, Tara. What brings you to Polyglot?"

"You."

Direct as always. In Tara, it was not a virtue. They had met four years ago when Philip had given a lecture at Zuhause University on Polyglot, and she had not left him alone since. Her eyes ran over him hungrily, and Philip had to keep himself from flinching. Tara had tired of college and now spent most of her time on the Landry worlds or off in space doing gods-knew-what, but at least five times each year she ran him to ground. She was rich, genemod beautiful, brilliant, and—in Philip's opinion—crazy. Or at least severely unbalanced.

He said, "This isn't a good time for a visit."

"It's never a good time, according to you. Are you still doing this ridiculous thing with the jeebees?"

He had never liked that name for the flying creatures, more like dragonflies than bees, that pollinated many of Polyglot's plants. The first settlers had used Terran names to "keep our homeworld alive forever." It had not worked, of course; after a hundred fifty years, Philip was one of the few who regularly accessed the historical databases. Civilization on the Eight Worlds was still too raw, and in some cases too uncivilized, for much scholarly research. But now everyone was stuck with names like "New California," "Galt," "bees." Even "month" was still used to designate four weeks of seven days each and "year" to mean fifty-two weeks, though the Eight Worlds had different rotation and revolution periods and varying numbers of moons.

He said, "This project is *not* ridiculous. The villagers—" he waved in the direction of the settlement of Adarsh and its mostly Punjabi descendants—"are making money by selling the jeebees' nectar, and the jeebees are keeping away the lions." Another ridiculous name—the predators native to Polyglot looked nothing like lions. Smaller, smellier, and far more dangerous to humans, they hunted in deadly packs and had killed children herding the genemod Terran goats that this relatively poor area depended on.

Tara said nothing, just stared at him with that sexual intensity that made Philip so uncomfortable—but was that because his body responded to it? So far, he had resisted her, although she invaded his dreams. Those green eyes, husky voice, body... Not for the first time, he cursed her beauty, and his own that had attracted her. He couldn't help the way he looked. Also, while he was at it, he cursed the Libertarian Landrys that did not control where their offspring went or what they did there. If Tara had been a Peregoy, he never would have met her.

She still watched him without speaking. The sun beat down; Polyglot had only a one percent axial tilt and most places were grassland or, near water, forest. Sweat formed at the back of Philip's neck. To relieve the tension, he raised his wrister and brought up a holo image. "This set-up—using pollinators to keep away predators and also produce income—was tried on Earth, only there the bees were real, the protectees were big animals called elephants, and the predators were us. See—this is an elephant."

Tara didn't move her gaze from Philip's face. "Did it work?"

"No. Poachers still wiped out elephants before the Catastrophe did. But this might work here."

"It won't. Human nature doesn't change. The best you can hope for is a temporary, carefully constructed truce that will fall apart eventually. The predators always win. Phil—"

"No, Tara," he said, somewhere between gently and irritated. "I've told you over and over again. No."

"But I love you."

"I don't love you. I'm sorry, but I don't."

"Do you love somebody else?"

This was what he dreaded. She was unbalanced, she commanded huge resources, she had the ruthlessness of Polyglot "lions" taking down unprotected prey. If Philip did fall in love with someone else, what might Tara Landry do to her, or to him? He considered Tara dangerous.

"No," he said. "Tara, leave me alone!"

"I can't," she said. "I won't. I know you want me—do you think I can't *tell*?"

Philip stepped back; when past conversations had gone like this, Tara had not hesitated to stroke his crotch, which had instantly responded. This time, however, she merely said, "Would it make a difference to you if I did something so wonderful that it saved millions more lives than your jeebee plan ever could?"

"What are you talking about?"

"I can't tell you now. Not yet. Phil, you don't know me. I'm as idealistic as you are. I *am*. We want the same good things for the Eight Worlds. With my money—and don't try to tell me your parents left you enough money because I know exactly what you inherited—you could do such great things for everybody! I would help you, not to do these fucking little experiments but real, large improvements and creations! I would—"

"*No*. Tara, I'm sorry, but no. Not now, not ever. I'm sorry."

He braced for the explosion, but it didn't come. She smiled sadly and said, "All right. I can wait."

"Don't." He turned away and strode around her toward the temple, the one place she would never follow. He expected a tantrum, but she said nothing.

The temple was empty, its coolness welcome. Philip's parents had lavished augments on their only child, spending most of their money on his genemods. In the temple's dimness, his infrared vision spotted the lion behind the altar. It had slunk in to grab bread left as an offering. Philip froze.

The lion crept around the stone altar, and he and it stared at each other.

Philip's muscle augments made him fast, but not as fast as a Polyglot lion. But these animals hunted in packs, not alone. This one might be an outcast. Gray and very thin, it had been reduced to eating bread. Possibly it was being hunted by its own kind, as the old often were. Slowly Philip moved away from the door and, just as slowly, reached for the gun at his waist.

He didn't need it. As soon as the doorway was clear, the lion streaked through it, carrying away the bread. Philip darted back outside to watch it disappear into tall grass.

Tara was still there.

She wouldn't come into the temple. Both she and the lion had agitated Philip; never had he felt less like meditating. But that's what meditation was for: to calm agitation. Although ever since that day five years ago, he had aimed at so much more.

He knelt on a faded cushion. The temple, its walls ornamented with unskillful drawings of various gods, had been built by late-arriving settlers who'd spent all their money getting to Polyglot, which was why they now occupied such a leftover, poor island. The temple was made of foamcast, cheap and durable. The treasured golden Shiva brought from Earth had been stolen almost immediately, and a local artisan had carved one of wood brought from a distant forest. This had sat on the stone altar for a hundred years, flanked by dim, bacteria-generated electric lights instead of candles. Like the lights, Hinduism on Polyglot had evolved in ways that no *pujari* would recognize, although followers still left offerings of bread, berries, and flowers. The heavy, pungent odor of yellow *thlek* blooms filled the temple.

Philip was not Hindu. He went to whatever place of worship existed wherever his work for the perpetually underfunded Polyglot International Environmental Service took him. As long as the place of worship was quiet, he could indulge his own peculiar religious practice, which had also evolved in the last five years.

Most people on the Eight Worlds were Rationalist, that dry substitute for the human impulse toward the sublime. Religion, Philip had realized long ago, provided two things: comfort through the unseen and a sense of community. Denial of all "superstition" negated both. The Rationalists had sought to remedy that problem by founding a movement with "services" consisting mostly of scientific information, along with the social events, charity endeavors, and solidarity once provided by churches, temples, mosques, covens, synagogues. The Rationalists were a great success, flourishing even on Polyglot, where older forms of worship also existed.

Philip had never liked Rationalist services. He appreciated science, of course; his training was in biology. But Rationalism lacked passion. In addition, he could never shake the idea, unproven but powerful in his mind, that there were other valid ways of perceiving and experiencing the universe. So he had tried Buddhism, Hinduism, Druidism, charismatic Catholicism—anything he could find. None of it satisfied him, although he did learn to meditate deeply.

Then, five years ago, it had happened, and not while he was meditating.

There were no words for "it," and Philip had stopped trying to find them after his stumbling explanations evoked only pity, or dismissal, or scorn. He couldn't even find words to clarify it to himself.

He knew all the biological explanations: meditation redirected blood flow in the brain away from areas that perceived bodily boundaries, resulting in "out-of-body sensations." Neuron-firing disturbances in the limbic produced religious hallucinations. He knew the psychological explanations: wish-fulfillment, sensory delusions, anxiety alleviation. He knew the philosophy: logic was one way of perceiving the world, but is it arrogant to assume it is the only way?

He knew what had happened to him.

No, he didn't know that—he knew only that *something* had happened, something as real and grounded as the cushion under him now. He had been in New Chengdu on assignment for the Environmental Service, walking by the Ocean of Aromatic Waters, named by the first inhabitants of the island. The waters might have been aromatic once, but this morning they smelled of dead fish washed up by a storm. Philip, barefoot, had just finished meditating and was thinking vaguely about lunch. All at once ocean, fish, and his own body disappeared. He was somewhere else, somewhere without form and possibly without substance, and in the presence of something calm, majestic, and so multiple that he could discern nothing individual, only a great whole of which he was now a part, as vast number of colors make up white light. He was somewhere definite in the universe, but he didn't know where.

Time did not exist, yet when Philip returned to his body, dusk had fallen and Polyglot's two moons cast silvery paths on a calm, dark sea.

He'd sunk down to the sand and tried to go back to wherever he'd just been. He couldn't. Ever since that day, he'd been trying to go back, so that he could understand what he'd touched. He'd never succeeded, and the master meditators he'd talked to had all tried to correct him: If he'd attained *satori*, there wouldn't have been other presences, nor a sense of physical place.

The masters were wrong. What Philip had experienced was just as real as this shabby Hindu temple, as the ache developing in his neck, as the planet turning under him. He would reach it again, maybe today.

And if he couldn't, he could at least stay here until Tara gave up and went home.

3

DEEP SPACE

The Peregoy cruiser approached the uncharted eleventh gate. *There*—it showed on the viewscreen, a gorgeous lacy shimmer against the blackness of space, its sensory data creating the same incomprehensible pattern as the other gates. David Gordon's fists balled in excitement.

David wasn't captain on the *Samuel Peregoy*; Sloan hadn't agreed to that. Well, much as David had wanted to captain her, the decision made sense. He'd never had the conn on something as big as this; the ship was undoubtedly armed in ways David wasn't familiar with; Sloan wanted to control, if only by proxy, whatever action might lie on the other side of this new gate. Peregoys were big on control.

At the command console on the spacious bridge sat Captain Magda Peregoy, some distant relative of Sloan's. Keep it all in the family. David had always thought it was weird the way all Peregoy kin had that same last name no matter who their other parent was.

So did the Landrys. Arrogant—not that arrogance was always a bad thing.

He sat beside the captain, watching the gate grow from an instrument detection to that mysterious shimmer an irregular kilometer across. Unlike many spacers, David had never tried to understand how or why the gates existed. The best guess was something to do with plasma cosmology and the quantum flux, whatever that meant. It didn't matter. The only things that mattered were that the gate existed, he had found it, and it was going to make him some degree of rich, depending on the planet that lay on the other side. It might be lush and fertile, a new part of the Peregoy empire, with David receiving a percentage of all immigration fees. It might be useful for mining. It might—worst case—be fit only for tourist viewing from orbit if, say, it was in such early formation that it was geologically violent. David would still get a percentage of fees. But he expected better than that; all planets beside gates had, so far, been habitable by humans even if, like the Landry mining planet New Hell, only barely.

"Thar she blows," David said. The captain and her crew ignored him. Maybe they didn't get the reference, or maybe they were just as much uptight pricks as Sloan Peregoy. No matter.

Sloan knew his business. David, accustomed to the bureaucratic licensing delays and credit problems that were the inevitable fate of his small-time expeditions from Polyglot, had been astonished at how fast Sloan had been able to create this enterprise. Less than a week to equip the ship with personnel and supplies. Then a few days on conventional drive through the

New California-Polyglot gate. A week to the Polyglot-Prometheus gate, farther away from Polyglot than any other gate from its planet. Why? No one knew. From the dwarf planet Prometheus, an entire month in deep space to this lonely shimmer much farther from Prometheus than other gates from their planets.

The executive officer said, "Captain, there's a ship following us."

"Identify?"

"Just a minute . . . got it. Class 6A vessel."

It was a small Landry ship. But then, David already knew that. Only—the ship was supposed to be here already, waiting at the gate, not just now arriving. Certainly not behind the *Samuel Peregoy*. That was the *plan*.

The captain said, "Full speed ahead. We can reach the gate first."

Disaster! The *Samuel Peregoy* would reach the gate first, go through, and claim the gate—depriving David of his chance to be part of history. And Tara had planned this so carefully! The Landry ship was supposed to be waiting at the gate. It was supposed to pass through simultaneously with the Peregoy ship, and both families would thus own the gate and the planet beyond. They would be forced to cooperate, which would be the opening wedge to defuse a rivalry growing steadily more dangerous. And David would be a part of that. He would be a fucking *hero*.

Although, on second thought . . . maybe this was better. In Tara's plan, all the money to be made from a new gate and a new planet would be split between the ruling families, with David taking his percentage from the Peregoy share. But if the *Samuel Peregoy* went alone through the eleventh gate, only Peregoy Corporation—which meant Sloan—would own the discovery. David's take had just doubled. Of course, now the new gate wouldn't help bring peace . . . but hadn't the Eight Worlds managed for a hundred fifty years to avoid an actual war? A few skirmishes in space, money spent building weapons, a lot of tension . . . but no war. It could just go on like that. Maybe this was better.

The exec said, "Gate perimeter imminent."

The captain said, "Proceed through."

The passage felt like nothing much: a shimmer on the screen, a nanosecond blip on the sensors, no different from any other gate. As a citizen of neutral Polyglot, David had gone through Peregoy gates and Landry gates. He hadn't yet gone through this one, nor even approached it ever before—despite the lies he'd told Sloan. Only Tara had gone through, when she had first found this gate. She could have claimed it for the Landrys but instead had chosen to set in motion this idealistic plot. When she hired David to approach Sloan, he'd been a little surprised at her scheme; when he'd known her on Polyglot, she hadn't seemed like the idealistic type. They'd had some good evenings in bars, some athletic sex, but then she'd fallen hard for some visiting lecturer at the university and tossed him out of her bed. Still, they'd kept in touch, and she'd always been interested in David's spacer exploits, especially the ones a bit outside the law.

"We're through, Captain," the exec said. And then, unable to keep surprise out of his voice, "Object just ahead!"

David felt his mouth form an O. *Not possible.*

No human had been through this gate except Tara,

once and very briefly. That's what she'd told him. That meant this object was ... had to be ...

"Tracking now!"

The object, magnified, skimmed across a viewscreen. David couldn't get a clear idea of its size. But it was clearly in orbit around the planet ahead, which showed heavy cloud cover. The orbital was cylindrical, featureless except for a short projection that was—had to be—a landing dock.

An alien landing dock. How had Tara not seen this? But she'd said she only stayed a moment beyond the gate, and the orbital might have been on the other side of the planet. But an orbital this close to the gate meant that the aliens—unthinkable word!—knew about the gate. Why hadn't they ever gone through it? Why were they unknown to the human universe?

It didn't make sense.

Captain Peregoy's voice held the undertones of someone exerting control to keep herself steady. "If we see them, they see us. Initiate contact."

The exec started a prerecorded message. Someone had planned for the improbable. The message sounded on the bridge and, David guessed, went out to the orbital on all possible wavelengths. First were tones giving a sequence of prime numbers, repeated twice, and then, "This is the Peregoy Corporation Space Service ship *Samuel Peregoy*, Captain Magda Peregoy commanding. We come in peace. Please answer."

On the bridge, tension prickled like heat.

Nothing.

The exec said, "No other objects detected in orbit, ma'am."

The orbital disappeared behind the planet, then

reappeared. The exec said, "Length is ten meters, diameter four meters."

The thing was small—smaller than Sloan's office. The message from the *Samuel Peregoy* repeated constantly for an hour. Were they conferring, down there on the planet? As it turned, David glimpsed the blue of ocean, plus a brown tip of land mostly still under cloud cover. Was anyone there? Maybe this was the sole orbital still in the sky after the civilization that put it there had decayed or perished. After all, that had happened on Earth. Only semi-savages were left on Earth, people whose culture had degenerated to practically iron age. David had read once, or maybe been told, that all sentient civilizations unable to spread to other planets would eventually destroy their own. Too many beings using up too many resources.

Captain Peregoy said, "Prepare to launch a scout to rendezvous with orbital."

A bubble of excitement rose in David's throat, heady as champagne. "Captain, you have four scouts aboard and you'll need one to streak back through the gate and file the Peregoy claim. You should reserve the others, in case anything happens to the first one going back—after all, the Landry ship is so close, just the other side of the gate. And I fly scouts, so I know that nothing you have aboard will be able to dock on that small platform. We don't even know how to secure the scout alongside—look, there's no apparent mechanism. But I can put on a suit and get over there on a vacuum sled. I can see if there's any way to open any door. You'd be risking only me, not a scout and not anyone from your crew."

The captain eyed him. "All right, Gordon. If you fail, we'll try something else."

He was expendable, now that he'd taken the ship to the gate location that Tara had given him. Maybe the captain even had orders to risk him first if any danger arose, thereby saving Sloan from paying David his future percentages. David didn't care. He was a spacer and this was what he lived for—along with the percentages, of course.

Ten minutes later, just as he finished checking and donning his suit, he entered the airlock, waiting for the ship to match trajectory with the orbital. When it did, the vacuum sled shot out, automatically following directions to rendezvous with the orbital. The *Samuel Peregoy* flew close beside. David saw its scout launch and fly back toward the gate. The captain was sending it back to file the Peregoy claim.

The Landry vessel still had not come through the gate.

David easily caught a projection on the side of the orbital. "A series of projections," he commed to the ship, "along the side above the loading dock. Conveniently spaced for handholds—lucky. But they don't seem to lead to any door . . . no, wait, there's something there, are you getting it on cam? A round hatch, you have to look really hard to find it . . . I'm pulling myself toward it."

"We have you on visual," Captain Peregoy said.

"Good."

David reached the hatch. He grasped a slight projection in the middle and pulled. Nothing. He twisted it, and the hatch easily opened. "I'm in. The opening is very small. Maybe they are, too—I'm barely going to fit through this hatch. No airlock. This isn't inhabited."

Odd. The orbital was big enough to enter, but no airlock.

"Received. Proceed."

David wriggled inside and floated. He brightened his suit lights.

"I'm in a completely bare area, a half-cylinder—the space is divided along its whole length. The interior sort of resembles an unfitted cargo shell. Absolutely nothing here . . . no, wait, there's a hole in the divider, at the far end. Going toward it now."

Captain Peregoy said, "Nothing? No equipment or markings of any kind?"

"Nada. Pulling myself through the hole headfirst . . . Christ, it's a tight fit. I see something at the far end of this deck . . . oh my God!"

His headlamp showed the machinery clearly, and David recognized it instantly. The timer light glowed red, enough light to see the small, distinctive, unmistakable manufacturing logo.

The bitch.

"Go!" he screamed into the commlink. "A Landry bomb! Get away! It's going to—"

The nuclear device exploded, vaporizing the orbital, David, and the *Samuel Peregoy*.

The scout plunged into the gate.

Tara watched the Peregoy scout emerge from the gate and speed away. Had it witnessed the explosion? Of course it had. Otherwise it would be the *Samuel Peregoy* coming back through the gate. She sat frozen at the controls of her small ship, the *Waterbird*, unable to move, able only to think, and to wish that she couldn't.

It wasn't supposed to happen this way.

A larger Landry ship, a day away from the gate, awaited orders. That was what it was supposed to do: wait. It had been waiting a week for Tara to arrive. The plan had been for Tara to reach the gate and issue orders. Those orders would have been for the Landry cruiser to match speed with the Peregoy vessel, so that both ships went through the gate at the same time, establishing a joint claim to the new planet. Then, once they'd spotted the orbital, both captains were supposed to do what any prudent captain would do: send down scout ships to investigate the orbital. Both scouts would be destroyed when they jointly breached the orbital. The two cruisers would witness that, as well as what Tara had seen when she'd gone through the gate the first time.

Lights on the planet below.

There was life down there. An alien civilization. Not capable of space flight; they had nothing in orbit and probably didn't even know the gate was there. But they would be assumed to own the orbital that Tara herself had put there on her second trip. The aliens would be assumed to have blown up Landry and Peregoy scouts. Necessary casualties. The aliens would be assumed to be the enemy.

The enemy of my enemy is my friend.

Landry and Peregoy united in a common cause, which they would win because how threatening could a civilization be if it didn't even have space flight? Landrys and Peregoys might eventually discover that the aliens hadn't planted the orbital bomb—but how? The evidence would be gone and the aliens wouldn't speak human languages. Even if they did learn English and denied the bomb, who would believe them? Anyway, by that time Tara would have created the alliance. No one would ever know that, but Philip would be impressed with her nonetheless: the heroine who had created peace by rushing the news to the Eight Worlds. That was what was supposed to happen.

But—the *Waterbird* had been crippled by a comet strike and repairs had taken so long that she arrived at the gate after, not before, the *Samuel Peregoy*.

But—the idiot captain of the *Samuel Peregoy* had somehow gotten his cruiser, not just a scout, blown up.

But—no Landrys had died, only Peregoys. Tara had created a war, but not against any unknown aliens.

"Ms. Landry, this is Captain Albrecht! Repeat, this is Captain Albrecht! Please answer!"

Slowly the voice penetrated Tara's mind. How long had the captain of the Landry cruiser been hailing her? How long had she sat, frozen, in her stationary ship? *Think*. She had to think.

"Ms. La—"

"Yes," she said. He would have tracked the *Samuel Peregoy* going through the gate. "We've lost the gate claim. Yes. Proceed to and through the gate to survey what planet is on the other side. We might as well get whatever information we can. I will wait to accompany you through."

"Received. Will comply."

Tara thought furiously. She had to salvage what she could from this debacle. Maybe there was still some way to turn Peregoy vengeance away from the

Landrys and toward whatever lived on the planet. Maybe the Peregoy explorer on the orbital—maybe David Gordon—hadn't had time to send a message to the scout before he was vaporized. If they hadn't realized the orbital was Landry...

"Ms. Landry," said the captain, sounding surprised, "we just received a delayed message from the Peregoy scout. It says, in its entirety, 'Landrys, you won't get away with this! We have a recording!' Your desired action?"

Tara forced herself to say, "No action. Proceed toward gate." The Peregoys had a recording. She was fucked.

Philip. She must keep Philip from knowing what she'd done. A good thing David Gordon was dead. He wouldn't have had time—she hoped—to name her specifically. The Peregoys would know this was a Landry act of war, but not which Landry.

Philip must never know.

She said, "Captain, change of orders. I'm going to proceed toward the gate. Wait for me to join you."

"I don't advise that you—"

A shimmer, a brief blip on the screens, and she was through.

Nothing—no debris, no clue that a deadly cargo shell and a doomed cruiser had ever existed this side of the gate. There was only the planet, below. Its cloud cover was dissipating.

The land along the coast of a continent gleamed with city lights.

4

GALT

Rachel Landry, CEO of Freedom Enterprises and head of the Landry Libertarian Alliance, strode through its glass and marble corridors. It had been too long since anyone had seen Tara.

Despite her age, she walked vigorously, long legs moving from the hips, arms swinging. Two techs scurried out of her way. She stopped by a large window overlooking the Galt spaceport. A research ship funded by Caitlin's division was just lifting off, bound for Rand's moon. Scientists aboard had a series of physics experiments planned for both the moon and the Galt-Rand gate. Once, long ago, Rachel might have been with them. By now, however, the physics she knew was probably all out of date.

Or maybe not. Most of humanity's hundred fifty years of space settlements had been devoted to building on the worlds gifted by the gates. Science had stagnated. Only recently had Freedom Enterprises been able to afford the luxury of pure research.

And the Peregoy worlds? Was that old horror Sloan Peregoy appreciably advancing science in his tightly controlled "benevolent dictatorship"? Rachel didn't know, although probably scientists on the three Landry worlds did. Peregoy, who tried to control everything and everybody, couldn't control the exchange of scientific knowledge, and Rachel, of course, would never try. The only control on Landry worlds was in the all-volunteer army, and that was Jane's responsibility.

The research ship rose into the sky. Immediately afterward, the protestors flooded back into the area, shouting their chants and activating their holo signs. A huge one in letters simulating red flames said GIVE US JOBS!

Rachel snorted. No one "gave" jobs. If you couldn't find one, then start some sort of enterprise yourself. There were whole sections of Galt and Rand still unclaimed, where an ambitious person could start a farm, a business, an entire town. This youngest generation . . .

No, that wasn't fair. There were plenty of self-reliant individuals in her granddaughters' and great-grandchildren's generations. Just not out there among the protestors. Still, decades, like eras, have moods, and the mood of this one was militant. It had been otherwise when Rachel was born, almost ninety years ago. Everyone had been caught up with working out the principles of this new, brave, Libertarian society on Galt and Rand and, later, New Hell. Free trade, free living, free people. Back then, they hadn't even had an army. But with the explosive growth of unfettered business had come not only prosperity but smaller, faster ships than the ones that had ferried the fortunate

from the dying Earth. That had led to competition
for more gates, to acts of piracy, to the necessity of a
military fleet. Now, however, a slowdown of business
had produced a recession. This was all cyclical, of
course, an inevitable blip of free-market capitalism,
but right now it was producing a lot of discontent.

Rachel craned her neck to see the last of the
research ship, but it had already disappeared, and
here was Annelise walking toward her with a tablet
in her hand. "Rachel—I was just coming to see you.
We have a problem."

When didn't they? Annelise, the eldest of Rachel's
five granddaughters, was heir to the leadership of Freedom Enterprises. As Rachel gradually shifted responsibility to her, Annelise's load of problems increased.
Before Annelise could start in on whatever the new
issue was, Rachel said, "Have you heard anything from
Tara in the last month or so?"

Annelise's mouth turned down at the corners. "When
do I ever hear from Tara? What's she done now?"

"Nothing that I know of. But she's been gone much
longer than usual."

"She'll be back when she gets bored. Nowhere but
Galt has enough amusements to distract Tara."

Not true—Polyglot did. Or might. Rachel had never
been there. Well, maybe after she retired.

Annelise's face softened. "Don't worry. She always
comes home. Although not, of course, to do any
useful work. You should never have settled that trust
fund on her."

Rachel didn't feel up to this old, old argument, nor
to pointing out that after Paul, her only child, died,
Rachel had felt mortality heavy on her heart and so

had settled money on all five of his daughters. She hadn't realized then that four of them would grow up to squabble continuously, while Tara, the youngest by fifteen years, would refuse to become involved with her sisters, with Freedom Enterprises, with the minimal government on Landry worlds. Or, as far as Rachel could tell, with anything else. Did Tara care about anything? She was a mystery to her grandmother.

Rachel said to Annelise, "What's the problem?"

"The refugee camp."

Of course. Rand was having one of the periodic plagues that affected humans on any world they had not evolved to inhabit. Microbes, evolving so much faster than humans, jumped species and adapted themselves to colonize these new hosts, which then developed immunity against them. Or not.

Rand, however, by the luck of the genetic lottery, had more pathogens that could colonize human bodies than did any other of the Eight Worlds. This particular epidemic, like the one that had killed Paul and his wife, was not responding to medication. Many had survived the disease. However, many more had used whatever resources they had to flee from Rand to Galt, where there were neither enough jobs for them nor, on a Libertarian world, any mechanisms to provide free food, shelter, health care, education. Private charities assisted because they chose to, and Rachel, moved by pity, had contributed to these. At the same time, she admitted to a scorn for able-bodied men and women who could not, or would not, think of ways to provide for themselves. Although the heart-rending holos of ragged and hungry children . . .

Annelise didn't appear to possess much pity. "The

refugees are holding two charity workers hostage until Freedom Enterprises provides them with, basically, a free living. Jane wants to send in the army."

This was bad. There had never been terrorists on Galt, where everyone was raised to assume responsibility for themselves and their children. The same was true on Rand, of course—or was it?

Rachel said, "Are the refugees mistreating the charity workers or threatening to kill them?"

"No, of course not!" Annelise actually sounded shocked; a free people did not terrorize each other.

"Then tell Jane no. The charity workers assumed the responsibility for going to the refugee camp, which means they assumed the consequences. But I want you to do two things, Annelise. Offer to loan refugees the cost of passage back to Rand now that the plague is over, provided that each one who accepts will sign a contract to repay over ten years at six percent interest. Second, hire a group to go to Rand in order to survey schools. I want a report on the state of teaching of, and adherence to, Libertarian principles. At every age level."

"Got it," Annelise said. "Did you ask Caitlin about Tara?"

This was a concession. Paul's five daughters mostly did not get along well with each other—and why was that? It was a mystery to Rachel, since each one alone was competent and even—periodically, at least—lovable, but none argued as much as Annelise and Caitlin. Caitlin, president of John Galt University, constantly wanted more money to run it than Annelise would put in the corporate budget. "A university is no different from any other institution," Annelise always said. "It should be self-sufficient."

"Only someone completely ignorant of higher education would think that," Caitlin retorted.

"I wouldn't know, since I never attended your university, did I? I was too busy taking over the business and raising three children."

"Your choice, right?"

Sometimes Rachel just wanted her granddaughters to shut up.

However, Caitlin was the only sister that Tara would even speak to. Tara seemed to respect Caitlin, who was less dogmatic than Annelise or Celia, less harshly judgmental than Jane. Caitlin reported that Tara had asked her all kinds of questions about the field of biology.

Rachel took a corporate flier the short distance to the university. Caitlin was teaching the one class she'd kept in addition to her administrative duties. It soothed Rachel to slip into the back and listen to the serious questions posed by these advanced students, even though Rachel knew next to nothing about virology.

"Hello, Gran," Caitlin said after everyone had left. She was pretty enough but not as stunningly beautiful as her four sisters. Her features, except for her unusually sweet smile, were unmemorable, and the bright green eyes of the others were faded to hazel with green flecks. Intelligent and imaginative, she'd been trained as a virologist and had chosen the academic life over business, and she ran Galt University to very high standards. But it was Caitlin's sense of balance that Rachel valued most. Balance sometimes seemed in short supply among the Landrys.

She was also perceptive. "Gran—is anything wrong?"

A lot was wrong, but Rachel confined herself to the

immediate problem. "Have you seen Tara? Or heard from her? She's been gone for months."

"No. Did you send a tracer to Polyglot?"

"No. Should I?" Getting a message to Polyglot meant sending a ship or a drone with the physical embodiment of the data through the Galt-Polyglot gate, then beaming it down to the Landry embassy on Polyglot, which would then trace Tara. To contact New Hell, two gates away, was even more cumbersome and time-consuming. Somebody needed to invent the ansible.

Rachel said, "Why do you think Tara might be on Polyglot?"

Caitlin hesitated. Rachel put a hand on her grand-daughter's arm.

"Caity, if you know something, tell me. I'm getting really worried about her."

"Well...all right. Yes. You remember I told you that Tara showed this sudden interest in biology, asking me all these questions, which I thought was pretty uncharacteristic. It turns out she's in love with some biologist on Polyglot."

"In love? And she wanted it kept secret? *Is he a Peregoy?*"

"No, of course not. He's a Polyglot citizen. But apparently he's not in love with her and she's doing everything she can to interest him."

Rachel didn't like the sound of that—with Tara, "everything she can" could be extreme. "What's his name?"

"I have only a first name: Philip. From the kind of questions Tara asked, he might be involved in some sort of environmental applications of biology, rather than pure research."

It wasn't much. But it was more than Rachel had had before. Only...

An embassy tracer might not be enough. She would have to send someone to Polyglot to find Tara, or at least this "Philip."

No—she would have to go herself. If Philip knew anything, he would be most likely to tell a distraught grandmother, not a stranger unconnected with Tara.

At the thought of leaving Galt, even on a mission like this, Rachel felt her spirits lift. She could have a short respite from the growing list of problems on the Landry worlds. Maybe even a chance to talk with a few physicists on neutral Polyglot, see if her knowledge of physics was as outdated as she thought. She could learn the latest research on the many mysteries of the gates. Maybe there were even new ideas on the biggest of those mysteries: why gates formed only beside human-habitable planets. Yes.

On the way back to corporate headquarters, Rachel wondered if the protestors were still waving signs and chanting, demanding things be given to them. Determined to bring down her society and its Libertarian principles.

The flier skimmed toward headquarters. The protestors were still there.

5

POLYGLOT

Philip paused on the beach to gaze back at the factory on the ridge, which belched black clouds against a bright sky.

Folly. Before him lay the kelp farm, producing sustainable, low-cost, nourishing raw material for a variety of foodstuffs. Behind him stood the same kind of polluting madness that, by ruining Earth, had sent humanity to the stars in the first place. Didn't anybody ever learn anything?

No, that wasn't fair. Polyglot, by decree of its eccentric discoverer a hundred fifty years ago, was open to any nation, which meant that it *had* nations with their different governments, flags, ideas about resources. The planet was basically one huge ocean dotted with lush islands, none quite large enough to qualify as a continent but nearly all large enough to host a colony with farming, mining, diverse biomes. Most of the city-states practiced at least basic eco-preservation, but Sparta was an exception. The founding family, a Greek oligarchy rich on Earth, had grown even richer by mining the plentiful ores on their island, manufacturing them into machine parts, and selling them to everybody else. The Spartans didn't seem to care what they did to Polyglot as a whole, and the weak Council of Polyglot Nations, for which Philip indirectly worked, couldn't seem to make them care.

It had been a frustrating two weeks, especially after his success with Adarsh. The villagers were happily selling jeebee nectar and the jeebees were keeping lions away. Whereas here in Sparta, Philip had completely failed.

And yet he had requested this posting. Sparta was Greek Orthodox, at least nominally, and Philip had heard of a Christian mystic living here, a woman who apparently not only acted as parish priest but also experienced something like the religious transports of Jeanne d'Arc, Saint Paul, and Saint Teresa of Avila. Even though Philip believed—mostly, anyway—the biological explanations that temporal-lobe epilepsy caused such transports, he was getting desperate. Five years without being able to re-experience whatever he had touched on that other Polyglot beach. Five years of seeking for something he couldn't name, or even adequately describe. Five years of a lunatic quest after the only thing he wanted, longed for, was driven to find, even as he questioned it. Why did he need so badly to touch something beyond this mortal life?

Why didn't everybody need that so badly? How could everybody else be satisfied with the pale imitation that passed as "reality"?

Maybe under the guidance of a Christian mystic instead of a Buddhist or Hindu...

And that, too, had been a failure.

Mother Ann Niarchos of Sparta Abbey had met him in a small, beautiful church with pews of polished wood, windows of stained glass, and intricate old-Earth images projected on the altar screen. Rain pattered softly on the roof. The priest listened to his story without interrupting or changing expression. She was middle-aged, plump, dressed in work pants and boots. She looked more like a mechanic than a cleric, but Philip had long ago learned that appearances meant nothing. Wasn't that, at heart, why he was here?

When he'd finished his long recitation, she said flatly, "You were blessed with grace."

Not his terminology, but the sentiment was right. "Yes, but I haven't been able to—"

"To have such grace given to you again? Why should you? Most people don't experience such heavenly bliss even once. Why are you so greedy?"

"It's not greed, it's—"

"It is greed. Gratitude is a virtue, young man. You should cultivate it."

Anger stirred in Philip. "You've experienced that . . . that grace more than once."

She snapped, "Yes, and with gratitude rather than any sense of entitlement. Even though your experience was only partial, you should—"

"Wait—what? How do you mean, 'only partial'?"

Mother Ann regarded him severely. "You told me you had a sense of a specific place and multiple presences."

"Yes."

"In a genuine mystical transcendence, there is no 'place' because one is taken into union with God, who is everywhere. There are no 'other presences' because he is One, indivisible. I'm willing to believe that you experienced something of that blessing, but from your own description, it was not the full experience."

Philip said nothing.

Her face softened. "You seem an eager seeker, but you're woefully ignorant. There are four levels of consciousness that a human can experience: wakefulness, the subconscious we access during dreams or drug use, the respite of deep sleep, and the mystical union with God. Are you sure you were not dreaming during your experience?"

"I was not dreaming."

"And now you're getting testy. You don't like hearing truth. That, too, will need to change if you're ever to join fully with the mind of God. You must learn humility."

His "experience" hadn't been the mind of God; no one sounded less humble than Mother Ann; Philip hadn't been on any of those "four levels." Nor "partially" stuck between them, like a malfunctioning elevator.

He said, "Then there's a fifth level. Deeper than the others, and I touched it. The building has a sub-sub-sub-basement."

"Are you mocking me?"

He was, but his native decency made him regret it. She believed what she believed. Philip stood.

"No, ma'am, I'm not mocking you. Thank you for your time. I'm going now."

"Go with God," she said, and the words had followed him out of the church into the rain. The next day he'd had his final, useless meeting on pollution control with a minor Spartan official who hadn't heeded anything Philip said. During the night he'd tried for hours to meditate, with no success.

Turning away from the factory on the ridge, he stopped. A woman walked along the beach toward him.

Tara. She'd found him again. It was her decisive walk, her dark hair. Philip drew a deep breath and braced himself.

But—no. As she neared, he could see that her body was thicker in the waist, her face much older. Rejuv treatments, yes, but those couldn't work miracles.

She said, "Philip Anderson?"

Her voice even sounded much like Tara's, low and husky, although this version carried more authority. He said, "Yes. You are . . . Annelise Landry?"

She smiled. "Thank you for that, but Annelise is my granddaughter. We all look somewhat alike—strong genes. I'm Rachel Landry. You know my youngest granddaughter, Tara."

Philip managed to nod. What was Rachel Landry, CEO of Freedom Enterprises and *de facto* owner of three worlds, doing looking for him on a beach on Polyglot? Tara had said her grandmother never left Galt.

She said, "When and where was the last time you saw Tara?"

"Has something happened to her?"

"That's what I'm trying to find out." The smile again, this time strained. "Anything you can tell me might help. Please."

A sudden breeze blew the dark hair into her mouth, and she whisked it out and made a little moue. Philip was conscious of her charm, of her genuine concern for her crazy granddaughter, of the steadfastness of purpose underlying her polite request—all qualities that Tara lacked. Tara was steadfast only in pursuit of him.

A wave broke on the sand and washed close to their feet. Rachel Landry did not move.

Philip said, "Director Landry, I—"

"Rachel, please. We aren't very formal on Galt." Again the smile, but she was watching him carefully. What augments did she possess? Heightened visual recognition of the subtle facial shifts that indicated lying?

"Rachel, I saw Tara over five months ago standard, here on Polyglot, at a Hindu village called Adarsh. I was working there. I work for—"

"Yes, I know."

Of course she did—she probably knew everything about him, including what he ate for breakfast. But why?

"Did you and Tara go to Adarsh together?"

"No. She often turns up wherever I am." He stared at her steadily, not wanting to disparage her granddaughter. On the other hand, maybe this dynamic matriarch could keep Tara away from him.

Rachel said, "She's stalking you."

"Yes."

"She wants you, and you want her to go away."

"Yes." Only later would he think it odd that Rachel had said "wants you" instead of "loves you." It indicated a depth of knowledge about her granddaughter that must have been painful.

"Tara didn't return to Galt when she said she would. She's now long overdue. Please tell me everything that happened when you saw her at Adarsh, plus the times before that, going back to when you two met. It may help. And then tell me what I can do for you in return."

Philip frowned. His information was not for sale; he was giving it freely. But then he realized that of course Rachel Landry thought in terms of exchanges, of deals, of contracts. That was how libertarian Galt, Rand, and New Hell functioned.

"You don't have to give me anything, Rachel. I met Tara at Polyglot four years ago, when I was giving a guest lecture at Zuhause University." He went through their whole history, not seeing how it would help, hoping that it would. She listened carefully, the green eyes so like Tara's never leaving his face, as the wind freshened and grew colder. She put on a thin-wrap sweater she pulled from a pocket; Philip imagined she was the kind of person who prepared for everything. Which meant, come to think of it, that she probably had a bodyguard or armed mini-drone somewhere nearby, and also that she was probably recording him every second.

"...and I think that's everything." And then, even though he hadn't wanted this to look like a contract, "Can you keep Tara away from me? She sometimes seems...well, a little unbalanced."

"She is," Rachel said, unflinchingly, and what did it cost a grandmother to say that? "But you must know that on Galt every adult has complete freedom to come and go as they choose."

Philip didn't believe that complete freedom could exist, but he said nothing.

"Thank you, Philip. But since I can't keep Tara away from you, let me give you something else in return for your help. You've been visiting temples and churches and Kabbalistic synagogues everywhere on Polyglot. Clearly you're looking for something: enlightenment, nirvana, samadhi, salvation, moksha, satori. An altered state of consciousness of some sort. You might find it, but it won't mean anything. However, if you want to persist even longer than you have, there is a new deep-brain stimulation technique being developed at John Galt University to treat schizophrenia. The researchers are looking for someone very experienced in meditation as a subject for part of their project. If you are interested, I'll make arrangements and pay for them."

Confusion took Philip. Could he reach that place he'd been five years ago through mechanical means? It didn't seem likely. But . . . he hadn't reached it any other way. Electrodes deep in his brain, stimulating implanted genemod cells developed from bacteria . . . the thought was repulsive.

The thought was alluring.

He was, he suddenly realized, more like Tara than he had thought. Their kinship was obsession.

Rachel cocked her head to one side, studying him, waiting.

To cover his confusion, he attacked. "Why do you say that an altered state of consciousness—" paltry words for what he had experienced!—"wouldn't mean anything?"

"I'm a physicist, or was. The mind arises from the brain, and whatever you find in any state of consciousness is just a temporary distortion of biochemical processes. That's reality." She smiled whimsically. "As one who experimented with psychotropic drugs in my youth, I know this."

He wasn't caught by the whimsy. "If you're a physicist, then don't you also know that on the quantum level, reality itself doesn't exist if you're not looking at it? Until there is an observer?"

"We don't live on the quantum level."

The wind was stronger now, whipping waves into whitecaps. Philip shivered. Rachel Landry waited for his answer, her arms crossed over her chest to keep her wrap from blowing open. Philip's mother, long ago, had stood in that same posture whenever she waited for anything. No two women could have been more different: the landscape gardener and the powerful director of the Landry empire.

He said, still stalling, "I don't think I told you anything useful to find Tara."

"You told me more than you think you did. Come on, Philip, I'm cold. Decide. Are you coming with me to Galt?"

"Yes," he said. "I am."

6

NEW CALIFORNIA

The message reached Sloan before the messenger. A scout from the cruiser *Samuel Peregoy* had sent it, heavily encrypted, as soon as the scout cleared the Polyglot-New California gate. The message had traveled at light speed; the scout, constrained by matter, would not arrive at Capital City until tomorrow. Sloan read the decrypted message, and then read it again.

> CLASS A COMMUNICATION
> CONFIDENTIAL TO DIRECTOR SLOAN
>   PEREGOY ONLY
> FROM LT. C. RICHARDSON, PCSS
> *Samuel Peregoy* proceeded through the unknown gate and was blown up, all hands lost including passenger D. Gordon, as Gordon attempted to explore an orbital around the planet. Gordon's last message in its entirety: "Go! A Landry bomb! Get away!

It's going to—" Visuals and audio attached. Landry vessel waiting outside gate; did not attempt to fire on me. Arrival at New California tomorrow ETA 15:00 Standard. Awaiting orders.

Sloan called Sophia. She glided into his office and viewed the message. The recording contained everything the scout had received from the *Samuel Peregoy* and everything Gordon had seen on the orbital, including the damning manufacturing logo on the nuclear device: Freedom Enterprises.

Landrys.

Sophia spoke first. "This is a clear act of war."

"Yes."

"They destroyed a PCSS cruiser."

"Yes."

Another long silence. Sloan watched the entire recording again, stopping it at every image of the planet, enlarging them, leaning forward to squint at the holo. The cloud cover was too heavy to see anything but blue and white swirls. He prolonged his viewing, and Sophia seemed to understand: The longer they studied the planet, the longer they could postpone a decision.

In a hundred fifty years, there had never been a war among the Eight Worlds. Only once had they even come close, five years ago. An unmanned Landry communication drone had disappeared going through the Galt-Polyglot gate, and Rachel Landry had accused Sloan of stealing proprietary information. Both fleets had gone on high alert. But the Landrys had been unable to come up with evidence, and Polyglot observation probes on both sides of the gate hadn't shown any Peregoy vessels anywhere near the gate. The crisis had passed, even though it had never been determined what happened to the drone. Sloan's opinion was that it hadn't really existed, since gates never malfunctioned, and that the Landrys had lied about the entire incident. Tensions between the two families continued, but to Sloan's mind, their enmity was more economic, a coveting of each other's resources, than physical.

Until now.

War. Unthinkable.

But Sophia said, "If we don't respond with force, this will be merely the opening attack. The Landrys will feel free to seize PCSS ships guarding our gates, or to vaporize more ships. All three Peregoy worlds will be at risk, and maybe also our research station on Prometheus."

"Yes," Sloan said again.

Wasn't he capable of anything more than that one bleak syllable? Apparently not. Sloan's throat knotted. He hadn't read much Terran history—Luis Martinez was always urging more on him—but he knew how terrible war could become, what costs it could exact from even those who won. But there was another, nagging consideration as well. Since the Landrys had set the bomb on the far side of the gate, they must have gone through it first. Therefore, gate and planet belonged to Freedom Enterprises. But it was innocent Peregoy blood that had been shed beside that gate, that had in a way *bought* that gate for the Peregoys. Sloan didn't know what lay under the unknown planet's cloud cover, but by rights of war if not of peace, surely it should belong to the Peregoys. And he wanted it.

"Immediately file a legal claim to the gate," he said to Sophia. "And order Lieutenant Richardson to come directly here tomorrow."

"That's not enough, Father. You need to declare war."

"Sophia—"

"You must."

Her face looked carved in diamond: hard, glittering. An unexpected chill ran down Sloan's spine. Immediately he suppressed it; he must not look weak in front of his daughter.

He said, "I want to talk first to Admiral Chernov and Planetary Defense Coordinator Clarke. Any possible military action will, of course, be confined to attacks at the Landry gates and defense of our gates." It would be unthinkable to take carnage to the surface of any planet.

"If we can confine it to gates," Sophia said.

"No 'if.' There won't be—"

SueLin burst into the room. "Grandfather! I need to talk to you right now!"

"No," Sloan said. "Later."

"No, now! That bitch Evelyn Jemison *cheated* on the bird competition, she used illegal genemods, I should have won but she—"

A bird competition. *Birds*. Sloan looked at his oldest grandchild, an adult but acting like an adolescent, spending all her time breeding and competing songbirds. Interested in nothing but her own petty triumphs. SueLin, the daughter of Sloan's estranged daughter Candace, also weak and ineffectual. SueLin, heir to the Peregoy Corporation after Sophia, who was childless. At one time, Sloan had hoped that Sophia would marry Luis Martinez. By now there were supposed to be plenty of Peregoy heirs, sturdy and smart and capable of looking after three hundred million people on three worlds. Instead, something—Sloan didn't know what—had ended the romance between Martinez and Sophia, and a vacuum-sled accident had taken Sloan's son Jonathan before he'd fathered any children. That left SueLin and her five-year-old brother, who could turn out to be anything but so far did not look promising.

Sloan made the decision he'd been contemplating for the last year. Martinez had once mentioned that Roman emperors and Norman kings had decreed their heirs, bypassing bloodlines when that seemed appropriate. Sloan was no emperor, but he had an obligation to ensure continued strong and benevolent leadership for those under his care. A sacred trust, in fact.

SueLin continued to rant about songbirds and "criminal cheating."

Sloan said to Sophia, "Call Security. Get her out of here. And file that claim on the eleventh gate."

Anyone else would have heard the astonishing words "eleventh gate" and seized on them. SueLin heard only "Get her out of here." She started to curse him, including insults Sloan had never heard before. Security arrived and seized SueLin.

"You'll regret this, you stinking old man! You can't treat me this way! I'm a Peregoy, too, and when this is all mine—let me go, you motherfucking bastard!"

The silence after she'd been dragged from the room felt solid, as if the air were not gas but some denser form of matter. Sloan found it hard to speak. But he did.

"You're right, Sophia. I'm going to declare war."

❖   ❖   ❖

Luis Martinez stood in the captain's cabin on the PCSS *Skyhawk*. The porthole had been deopaqued, but Martinez ignored the view of New California turning below his ship, the wallscreen that had blanked minutes ago, the expensive but sparse furnishings of his cabin. His face furrowed with thought. Someone knocked on the door, which said, "Lieutenant Commander DiCaria."

"Open."

Martinez's executive officer, Zachary DiCaria, entered and saluted. "You sent for me, sir?"

"Yes. Sit down, Zack. We have orders."

DiCaria's eyes gleamed, light brown against his dark skin. Martinez considered him a rising star—intelligent, loyal, and vigilant—and both of them knew it.

Martinez said, "Ten minutes ago I finished speaking with Director Peregoy. He had just finished meeting with Admiral Chernov and Defense Coordinator Clarke and is summoning the corporate Board of Directors immediately. An eleventh gate has been discovered, about a month out from Prometheus and three months from New Utah in its current position. Peregoy Corporation is claiming it. The Landrys went through first, lured the *Samuel Peregoy* through the gate, and blew it up. All hands lost except a scout pilot, who reported to New California. Two hours from now, the director will declare the Landry attack to be an act of war."

For a long moment, DiCaria said nothing. Then, "What are our orders?"

Martinez knew officers, including the ancient Admiral Chernov, who maintained strict and formal distance from their staff. In this, they copied the director. Martinez, however, had always chosen a different course, and it was what had made him so valuable to Sloan Peregoy. Martinez studied his officers carefully, chose a few to trust, and worked with them closely. Not without military discipline, of course, but cultivating a two-way openness that encouraged their observations and opinions. He'd learned a lot that way. DiCaria had been promoted quickly in part because he, in turn, cultivated the trust of the NCOs aboard ship. What DiCaria learned, he passed on to Martinez.

Not that the director was wrong in his basic approach to the worlds in his care. Sloan understood the necessity of preventing the ecological and scientific disasters that had destroyed Terra: climate change, resource exhaustion, species extinction, desperate and annihilating biowarfare. Avoiding those on the limited land surfaces of the three Peregoy worlds required unrelenting control of the economy, the population, and science. In addition, people had to be planned for, including those in each generation who turned out to be helpless or stupid or ruthlessly exploitive. The first were cared for by the corporate state. The second were helped to simple jobs that paid enough to maintain themselves with dignity. The third were stopped, harshly if necessary. The result of so many obligations was the vast set of interlocking rules that regulated the Peregoy planets. Too strict rules, some said, but they worked. Mostly.

Martinez went one step further. Unlike the director, Martinez read a lot of Terran history. He understood, if Sloan did not, that the populace's reactions to rules were also important. Sometimes, those reactions were critical.

He said to DiCaria, "We leave at sixteen hundred hours to guard and defend the new gate. Two other

PCSS cruisers go with us, the *Zeus* and the *Green Hills of Earth*. I am Fleet Commander for this OpOrd. What I want from you, Zack, is a reading on the general attitude of the crew. They're not getting the chance for a final leave with their families before we depart, and those on leave and too far away to return to ship will be left behind. A replacement roster is already on the way upstairs, including an officer to replace Lieutenant Jones. I'll want your recommendation on whatever your non-coms tell you about crew attitude toward war."

"Yes, sir. Captain—is the director firm in this? Might not meeting with the board change his thinking about...about war?"

DiCaria's question told Martinez more than the young man suspected. It wasn't only the crew's attitude that Martinez needed to understand. He said crisply, "I'm only privy to what I was told. If anything changes, I'll inform you."

"Yes, sir."

"Dismissed."

After DiCaria left, Martinez drew a small, e-locked box from his pocket. Sloan had sent it upstairs by special drone. The box was marked PERSONAL. "Don't open it," Sloan had said, "until you're departing this new gate to return to New California." It wasn't like Sloan to be mysterious, and Martinez would have sworn that the old man's face on viewscreen had looked embarrassed. Why?

He locked the box into the safe in his cabin and turned to the viewscreen. New California's one continent was just turning into sight. Martinez gazed at the continent below, its lush green forests and three cities and outlying islands in the clear blue sea. He'd been born on Linda Vista Island, to one of three families with a license to colonize that lovely, semi-tropical Eden. His parents were buried there.

They'd been basix farmers, so inept at farming that their agribusiness had grown smaller and more in debt each year, until finally it failed completely. It shouldn't have; the firm that had purchased it had doubled, then tripled, crop yield over the next few years. The fault had lain not in the farm but the farmers. Both had been disinclined for work or sacrifice. They had followed pleasurable pursuits instead, harmless enough but distracting, until finally they'd distracted themselves into the relative poverty that Peregoy Corporation safety nets permitted, and their teenage son along with them.

He'd hated them for that, for years. Only time had brought him to appreciate the one sacrifice they had made: to send him to spacer college. He had done well enough to forgive them, and eventually he'd made their last years happy with a small, perpetually messy house by the North Ocean, where they had partied too much and bragged to everyone about their wonderful son.

Martinez owed everything to Sloan Peregoy. He'd come to Sloan's notice in college; Sloan had always had an eye for talent. Sloan had mentored him, promoted him, made sure the promotions were both deserved and honored by jealous colleagues. Martinez could not say that he and Sloan were close; Sloan got close to no one except his daughter Sophia. Martinez was well aware that at one time, Peregoy had hoped he would marry Sophia and produce better heirs than Sophia's sister's kids, never mind that Sophia was twenty years older than Martinez. Her eggs had been frozen, and probably still were, since Sophia never showed any interest in him or any other mate, male or female. Martinez had married Amy instead. Since her death, there had been no one else, and never would be. He was married to the fleet now.

But . . . *war*.

Gods and Rationalists help us all.

7

GALT

Philip had been on Galt before, but not like this.

On his first two trips, he'd been a student, once working his way caring for life-support algae on a creaky and antiquated cargo ship, once as an intern with a summer biology expedition to a dying ecosystem on an outlying island. Both times he been at the bottom of the status ladder, doing whatever no one else wanted to do. Both times he'd slept rough and eaten when and what he could. He hadn't minded; he'd been twenty.

The third trip, three years ago, had been to attend an environmental conference at the university. By that time, Philip had a job, the small inheritance from his parents, and a girlfriend. None of those things had lasted, and the trip had been just one more lackluster round of endless theoretical papers, almost totally divorced from actual environments. Accommodations, though not as crude as on a freighter, had been pretty basic.

Rachel Landry's personal ship, the Landry Libertarian Alliance Security Corps ship *Blue Flame*, had staterooms, crews' quarters, a chef, robocleaners, a live steward. There was a billiard table, a game he'd never heard of, which wasted the cubic feet of an entire small room. Philip turned out to be surprisingly good at it. He played with off-duty crew. Rachel had no time for him, presumably running the Landry worlds from her quarters. The night before planetfall, Philip got slightly drunk with the steward, who was very drunk.

"So," Johnston said, lining up his shot, "what're you shooing...doing here?

Impossible to explain. What could Philip say: "I'm a seeker, looking for the fifth level of reality, the true substrate of the universe, the panconsciousness"? True but incomprehensible, sometimes even to him. He merely smiled.

"Thought so," Johnston said, with deep satisfaction. "If I looked like you... But isn't she a little old? Hope you're getting paid enough."

Philip blinked. "Uh, no...Rachel...we're not lovers! I'm a biologist."

"All biology, isn't it?" Johnston missed his shot by at least six inches.

Philip thought of walking out. He thought of slamming his cue stick against the table, possibly breaking one, or both. He thought of using this opportunity to obtain information.

He said as he aimed for the number four ball, "I hear there's trouble on Galt."

"Oh, you don't koe...*know* the half of it. Protests all over the damn planet."

"What about?"

"Not enough jobs, no government help . . . well, hardly no government, is there? Dawg eat dawg. I tell you, I'm damn lucky to have this job." Johnston's face clouded; a fear had penetrated the fog of his inebriated brain. "You aren't going to tell her what I said, are you? I know you two aren't fucking."

"Won't say a thing, I promise," Philip said, from equal parts pity and distaste.

"Thanks. Hey, what part of Pogyglot . . . Polyglot you from?"

Philip sank the four and aimed at the ten. "Albion."

"Don't know it. They got real government there, that helps people to jobs?"

"Sort of. Halfway between Landry libertarianism and Peregoy corporate dictatorship."

Johnston spat on the deck. "Fucking Peregoys. We should blast 'em all to hell."

Philip straightened up from the table. This was unexpected. "Why?"

"Why? Because they want to take every little thing we got, that's why!" He rammed the cue ball so hard it careened across the table and leapt off. "Aw, game's over. Gotta go. You won't . . . you know, say anything to her?"

"No. I promised. I—"

The captain's voice cut him off, booming throughout the ship. "This is the captain speaking. Six weeks ago, a Peregoy Corporation cruiser on an exploration mission was accidentally destroyed in deep space, and New California has issued a declaration of war against the Landry Libertarian Alliance. I repeat, we are now at war. Within the hour, CEO Landry will issue a statement to the citizens of Galt, Rand, and

New Hell. As of now, this ship will assume wartime duties, regulations, and security. All crew, report immediately to the wardroom."

The steward, instantly sober, said, "Aw, shit."

Philip felt stunned. Wartime regulations and duties? The Landrys had such things in place, ready to go "as of now"? Did that mean war had been anticipated? Had Rachel expected this?

And why had a Peregoy cruiser, rather than a much smaller research ship, been on an exploration mission? Exploring what?

The only person who could answer those questions was Rachel, and Philip understood that he had no chance of getting time with her now. Even finding Tara would be secondary to war. Wherever Tara had gone, she wasn't...

All at once, he had a suspicion of where she might be. The suspicion grew—not enough to fight his way into Rachel's sanctum, but still a definite possibility. What should he do with it?

And what would now happen to him, marooned on Galt with little money and no assistance from the woman who had just become the commander-in-chief of a private navy at war?

Philip needn't have worried. An officer met him at the departure lock with a credit chip, an address, and a hasty message from Rachel: "Give this recording to Dr. Hampden at Galt University, the Institute for Brain Research." Rachel hadn't forgotten him.

He took a maglev from the spaceport to the university. Life had undoubtedly been altered drastically in the Landry fleet, in the offices of power, at unseen military bases. But even though the announcement of war had been made hours ago, life in the city seemed more affected by civil unrest than by any fear of attack.

Three years ago, he'd seen poverty, disaffection, and addiction to the tempting array of street drugs that masked poverty and disaffection for a few hours. However, the city now looked tenfold worse. From the train window he saw people, thin and sunken-eyed, camped on littered sidewalks. Some seemed to be families with children. In a park a group of protestors marched around twelve-foot-tall holosign: GIVE US JOBS! The holosign flickered, shone brightly again, then abruptly vanished.

The man in the next seat looked up from his tablet and snorted. "Parasites can't even protest well."

The train hurtled beyond the press of buildings, past fields dotted with litter and cheap foamcast tents. Philip leaped to his feet. "Oh my God!"

In the middle distance, two women ran toward the maglev. As Philip watched in horror, they threw themselves in front of the train. In an instant they were gone, and a lake of dirty water flashed past. Philip demanded of the man, "Did you see that? Those women killed themselves!"

"Martyrs to the cause." His lip curled.

"What do you mean?"

The man looked at him more closely. "You're not from Galt."

"No. Polyglot."

"Not a good time to be a tourist, with war just declared."

"I'm not a—what did you mean, 'martyrs'?"

"These are all refugees from Rand. They came here

expecting the unearned hand-outs they couldn't get there, and since we don't support parasites who won't work, they try to manipulate public opinion with these public suicides. That little stunt was being carefully filmed, you can be sure of that, and the film will be used as propaganda. Which will backfire, of course."

"But if they want jobs—"

"They don't, no matter what they say publicly. What they want is for those of us who do work to support them. That won't happen." He went back to his tablet.

Philip hated him too much to say aloud what he was thinking: *War will create more jobs.* It always did, throughout history. He looked at the man's clean-shaven face, smug even in repose, and felt slightly sick. If Rachel hadn't, even in the midst of crisis, remembered Philip, he might have been in the same position as those refugees, and just as subject to the supercilious cruelty of people like this.

Whose basic ideas of total self-reliance Rachel presumably shared, promoted, ruled by.

By the time the train stopped at the university, Philip was in an internal rage of social indignation, fear, and hunger. If it were possible, he would leave Galt immediately and forget this stupid idea of brain implants. Since a brand-new war ban on unnecessary travel made it impossible, he found a dining hall, ate, and went to look for Dr. Hampden.

"That way," a hurrying student said, pointing. "Can't miss it."

"Oh, you have wrong directions," another said fifteen minutes later. "You go through that building there . . . wait, I'll walk you there."

Oddly, this calmed him down. These students might

be heartless Libertarians, but they behaved like all other students he'd known, and had been himself: willing to help, courteous to a stranger. And the campus was beautiful, shaded by Galt's native trees like giant ferns, bright with beds of genemod flowers, glowing in late afternoon light from the sun. It glinted off the plastiglass windows, turned the foamcast walls to mellow gold, suffused the warm air with the spicy scents of flowers. Still, he was aware that only those who could afford the fees attended university. Hired security forces kept out those who could not.

Tara Landry had turned her back on all this beauty and protection to go to Zuhause University on Polyglot, a much more diverse and raucous college. Philip wasn't surprised.

The Institute for Brain Research was a building of stone, not foamcast, with simple arches forming a colonnade on all four sides. People sat on railings or stone benches, talking earnestly. He found Dr. Hampden's office on the ground floor and knocked. The door said, "Just a moment, please." When it opened, Philip was looking at a woman only a few years older than himself. "Yes?" she said.

Brown eyes, rather dull brown hair tied back, dressed in dark pants and a green tunic, she was in no way remarkable. Neither pretty nor plain, short nor tall, skinny nor fat. Yet Philip felt he would have noticed her anywhere: her confident carriage, alert expression, intelligent eyes. This was someone who knew who she was and what she wanted to do, but was not going to trample others to get it. She was the antithesis of the man on the train. She was the un-Tara. Nothing in her manner suggested either impatience or the kind of female reaction Philip usually got to his spectacular genemod looks.

"Yes?" she repeated.

He'd been standing there like a fool. "I'm looking for Dr. Hampden. Rachel Landry sent me."

If that impressed her, she didn't show it. "I'm Dr. Hampden."

Philip had regained poise. "My name is Philip Anderson. I have a message for you from Ms. Landry."

He handed her the chip and she listened to it. Someone within called, "Julie?"

"Just a moment, Cy." She turned her gaze on Philip. "You've volunteered to be a deep-brain implant subject? Why?"

"That's not an easy question to answer."

"We're most certainly not going forward without an answer. Which will be followed by a battery of physical, mental and psychological tests. This lab is not a whimsical hobby of Rachel Landry's, nor of university president Caitlin Landry. Neither one makes scientific decisions for me, and I need to protect the validity of my research and its methods."

"I understand," Philip said. He'd touched a nerve. But if a favorable decision rested with Julie Hampden, then he would convince her that he was healthy, sane, and possessed of a convincing reason to undergo an experimental messing with his one and only brain.

Yeah, right.

"Dr. Hampden," he began, "may I ask how familiar you are with—"

"Julie," a man said, crowding into the doorway, "this can't wait. Post-op called. Subject Six had an epileptic seizure."

"All right. Yes. Mr. Anderson, sit down over there and wait. It might be a long wait, unless you'd rather come back tomorrow."

"I'll wait," Philip said. Silently, he completed his own question: —*with Varennes's theory of the inter-section of quantum entanglement and the collective unconscious?*

She would never accept him as a research subject. And if she did, would he too end up in a post-op epileptic seizure? On this Libertarian planet, where each person was allowed to make decisions about his or her life and there existed no governmental controls, just how experimental *was* experimental science allowed to be with human subjects?

Who was crazier, him or her?

Two weeks later, Philip lay on a gurneybot, waiting to be taken into the operating room. His shaved head was covered by a thin helmet he couldn't see and his hands were strapped down to prevent him from touching the helmet. The room was too cold. The gurney was too hard. He felt like a trussed, decorated, chilled chicken readied for sacrifice to some mechanical god. There was no other place on the Eight Worlds that he would rather be.

Julie Hampden, swathed in sterile garb, suddenly loomed over him. All he could see of her were two brown eyes, but his heart leapt. He said, "I didn't think you'd be here."

"Me neither. Your surgeon gave way only because I got permission from Caitlin Landry herself."

Philip smiled. He wanted to kiss her eyelids. He wanted to rip off her scrubs and then everything else.

He wanted to ignore the careful protocol that had kept them from so much as touching hands during all his pre-op tests. He wanted more of whatever drug they'd already given him, because this recklessness was a drug reaction—wasn't it?

He didn't need more drugs to tell her how he felt, how he'd been feeling since the moment they met. "Julie—"

She cut him off. "No. Don't."

"But—"

"You're drugged, Philip. Don't talk." She smiled. "Unless it's about physics."

"It's not. I—"

"Look at this." She held up a tablet, which held an image of green and red worms.

Her rejection should have made him feel bruised, but it didn't. They both knew what lay between them. It would happen, when he was no longer her research subject. Everything would happen at exactly the right time!

Only, what if, afterwards, he—

"Philip, don't get amorous. It's a side effect of the drug. *Look* at this. Do you know what it is?"

"No." Sulky now. He didn't seem in control of his emotions. He was as bad as Tara. Tara—where was she? Had he remembered to tell Rachel Landry—

"Focus, Philip. Be *you*. This is an electron micros-copy image of neural connections. This is what the implants are going to boost."

Of course it was. Did she think he didn't know that? Why was she telling him what they'd spent so much time discussing already?

He realized the answer: Because she'd wanted to be

with him during the operation, but she didn't want to discuss anything personal. The green-and-red worms were a distraction. She wanted him to be detached, cerebral. He wanted desperately to please her. Only all at once it was hard to think, hard to talk.

Fucking drugs.

He said, "Gamma waves," and she smiled.

"Yes. Gamma waves."

That was what the operation was for, yes. The brain produced them naturally. They aided memory, the immune system, concentration. Deep-brain stimulation from implants had been used even on old Earth to combat a growing list of ailments and memory problems. Serious meditation dramatically increased cerebral production of gamma waves—but not, for Philip's purposes, enough of an increase. The implants would boost that production.

Someone started the gurneybot moving. Julie walked alongside. Philip wanted to say something, but he couldn't find words. Finally he mumbled, "Physics . . . of nothingness." She didn't hear him, or she chose not to respond.

But Philip knew what he meant. The physics of nothingness was why he was here. Julie was interested in his brain. Philip, who'd spent every spare minute reading as much physics as he could understand, was here for the void.

Which didn't exist. Even "empty space" roiled with gravitational waves. With particles that popped in and out of existence, brief excitations in fields of energy. With non-locality and unseen dark matter. With energy that became particles and particles that became energy. Everything in the universe was entangled with everything else; particles existed in all states at once until observed, and observation changed the whole system, even the dimension of time, so that effects could happen before their causes. It was a seething *jungle* out there, and he was a blind man trying to stumble through it encased in a cage of meat.

But the number of potential neural connections in a human brain, which also operated partly at a quantum level, exceeded the total number of... something. Stars in the Milky Way, maybe? Julie had told him that—hadn't she?

There was something he wanted to say to Julie, to himself, something written by someone... Eddington? Yes, Arthur Eddington... but what?

Then there were people moving around him, and very bright lights, and someone saying, "Breathe," and then a genuine nothingness.

He woke, slept, woke again. The third time, he lay in a hospital bed, in a small room with dimmed lights that were nonetheless still too bright. Monitors hummed softly around him, and footsteps went by in a corridor. A man laughed, low and pleasant, and said something Philip didn't hear clearly. The footsteps receded.

He was alone.

He touched his head: bandages under some sort of thin film. A nurse appeared, somehow looking both compassionate and stern. "Mr. Anderson? You're awake. I'm going to ask you some questions, all right?"

As if Philip had a choice. But he said, "Sure." He wanted to get this over and again be alone.

When the simple questions were over, sternness took over from compassion. The nurse said, "One more thing, and it's very important. Dr. Hampden left word that when you awoke, you are not to try to meditate yet. Wait until after both the doctor and she have seen you. All right?"

"Yes."

"Repeat back to me what I just said."

Philip did, word for word. The nurse fussed with machinery for a few minutes and then left.

Philip began to meditate.

Clear his mind, concentrate on his breathing, let the emptiness-that-was-not come as everything else faded away. It was surprisingly easy, easier than it had ever been before, but then he had to push away the elation he felt. Elation wasn't emptiness. Push away everything, let his mind just be. . . .

Time passed. He touched something.

A second later, it was gone.

With a deep shudder, Philip returned to himself. Daylight flooded the room. Julie, two of her researchers, and a doctor stood by his bed. The researchers were absorbed in the screen displaying his brain waves. The doctor looked grave. Julie looked quietly furious.

Disappointment tsunamied through Philip.

Julie said tightly, "You were told not to do that."

The doctor said, "There doesn't seem to be any harm done."

Philip said nothing. Whatever had just happened had been brief, partial, unsatisfactory. Nothing like the transforming experience of five years ago. Yes, he had touched *something*, but he couldn't sustain it, couldn't understand it, had gained nothing from it.

A researcher said, "Increased production of gamma waves, yes, but fitfully—look at this graph. He wasn't—"

Philip stopped listening. He closed his eyes. For *this* he had machinery in his brain—for a graph that didn't even excite researchers all that much?

Then the researcher said, "I wonder if there's a learning curve. If he can control the gamma wave production with practice. We need to set up a schedule that controls for variables."

Practice. Like a concert pianist, an athlete, a dancer. Practice and discipline. And then maybe...

Philip opened his eyes. "Yes," he said.

8

PROMETHEUS

DiCaria said, "There they are, sir."

The Landry warship showed as a blip on a datascreen of the *Skyhawk*. Technically, of course, it was not a warship since it belonged to a corporation fleet and, until now, there had never been a war. But call it what you will, Martinez had no doubt that it was just as heavily weaponized as his own vessel.

Martinez said, "Arm weapons."

"Armed."

"Countdown at twenty units from firing range."

"Yes, sir."

The *Skyhawk* hovered on the Prometheus side of the Polyglot-Prometheus gate. Martinez's three-ship fleet had raced from New California through the gate to neutral Polyglot, spent a week reaching the Polyglot-Prometheus gate, and passed through. The most remote gate and—until now—the farthest away from any planet, it had been the last one discovered, barely fifty years ago. It led only to the dwarf planet Prometheus, or so everyone had assumed.

Prometheus orbited the same star as New Utah, although so far away that the planet was frozen, a small ball of rock and ice. It shone with thin layers of carbon monoxide, methane, and nitrogen over water ice. Tholins, darker areas caused by charged particles falling on mixtures of methane and nitrogen, dotted the surface, as did craters and shallow mountains. It made for a bleak environment, totally unlike anything else near a gate. The only thing on Prometheus was an underground Peregoy research station on a hundred-year lease from Polyglot, which owned Prometheus. Neither Polyglot nor Peregoy Corporation had stationed defense ships at the gate, since the barren planet below held nothing of real value.

Until now.

Control the Prometheus gate and you controlled the most direct access to the newly discovered eleventh gate. The eleventh gate could also be reached from New Utah, but that was a three-month voyage through deep space. Martinez sent his other two ships, the *Zeus* and the *Green Hills of Earth,* to the new gate, as per Sloan's orders. The *Skyhawk* lingered here, gambling that this critical access point was where the Landrys would attack in the first battle of the war. He would, if he were a Landry captain. In addition to the weapons on the *Skyhawk*, Martinez had backup from the planetary defense weapons. They weren't much, but the Landry captain might not expect them to exist at all.

And here came a Landry cruiser, newly emerged from the Polyglot-Prometheus gate.

"Twenty from firing range," the lieutenant said.

Martinez felt in his own skin the muscle-tightening of everyone else on the bridge. This was what they had trained for and had never yet had a chance to exercise. On New California, more ships were being hastily constructed; in war you always lost some battles. Martinez did not intend to lose this one.

"Eighteen," the lieutenant said.

Mounted on the bulkhead was a permascreen with Sloan Peregoy's portrait. Martinez had never liked that; it reeked too much of veneration, with overtones of Lenin and Mao and other dictators. Sloan Peregoy, that intelligent but limited man, did not read enough history. But Martinez had never had the portrait removed. Standard fleet equipment.

"Sixteen."

Sloan stared out, level-eyed and unsmiling, at Martinez.

"Four—aaahhhh!"

A blast of light on all viewscreens, soundless except for the sickening *SLAM!* against the ship.

"We're . . . hit," said the gunnery officer. She'd been thrown to the floor, tried to raise herself, and collapsed.

"Retreat!" Martinez said. "Straight-line retreat!"

The *Skyhawk* had not lost power. Wherever they'd been hit, it hadn't been in the drive. Martinez, who'd kept his seat, watched the moving blips on the data screen. If this new weapon had an even greater range, or the Landry ship a greater speed . . .

Because it had to be a new weapon. Nothing in the Peregoy arsenal had that long a firing range, *nothing*. This was what Martinez had been afraid of and had argued about with Sloan, arguments that Martinez had lost.

The Landry ship didn't pursue the *Skyhawk*, nor fire again. The brief battle was over—the first of the war, and Martinez had lost. He watched another Landry ship emerge from the gate into Prometheus space. Both went into orbit around the gate, out of range of the pitiful planetary defense weapons. The two warships weren't interested in Prometheus, or its scientists. They wanted only to control the Polyglot-Prometheus gate.

There wouldn't be Landry ships on the Polyglot side, which was neutral space, but there didn't need to be. The Landry Libertarian Alliance now controlled the most direct access to the eleventh gate and whatever lay behind it. What the hell was this new weapon, and what else could it do?

"Damage report," he said. "All sections, damage report. Gardwell, the drive?"

"Undamaged, sir." Gardwell's face appeared on a viewscreen.

"Available speed?"

"Maximum, sir."

"Good. Helmsman, set a course for target destination." Sloan Peregoy's intel said one month from Prometheus to the eleventh gate.

A medical team arrived on the bridge for the gunnery officer, who'd broken an arm in her fall and was irritable about it. "I'll be back as soon as it's set, sir."

The damage reports came in. Not as bad as he feared; perhaps the Landry ship had fired too soon. Perhaps the new weapon, whatever it was, was too new to them as well. Perhaps—with any luck—this was a prototype, and they didn't possess more.

But the *Skyhawk* had lost three crew members and a part of a cargo bay.

As Martinez made the dozens of necessary decisions, a part of his mind would not let go of his thoughts about Sloan Peregoy. Martinez had told him, in the respectful terms that were the only ones Sloan would listen to, that the tight corporate control on the Peregoy worlds might have unintended consequences. Communications were controlled. The environment was cared for and protected. Jobs were provided for all. Indoctrination of children was heavy. Capitalism was tightly regulated. Order and respect were emphasized. None of that, although it forced planetary peace and eliminated want, created the atmosphere needed for creative innovation.

The Landrys, whose Libertarian worlds and unregulated capitalism allowed for virtually anything to be created, tested, and revised no matter what it did to people or planets, were shortsighted but better at innovation. They had innovated themselves a new weapon, and the *Skyhawk* had lost its first and only battle.

Prometheus and its shimmering gate dwindled on the viewscreen until they disappeared.

Martinez brought up the data on his three dead crewmen. Dean Chimenti, Warrant Officer, wife and two children, file request for burial in space.

Janice Flewellen, Spacer First Class, parents on New Yosemite, file request for body to be returned there.

Daniel Chapman, brother on New California, file request for burial in space.

Martinez would write to each of the relatives and send the letters with his official report. "Mr. DiCaria," he said to his exec, "take charge of funeral arrangements."

Unintended consequences.

9

GALT

News of the victory at the Prometheus gate reached Rachel on Galt eight days after the battle. Interplanetary communication was, she thought and not for the first time, a throwback to pre-industrial humanity on old Earth, when news must travel by horse or runner or raven. The gates had their drawbacks.

"Grandma?" commed Jane Landry. Jane, the granddaughter in charge of corporate security, had renamed her division the War Department. "Didn't you hear me? I said we're now in possession of the Polyglot-Prometheus gate! And we have proof that my K-beam prototype works!"

"Yes, of course I heard you," Rachel said, eyeing Jane. "That's good news. Or as good as war news can get, anyway."

Jane tilted her head and scowled. You just never knew how your children would turn out, and certainly not your grandchildren. As a child, Jane had been the plainest of the five granddaughters, dumpy and sullen. Now she was by far the most beautiful, with the Landry dark hair in effortless deep waves and the Landry green eyes darkened to a sometimes disturbingly bright emerald. Jane was also, with Tara, the most intense of the five. As tensions between Peregoys and Landrys had grown over the years, Jane had increased and improved Freedom Enterprises' security division and then had—seemingly overnight!—morphed it into a full-grown military organization. But she saw all events without shades of gray and for that reason, Rachel didn't confide the two things distracting her from this first dubious victory: its implications and the repeated messages from Philip Anderson.

The K-beam prototype developed by Jane's "military research corps," also recently renamed, was by her fevered account a success. But it had not destroyed the Peregoy cruiser. That meant that before long Sloan Peregoy would learn of the brief battle, if he hadn't already. Jane tended to dismiss Sloan: "His ass is clenched so tight he couldn't shit out new weapons or new anything." The wisdom on Galt was that the Peregoy totalitarian dictatorship, no matter how "benevolent," could never match the enterprise and accomplishments of a free people, or of a voluntary military rather than a conscripted one.

These ideas seemed borne out by Jane's victory at the Prometheus gate, and once Rachel would have agreed. But escalating protests, one of which she could see from her office window this very moment, were undermining her certainty. Demonstrations about the deaths of the two refugee "martyrs" who had thrown themselves under a maglev—*choosing* to do so!—had not let up. Rachel was disturbed by what seemed a mounting dissatisfaction on Galt by those who, instead of assuming responsibility for their lives, wanted the Landrys to provide for them. She knew enough of Earth's past to know that from strong enough dissatisfaction could grow revolutions.

There was, however, no way to impress any of this on Jane, who burned with war fever.

Nor could Rachel explain to anyone else why she was disturbed by Philip Anderson. He had called six times since his arrival on Galt, and she had taken none of his calls. No time, and his ridiculous quest was a low priority, to say the least. But the last message, which arrived just moments before Jane had burst into Rachel's office, had held not only a note of exasperation but a lure to get Rachel to return the call: "Please call me . . . it's . . . I didn't want to say this before because it's so tentative . . . but it's about Tara."

"Grandma!" Jane said. "I'm explaining my next strategies to you! Were you listening?"

"Yes," Rachel said, although she hadn't been, not carefully. It didn't really matter. Rachel was still CEO of Freedom Enterprises, but Jane had autonomy for her division, and she had capable—if inexperienced at war—fleet captains.

"Good." Jane, as usual, broke the link without ceremony.

Rachel called Philip on what he did not have access to: an encrypted link. He answered immediately, and his face—really, a man should not be that handsome, genemod or not, it made him look like a caricature from some romantic holodrama—appeared on the viewscreen on Rachel's desk.

"Philip. Sorry I didn't return your call earlier. It's busy here. What about Tara?"

If he was disconcerted by her abruptness, it didn't show. "I think I know where she may be now. It's only a guess, but I thought I should tell you."

"Yes. Where?"

"On Polyglot, at a small northern village called Adarsh, where I told you that I saw her last. Again, I'm only guessing that—"

"Why do you think she might have returned there?"

He grimaced, and then looked as if he regretted the grimace. "Because that's where I'm supposed to be. She knew I was scheduled to return about now to check on an experiment the International Environmental Service is running with pollinators and lions."

"You think she might have gone there solely because you might be there?"

"It sounds egotistical, but...yes. I do. I could be wrong."

Rachel had a queasy feeling that he wasn't wrong. She hadn't fully realized how disturbed Tara was. Or how lonely.

"Thank you, Philip. Bye."

After she hung up, she realized she should have asked him how the deep-brain implant project was going. Tara had driven all else from her mind. But probably it didn't matter; Philip might gain something from the implants, and the university might gain knowledge, but it was impossible that implants, tools of the physical universe, could deliver all the wish-fulfillment aims he hoped for.

Which was also true of the victory at the Prometheus gate. Too bad that Rachel could never convince Jane of that.

She set about arranging for a trusted aide to go to Polyglot and find Tara.

10

NEW CALIFORNIA

Sloan said to Sophia, "Are you sure?"

"Of which part?" she said, logically. "The battle or the planetary-development station?"

"Both!" He heard his agitated tone, breathed deeply, and brought himself to calm. Although Sophia was the one person he ever allowed to see his self-control slip, he still didn't like it when it happened. But this was a double portion of bad news.

Sophia said, "I'm sure, sir. Of both." In the corner of the room the wolves regarded him steadily from their yellow glass eyes. Beyond the window, one of New California's small, fast moons shone faintly in the evening sky.

Sloan said, "All right. Give me the details."

She recited what they both already knew in order to give him time to recover himself, a courtesy that Sloan didn't like because it was so recent. As if she thought he deserved extra care now because he was old. "The gist is that the Landrys had some sort of new weapon with a greater range than ours. A Peregoy resupply ship going to Prometheus was hit as soon as it went through the Polyglot-Prometheus gate, but an info drone got back through, and its recordings were received by our own people on Polyglot. The supply ship was vaporized. No intel on what happened to Luis Martinez's fleet. They might be gone, too."

Luis—perhaps dead. Prometheus lost. Were the scientists and support personnel at the research station now prisoners of war? How would the Landrys treat them? Did an undisciplined, every-person-for-themselves government take prisoners? All of this, like war itself, was unmapped territory.

Luis.

He made himself say, "What information about the planetary development station? Which station?"

"The one here in Capital City. Civil defense plans have been announced on all our worlds and people are reporting for wartime assignment—so far. But here, less than half of the summoned recruits have reported in."

Sloan blinked. Every young person served in Planetary Development for two years, working on infrastructure or environmental protection or the disaster response. Everyone also remained eligible for recall until they were fifty. That had happened during the last plague, during Hurricane Eris, during the big push to develop Sevigny Island. Everyone left their lives and reported in when requested, knowing both that their planet needed them and that the compensation they received would match what they had been earning. No one refused to report when called. It was a solemn duty.

It was also futile to try to avoid. On the Peregoy worlds, unlike the slapdash Landry chaos, everyone had to produce their citizen I.D. to do anything, including buy food. Sloan's intelligence agencies could track anyone, anywhere on the four worlds populated by Peregoy citizens.

Three worlds, now.

Sophia continued, her beautiful face as impassive as those of the dead wolves. "The refusers say they won't go to war. That the two years already given to Planetary Development didn't include any mention of military action. That this is not what they signed up for. That the increased taxes for the war effort is enough for them to give."

"They don't decide what is enough to give! I do!"

"Yes, Father. But if I may say so, sir, Peregoy Corporation has taken care of them all their lives. We provide jobs, basic income, health services, education—"

"Of course we do! That's what a good government does!"

"Yes," Sophia said, as Sloan turned his face away in confusion and sudden shame at his unseemly outburst.

Tactfully, Sophia pretended to not notice, continuing with her report. "I would offer this for your consideration: People who have always been coddled are less likely to risk true danger. The protestors are saying they're pacifists. They would rather be jailed than serve. That's fueling more protests and demonstrations."

Sloan watched the moon disappear below the horizon. The silence lengthened. Finally he said, "I'm disappointed, of course. But swift action is necessary. Has anyone involved in protests, on either side, been hurt so far?"

"No."

"But they might be soon. Arrest all the leaders. Is there a leader? Who?"

Sophia said gently, "That's the other part of it, sir. The resistance was organized by SueLin."

He said, a retort as automatic as whiplash after a blow, "SueLin couldn't organize a dinner party!"

"Then she's lent her name to someone else's organization."

"Arrest her immediately, and bring her here."

"She's in hiding, sir."

"In hiding? How?"

"Probably with sympathizers who have taken care not to identify themselves with the resistance movement for just this reason."

"Have John Patel in intelligence find her. Priority one. Then bring her here. Tell Defense Coordinator Clarke I want to see him here, as soon as possible. Right now, if he's nearby."

"Yes, Father." Sophia turned to leave.

"No, wait—one more thing. You said that 'everywhere else people are reporting for wartime assignment—so far.' What did you mean?"

"What I said." All at once Sophia's cool façade melted. She came to Sloan's desk, put both manicured hands on it, and leaned forward intently. "Father, you know I agree with you about everything important. You're a wonderful steward of Peregoy Corporation and its people. But it's possible to get so caught up in ensuring everyone has the necessities of life that you infantilize them. People like SueLin—they have tantrums when they have to do something difficult because everything has been smoothed for them. And I think we have more people like that than you realize. This insurrection could spread beyond Capital City."

Sloan had never seen his daughter so intent. Her criticism stung, but he also knew it was just. He said, "What are you suggesting? I'm going to break this so-called 'resistance.'"

"I know you will. But you also need something bold to galvanize citizens *and* to show the Landrys that they can't just take our gates and our planets. To show people, theirs and ours, that Peregoys are not soft lapdogs."

"You have something in mind, Sophia?"

"I do."

"What is it?"

She straightened. "You know I play chess to relax."

"Yes." Chess had never seemed to him very relaxing: war by other means. But Sophia was good. The only person that Sloan had ever known to beat her was Luis Martinez.

"In chess, when an opponent has the superior position and you can't attack his major pieces directly, you attack the pieces protecting them. In effect, you weaken the opponent by depleting his reserve resources. If it's unforeseen, that's even better."

Sloan disliked analogies. "I'm not following you."

"Capture the Polyglot-Galt gate."

He stared at her. She was serious.

"Use the PCSS to create a plan to seize the Polyglot-Galt gate and then defend it. Polyglot vessels can come and go, as can ours, but no Landry vessels. They rely on Polyglot for information, some raw materials, and markets. For all we know, the new Landry weapon was developed at John Galt University—it's the oldest university and has the best research facilities."

"Sophia...you can't be serious. Polyglot is neutral."

"And it can stay neutral. You're not going to take over the planet, just its gate to the Landry worlds. It's because Polyglot has always been neutral that they haven't put a strong defense force there. The Polyglot Council of Nations will protest, of course, but we can say we're offering protection from the new Landry weapon, which we are. We can also offer them whatever else you think is necessary. You're good at making deals."

Sloan said nothing, thinking.

"Will you at least discuss it with Coordinator Clarke when he arrives? And with Admiral Chernov? Not that he's any use; he's doddering and you should retire him. You really should."

"I will at least discuss it with General Clarke."

"That's all I want." She smiled at Sloan.

The smile changed her whole face, lighting it. Sloan thought, not for the first time, what a shame it was that Sophia had not married someone like Luis Martinez and produced heirs for Peregoy Corporation. That was the marriage that Sloan had intended for her. But Sophia seemed to be one of those people with a very low sex drive, and she'd always made it clear that running the corporation was far more interesting to her than motherhood. With Sloan's son dead of plague, it had been left to Candace, with the weakest character of his three children, to produce heirs. Thus, SueLin.

The door said, "Planetary Defense Coordinator Lucius Clarke requests admittance."

"Admit," Sloan said.

11

THE ELEVENTH GATE

The *Skyhawk* streaked through normal space, trailing the two Peregoy ships that Luis Martinez had sent ahead to the new gate. He was in retreat, tail between his legs, and everyone on the bridge kept their eyes firmly on their consoles and viewscreens. Their first battle, and they had lost.

"Landry ships remaining behind at New Prometheus, sir," said DiCaria.

"Continue monitoring as long as possible. Report a no-change status every five minutes."

"Yes, sir."

Of course the Landry warships weren't following. They remained to control the Prometheus gate, which now was Landry territory, along with the research station on the planet below.

"Lieutenant DiCaria, contact both the *Zeus* and the *Green Hills of Earth* on the encrypted channel."

"Yes, sir . . . Captains Vondenberg and Murphy on commlink."

In quick, clipped sentences, Martinez explained what had happened at the battle. Such dryness for what should never have happened at all.

The Peregoy claim to the new gate had been filed on Polyglot. Yes, technically the Landrys had gone through the gate first, but they had used it as an ambush and so clearly forfeited their claim. Martinez had served with officers who died on the *Samuel Peregoy*, good men and women who had been slain by Landry treachery. It was difficult to keep the dispassion in his voice.

He concluded with his orders: "Deploy a scout to inform the command at New Utah, with instructions to send a full report to Sloan Peregoy. All available sensor data from the attack is attached. All three Peregoy Corporation worlds must increase gate defenses."

The scout would have to make the three-month voyage to New Utah and then go through two gates to reach New California. There was no faster way to send information. It would also cost Martinez one of his three scouts. Why hadn't the damn physicists figured out faster-than-light communications?

"The *Zeus* and *Green Hills of Earth* will proceed to the new gate with all possible speed. If you encounter Landry ships at the gate, retreat as soon as they are detected and wait until this vessel arrives. We don't know how many of this new weapon the enemy possesses. If no Landry vessels are detected, send a probe through the gate to determine possible enemy presence on the other side. If the probe does not return, retreat and wait.

"If the probe does return, send a scout through the gate. If no enemy presence is detected planetside, both the *Zeus* and the *Green Hills of Earth* are to proceed through the new gate. Use thrusters to remain as close as possible to the planetside of the gate. When the *Skyhawk* arrives, we will proceed through the gate while constantly emitting an encrypted signal, being sent to you now along with a random-generator program to change the signal often. If any vessel not emitting that signal comes through the gate, fire immediately and destroy it. Our best chance is to attack before the enemy knows we are there."

Captain Edward Murphy said from the *Zeus*, "Any vessel at all, sir?"

"Yes. Even if it's a Peregoy ship—it could merely be disguised as one. Peregoy, civilian, Polyglot, pirate—destroy it. I don't anticipate that contingency, but those are my orders."

"Yes, sir."

"I shouldn't be more than a standard day behind you. But that one day might be critical."

He answered their questions, which were intelligent and thorough, especially Captain Elizabeth Vondenberg's. He had strong hopes of her. She could one day lead the fleet.

If they won this war. If they survived this war. If there was still a Peregoy fleet to lead.

The *Skyhawk* crept cautiously toward the new gate. There was nothing here to impede the ship's scanning signals, only empty space. Nowhere for a Landry ship to hide.

There were no Landry ships in evidence.

So either the three Peregoy vessels had succeeded in being first to reach the eleventh gate, or the enemy had outwitted Martinez's ruse with one of their own. Martinez had spent the month-long flight thinking over and over of all the possible ways the enemy might engage. Still, if the initial report had been accurate, the surviving scout from the *Samuel Peregoy* had detected only one vessel on the space side of the new gate, a small Landry craft. It must have set the bomb. Martinez had no idea where the little ship had gone next, or who had been aboard.

There it was, the eleventh gate, shimmering against the blackness. Identical to and as mysterious as the other gates, it differed from them only in having no planet on this side. In a hundred fifty years, the best minds on seven worlds had not learned how these gates formed, how they worked, why they existed only beside planets that could support human life. Nor why Prometheus was the exception. Was it to eventually lead humanity here?

He said to his exec, "Emit signal constantly."

"Emitting constantly."

"Prepare all weapons to fire on command."

"Prepared."

"Prepare to enter gate."

"Prepared."

Martinez found he was holding his breath as the *Skyhawk* entered the gate. He made himself breathe. Adrenalin coursed through his body, quicksilver. The shimmer took them, and then they were through.

No attack. No debris. Only the *Zeus* and the *Green Hills of Earth*, holding their fire.

Martinez said crisply, "Captains Murphy and Vondenberg, report."

Vondenberg answered. "No sign of the enemy, sir."

"Stay in position and prepared to attack. Other intel?"

"Yes, sir," Murphy said, and Martinez would have sworn his voice held an undertone of fear. "Two observations, sir. First, the planet appears to have only one gate, not two."

Nothing startling about that. New Utah and New Hell, at the edges of the frontier, each possessed only one gate. So had Prometheus, the most remote human world until this new one, so far out from the dwarf planet, had been discovered.

Murphy continued, and now the fear—or was it wonder?—sounded more strongly. "Sir, the planet is covered with clouds, as it usually is, but a few hours ago they cleared and... wait... there, sir! Look!"

The planet below lay between its star and the *Skyhawk*, its night face turned toward the ship. Clouds covered all of it that wasn't dark water. But as Martinez watched, the clouds shifted rapidly; there must be really high winds down there. A clear patch of coastline emerged along the twilight zone between day and night.

The land twinkled with bright lights.

12

GALT

A grandmother was not supposed to favor one of her grandchildren over the others. Certainly she was not supposed to dislike one. That was the conventional wisdom.

Conventional wisdom was so often wrong.

Rachel Landry's favorite was, and always had been, Caitlin. Caity was the brightest, the most sensible, the sanest. From early childhood she'd shared Rachel's interest in science, bringing her grandmother bugs to identify, drawings of star patterns, questions about why water ran only downhill. She'd taken a degree in biology although, like Rachel herself, Caitlin had been coopted by necessity into administering Freedom Enterprises' vast holdings. Now she ran Galt University. Family concerns always came first.

Annelise, the oldest and Rachel's heir, was also sane and sensible, although without Caitlin's imagination. Annelise made an excellent administrator.

Celia, the second oldest, had left Galt right after university and never returned. She'd married a mining engineer and now ran the corporation's mining operations on New Hell. Rachel should be grateful for that, since New Hell was hot, dusty, and unpleasant, and few people wanted to stay there permanently. Celia and her husband Roger Liu did. Sometimes Rachel felt guilty that she didn't really miss Celia, who's always been stand-offish and judgmental. A prig, really.

That left Tara and Jane.

Jane Landry stood in her grandmother's office, alternately pounding her fist on the desk and pumping it into the air. The most beautiful of Rachel's granddaughters resembled at this moment a malprogrammed bot with rabies, a disease that had unfortunately traveled with colonists from old Earth. "We got it!" she shouted, too loudly. "We fucking took the Prometheus gate and shit all over Sloan Peregoy's ugly face!"

"Jane—"

"That fucker's days are numbered!" *Pound pound pump pound.* "The K-beam did it! I did it! You remember that you didn't want to risk developing it on ... c'mon, Gran, look a little happy about this! It's a fucking victory! Don't you understand what taking that gate *means*? Peregoys can't get from Polyglot to Prometheus to use Prometheus as an easy jumping-off point to the new gate! They'll have to—"

"Don't patronize me," Rachel said coldly. "I know what the Prometheus gate can be used for."

Jane was immune to coldness. "Then look happier! And the K-beam, that you opposed, isn't the only new weapon we're developing on Rand! We—"

"Jane, *stop*. I'm happy about the victory. You were

right and I was wrong. That doesn't mean I'm happy about going to war. War is—never mind, we've been over this before. The Prometheus battle was over days ago, and it's not why I called you here. What about Tara?"

"Oh. Her." None of the sisters approved of Tara, but Jane's dislike, like all her negative emotions, was malevolent. But when Rachel's private intelligence network had been unable to locate Tara on Polyglot, Rachel had been forced to turn to Jane's military intel.

"Jane, did you find Tara?"

"Yes. Cowering in her ship in space."

Rachel held on to her temper. "Cowering? Why?"

"I don't know."

"Well, is she on her way here?"

"Yes. I had her captured and—"

"'Captured'?"

"She didn't want to come."

Rachel moved toward her granddaughter. "Jane, if you hurt her in any way—"

"Nobody hurt her. My troops wrestled her onto a transport. She'll be here next week and you can coddle the precious, bungling infant all you want."

"Good. Thank you." Rachel would get no more useful information from Jane. "What I wanted to talk to you about is—"

The door burst open and three of Jane's soldiers charged in. "Ma'am, the building has been breached. Come with us to the flyer on the roof."

Breached? Rachel said, "Window, clear!" It deopaqued and Rachel nearly gasped. Protestors swarmed over the fence, hundreds of them—thousands? How was this possible?

Jane said, "The alarms?"

"Remotely disabled, we don't know how. Come now."

Jane said, "No. Drive them off. Fire at will."

"No!" Rachel whirled from the window. "Hold your fire! Those are our people!"

"Those are criminals attacking private property!" Jane said, much angrier at her grandmother than at the mob. "And I'm in charge of defense!"

"And I'm the CEO. Jane, order your captains to hold their fire or I will."

Jane and Rachel locked gazes. So much was in that gaze, personal and political and ideological. Rachel owned Freedom Enterprises until she passed it on to Annelise. She could remove Jane from power. It wouldn't be easy, but with Annelise and Caitlin on her side, Rachel could do it, and both she and Jane knew it.

Jane said over her implant, "Captain Voskitch, hold all fire unless fired upon. Report situation now!"

A deep male voice filled the air. "Situation controlled, ma'am. The rebels got only as far as the lobby. We have their spokesperson and they are laying down arms."

Rebels.

Arms.

Rachel looked back at the window. The rush over the fence had slowed, and people milled around the courtyard; orders must have been passed to them from their leaders. It seemed that she could feel, taste, their disappointment and anger.

She said to Jane, wordlessly restoring her to command, "Please have the spokesperson brought up here."

Jane gave the order, along with a string of others. Her granddaughter had always been able to think quickly. Intelligent, fearless, innovative, and, Rachel now saw, dangerous to everything Freedom Enterprises stood for. Libertarianism reluctantly needed both police and an army, human nature being what it was, but the freedom and individual responsibility embraced by all citizens were supposed to keep policing to a minimum. Until recently, they had.

Without saying good-bye, Jane strode from Rachel's office. Two of her soldiers remained. Rachel watched the protestors, although she couldn't hear what they said. The window, she remembered, had been replaced a year ago, at Jane's insistence, with a polymer strong enough to withstand gunfire. Her stomach churned.

When two soldiers brought in the "rebel" spokesperson, he was a surprise. Younger than Rachel expected, he had the smooth, almost poreless skin and large, glowing blue eyes of expensive genemods, yet he wore an exaggerated version of the old, patched rags of the very poor. An affectation. Effective with his followers?

"Let him go," Rachel said to the soldiers, who obeyed immediately. The boy stared at Rachel, as fearless as Jane.

Was it that the young hadn't yet learned enough to fear?

"I'm Rachel Landry."

"I know who you are."

"Fine. Who are you?"

Rachel half expected no answer, or perhaps a sneer, but he said, "My name is Ian Glazer. I'm the regional spokesperson for the United Citizens for Responsible Government."

There was an actual organization, with "regions" and a name that cleverly echoed Libertarian principles. And "Glazer"—it rang a faint bell. Then Rachel remembered.

"You're Jeff Blaine and Susan Glazer's son."

"Yes. But they have nothing to do with the UCRS."

Obviously. Blaine & Glazer was a successful, very rich manufacturing family on Rand. That explained Ian's genemod looks. Rachel said, "What are you doing on Galt?."

"I came with the plague refugees from Rand. I speak for them and for the underclass on Galt. Rachel, we demand justice. The rich have so much and the poor, including the refugees, are becoming much poorer."

"So make yourself—or, rather, themselves—richer. Get jobs. Start a business. Farm or ranch on unclaimed land. Show some initiative instead of expecting handouts. That's how everything else on Freedom Enterprise worlds got built."

"And it only worked while there was still available *arable* land, and expanding businesses, and no plague. Now there are none of those things, and the refugees from Rand spent whatever money they had to get off planet so they wouldn't see their children die—can you blame them? Freewheeling Libertarianism worked once on the Landry worlds. It doesn't anymore because resources aren't infinitely expandable, and because it's fundamentally unjust—to people, to their circumstances, to the environment. Have you seen what mining and fracking have done to New Hell?"

Rachel had not. She received reports from Celia but had not been to New Hell, or even Rand, in maybe thirty years.

Ian Glazer wasn't done. "In another decade, New Hell will be unlivable. It doesn't have that much land mass, you know, and most of it is being destroyed. How is that 'taking individual responsibility' in the grand old Libertarian fashion? No regulations mean maximum exploitation!"

Now the sneer was evident. And Rachel knew that environmental destruction had always been the weak link in Libertarianism. But what was the alternative— Peregoy dictatorship?

"The environment isn't the worst of it, no matter what you think," Ian said, as if reading Rachel's mind. "The children are. Visit a refugee camp here on Galt. See how starving kids with no medical attention affect your ideology, CEO Landry."

"Children are the responsibility of those who chose to have them. If you can't care for them, don't have them. It's all about individual choice, Mr. Glazer."

Ian continued as if Rachel hadn't spoken. "Here are our demands. First, delivery of food daily to the refugee camps. Second, a Freedom-Corporation-sponsored jobs program. Third—"

"I can't create jobs that no one needs done. Most businesses are so fully automated that—"

"Which is part of the problem. Create jobs to clean up the environment."

"Paid for by whom?"

"You have the money!"

"And we've earned it by providing actual goods and services. Just like your parents did. If it weren't for their hard work, you wouldn't have the education to organize and lead that rabble I saw out there. Let them work, too—there will be war work now. Or join the military and be taken care of that way."

"No one in the Movement will either join the military or work in a factory making war goods."

"You will if you get hungry enough."

"No, we will not." Ian leaned forward on the balls of his feet, like a fighter. Even though his wrists were tangle-foamed together, both of his guards tensed. "You'll be surprised by how many of us there are already, and how many there will be. We know that not participating in your war is the best—the only—card we have to play with your ilk, and we're going to play it no matter what the cost. The future is at stake."

For a second, Rachel felt a frisson of fear. If the army and the corporate fleet rebelled under this class-traitor upstart . . . But, no, Ian Glazer was just blustering. More than that—he was counting on Rachel's own ideology to not lock him up this instant. Libertarianism allowed people to bluster. Jane's space corps, loyal, had taken the Prometheus gate. And the protestors beyond the window, having failed to breach the building, were dispersing.

She said to Ian, "We'll just have to wait and see, won't we?"

"Yes."

"Sergeant, escort Mr. Glazer out of the building and off Freedom Enterprises grounds."

Ian said nothing more. Three minutes after he'd left, Jane strode back into the room. Manic exultation and anti-protest bloodlust had both left her face. She looked carved from stone.

"Mother, I have bad news."

"Tara?"

"No, not Tara. Fuck, when will you . . . never mind. This is war news, and it's bad. Peregoy ships have taken the Galt-Polyglot gate."

For a moment, Rachel couldn't think what Jane meant.

"Did you hear me? The Peregoys attacked our ships at

the Polyglot-Galt gate. My fleet didn't have the K-beam because so far we have only the one prototype that I rushed to Prometheus, and because Polyglot is supposed to be fucking *neutral*. Sloan Peregoy has violated over a hundred years of interplanetary contract! Now the only way anyone on Galt can reach Polyglot is by going the long way around through the gates around Earth!"

Rachel managed to say, "Have you—"

"Sent more ships to defend the Galt-Terran gate? Of course I have. But this will slow down both my war effort and the economies of both the Libertarian Alliance and Polyglot."

"Polyglot will protest it. The Council of Nations won't let Peregoy keep the gate."

"Polyglot has no real army or navy. They're too busy preserving dead cultures to act together on anything. We'll have to take back the Polyglot gate ourselves."

"Can you—"

"I don't know. Meeting of my chiefs of staff in ten minutes. Are you coming?"

"Yes. But first, Jane—before the gate was captured, did Tara's ship pass through to Galt?"

"Fuck it, Mother, at a time like...yes, it got through. She'll be here tomorrow." Jane stormed out.

Rachel stood quietly for a long minute. For two, three. Then she said to the wallscreen, "On. Where is Jane Landry meeting with her chiefs of staff?"

"Conference room four."

"Thank you." Stupid to thank a building, but Rachel had always done so. She put her hands on either side of her head, over her ears, as if to shut out din that only she could hear. It didn't help.

She left her office for conference room four.

13

GALT

Everything Philip did was monitored. Everything.

Biosensors stuck to his skull, his chest, his wrist, his armpits, his nostrils, the insides of his mouth, even his cock. They swarmed in his blood. None of them were intrusive, none interfered with anything he wanted to do, but he was nonetheless constantly aware of them. Sending signals, revealing his bodily functions to researchers at the Institute, tying him to his body. Three times a day he reported to a lab where his fluids were collected, his reflexes tested, his mind grilled to see if, and how, it was functioning. It was all the price of the deep-brain implants.

Which he could barely use.

Once or twice, meditating in a room with a two-way mirror, he thought he might have reached the fourth level of brain activity, the meditative state, which he used to be able to reach regularly. The fifth level, where he touched that Great Unknown, wasn't even a glimmer.

After each session, he met with Julie, who shook

her head. "Your brain waves are those of full, wakeful alertness."

"I don't feel alert."

"You don't look it, either."

"I know what I look like. Shit. How do you expect me to sleep knowing that every snore and fart is being reported to you?"

She smiled. "Actually, I don't hear about the farts."

Philip gazed at her, and a second later was horrified to feel his cock rise. That would show up on the biosensors. But the desire that he always felt in her presence—to touch her hand, kiss her mouth—was so strong that it had to manifest itself somehow. Damn, it had been too long since he'd felt a woman's skin next to his own. And he had a dim memory of saying something to her just before he went into the OR, something he shouldn't have said according to the rules Julie had laid down. She kept strictly to those rules.

She rose. "Go back to your room and rest, Philip. Lab tests in an hour."

"Julie—"

"Rest." But there was a shine in her brown eyes, a swing to her walk as she left the room. Philip, for good or ill, had known a lot of women. His looks had made that easy. Julie wanted him as much as he wanted her, but she was a professional.

He went back to his room and lay on the bed. The images that crowded his brain had nothing to do with meditation.

Fuck this. Two weeks had passed since his operation, and after that first brief stirring in the dark recovery room, he might as well have been trying to build old Rome with his mind.

Quietly he rose from his bed and opened the door. No one in the corridor. He went down the hall to a bathroom, but not the one attached to his room that measured his feces and urine and saliva. In a stall, he removed every external sensor from his body, then sprinted down a stairwell and out an emergency door. Which would, of course, alert Security. He ran toward a little wood separating the Institute for Brain Research from the university campus, barreled through the wood, and entered the first building he saw. The entrance had stairs leading to a basement corridor. Doors, most of them locked. However, an unsecured door led to an underground room with a table, chairs, sofa, fridge, InstaBake—some sort of break room for employees. A duty roster glowed on the wallscreen. Three names were listed, all with duties in, he hoped, other buildings.

Philip turned off the lights and lay on the sofa. It smelled of old sweat. Sensors still swarmed in his blood, but sensors were not spaceship commlink devices. Surely their range was limited, and surely he was now beyond it.

He slowed his breathing, concentrated his mind, and began to meditate. He couldn't get there. The tension of leaving the Institute prickled at him like ants. Contracts were pretty much the sole regulators of life on Galt, and he was breaking his.

Five minutes later, the door flung open and Julie entered with a serious security bot, the kind programmed to restrain and carry off mental patients or criminals. "Philip!"

He sat up, allowing himself the relief of anger. In the dim light from the corridor, she was a curvy silhouette, and anger somehow morphed into that other agitated state, desire.

"I can't do it, Julie," he said furiously, desirously. "With all of you watching me and controlling me and denying me—I'm not a bot, damn it! You had a tracker in my clothes, didn't you? I'm not a criminal, a child, or a machine! And a mystic state isn't something you just order up like a chicken dinner!"

"Deny you!" she said, just as angry as he was. "What have you been denied? You got the brain implants you swore you wanted, got them for *free*, and in return all you have to do is—what are you doing?"

Adrenalin propelled him off the sofa. He put both hands on her waist. "What have I been denied? You know what. Go ahead, order the bot to knock me out and carry me back. Do it."

She didn't. He felt her body shudder, then melt against his. Her hair smelled of some spice he couldn't name. She said in a husky voice, "Code 17. Bot off."

He forced himself to say, "Julie, I don't want you to if you don't—"

"I do." She kissed him, so hard it bruised his mouth.

"But if your job—"

"Shut up," she said, and he did.

Afterward, Julie fell asleep. Philip, surprised and pleased by the intensity of her, lay awake on the cramped, musty sofa. She was going to be remorseful when she woke, he knew that. He also knew that he was not.

All the tension had left him. One arm and one foot dangled over the edge of the tattered sofa, his entire body in a relaxation so deep that he felt boneless.

Head, limbs, torso—all so heavy that he could not have lifted them if he wanted to, and he did not want to. Julie's body, unseen in the total darkness, lay against him, her breathing deep and regular. Her breathing filled the world, was the world.

Philip rode on her breath to somewhere else.

A moment of surprise, and then he let it happen. He was in the dark room, where his body stayed. But his mind—his consciousness—lifted and soared. He saw nothing, his eyes left behind with the rest of his matter, but matter was not the only element of the universe. Matter was secondary, a temporarily congealed form of energy, the result of collapsing waves. Energy was primary, the original force, entangled since the Big Bang. Energy was primal.

Philip rode the entangled energy of the universe.

He brushed something. Afterward, he could not say what it was—or what they were. Many, millions, of *something*. Impossible to put a name to. But there was matter here, too, or rather the possibility of matter, the probability—and the moment he tried to put a name to the matter, it shifted under his touch and he was back on the sofa in the dark.

Tears ran down his cheeks. It had happened. Not like it had five years ago; that had been only a shadow of this. Now he'd gone past that elusive, so-long-sought consciousness to an unsuspected, even more basic state. The substrate underlying the structure of the universe and unifying its forces. And now he knew for sure. There *was* something out there, something more. And he had touched it, even if he could not sustain that touch.

"Lights!" Julie's voice said, and the room flooded

with unwelcome glare. She bolted upright, her naked shoulder wet with his tears, her face creased with worry.

"Philip, what is it? I'm not angry, the sex was my choice, too. It shouldn't have happened but it doesn't have to abort the experiment.... Philip?"

He said, "Energy doesn't collapse into matter unless there is an observer."

The worry creases on her forehead deepened to fissures. "What? Are you all right?"

"Yes," Philip said. And then: "They're out there. I have to find them."

He could not. He tried and tried, and all he found was frustration.

He tried again.
And again.
And again.

Julie had gently refused more sex. She deeply regretted what she regarded as her "exploitation of researcher-subject trust." Philip, who didn't regret it at all and did not feel exploited, had then tried masturbation to bring him to the same relaxed, uninhibited state that had led him to whatever deep reality he'd touched while on the basement sofa with Julie. Masturbation had failed. Endorphins from frantic exercise had failed. Meditation had failed. Psychotropic drugs of various types had failed, leaving him groggily confused about any level of reality whatsoever.

Frustration. Nothing but failure and frustration.

14

THE ELEVENTH GATE

Martinez gazed at the planet below, the unknown world beyond the eleventh gate. His glimpse of lights along the coastline had been brief before clouds rolled back in. But he had seen the lights; everyone on the *Skylark* and *Zeus* and *Green Hills of Earth* had seen them. Clustered lights, as in a city, along the dark waters of the coast.

Could humans from old Earth somehow have discovered unknown gates between Terra and here and launched a colony before Polyglot had even been settled? No, that wasn't possible. Earth's death agonies had been swift by extinction standards, but not instantaneous. It had taken four or five generations for desertification, biowarfare, rising oceans, famine and, finally, all-out war to kill Terran civilization. By the time the nuclear weapons were launched, Polyglot had been colonized, and both Samuel Peregoy and Kezia Landry had taken their differing governmental

philosophies from Polyglot to the new worlds of Galt
and New California. The long Terran exodus had
been documented for generations. No lost colony had
emigrated to this undiscovered planet.

Whatever was down there was not human.

Martinez turned from the viewscreen to planetary
data from atmospheric probes and visual surveillance.
More reason why this was not a rogue human settlement. The planet more closely resembled one of
Saturn's moons, Titan, than it did Earth, with high
concentrations of nitrogen and methane, although the
atmosphere also contained some complex hydrocarbons.
The inhospitable world had a low surface temperature,
clouds of methane ice and cyanide, dunes of hydrocarbons, oceans of liquid methane. It was the first planet
beside any gate that was not habitable. Whatever built
those cities did not have human biology.

Could this entire "city" be a Landry trap, as the
initial booby-trapped orbital had been? Martinez didn't
dismiss the idea, but neither did he give it much
credence. Too elaborate.

Martinez kept his three-ship fleet on alert, ready to
either dart back through the eleventh gate or to return
fire. Scouts kept watch on the deep-space side of the
gate. So far, nothing had happened. The aliens didn't
seem to have anything in orbit, so perhaps they were
pre-space-age. They might not even know that they
had a gate, or that the Peregoy ships hovered near it.

Martinez considered. His orders were to hold the
gate against any Landry incursion, not to make contact with aliens. On the other hand, neither Sloan
Peregoy nor anyone else had imagined there could *be*
aliens here. Maybe there were not, because time-lapse

monitoring from high orbit as the planet rotated showed that there was only the one city, and its lights never varied. None turned off during daylight hours, and no additional lights switched on.

Nobody was home.

He made a decision. "Lieutenant, open all possible broadcast frequencies."

"Yes, sir."

"Send prime numbers three to sixty-seven, followed by this message: 'This is the Peregoy Corporation Space Service ship *Skyhawk*, in orbit above your planet. We come in friendship.' Repeat sequence at five-minute intervals until instructed to stop."

"Yes, sir."

Nothing. Five hours later, ten hours, still nothing. Were they conferring down there—if there even was a "they"?

At any moment, Landry ships could approach the eleventh gate from Prometheus.

Sloan Peregoy didn't want only the gate for Peregoy Corporation—he wanted the planet. If it was as useless to humans as it seemed, and if it had no other gates around it leading to anywhere that was useful, then Martinez's three warships were better deployed elsewhere. The loss of the Prometheus gate meant it was going to take Martinez much longer to return to New California. He would have to travel to New Utah, a three-month trip, and then through two more gates. Martinez couldn't receive orders from Sloan, not here. He needed to decide if this planet was worth holding on to or not, and he needed that information before he lost forces defending a useless piece of real estate against the enemy.

"Lieutenant, continue broadcasting. Meanwhile, we're sending an exploratory team to the surface."

He couldn't go himself, of course. He wasn't an expendable young hotshot, and it made no difference that he had never wanted anything as much as to be on that exploratory team. Instead, he stayed on the *Skyhawk* and received the radio and data communications as the three chosen took their scout through the cloud cover.

"We've landed at the edge of some structures," Lieutenant Maxwell Gruber said. "No sign of life of any kind."

The structures were low, circular, with ridged walls tapering to flat tops. They seemed arranged randomly, as if someone had tossed a bunch of huge, dun-covered bottle caps beside the sea. The lights glowed on the tops of the structures. No streets or walkways snaked between structures, and Gruber detected no plant life of any kind. The ground beneath the scout was sand over rock. Methane haze drifted above distant mountains.

Martinez said, "Wait one hour for signal or approach."

Gruber did. Nothing.

"Send the reconnaissance bot from your vessel and proceed with caution."

A clumsy looking object of metal and polymers, which was not nearly as clumsy as it appeared, continuously transmitted data as it made its way to the closest of the alien structures. Gruber dutifully reported what was already clear from the data stream. "No visible doors or other sorts of entrances, sir."

"Continue reconnaissance."

The image from the scout became eerie: a human substitute wandering among giant dun bottlecaps, one looking as solitary as the other. A child's nightmare of abandonment among the familiar turned grotesque.

Sonar revealed nothing underground. The bottlecaps themselves contained shadowy substructures of some kind, utterly unfamiliar. Other scans revealed no additional detail. No gears, joints, radioactivity, sound waves, digital activity. Nothing at any wavelength.

And yet Martinez had the stubborn idea, utterly unfounded, that the bottlecaps were not dead. No way he could know that—but it persisted.

Gruber said, "I can try a breach."

It was the next step; the robot carried explosives. Martinez considered. How far could he stretch Sloan Peregoy's original orders? And if something unimaginable did inhabit the bottlecaps, an explosion might provoke retaliation. Or, at a minimum, fully justified distrust.

"Negative, Lieutenant. Recall the 'bot and return to the *Skyhawk*."

"Yes, sir."

Without direct orders from Sloan Peregoy about the situation, Martinez made a judgment call. He would remain here with his three-ship fleet to defend the gate. A scout would return to New California, carrying Martinez's report.

He was aware of, but did not give undue weight to, his own desire to see what might happen next on the planet below.

15

NEW CALIFORNIA

It was surprisingly hard to find SueLin, which argued that the "resistance" organization was larger than Sloan had suspected. Perhaps, Sophia's chief of intelligence suggested, it was organized into cells, each with no direct knowledge of most of other cells, so that the people who had been interrogated had said nothing useful because they didn't know anything useful. If so, that suggested a sophisticated level of organization. But, then, organization was what Peregoy worlds did. But not what SueLin did. She was pawn, not queen.

At any rate, the resistance no longer topped Sloan's list of concerns.

Captain Ananya Batra said, "Approaching the New California-Polyglot gate, sir."

Sloan sat behind her and the copilot on the tiny bridge of Sloan's personal ship, the *Acropolis*. Class 6A vessels were unarmed—mostly—and modified as the owners wished. Sloan's included two cabins, crew quarters, and a common area with small galley, all of it comfortable but not luxurious. With him were a multilingual translator and six elite bodyguards, augmented and so well trained that they did not need to carry weapons. Of course, neither bodyguards nor weapons were allowed where he was going, but they were comforting on the trip and useful when conducting business on Polyglot, although Sloan did not intend to do much of that. He had a mission here.

He had not left New California in two decades. Sophia often visited New Yosemite, but mostly Sloan relied on his network of corporate vice-presidents and planetary operation officers, chosen with supreme care and monitored constantly. Sloan was, after all, almost ninety, and rejuv could do only so much. Still, he was pleased that he had stood so well the trip from New California to the orbital port. Rising up the gravity well had hurt, but not broken, his old body.

This trip to Polyglot was imperative. The Peregoy fleet had violated Polyglot neutrality by taking the gate between Polyglot and the primary Landry world, and the Polyglot Council of Nations was furious. The presence of Sloan Peregoy himself wouldn't be enough to mollify them—even though it was the Landrys, not the Peregoys, who had started this war. Polyglot didn't care who started the war. The Council of Nations cared only that war not violate their neutrality. However, Sloan planned on adding considerable sweeteners to his explanations. He was going to turn a violation into a negotiation, and negotiating was what he did best.

Captain Batra exchanged terse communications with the one Polyglot cruiser on this side of the New California-Polyglot gate, as well as with a Peregoy cargo ship approaching the gate from Sloan's left. He watched the cargo ship, the *Quasar III*, as it disappeared into the shimmer of the gate. He hadn't realized how much he missed seeing that shimmer. A holoview was not the same. The gate was beautiful, insubstantial silver lace in the blackness of empty space.

Batra said, "Entering the gate, sir."

A brief moment of suspension, and then they were through. Polyglot lay below them, green and blue, its generous continents sparkling with evening lights. If Samuel Peregoy had had such a world, if he had reached this planet first instead of the lunatic who had discovered the first gate and indiscriminately opened settlement to everyone, the Peregoy empire might now rule all eight worlds. If—

The copilot gasped.

Sloan leaned forward in his seat, trying to see over the copilot's shoulder to the datascreens. The copilot stared, rigid. Batra frowned deeply. For a long moment, Sloan didn't see what was wrong: no alarms sounded, no other ship appeared on the viewscreen, nothing fired at them. Then he realized it was not what was present that mesmerized both pilot and copilot, but what was absent.

The *Quasar III* had not emerged from the gate.

"Captain Batra..." Sloan began, and was ignored. Batra was giving rapid, incomprehensible orders. Screens flashed with data and with panning views of space. Finally the copilot said, "She's gone, ma'am. No debris, no residual radiation, nothing. She wasn't destroyed on this side of the gate."

Sloan said sharply, "The cargo ship was destroyed *inside* the gate?"

Batra said, "It would appear so, Director."

"Do you know of anything that could do that?"

"No, sir."

"A new weapon then? A Landry weapon?"

"Unknown."

Cold filled Sloan's belly. If the Landrys could destroy ships inside gates . . . catastrophe. Not only would warships be lost, but communication scouts and cargo vessels. Commerce among the Peregoy Corporation worlds would be crippled.

But . . . wait. He was on the Polyglot side of the gate. The Council of Nations would be just as outraged as he was. In fact, next to this Landry violation, the Peregoy taking of the Polyglot-Galt gate would become less important. Sloan could use this, exploit it, to enlist Polyglot on his side in the war. He had personally witnessed this war crime against a civilian ship. The *Acropolis* might just as easily have been the victim of this new weapon. Perhaps that was even what had been intended, and the *Quasar III* had been unwittingly attacked instead. Innocent lives lost . . .

"On," he said to his wrister. "Crew list for the *Quasar III*, with pictures and brief bios."

With any luck, at least one of the dead would be young, attractive, and sympathetic. That would be the image to present to the Council of Nations. He or she might even be—have been—a Polyglot citizen. With any luck.

Sloan's ship dropped toward the planet.

16

GALT

Jane's soldiers brought Tara to Rachel's apartment at the Landry compound.

Her apartment occupied the entire top floor of the six-story structure five kilometers from Freedom Enterprises headquarters. The building sat in the middle of the compound, surrounded by flowerbeds, moonthorn trees, and the bright houses of Landry granddaughters, grandchildren, and cousins. Twenty-five years ago the entire walled compound had been rebuilt for the second time, these lavishly curved buildings replacing the more modest stone-and-wood ones that had once displaced the first settlers' foamcast habitats. Every wall of Rachel's penthouse was clear plastiglass. When it was deopaqued, she could see as far to the north as the spaceport; to the south, the Suno Mountains. The compound's formidable security was practically invisible.

She'd chosen to decorate her apartment without

either programmable holograms or Earth antiques, the
usual choices. Her walls were hung with paintings and
collages created on Galt, mostly seascapes although
she had one priceless Garafoli nude. Rugs in warm
colors covered the floors; the sofas and tables were all
hand-made and exquisite. In one corner of the main
room, beside the bar, bloomed a garden of deep red
boli flowers. Rachel stood in the middle of the room,
fists clenched, waiting for Tara.

The door said, "Three people approaching: Lieu-
tenant Jared R. Jennings, Freedom Enterprises Security;
Private James K. Tollers, Freedom Enterprises Security;
Tara Kathleen Landry, citizen of Galt."

"Open," Rachel said.

Jennings was tall and bony, all whipcord muscle.
Tollers was huge, with the look of serious augments.
Did Jane think that Tara, who looked like a defiant
doll between them, needed such formidable captors?
Rachel's irritation with Jane, a flourishing tree, grew
another branch.

"Ma'am, Lieutenant Jennings, sent from—"

"Yes, Lieutenant. Leave her here, and thank you."

"Ma'am, my instructions from the commander-in-
chief are to remain beside Ms. Landry to—"

Commander-in-chief? When had Jane given herself
that title? Rachel said, "And *I* am dismissing you,
with my thanks."

Rachel was CEO. The lieutenant saluted and left,
taking Private Tollers with him.

Tara stood with her chin lifted, her whole body taut.
She'll attack before I can, Rachel thought, because
when had Tara ever employed any other tactic?

"What the fuck gives you the right to have me

arrested and brought here against my will? I'm an adult! You always talk about freedom and individual choice and then you have the *gall* to—"

"Freedom doesn't include the choice to start a war. Because it was you, wasn't it? You had a larger ship, the *Caroline*, accompany you from Prometheus—I checked the manifests, and I've talked to the captain. Your orders were for him to have one scout ready to deploy, an order you never gave. I've seen the recording the Peregoy scout sent and the *Caroline* intercepted. A Landry *bomb* on the other side of the eleventh gate. Tara, do you understand what you've done? How could you? Murder over *three hundred people*, and when you knew—must have known!—how dangerous things already were between us and the Peregoys. A war, Tara! Now thousands more might die, and we've—"

"I didn't mean to!"

All at once, before Rachel's eyes, her granddaughter crumpled. Rachel had not seen her do that since Tara was eight years old.

"It was an accident! I didn't mean to!" She sank to her knees, covered her face with her hands, and sobbed.

Rachel was not going to be bought off with histrionics. "An 'accident'? How do you accidentally booby-trap an orbital you yourself built at a gate that you yourself discovered?"

"Are you going to tell Jane? Will she put me in prison?"

Rachel seized her by the shoulders and hauled her upright. "Answer me! Tara!"

Tara sobbed louder and threw herself into her grandmother's arms.

A hundred tender memories ignited by her granddaughter's body against hers: Tara as an infant, winding her tiny fist around Rachel's finger. A one-year-old, a sweet sleeping weight on Rachel's shoulder. A three-year-old, wailing, "Gammy! Fix it!" A six-year-old, blindly seeking consolation when her mother died.

Gammy, fix it. Not this time. Gently Rachel disentangled herself. "Tara. Talk to me."

More sobs. It seemed to Rachel that she heard genuine remorse in those sobs—or did she only want to hear it? Certainly she heard fear. She waited; even the worst crying jag ends eventually.

When it did, Rachel waited, stony.

Tara said, "Can we sit down?"

"No. Tell me what happened."

"It *was* an accident." Now Tara's brows lowered, defiance replacing fear. "Even if you don't believe me. But then, you never do."

"Not true. Tara, what happened?"

"I set the bomb, yes. I discovered the gate and I saw an opportunity to make peace between Peregoys and Landrys. Surprises you, doesn't it? You've always been so ready to think I intend the worst! But I was trying to make peace!"

"By destroying a Peregoy cruiser? Come on, Tara."

"It's true! The bomb wasn't supposed to destroy a cruiser! I discovered the new gate and I knew both us and the Peregoys would want wherever it led. To the new planet beyond the gate. So I went through the gate, and then I returned later with a small orbital and the bomb, and then I got an old friend to go tell Sloan Peregoy about the gate. Then—"

"What old friend?"

"Nobody you know. Knew. Anyway, I hired the *Caroline* and sent it there and I went there on my ship, the *Waterbird*. The plan was to wait until the Peregoy ship showed up, and then time it so that two scouts, ours and theirs, went through the gate together, racing to claim the gate. The bomb was timed to go off a certain length of time after the orbital's sensors registered a ship. Both scouts would be destroyed, and all trace of the bomb."

"And how would that—"

"Let me finish! The *Waterbird* took a comet hit. We arrived there too late. The *Samuel Peregoy* went through—what kind of idiot captain doesn't send a scout first? It wasn't supposed to happen that way! I thought that when both scouts were destroyed, the Peregoys and Landrys would unite against a common enemy. You know: 'The enemy of my enemy is my friend.' I could bring peace between them and us!"

"Unite against a common enemy? What common enemy? You were willing to kill two pilots for some phantom enemy? And just because a scout from each side was destroyed, that wouldn't necessarily mean—"

"No, not 'just' that. I thought we'd all unite against the enemy because there is one. Or at least, could be one."

"Who?"

Tara spoke as if the words were wrung out of her. "Whoever is down on the planet. Because when I went through the gate the first time, I saw lights down there. Lights of cities. That's what happened. Now do you believe me? I was just trying to make peace!"

Rachel moved to a sofa. She had to; her knees were giving way. "Lights?"

"Yes! Send a ship to check, if you don't believe me! We own the new gate because I went through first, and we own the Prometheus gate because Jane won her stupid battle, but she gets credit and I get shit! It's not fair!"

Tara began pounding the side of her own head with her fist. More histrionics? No. She picked up a heavy glass sculpture and struck herself. Rachel leapt up, crying, "Security!" A moment later Lieutenant Jennings, who hadn't left after all, burst into the room. But Rachel had already knocked the sculpture out of Tara's hand. It hit the rug, bounced, and rolled. Blood gushed from Tara's head. She started to scream: "Philip! Philip!"

"Call medics," Rachel gasped. Then, with every bit of will she had, she said, "Wall on. Summon Annelise Landry and Jane Landry here. Code One. Repeat, Code One."

"Gammy!" Tara screamed. "Fix it! Oh, fix it!"

Rachel couldn't answer. Her throat had closed too much for speech.

Fix it.

How?

Annelise came immediately. Jane did not. She'd sent a prerecorded message informing Rachel that Jane had already dispatched ships to the new gate, although if the Peregoys had launched into deep space from Prometheus before the K-beam captured the Prometheus gate for the Landrys, then Peregoy vessels might get there first. There was no way to know until reports came in. In the holo, Jane wore an even more elaborate uniform: green and gold, with epaulets on the shoulders and four stars on the breast.

Tara had been sedated and hospitalized. *A psychotic break* was the initial diagnosis. At the look on Rachel's face, Annelise glanced away, down the long corridor of Galt Hospital Center, and then reached for her grandmother's hand.

Rachel did not tell Annelise what Tara had done at the eleventh gate. Time enough for that later on. She let Annelise lead her to a waiting room, a small space furnished with the kind of conformachairs and "soothing" walls that Rachel despised. She leaned her head against the back of the chair, which tried to morph into a comfortable shape. Fucking chair. There was no comfort here.

War. Because of course Sloan Peregoy would retaliate.

An hour later, when Rachel had been told by the doctors that she could not see Tara, Rachel returned to her office. She'd just poured herself a strong drink when Annelise, who'd supposedly gone home to her family, entered the room, looking deeply troubled. She said, "Gran, I'm afraid I have more bad news. I wanted to give it to you in person."

"From Jane?"

"No. From the Polyglot Council of Nations. The Peregoy ships controlling the gate allowed it through."

"They did?" That didn't make sense, since surely the message was a condemnation of the outrageous Peregoy violation of Polyglot neutrality.

Annelise had already decrypted and listened to the message. She laid the datacube on Rachel's desk, next to her drink.

Rachel made no move to touch it. "Tell me."

"It's signed by all twenty-six city-states on Polyglot. A universal condemnation of whatever weapon we used to destroy the Peregoy cargo ship *Quasar III* inside the Polyglot-New California gate. They're demanding that we surrender the weapon and also make reparations to Peregoy Corporation."

"*What?* I don't understand."

"Nor do I. Has Jane—"

And the K-beam, that you opposed, isn't the only new weapon we're developing on Rand! Jane had said that to Rachel. But—

"No," Annelise said with uncharacteristic violence. "She *wouldn't*. Not without telling me she was developing such a thing. Which isn't even possible! We know nothing about how the gates work, nothing."

"Send again for Jane."

"I will, but I don't think she'll come. She's on Rand, at the shipyards, overseeing her new navy."

"If she's done this—"

But Rachel didn't believe it. Annelise was right; the gates were still complete scientific mysteries, and Jane's scientists couldn't manipulate one to destroy a vessel inside itself. If anyone, anywhere, had made such a breakthrough in physics, Rachel would have heard about it.

That left only the Peregoys. They might have destroyed their own vessel—after all, why not? Tara had done the same thing, and Sloan might have wanted a controversial act to blame on the Landrys. That must have been what happened.

Rachel, who had not slept well for days, knew she would not sleep at all tonight. War, deception, escalation, betrayal—This was what had destroyed Earth, what the settlers had hoped to escape with their brave new civilizations.

Annelise had been listening to her implant. "Gran," she said softly, "I'm sorry to have to tell you this at such a time, but protestors have stormed and taken over the foamcast factory at Reardon. They're demanding to meet with you now."

17

POLYGLOT

World government was never really either.

Sloan Peregoy, seated as a not-at-all-welcome guest at the Polyglot Council of Nations, watched Council members file in, most of them a few minutes late. Inexcusable—everyone knew this was a critical session for the entire Eight Worlds, even though this "government" had limited power over the actual government of Polyglot's twenty-six nations. Two of those nations didn't even belong to the Council, maintaining some sort of ethnic purity by limiting contact with everybody else. Ridiculous. A planet couldn't be governed efficiently and benevolently when twenty-four city-states had to argue over every detail. Not that Sloan, right now, could be considered a "detail."

The delegates wore a bizarre variety of business tunics and what Sloan supposed were "native costumes" from old Earth—why? It had been a hundred fifty years since the Escape began. If Samuel Peregoy had been the first to claim Polyglot instead of that lunatic nationalist Patrick Fenton, this planet would look much different now. Assimilation aided identity and reduced conflict.

Conflict . . . but he wasn't going to think now about SueLin and her ridiculous "resistance."

"Greetings, Director Peregoy," said this year's Council president Allie Bakshi, a middle-aged woman in a crimson sari. Another problem with Polyglot: a different leader every two years disrupted any continuity of policy. And not everyone in the Council spoke English. Sloan saw no translators except his own; they were probably linked to their principals through earplants. Ridiculous. A planet should have a universal tongue.

However, Sloan did approve of the Council chamber. Made of stone and foamcast, it somehow managed to look impressive without ostentation or wasted expense. A high, wide dome roofed with invisible plastiglass, so that it seemed they were under open sky. Unadorned white columns in a colonnade around the perimeter, with the huge circular table, a hollow O, in the center. To one side was an observer or guest section behind a low polished railing. The only decorations were tubs of healthy native plants from the different island nations of Polyglot. Simple and yet majestic, conveying authority. Sloan would tell his architects.

President Bakshi rose and made a ritual speech in excellent, musically accented English. A few minutes into her remarks, a ripple of astonishment spread around the table and through the subordinates in the colonnade. Sloan turned to follow the gazes. Rachel Landry and two bodyguards walked toward the table.

Sloan felt his upper lip lift and his nostrils spread.

Almost a low growl formed in the back of his throat. He controlled himself, betraying nothing. What was she doing here? She must have come the long way around, through the Galt-Earth gate to Terra and then the Earth-Polyglot gate. Damn the Council for insisting that he delay his presentation a week until every single last member had arrived from their insignificant nations!

A man stopped Rachel Landry and spoke to her. She nodded. The two bodyguards left; personal security was not permitted in the chamber, and weapons nowhere on Council grounds. Although there was no telling what hidden and unknowable weapons Landry had on her person; everyone knew it was unregulated mayhem on Galt. And this woman had somehow devised a way to destroy an entire cargo ship during transit through a gate.

President Bakshi spoke to the Landry woman, after which she was permitted to take a seat in the same guest section as Sloan, although not beside him. Several other people sat between them. President Bakshi resumed her place at the table, still standing.

"You all know why we are here," she said in English. "Director Peregoy, of Peregoy Corporation, has traveled from New California to defend Peregoy Corporation against the grave charge of violating Polyglot neutrality. This is not a trial, but Director Peregoy understands that he could be detained on Polyglot if the Council so votes, until Peregoy Corporation ends its illegal seizure of the Polyglot-Galt gate and also pays sufficient reparations to Polyglot. These acts are unprecedented in the history of the Eight Worlds, and all Council members are encouraged to not underestimate their significance. Then, quite unexpectedly but in the interest of fairness, we will hear from Rachel Landry, CEO of Freedom Enterprises and head of the Landry Libertarian Alliance. Director Peregoy, you may begin."

Not an impartial introduction, but no more than Sloan had expected. The faces watching him, brown and black and white, were wary and hard-eyed. It was important that he not underestimate them, even though he considered them a disorganized pack of misbegotten idealists, surviving only because Polyglot happened to be the largest, lushest, and best favored of planets.

"Members of the Council of Nations, thank you for allowing me on Polyglot and for agreeing to hear me this afternoon. President Bakshi has named a grave act on the part of Peregoy Corporation, and she is correct. I very much appreciate the opportunity to explain to you three circumstances concerning Peregoy violation of Polyglot neutrality.

"The first you already know, although perhaps not in detail. Peregoy Corporation declared war on the Landry empire—a war *we did not start*. A Peregoy ship, the *Samuel Peregoy*, went through the new gate discovered beyond Prometheus, and discovered there a small orbital around a new planet. A scout ship made contact with the orbital and one man boarded it. Immediately afterward he, the scout, and the Peregoy cruiser were blown up by a bomb on the booby-trapped orbital—a *Landry* bomb. We have proof of this, and the Landrys have never denied it."

Sloan paused and looked directly at Rachel Landry. All gazes followed his. If she denied it, he had the recordings to play. Revealing her to be a liar, in addition to a murderer, could only help his cause.

She said nothing.

Sloan continued. "Three hundred people died aboard the *Samuel Peregoy*, including my cousin Magda Peregoy. If that had been a Polyglot cruiser wantonly destroyed, what would the response of Polyglot have been? You are a neutral planet—but in the face of a direct, brutal attack on a Polyglot ship, would you not have responded? Your citizens depend on their leaders for their safety, each and every precious life in each and every one of Polyglot's twenty-four nations."

There—an appeal to nationalism, a driving force on Polyglot. Nationalism stupidly fragmented worlds, but it was useful to Sloan now.

"But why, you're probably asking, wage this war by taking the Polyglot-Galt gate, violating Polyglot neutrality? The second circumstance guided that decision. You know that the first battle of this war occurred at the Prometheus gate, Polyglot territory under lease to Peregoy Corporation. We lost that battle, and the gate. What you may not know is that the Landrys deployed a new weapon, which we have since learned they call the 'K-beam,' with a firing range much greater than anything possessed by either the Peregoy or Polyglot fleets. This weapon is, quite literally, capable of defeating any ship anywhere in space—which of course includes Polyglot's four gates. Peregoy Corporation decided it must act quickly to protect both our planets and Polyglot, and so took the Galt-Polyglot gate to prevent any ships equipped with this weapon from attacking Polyglot neutrality, on which we all depend. The only way to protect Polyglot is to wait on your side of the gate and destroy any Landry ships coming through from Galt before they can deploy this brutal new weapon."

A rising murmur among the Council. Before it could swell, Sloan held up his hand. "So why didn't we inform Polyglot of this weapon and let them decide if they wished Peregoy to defend your planet? *No time.* We had no idea when the Landry Alliance would attack next, or with what. And subsequent events proved us right. But before I get to that, the third circumstance, let me say that, even if time-driven, Peregoy Corporation's unilateral decision to take the Polyglot-Galt gate was a violation of Polyglot's rights, for which I'm prepared to make reparations. For every Polyglot ship carrying goods to a Peregoy world, Peregoy Corporation will pay ten percent over and above the goods' value. Half of that will go to whatever entity, whether corporation or state, is registered as the vessel's owner. The other half will be paid directly to the Council of Nations. Thus will Peregoy Corporation demonstrate its good faith toward, and solidarity with, Polyglot."

A cacophony of voices. Again, Sloan held up his hand.

"Please, let me finish. The third and most damning circumstance is yet to be named—although I know that you already are aware of it. The Peregoy cargo vessel *Quasar III* was destroyed within the Polyglot-New California gate by yet another new Landry weapon. Your own surveillance drones, like ours, have shown that. The *Quasar III* entered the gate on the New California side, and never came out the Polyglot side. Why do I think that the vessel's destruction was caused by a Landry weapon? Because Peregoy Corporation, obviously, would not destroy our own ship. Nor would neutral Polyglot. In a hundred fifty years, no gate has ever malfunctioned. That leaves the Landrys, with whom my corporation is at war. What is the obvious conclusion?

"And who is next? One of your ships, to bring Polyglot under Landry control? Libertarians, as you well know, do not believe in the rule of law, only in individual self-interest. If Polyglot is vulnerable, they will take it. And more lives will be lost, lives like these."

Sloan held out a portable holoprojector and activated it. Four holos jumped out, life-sized on the Council chamber floor. Two older men, a middle-aged woman, and a young man. "Captain Joshua Murphy of New California, commanding the *Quasar III*. Warranty Officer Chloe Wang of New California. Spacer first class David Twenge of New Yosemite."

As he named each, the holo disappeared, leaving only the last, a handsome young man with pale brown skin, very white teeth, and a mop of thick hair. He smiled from his illusion of light, then waved one hand.

"Spacer Scott Richard Schneider, of Zuhause, Polyglot."

Now the cacophony was unrestrained. Zuhause was among the richest of Polyglot's nations. Schneider's expression was eager, open, a young person avid for life. A citizen of Polyglot's largest nation, New America, would have been better, but Sloan was glad to have gotten Schneider.

Over the clamor rose a single voice, climbing to a shriek. "No!" Rachel Landry screamed. "It wasn't us! There was ... once before ... Tara ..."

She clutched at her chest, staggered sideways, and fell.

People rushed to her. For a moment, indignation held Sloan immobile—how dare she steal his speech like that? And with a staged, melodramatic collapse? Then he saw that it was not staged. Rachel Landry, a decade older than Sloan, had had a heart attack.

For an instant, mortality brushed him with cold wings. Then he stepped forward, pasting concern onto his face. "A doctor! Send for a doctor!"

His mind raced, calculating whether it would be better or worse if Rachel Landry died. Would that create a martyr? Or create weakness on Galt due to confusion and rivalry among the Landry grand-daughters?

How should he play this now?

18

GALT

Philip lay on a blanket hand-woven of rough juba fibers in a field of experimental crops at the edge of the university campus. Stars glittered above him, impossibly high. He couldn't name any of the Galt constellations, so different from those of distant Polyglot. Around him rose the scent, pungent but not unpleasant, of whatever plants grew in the darkness. Unseen fronds rustled softly. Beside him on the blanket, wetting its design with its last spilled drops, a bottle of the strong local wine lay on its side. It was not the only bottle.

Maybe that would free his mind. Nothing else had. He was desperate. Also very drunk.

A meteor streaked across the field of stars.

In the distance an animal made a quick, harsh noise.

Something small and many-legged skittered across his outflung hand.

He could not get there—wherever "there" was. With the presences. To the basement level of reality, down there among the old crates and dusty broken machinery. Or whatever. It didn't matter how he thought of it, because it was beyond conscious thought. Beyond words. Also because he was such a failure at getting there, wherever "there" was...

Fuck it. Why was he the only person on the Eight Worlds who wanted this? Was he the only person? Was he really that weird, abnormal, out of his mind?

Yes.

No. "Out of his mind" was where he wanted to go, and couldn't.

He was just about to give up, stagger back to his university room, and sleep off the wine, when the stars began to swirl above his head. They circled slowly, a stately minuet, then moved toward each other to coalesce into a shining globe until, all at once, Philip was among them, was them, was everywhere and nowhere.

A presence, registering surprise. No, not a presence, *presences*—or not. But Philip was among them, was them. They made, or were beside, or clustered around, a door. A portal, an entryway, wide open. Philip turned his attention to it, this thing of energy. It closed around him, taking him in. Then it vanished, or he did.

None of those words described what had happened, or how. There were no words for something so beyond language.

He lay on the blanket, now soggy with morning dew. His body felt stiff and cold; his mouth tasted sour with last night's wine. Thin strips of color stained a gray sky.

Slowly, Philip creaked upright. He had been there,

at the fifth level of awareness, the substrate underlying the universe, among...what? He didn't know. But he'd been there, and now he knew they existed. Not just as energy, but as energy's condensed twin, matter in some strange form. Not just in timelessness, but in time—his time. Somewhere. He had touched...something. He had done...something. He had been *there*.

Philip limped toward the lighted building beyond the field. He was elated, confused, hung over, apprehensive, and very, very hungry.

Philip and Julie sat in her office at the Institute for Brain Research, he on a chair with a too-hard back and she barricaded behind her desk. As if, he thought bitterly, she needed more barriers than the emotional ones she'd already erected between them. Maybe she did.

The office was preternaturally neat and elegant in its simplicity, like Julie herself. She wore a dark blue business tunic that was neither tight nor loose, a necklace of light blue stones, her hair in a tight chignon. She looked untouchable.

"Julie—" he began, not even trying to keep the pleading out of his voice. Bad enough that he was still hung over, and looked it.

"No," she said crisply. "I called you here to tell you that this phase of the research study is finished. We have all the data about your implants that we need."

He felt a smile split his face. "Good! Then you and I can—"

"No, Philip. What happened was a breach of professional ethics. My fault entirely. There will be follow-up phases to the research in a few months."

"And you'll be doing that, too?"

"Well...no. I have a different project, now that we're at war. I'll be—"

"I don't care," he said, anger turning him rude. "So you and I could see each other again, you just don't want to."

She said nothing.

"It's because of what I've told you happened, isn't it. My sensing—no, *touching*—something out there. Leaving my body to do it. You think I'm crazy, and you don't want to get involved with a crazy person."

"Not 'crazy.' But delusional, yes. I'm sorry."

She was—deeply sorry, and Philip didn't care. The first woman he ever thought he could love, and she was kicking him away because of what was, in fact, the most important thing about him.

"Philip—it's the brain implants. They've intensified your neural pathways, so that you believe even more deeply what was never true in the first place. You're a wonderful person, but the—"

"But nothing," he said, and rose because he couldn't bear to look at her any longer. It was the old, old divide between materialists and mystics, those who thought the mind was nothing more than the actions of the brain and those who knew differently because they'd experienced differently. Experience that could not be measured, could not be replicated at will, could not even be described in words or numbers—and so, to the scientific mind, did not exist.

Philip left. Julie did not try to stop him. He heard her sob just once, a sharp catch of breath, but he didn't turn around.

19

THE ELEVENTH GATE

Cloud cover, denser than before, wrapped the planet in mystery. No sensors on the *Skyhawk* registered any different data than before Martinez had sent the scout to the surface. He finished his report to Sloan Peregoy, summoned Lieutenant Gruber to his quarters, and gave him orders and codes to get it directly to Sloan or Sophia Peregoy, via New Utah. Gruber would have to spend three months alone in space, but Martinez had picked him carefully. The lieutenant could handle it.

Martinez went to the bridge. He had nothing to do there. He had nothing to do anywhere. No Landrys had appeared through the eleventh gate; no aliens had appeared on the planet; no further instructions had, or could as of yet, come by scout from Sloan. Had the new Landry weapon captured more Peregoy gates? It was frustrating not knowing what was happening elsewhere, since nothing was happening here.

I am not built for inaction, Martinez thought, not for the first time. All his life, he'd counted this as his greatest personal challenge: to wait patiently, to restrain his overflowing energy until the best time to act. He thought that, by and large, he had learned that difficult lesson, but not easily.

On the viewscreen, he watched the scout launch from the *Skyhawk* and fly toward the gate. Vondenberg and Murphy were undoubtedly doing the same, also victims of inaction. During the past two weeks, Martinez had sent two more expeditions down to the planet, searching for something—anything—to put in his report to Sloan. There was nothing. Finally, he had to send yet another of his limited number of scouts.

"Approaching gate," Gruber said.

That lovely, strange, inexplicable shimmer.

"Entering gate . . . wait . . . *what*?"

Everyone on the bridge snapped up straighter. The scout hovered at the edge of the shimmer.

"Gruber," Martinez said sharply, "what's wrong? Do you have a malfunction?"

"No, sir—the gate has a malfunction. It won't let me enter!"

"Send ship data!"

It was already arriving. The scout's drive labored at maximum power. Nothing happened.

"Sir, I can't see anything different, but it's like the gate is suddenly pushing me away. Matching my power so I can't move forward. Is that possible?"

"It's never happened before. Retreat and approach again."

He did. Martinez watched the sensor data, which told him nothing. The gate was not emitting any different radiation, but it was not yielding. A new Landry weapon? But drones patrolling the space-side of the gate had not reported any Landry ships approaching; nor had the scouts sent periodically to check on the drones. Martinez was no physicist, but surely it wasn't in the scope of human knowledge to just close stargates?

He glanced at the planet turning beneath them. Inhuman knowledge?

An hour later, the scout still had not been able to penetrate the gate. Nor had probes or drones, no matter how small. Martinez ordered the scout to return to the *Skyhawk* and the bridge crew to fire drones at the gate every hour. Tension on the bridge, and undoubtedly throughout the entire warship, stung like tiny needles on the skin. But no one—at least, no one on the bridge—voiced the question.

What if the gate was permanently closed?

Life supplies on Martinez's three ships were not infinite.

Drone after drone failed to penetrate the gate.

After eight hours and sixteen minutes, when Martinez had been awake for twenty-five hours, a drone sailed into the maddening shimmer and disappeared.

"Yes!" the helmsman burst out, followed by, "Sorry, sir."

Martinez barely heard her. He studied the sensor data, which showed no detectable change in gate information. He sent Gruber through the gate with instructions to wait for an hour before leaving for New Utah. Gruber's scout cleared the gate. Next trial was the *Zeus*, which also passed back and forth easily through the gate.

None of it made any sense.

Gruber left with his report, and for the next few days, Martinez tested the gate often. It functioned normally. Scouts went through and back to report that there was nothing to report. Boredom resumed.

One evening, just before ship's lights dimmed for the "night," Martinez went to his cabin, opened the safe, and took out the small box Sloan had given him on New California. He stared at the bold lettering: PERSONAL. Sloan had told him not to open the box until Martinez departed New Utah for home. However, Martinez didn't see why he should delay. Either he was never going to reach New Utah and so never depart it, kept on perpetually resupplied duty guarding this alien planet, or else the Landrys would eventually show up and vaporize him with a weapon he could not match. In his current mood, neither alternative seemed worse than the other. And he was curious. And anything PERSONAL was not official orders.

He opened the e-box with the code that Sloan had given him.

It contained a datacube and a folded piece of paper labeled TRANSCRIPT OF ENCLOSED HOLO-RECORDING. Sloan being meticulous about backups. Martinez could read much faster than Sloan could talk; he opened the paper first. It was brief, hand-written in Sloan's formal, slightly pompous style:

TO LUIS MARTINEZ FROM SLOAN PEREGOY:

This is to inform you that I am disinheriting both my grandchildren, SueLin Serena Peregoy and Tarik Ryan Peregoy. My heir to

Peregoy Corporation is my daughter, Sophia Kenly Peregoy. Should she die without issue, as seems likely, my heir will be you, Luis. I am executing legal documents to that effect on New California.

This may surprise you. However, it was you who told me about the Roman emperors and Frankish kings who chose their own successors, bypassing blood kin when necessary for the good of the state. After Sophia, you are the person I trust most to guide the Peregoy worlds in the ideals we both believe in: care of and employment for every citizen plus stewardship of the planetary environments, all ensured by a strong hand at the top exercising ceaseless vigilance.

By the time you return to New California, I hope we have won the war with Landrys. I will then prepare my vice-presidents to accept your eventual stewardship, as will Sophia, who agrees with me about your inheritance after her. My kin will be provided for, the funds tied up in such a way that they have its use but no control over Peregoy holdings.

I do this for the good of the worlds in my care.

Sloan Richard Peregoy

Martinez sat down, stood up, took a few aimless steps. Surprise put him on automatic pilot, not aware of what he did. When he returned to himself, he read the letter again, then viewed the holo. It consisted only of Sloan reading the same letter, his face impassive as ever, his voice dry.

Him. Luis Martinez. To inherit the Peregoy empire.

He'd known, of course, that if he'd married Sophia, his influence would increase. Not, however, all that much—Sophia Peregoy was a woman who kept firm control of what was hers. But now, if Sophia died before him . . .

Did he even want Peregoy Corporation? Did he want to run three planets—or four, if he could keep the one rotating below his ship—instead of, as he'd hoped would be his future, eventually becoming admiral of Peregoy Corporation Space Service?

He didn't know. He wasn't sure of anything: not what his future should be, not if he would survive to have a future, not why Landry warships hadn't yet arrived here, not why the stargate had closed and then opened again.

He shut down the holo, held the letter in his hands as if it were a bomb, and watched the cloud-covered planet turn slowly on its invisible axis.

20

GALT

The nurse bot brought Rachel another blanket and laid it over her. Its mechanical voice said, "Can I bring you anything else?"

"No," Rachel said. She didn't like human-shaped bots, not even those manufactured by a Landry subsidiary. In her penthouse, she permitted only cleaning bots, which were shaped like ottomans with tentacles. All five granddaughters laughed at this "weird quirk." However, no one was laughing now.

Rachel remembered nothing of her heart attack, the hospital on Polyglot, or the emergency trip back home. Sloan Peregoy had allowed a "compassionate exception" to allow her ship through the Polyglot-Galt gate. As if that old reprobate were ever capable of compassion.

She lay in a room at the top of Galt Hospital Center, a cheerful, flower-filled room with yellow curtains open to a lovely view of the mountains. The room was designed to raise the spirits of patients more capable of cheer than Rachel. She was supposed to remain quiet and unstressed.

Not possible.

"System on," she said, and the wallscreen brightened. Rachel said, "Perform retinal ID. . . . Locate and summon Tara Serena Landry."

"No," the wall said.

No? "Access Freedom Enterprises data."

"No," the screen repeated, and a human nurse rushed into the room. "Ms. Landry, you must remain quiet. Visitors must be approved by Dr. Coleman and all visits monitored."

"Fuck that," Rachel said, and realized she sounded like Tara. This wasn't the nurse's fault. "I'm sorry. But I want my granddaughter Tara brought to me—she's in the mental-disturbances area of this hospital—with whatever attendants are necessary. My orders override the doctor's."

"I'm afraid not."

For a moment, Rachel could not process the words. Her orders always overrode anyone else's. Then she saw how frightened the young nurse looked, and how hard she was trying to hide her fright. Rachel changed tactics. "Is my oldest granddaughter, Annelise Landry, on the approved list?"

"Yes."

"Good. Summon her." Calm, sensible Annelise—of course she was on the list. Caitlin would be, too, and Rachel would see her soon. Caity always cheered her up. But it was Annelise who would know what was happening with Freedom Enterprises, with the protests, with the war. It would have been Annelise who decided who was on Rachel's visiting list. Rachel didn't even ask about Jane.

When Annelise arrived from headquarters, Rachel smiled, looked serene, and made sure her voice sounded strong. "Hello, dear heart."

"Oh, I'm glad to see you looking so much better, Rachel."

"I feel better. But I need to know what happened on Polyglot, what's happening now. Not knowing is causing me more tension than knowledge would."

Annelise nodded. It was how she herself would have felt. "Sloan Peregoy—do you remember his speech to the Polyglot Council?"

"Perfectly."

"Yes. Well, it succeeded. Peregoy Corporation and Polyglot are now in loose alliance, although Polyglot is 'keeping its neutrality.' A contradiction, of course, but everyone pretends to accept it. Such an alliance can't last."

Annelise watched her closely, undoubtedly looking for signs of agitation. Rachel was careful to show none, although under the extra blanket, she clenched both fists hard. "Go on."

"There's been a good result, though, of that alliance. Protests against us here on Galt have almost stopped. The war has created a lot of new jobs—Jane and Caitlin have seen to that. Jane is building the fleet, and Caitlin is organizing civil preparedness in case of attack. The—"

"Funded how?"

"By Freedom Enterprises, of course. We have to."

"Yes. So no more protests at headquarters?"

"Oh, some, of course. The would-be parasites still

resent us Landrys. But the protests aren't like before, and Jane's deputies are . . . are doing a good job of quelling them."

Rachel, hyper-alert and completely familiar with her granddaughters, said, "What about Jane? There's something you're not telling me."

"No, nothing."

"I don't believe you, Annelise." She kept her tone reasonable, but dread slid through her. Jane, with her new uniform and her new title of Commander-in-Chief and war fever burning in her eyes . . .

"Oh, another thing you'll want to know: Celia's son Savron is getting married to a mining engineer, that young man . . . What was his name? Oh—Dennis. Unfortunately, the wedding will be on New Hell and with the new travel restrictions of the war—"

"Annelise. What about Jane?"

"Aren't you interested in your great-grandson's wedding?"

"Yes, but not now. *Jane.* What is she doing? What aren't you telling me?"

"Nothing. You're getting agitated, Rachel. Rest now. I'll look in on you tomorrow."

"No. Now. What about Jane? Tell me—I'm still CEO!"

Annelise stood at the foot of the bed and looked steadily at her grandmother. Rachel saw the thing it was easy to forget about Annelise: under the calm face and gentle voice was the same unyielding stubbornness as Jane, as Tara, as Rachel herself. Tara and Jane were all sharp spikes; Annelise was a smooth wall. The only way to breach that wall was through appeals to logic and tradition.

Annelise said, "While you're incapacitated, I'm acting CEO. It's in the corporate by-laws. Rest, Rachel." She glided from the room.

"Come back here, Annelise! Come back here now and listen to—"

The nurse rushed in. "Calm yourself, Ms. Landry! Your heart! No, you can't get up, you—"

"I am getting up! And I'm going to fight you and everyone else, I'm going to throw things, I'm going to fire all of you if I don't see my granddaughter Jane right now!"

Dr. Coleman was summoned. Rachel, with a super-human effort, quieted herself. With a combination of threats, ersatz calm, and authority, she bargained with him, all the while feeling sorry for the poor man, but not sorry enough.

The doctor gave her access to Freedom Enterprises data, under supervision.

Rachel learned that Jane was off-planet, having gone through the Galt-Earth gate and then, instead of going directly on to Rand through the Earth-Rand gate, had gone down to the Terran surface. Earth? Why would Jane, in the midst of war preparations, go to that ruined and barely livable planet? All Earth could offer were bands of strange, radiation-poisoned people who refused to leave humanity's first home, surviving at practically a subsistence level.

Rachel said sweetly to the nurse, "I'd like to see my granddaughter Caitlin. I'm sure she's on the visiting list. And she's right here, at the university."

"I'll see what Dr. Coleman says."

He said that Rachel needed to rest first, but that Caitlin could come in the evening. Rachel stamped down a sharp reply and obediently closed her eyes. To her own surprise, she did sleep, and woke feeling refreshed by both her nap and the sight of Caitlin sitting quietly beside Rachel's bedside, reading on a tablet.

"Caity."

"You're awake. How are you, Gran?"

"Better now that you're here."

Caitlin smiled. Rachel appreciated the sweetness of Caitlin's smile, but not as much as her sense of balance. Balance was in short supply among the Landrys.

Rachel got right to the point. "What is Jane doing on Earth?"

Caitlin's brows shot up. "I didn't know Jane had gone to Earth."

Another door closed.

"She has. You really don't know anything?"

"I would tell you if I did."

True. Rachel said, "Then tell me about the civil preparedness program that Annelise said you're in charge of."

Caitlin did, concluding with, "But don't give me too much credit, Gran. I've mostly farmed the prep out to committees, who are doing the job well." She took a deep breath. "I've been spending time at the refugee camp. The one closest to the university."

"Why?"

"Conditions there are deplorable. They . . . no, don't look like that. I'm not going to argue Libertarian principles with you, not again. Your doctor said to keep my visit short and—his exact words—'non-threatening.' I don't know what he thought I would threaten you with."

"A knife."

"An axe."

"A torpedo."

"More likely," Caitlin said shrewdly, "a balance sheet. The ultimate weapon."

Rachel laughed, which hurt but was worth it.

They bantered more; Caitlin was the only one who understood Rachel's jokes. Rachel cheered up but didn't lose sight of her main objective. When Caitlin left, Rachel had her summon the doctor on duty. Rachel had risked her life with her earlier tantrum, or so they said, and she wasn't going to waste that until she found out what she wanted to know.

"Dr. Coleman, I want to see my youngest granddaughter, Tara. She's in the mental-disturbance ward of this hospital."

He folded his lips into such a thin line that they seemed to disappear. Finally he said, "All right. Tara Landry is recovering well. She can be brought here for a short visit, under supervision, if you promise not to get up again."

A contract. "All right."

Tara was not exactly "recovering well;" she was obviously on serious medication. She was escorted in, sat in a chair beside her grandmother's bed, and smiled gently. Her nurse, who might have also been her guard, withdrew to the window and tactfully studied the distant mountains as if trying to move them.

"Hi, Gran. How are you?"

"I'm—"

"I'm doing much better, and my nurse is nice." Tara began a long, irrelevant story about the nurse and a breakfast tray of pancakes. Rachel saw that whatever Tara was on made her talkative. So not a sedative but some other, newer influencer of brain chemistry. How distractible and uninhibited did it make Tara, who had always been interested in anything discreditable about her sisters? How much could Rachel learn?

Rachel had thought long about exposing Tara's monstrous act of setting the bomb at the eleventh gate. Galt had no courts as such; each settlement administered justice as it saw fit. In the capital, Freedom Enterprises' security division caught, tried, and imprisoned wrongdoers, empowered by the corporation that owned the city. Those who didn't like that were free to move elsewhere. Rachel and Annelise could pardon anyone they chose.

Tara had committed murder.

On the other hand, everyone who'd died at the eleventh gate had arrived there on a Peregoy warship, and killing enemies in wartime wasn't murder—was it? Also, Tara was clearly mentally ill, and had been for a long time. Was she responsible for her actions? Or was Rachel, who had not seen in time how unbalanced Tara had become, really the one responsible?

In the end, Rachel had chosen to say nothing about Tara's bomb. That might not be an ethical decision— Caitlin would certainly think it was not—but Rachel determined to spend her resources on stopping this war, not on providing Sloan Peregoy with more propaganda to carry it on.

"Tara," she said when the pancake story finally ended, "Annelise was just in to see me."

Tara made a face.

"She told me that Savron is getting married. But she wouldn't tell me about—"

"I'll never marry. Philip didn't come. I waited and waited at Adarsh, but he didn't come."

"No. About Jane—"

"He'll never come. He doesn't want me. He wants that stupid mysticism of his, when he touched the stars five years ago. Or something. He can't even explain it properly! Why would you want some fucking thing that happened five years ago instead of a real life? And now I don't even know where Philip is!"

Tara was getting agitated. Her guard turned from the window. Rachel, who knew that Philip Anderson was in the city at the Institute of Brain Research, reached for Tara's hand. "I'm so sorry, dear heart. But don't get upset now or you'll have to leave."

Tara ignored this. She gripped Rachel's hand and leaned forward. "That fucking mysticism. Five years ago. It was Fourmonth 16, and that's tomorrow again, and I don't know where he is."

"I'm sure he's all right."

"Really?" Tara said, her gaze suddenly much steadier. "Will you find him for me?"

So Tara was not as disconnected as she seemed. Had Rachel just been played? As she hesitated, Tara tossed her hand back.

"You won't, will you? You won't find him. Jane can find a Peregoy on old Earth, and you can't even find Philip on Polyglot!"

"Jane found a—which Peregoy?"

Tara's face creased with cunning. "If I tell you, will you promise to find Philip?"

"Yes." Rachel sacrificed Philip. Besides, she hadn't said when she would find him. "But you have to tell me everything about Jane. And how do you know it?"

"People talk. I hear them. Sometimes they don't know I'm there, listening. I creep around, and as long as I'm good, they let me. I get to the Link. And I can hack real good."

What kind of security went on in the mental-disturbance ward? Although all at once Tara didn't actually look all that disturbed, except for her obsession about Philip. Certainly Tara didn't look dangerous to herself or anybody else. And this was Galt, where personal freedom was all.

Tara started to rave about Philip, his handsomeness and intelligence and general godliness. Rachel interrupted with a bargaining technique she'd used with all her grandchildren when they'd been younger. "Tell me three things, just three, that I don't know about Jane, in return for my promise to find Philip."

"All right." Tara thought, evidently wrenching her thoughts away from Philip. "First, she's investigating what happened at Prometheus gate."

"You mean that her K-beam let us seize the gate?" That was old news.

"No, what happened ten days ago. Everybody is talking about it. The gate all of sudden closed for over eight hours. Just wouldn't let ships through. Then it opened."

Rachel blurted, "That isn't possible."

Tara shrugged. "Everybody says it happened. My nurse—"

"All right." Rachel didn't want a return to the pancake story. "That's one thing. Now tell me about the Peregoy that Jane found on Earth."

Tara grinned maliciously; she was still Tara. She glanced at her guard and then lowered her voice—yet another indication that Tara was not as disconnected from reality as she pretended. "Well, Jane didn't exactly find her. Not yet. But she knows that SueLin Peregoy is on Earth."

Rachel, not able to help herself, gasped. "How do you know?"

"Can't tell you. It's secret."

Was it true? Why would SueLin Peregoy, about whom Rachel knew very little except that she was Sloan Peregoy's granddaughter and the eventual heir to Peregoy Corporation, be on Earth? Tara must have made this up. Could Rachel trust anything Tara said?

"And the third thing," Tara said, "is that Jane and Annelise don't want you to be CEO anymore. They don't think you can do it since your heart attack. I know because I'm still on the family encrypted channel—remember? You put me on so I'd get interested in Freedom Enterprise's stupid business dealings. Well, I'm not. But I listen sometimes because my doctor thinks it will get me involved with the family. She doesn't know what I actually hear. That's how I learned about SueLin Peregoy, too. She was leading protests against her grandfather, maybe trying to seize power. That's what Jane thinks."

Rachel's heart began thumping wildly. She tried to make herself relax. Biosensors alerted the staff and the nurse strode into the room. "That's enough, Ms. Landry. Your grandmother needs to rest and you need to leave."

Tara didn't argue. She rose, put her finger to her lips, and whispered, "Remember—you promised to find him for me."

The nurse summoned Dr. Coleman, who prescribed something in a syringe. Rachel submitted, She needed her body calm as her mind raced.

SueLin Peregoy on Earth.

Annelise and Jane believed that Rachel was no longer capable as CEO.

Regret pierced Rachel. She'd missed her chance to remove Jane from power, and now it was too late. Rachel was a helpless old woman in a hospital bed.

No. You'll get well. Think about something else besides yourself. Think bigger.

The Prometheus gate had somehow closed for over eight hours. Was that another new weapon of Jane's that she'd been testing at the far edge of the frontier? Rachel had been a physicist, still read the latest research when she had time. No, it wasn't possible that some new weapon could manipulate the totally unknown physics of the gates. So whatever had happened a tenday ago, it hadn't been that.

Just before the sedative took her, Rachel had another thought.

The *Quasar III*, disappearing into a gate and never emerging.

A gate "closing" ten days ago.

Fourmonth 16, almost five years past. She remembered Fourmonth 16.

No, not possible.

"I need access to..." she began, just before the drug took her.

21

GALT

Days and nights of grief.

After Julie discarded him—that's how it felt, yes—Philip left the university, rented a cheap room in the city, and tried to touch again whatever he'd reached while lying, drunk, in that field. That touching had happened at night, so he bought sleeping pills, slept all day, tried all night. He experimented with drinking, then fasting, then lying for hours in a warm bath. Nothing worked. He meditated on his bed, outdoors in a park, on the roof of his boardinghouse, almost tumbling off its steep pitch. He began to wonder if Julie was right, and he was becoming crazy. His obsession reminded him uncomfortably of Tara.

He paid no attention to news, including the war, which seemed just as remote as what he now thought of as metaconsciousness. He barely ate, growing thinner. He stopped shaving or having his hair cut. Some days he didn't shower. The room, already musty with stale odors, grew mustier. The window had been painted shut. Philip's money was running out.

I have to stop this.

I can't stop this.

When he wasn't trying to connect to the universe—and how stupid that sounded, even—he read physics on his tablet. He couldn't afford access to scientific journals, which—like everything else on Libertarian Galt—were not free. But the university library had vast archives, many of them from old Earth. Philip read about two-hundred-year-old theories, never proven, as the slow train wreck of the Terran collapse took scientific inquiry down with it.

Physicist Gregory Matloff's idea of a "proto-consciousness field" extending through all of space.

Bernard Haisch's rogue theory that quantum fields produce and transmit consciousness in any sufficiently complex system, organic or not.

John Wheeler's "participatory anthropic principle."

Much older, Roger Penrose's argument that quantum events in the brain link self-awareness with the cosmos.

And oldest of all, Albert Einstein's "cosmic religious feeling."

Although what Philip felt, what he touched, was not religious—was it?

He meditated again. Nothing.

But once, he did succeed, at least partially. Definite contact, but he couldn't sustain it. He was like a drowning man who gulped one lungful of air before the waters again closed over him. And he couldn't go there again. But he had touched it, or them, and that emboldened him to keep trying.

He was lying on the bed with a plate of congealed

food on the floor beside him, waiting for night, when someone knocked on the door. The room was not electronically wired. Philip leapt up and flung open the door. "Go away and leave me alone!"

Two men, both in Freedom Enterprises security uniforms. "Philip Anthony Anderson?"

"Go away!" He started to slam the door. One of the men deftly blocked him.

The other said, "Philip Anderson, I have a message for you from Freedom Enterprises CEO Rachel Landry. She wants to see you immediately. We'll take you there, sir." He handed Philip a datacube.

Rachel Landry? Hadn't Julie told him that she was very ill, that the Landry granddaughters were running the corporation? He hadn't really listened.

Curiosity pricked him. Also, he was nearly flat-out broke. Rachel had brought him to Galt; perhaps she would fund his return home. Although wasn't the Galt-Polyglot gate now in Peregoy hands? Philip slid the tiny datacube into his wrister. The two men didn't turn away, so presumably they already knew what the cube contained.

The visual was not Rachel's face, but a holo of a gate against a miniature star field. Her voice said, "Philip, please go with these men. I have a way for you to get what you most desire."

He blinked. Probably the guards thought that meant sending him back to Polyglot. Philip knew better.

He said, "Give me five minutes to shower and pack."

They drove him out of the city. Philip smelled the sea long before he saw it. The security men would answer no questions about why Rachel was here, away from the city, instead of in a hospital or at her apartment in the Landry compound. If one of the guards hadn't already spoken to him, Philip might have thought they were both mute.

They passed through a gate in an electronically fortified wall and up a winding drive bordered with flowers. The rich on Galt, with none of the taxation taken for granted on Polyglot, certainly did themselves well. The house sat on a cliff above the ocean, with a gorgeous view of blue water dotted with distant islands. Rachel greeted him in a wide, plastiglass-walled room. She lay on a sofa, dressed in a long-sleeved top and calf-length filmy skirt the same color as the sea, made of some material that probably cost as much as Philip's weekly salary. She looked paler and thinner than he remembered.

"Philip. Thank you for coming." She flicked her eyes toward the guards, who immediately left the room.

"It didn't seem I had much choice. Would you have kidnapped me?"

"Yes. This is that important."

Her directness reminded him of Julie, which hurt. "What exactly is so important?"

"Not here. Help me up."

He gave her his hand. Carefully, as if she'd aged decades in the months he'd been on Galt, she rose to her feet, leaning heavily on his arm. He said, "Are you well enough to stand? Shouldn't you have a carrybot?"

"No, and no. Take me to the elevator. Over there."

A small plastiglass elevator took them down the cliff face. The beach below them was pure, pale blue sand. Dyed to match the water and sky, he supposed, and grimaced. What chemicals had it put into the environment?

They left the elevator, Rachel again took his arm, and they walked slowly toward the water. "We can talk safely here."

"Who would, or could, overhear you in the house?"

"Oh, you'd be surprised."

Drones flew noiselessly overhead, each bearing the Landry logo. Philip didn't know if they were eavesdroppers, security, or possibly fakes bearing Peregoy bombs. Rachel ignored them.

At the water's edge she sank gracefully onto the sand, her filmy skirt billowing around her. "We can talk here. The surf masks pretty much all sound. But cover your mouth, like this, so your lips can't be seen."

"Rachel—is all this necessary?"

"Yes. I need to ask you some questions, and to give you some vital information. What happened to you on Fourmonth 16 five years ago? And at what exact time, Earth-standard?"

Philip stiffened. How had she known that? Tara, of course. But why did she, another materialist like Julie, want to know with such evident intensity?

Fuck it. He saw no reason not to tell her. "I had a mystical experience. I touched something out there that I'm now calling the metaconsciousness. Go ahead, roll your eyes."

She didn't. "What happened four weeks after your surgery? No, don't ask questions yet, just tell me."

"I touched it again." *After sex with Julie*, he didn't say.

"And on Fourmonth 5 of this year?"

"Yes. Rachel—"

"Tell me everything about those experiences. Don't leave anything out, especially not exact dates and times. It's vital, Philip, to every one of the Eight Worlds."

Bewildered, he told her. Her manner as she listened was so different from the last time they'd talked, so attentive, that he gave her all of it: the presences, the image of the door—"My image, not theirs"—the many failures, this morning's flicker of success before her guards interrupted him. He finished with, "They're there, Rachel. I'm not crazy. They exist, both as meta-consciousness and in or near a physical place. I had a brief impression of aridity, lifelessness, vague rounded shapes—I know how that sounds. *But I am not crazy.*"

"No. I wish you were. It would be easier." Then she was silent so long that Philip scowled.

"All right, your turn. Talk. What is this about?"

She dug her fingers deep into the blue sand. "You know that the biggest mystery about the gates, other than how they work, is why they exist only beside planets on which humans can live. The odds of that occurring naturally are . . . well, greater than the number of stars in the universe. It can't be a natural phenomenon.

"On Fourmonth 16 five years ago at 16:03 standard, a Freedom Enterprises drone entered the Galt-Polyglot gate and never came out. At first we Landrys thought that Peregoy Corporation had something to do with the disappearance, but no Peregoy ships were anywhere near there, and it never happened again. We didn't Link anything about the accident because there was, literally, no information.

"On Fourmonth 5 of this year, the Prometheus gate, which Freedom Enterprises now controls, closed for eight hours and sixteen minutes. Just closed up, so that no ships could enter it. That started, as close as I can discover, around one in the morning, Galt time.

"Before that, four weeks after your surgery, something else happened. A Peregoy cargo vessel, the
Quasar III, entered the New California-Polyglot gate
and disappeared. Never emerged on the Polyglot side.
The *Quasar III* carried a crew of four, now presumably all dead."

"No. *No*. That wasn't me!"

"Are you sure?"

He wasn't. His mind raced. Five years ago, his first
mystical experience, on the beach at New Chengdu.
Four weeks post-surgery, lying with Julie after sex, loose
and free and *gone*, immersing himself in the shimmer.
Fourmonth 5, when he lay all night in the field beside
the university and, for the first time, fully touched what
lay below all known reality. A door, a portal, that he'd
felt open, and close. He put his hands over his face.

Rachel pulled them away. "No time for grief now.
It wasn't anything you did deliberately. Philip, listen
to me . . . can you control what you do to the gates?"

"No!"

"Can you learn to control it?"

"I don't know! And how many people will die while
I practice? Only . . ."

"Only what? Tell me!"

"Last time, I almost touched . . . no, I *did* touch
the metaconsciousness. There was a . . . a beckoning.
To a place where they exist. Materially, I mean. Or
did exist. Or something."

Above the ocean, something sped toward them, low
over the water and very fast.

Rachel seized his arm. "Quick, we don't have much
time. If you went to that place, do you think you
could improve your control over the gates?"

"I don't know. How could I know? Where is such a place? Rachel, this is crazy!"

"You think I don't know that? But we don't have much choice. I think your place is the new planet, the one behind the eleventh gate. The gate that started this war."

And all at once, Philip knew that it was. That's where they were, the Others. That was the beckoning.

The speeding craft was a drone, closer now. Rachel said directly into his ear, "I'm going to send you there. You're going to learn, as fast as possible, to control the gates. And then close them all."

"What?"

"You heard me. No, don't tell me how ridiculous that is. It's our only chance."

"Our only chance of what? And how can you send me to the new planet—don't the Peregoys control it?"

"Yes. You and I are going to Polyglot. Sloan Peregoy is still there. We're going to bargain with him."

Philip just stared at her. The drone circled, flew in to descend beside them.

"Quick, they're almost here. That thing can hear a whisper a mile off. Kiss me."

He gaped.

"It's the only cover I can think of. She'll believe it." She leaned toward him.

Her lips were dry, thin, old. Her spindly arms went around him with surprising strength. Philip was afraid of hurting her. But her voice was just as strong as her arms. "It's my granddaughter, Jane. We have to get to your 'presences' and close the gates, Philip. Jane is building more ships and K-weapons. She's preparing to destroy the Peregoy fleet and, after that, every last city on New California."

22

POLYGLOT

Sloan hadn't intended to stay this long on Polyglot. But maintaining the alliance between the Council of Nations and Peregoy Corporation took constant negotiating, placating, visiting of endless officials from endless nations, which only proved how much more effective single-family rule was for everybody. Good thing Sophia was so capable of governing in his absence. Drones came daily with updates from New California. He and Sophia were managing.

He also hadn't intended such a long search for SueLin. It was ridiculous. There was nowhere on the Peregoy worlds where she could go undetected, and she certainly wasn't on any Landry planet. So she was either in space or on Polyglot, and Sloan was spending too much time every day recruiting searchers here.

Nor had he intended the war to go so quiet. The longer that the Libertarian Alliance waited to counter Sloan's alliance with Polyglot, the longer they had to build more K-beams, plus whatever Landry weapon had swallowed the *Quasar III* inside a gate. Nearly every night, Sloan lay sweating into the darkness over what that could mean. But he and Sophia were doing all they could for defense of Peregoy gates, planets, fleet, and citizens.

It wasn't enough.

"Two people requesting admission, sir," the wall said.

Sloan frowned. He was in his rooms at the hotel beside the Council of Nations, in his bathrobe, eating breakfast at a small table beside the window. Breakfast was Sloan's planning time; not even his bodyguard was allowed in the room. Unlike his system at home, this one did not I.D. visitors. No one should be bothering him until he arrived at his office in a Peregoy Corporation subsidiary. The screen showed two figures standing in the hall, a tall man and a shorter person of indeterminate gender in a high-collared tunic and large hat. Anyone without weaponry could enter the lobby of the hotel without scanning and take the elevator to corridors upstairs. Ridiculous.

Sloan snapped, "Identities!"

The short person answered. "I'm Rachel Landry, Director Peregoy."

A twisted joke. Sloan was about to summon Chavez when she said, "It is me. And I have your granddaughter SueLin and I want to talk to you about that. The building has already vetted us for weapons. It's important, Sloan."

He stiffened at the effrontery of her using his given name, but his mind raced. It couldn't be her. Rachel Landry would have been identified at the stargate or the spaceport—she was a *war criminal*, a label that until recently hadn't even existed on the Eight Worlds. Nor could she "have" SueLin. Not possible.

She said, "Your granddaughter was captured on Earth, hiding in the mountain bunker you maintain in what was old California. The entry code is 650723J. The bunker, which has now been destroyed, contained copies of the boyhood diaries of your great-great grandfather, Samuel Peregoy."

No one could have known that who hadn't actually been in the bunker. Sloan fought off a swoop of vertigo, then called Chavez and his backup in their adjoining apartment. He said to the images on his wallscreen, "Strip to your underwear or I won't open the door."

They did. "Rachel's" body was thin, wrinkled, old. The man was well-built but didn't seem heavily muscled enough for a bodyguard. Augments? Sloan's men had them, too. He told the door to open.

"Thank you," the woman said. Her face looked nothing like Rachel Landry's. She staggered slightly and the man supported her. "I must sit down."

Sloan nodded toward the sofa. She sank into it, breathing heavily. He said to the man, "You sit, too." Harder to attack that way. The man sat. He was very handsome; was this a Landry grandson-in-law that Sloan hadn't heard about? "Who are you?"

"My name is Philip Anderson. I'm a citizen of Polyglot. Rachel doesn't look like Rachel because in order to travel from Galt unrecognized, she had facial surgery and retinal transplants, giving her a new scan."

Damn. That tech didn't exist on New California. If it spread—and such things always did—it was going to seriously complicate security everywhere. And why was a woman who'd had a heart attack a month ago having repeat surgery? "Freedom" gone insane. One's health mattered.

He demanded, "Tell me about SueLin. If in fact you are Rachel Landry and you're telling me the truth."

"You know I am, Sloan. I'm here about SueLin, yes, but also much more than that. I have a story to tell you, and I've risked my life to come tell it. Philip is a part of that story."

"I'm not interested in Landry stories."

"You are in this one. And in something else: My granddaughters Annelise and Jane control Freedom Enterprises now, since my heart attack. Jane is building new ships equipped with K-beams, building them as fast as possible. She's going to destroy your entire fleet with them, and after that, attack New California. And you know it."

His nightmare, made clear by this detested woman. But Sloan kept his voice level. "You expect me to believe that you're opposed to her doing that?"

"Fuck it, Sloan, do you think I wanted this war?"

"You began it."

"No. The war is an accident by a mentally disturbed person who thought they were facilitating a joint Landry-Peregoy attack on aliens on the new planet, which you must know by now has a city there. You—"

"What person?" David Gordon, who had sold Sloan on the "investment opportunity" in the first place?

"It doesn't matter. You learned about the alien city before we took the Polyglot-Prometheus gate, didn't you?"

He had, but didn't know that she possessed that information. What else did she know? He said, skepticism frosting his voice, "Who is this mentally disturbed person who allegedly started the war?"

Rachel ignored his question and continued, though it was clear the effort cost her. "Sloan, what kind of civilization do we have where one deranged person can ignite an interplanetary war? He isn't Gavrilo Princip or Helen of Troy, for God's sake!"

Sloan didn't know who either of those people was. Luis Martinez would have known.

The man, Philip Anderson, said, "Rachel, do you want another pill?"

"No. Sloan, listen to me. Hear me. We're well on the way to duplicating all the political mistakes of old Earth, with the same catastrophic results. But we have a chance to stop it now."

"Oh? And how might that happen?" Polite sarcasm and patent disbelief. Always a good tactic: belittle the enemy.

"But we could. Here and now. The two of us."

"No." Such a simple word to change the destiny of the Peregoy worlds—and for the better. Sloan would be such a better steward of Galt than the Libertarian Landrys, who did nothing—nothing!—for their own people. And even if he didn't gain Galt, he was not going to be tricked into giving Rachel Landry and her dangerous granddaughter Jane a chance to gain, or destroy, New California.

He added, "I'm more interested in SueLin than in any Landry scheme to 'end the war.'"

"They're . . . related." She was gasping for breath now. "Philip . . . will tell you."

He did, a long fantastic tale of coincidental dates, delusional ability to control gates, mystic nonsense. And Rachel believed all this. So the bomb planter wasn't the only one who was mentally disturbed; had it been another Landry? There must be bad genes in the family.

When Anderson finished his ridiculous fandango, Sloan merely shook his head.

Rachel, who'd swallowed a pill, looked stronger now. She said, "So here's my offer. You send Philip on a Peregoy ship to the new planet. That's all you have to do. In return, I'll bring SueLin to Polyglot and give her to you."

"But you are no longer CEO of Freedom Enterprises. You just said so. You don't have any power."

"Doesn't matter. My granddaughters didn't capture SueLin. I did, with private resources they don't know about, and no one else knows where I'm holding her. You have nothing to lose, Sloan."

This was true. He would get SueLin back to deal with in his own way, without creating a martyr to her subversive cause. Rachel Landry couldn't know about the disturbing reports Sophia was sending of conscription refusal among the spoiled younger generation who wanted government care without having to actually defend it. Sloan would get back his rebellious granddaughter so he could properly and publicly disinherit her in favor of Luis Martinez. Meanwhile, this half-cracked, would-be mystic would change nothing at the eleventh gate. Sitting there in his underwear, feeding pills to a feeble old woman, Anderson looked more pathetic than anything else. And the whole fandango would buy Sloan time to deal with the Landry fleet and its new weapons. Also to move critical financial operations to Polyglot. Jane Landry wouldn't dare attack neutral Polyglot.

He said, "Before I agree, you will give me the

technology for changing retinal patterns, along with SueLin."

Philip said, with too much dismay to ever be even a passable negotiator, "But if you get her first, you could just refuse to take me to the new gate. Double-cross us."

Sloan ignored him, the ignorant puppy. "Ms. Landry?"

"I'm going to trust you, Sloan, and give you SueLin first. Not, however, the retinal transplant tech. That's not on the table. But I'm going to inform the Polyglot Council of Nations about the deal we're striking, and request that they monitor it. I don't think you'd like it known to Polyglot businesses that you don't honor contracts."

The puppy could learn from her, even if she was feeble and maybe dying. Sloan said, "Then we have a deal. Mr. Anderson, you leave tonight from Polyglot. Although it will take a fairly long time, since you'll have to go the long way around, through gates to New California, then New Yosemite, then New Utah, then the long space trip to the new gate—in all, over three months. Freedom Enterprises controls the much quicker Prometheus gate."

"Yes," Rachel said, "and I can't get a Peregoy ship safe passage through it. But a Polyglot ship can use the gate. You have an alliance here, Sloan. Put it to use. Get Philip on a Polyglot ship to Prometheus and I'll guarantee safe passage for a three-person scout through the Prometheus gate and then on to the new gate. Do it before my granddaughter Jane gets around to taking that gate away from you, too.

"To all our peril."

23

GALT

One week. That was the time for the Peregoy vessel carrying Philip Anderson to reach the Polyglot-Prometheus gate, pass through to Prometheus, and then begin the four-week trip into deep space to reach the eleventh gate. Five weeks total, and Rachel could think of nothing else. Which was unfortunate because there was a lot else to think of.

Three days after she left Polyglot, she still felt weak. However, business did not wait for weakness to pass. Rachel worked from her penthouse apartment in the Landry compound. People came and went. She was no longer CEO, but courtesy reports came in from Annelise and—more important—from Rachel's private intel networks, unknown to Annelise or Jane. Sometimes it was useful to know what was going on that her granddaughters and Freedom Enterprises VIPs might not wish to share. Between bouts of work, Rachel raised her eyes to the window, watching a storm gather over the plains to the west. High anvil clouds—there would be thunder and lightning.

"House, open the study window." All at once she wanted to feel the gathering humidity, the electric tingle in the air. It rushed in, warmer than usual, heavy with coming rain. Rachel breathed deeply. How long since she'd stood outside in a thunderstorm, letting it pelt her, laughing at the sky?

Years. Decades. She was so old.

The door said, "Terry Mwambe asking for admittance."

"Admit."

Mwambe, one of the most trusted people in Rachel's private network, entered the room. If it was useful to know what things were going on, it was even more useful to have people who could do something about those things.

"Ma'am," Mwambe said. He was tall, strong, augmented, with very dark skin and hair dyed bright red. Hardly inconspicuous, but that was intentional. Hide in plain sight.

Rachel said, "SueLin Peregoy?"

"Delivered and received on the designated orbital. Operation completed as planned."

"Thank you." Sloan had his granddaughter back, and Philip Anderson was launched on his incomprehensible mission. Rachel dismissed Mwambe and turned to something she could understand, the Freedom Enterprises aggregate quarterly audit.

She scowled. Something here was not right. The audit flagged huge withdrawals from Caitlin's personal account, which Caitlin had a right to do, supplemented by smaller, discrete transfers from general operating funds, which she did not. The funds had then been paid to a number of companies, none of which made sense. Rachel summoned her.

While she waited, she lifted her hair off the back of her neck; air from the open window was so hot. Unusual for Galt, which had such a small axial tilt that it was seasonless, a constant paradise. But even paradise had weather fronts. Rachel didn't close the window. The garden fragrances were worth the heat and humidity.

Caitlin arrived and hugged her. "Gran! You're looking much better."

"And you're a sweet liar."

Caitlin grinned. It was an old joke between them: Even as a child, Caity had only lied to make other people feel better, never to save herself from punishment. Rachel looked at her granddaughter with pleasure. Caitlin wore a pale long tunic of some synthetic material so light that it floated with every movement, along with a complicated necklace of pale stones. She looked cool and competent, but without Annelise's rigidity. She also looked defiant in a Caity sort of way, without belligerence.

Rachel said, "So what are you building at the university that you haven't told me about?" The funds had gone to contractors, some of whose companies had not existed a few months ago.

Caitlin said, "It's not at the university. It's at the refugee camp."

"So I suspected. Tell me, Caitlin, as you should have done before now."

"I don't have to report how I spend my personal monies."

"No. But you've transferred funds from Freedom Enterprises."

"Yes. I was going to tell you about those, as soon as you got stronger. I didn't realize you'd recovered so quickly."

Rachel hadn't, but she knew she looked as if she were more healthy than she actually was. Caitlin leaned forward and put her hand on Rachel's arm. "Gran, I was making conditions tolerable for the refugees. Basic housing, food, medical care. You didn't see the conditions at those camps."

"The refugees should have stayed on Rand. Millions did, helping the plague-containment effort instead of abandoning it. The refugees made their own choices. They were told that the economy here couldn't absorb them, but they came anyway."

"And mostly sold everything to do that. They were protecting their children!"

No use to argue with Caitlin about kids. She went soft and mushy over them, and why hadn't she produced any of her own? Rachel knew the answer: Caitlin was a secret romantic. She'd waited—maybe still was waiting—for the right mate, and he had never appeared.

Rachel said, "When did all this begin?"

"Months ago. Two women at one of the camps got so desperate that they threw themselves under a maglev to bring attention to conditions in the camp. They *killed* themselves."

"I remember the propaganda holos. I also remember that a refugee camp held two charity workers hostage and then mysteriously let them go. Did you pay a ransom?"

"No," Caitlin said. "That would only encourage more kidnapping. I don't know what happened there."

At least Caitlin's charity hadn't overrun her common sense.

Rachel changed tactics. "All right, you established free services at the refugee camps. That doesn't account for the enormous sums that went into 'Dyer Foamcast Contracting,' which doesn't exist."

"No. I had to create a company that would get past Annelise's accounting programs, at least for a short while. Dyer Contracting is a shell to buy passage on various small cargo vessels that normally carried trade to and from Polyglot. Since Peregoys captured the gate, many ships are idle. They're glad of the business."

"You're paying to send the refugees back to Rand. With your own money—and mine—on small cargo vessels."

"Jane has commandeered everything that can be retrofitted as warships." Caitlin's grasp on Rachel's arm tightened; her voice vibrated with passion. "Gran, these are our people. They can't just rot here, away from their homes."

"Caitlin, these are individuals who made their own choices, bad or not, and it's not your job to rescue them." But Rachel knew her voice lacked conviction.

Caitlin knew it, too. She stroked her grandmother's hair. "I'm sorry you found out this way, Gran. I was going to tell you."

"After the rescue operation was over."

"Well—after it was far enough along to finish up successfully." Caitlin grinned. She had a fine grin.

Rachel said, "I don't know."

"Don't know what, Gran?"

"Anything." *Philip Anderson*. "I don't know anything at all anymore."

"You're tired. Shall I take you home? Do you want me to call for a gurneybot?"

"Not *that* tired. I'm just going to take a nap on that sofa."

Caitlin could take a hint. She left, kissing her grandmother tenderly. The light material floated around her young body. Young? Yes, thirty-five was still young. Ninety-six was not.

Rachel lay on the sofa. Beyond the window, the sky at the horizon had whitened to the color of bone, the clouds were piled even higher, but the storm hadn't broken.

Not yet, Rachel thought. *Not quite yet.*

24

THE ELEVENTH GATE

Martinez, fortunately, was already on the bridge when his farside scout emerged from the gate, emitting the prearranged Peregoy signal. The scout pilot commed his alert: "Polyglot vessel approaching the gate! Coming from Prometheus gate. Class 6A ship."

A small Polyglot vessel? Neutral Polyglot, and coming from Prometheus? The loss of the Prometheus gate to the Landrys still stung. He said, "Approach distance?"

The scout pilot gave it: thirty hours out. Martinez had two scouts and three unmanned probes on the space side of the eleventh gate. The second scout would already be moving toward New Utah, away from any danger. Was Polyglot now in alliance with the Landrys?

There was nothing to do but wait. Surprise was his only advantage. Possibly the Landry vessel didn't know Martinez was here. He could hit the ship as it came through the gate, before it had a chance to assess the *Skyhawk's* position and deploy its new long-range weapon, if it had one. Could the new weapon even be fitted onto a small vessel rather than a warship? Martinez didn't know but was taking no chances. His orders were to allow through the gate nothing but Peregoy vessels emitting the coded signal. He watched the exec's instruments, trained on the delicate shimmer of the stargate.

Thirty hours later, a drone emerged and was immediately vaporized—but not before the *Skyhawk* had detected the Peregoy signal.

The artillery officer burst out with, "What the hell!"

Indeed. Had the Landrys cracked the signal? It was changed every day, based on a randomly generated program known to only Martinez and Peregoy headquarters. Had New California been taken by the Landrys? Was this the end of the war, and Peregoy Corporation the loser?

Or...

The drone had not been able to send position data back through the gate. Whoever sent it couldn't know the drone had just been destroyed. Martinez still had the advantage of surprise.

"Mr. Conway," he said to the artillery officer, "if anything else comes through the gate, delay firing for two seconds. If it emits the signal, delay until I give the order to fire."

"Yes, sir."

A minute passed. Two. A ship emerged from the gate, a Polyglot craft emitting the Peregoy signal.

"Don't fire!" a woman's voice cried on all-frequency broadcast. "This vessel is not armed! We come from Sloan Peregoy!"

DiCaria looked at Martinez; the exec clearly thought it was a Landry trick. But DiCaria didn't know everything.

Martinez snapped, "Give verbal classified code!"

The voice said, "Wolves hunted at night."

Correct. What was Sloan doing? Why send a Polyglot vessel? The only possible reason was to arrive here faster than any ship coming from New Utah; a Polyglot scout might get permission to use the Prometheus gate. But why would the Landrys grant that? Martinez said, "Hold fire. Vessel, use visuals. Identify self and intentions."

A wallscreen brightened, showing the bridge of the small ship. A pilot in the uniform of the pathetic Polyglot space fleet. Two Polyglot crew. A man in civilian tunic, whom Martinez had never seen before.

Before the pilot could reply, the civilian said, "I'm Philip Anderson. I'm here on a . . . a special mission authorized by Sloan Peregoy. I have a data packet for your eyes only, Captain Martinez. This vessel carries no weapons at all. I don't know if you have the means to verify that without boarding us."

Martinez didn't. "Send your retinal scan and those of everyone else aboard."

"There are only we four." Each of them leaned into a retinal scanner, which beamed the intel to the *Skyhawk*. The computer identified the three crew; Polyglot shared spacer information with all Eight worlds. The civilian, Philip Anderson, was not in the database.

Martinez said, "Why are you arriving on a Polyglot vessel from Prometheus?"

"It was faster," Anderson said. "Rachel Landry and Sloan Peregoy agreed to cooperate on sending me here, which is why this ship has the Peregoy signal but comes from Landry-occupied Prometheus. Look, Captain Martinez, I know that sounds suspicious. Why would Rachel Landry and Sloan Peregoy cooperate on anything, and how did they do that? Please allow me to send you Director Peregoy's data. He says you have the code to break the encryption. He also said to advance the gate code to the next iteration because now it has been compromised."

Martinez scowled; that had already been done. He didn't need this civilian enigma to tell him his business. "Send data now. Hold position until I order otherwise."

"Holding position, sir," the Polyglot pilot said. She, at least, understood military procedures.

The data arrived. Martinez read it on his wrister. Read it again.

His orders came authentically from Sloan Peregoy. What the hell was the old man thinking? But the orders were clear, and Martinez had no choice but to follow them.

To DiCaria he said, "Dispatch a team to rendezvous with the Polyglot vessel, board, verify absence of weapons, and bring Philip Anderson aboard the *Skyhawk*. Include Dr. Glynn—she will perform full bioscans and complete body search on Anderson. Only when she's satisfied can anyone on the team return to the *Skyhawk*. Anderson is to arrive here with nothing, including clothing. If he refuses, the scout is not to board and will return without him and await further orders."

From his face, Martinez knew that DiCaria understood what he wasn't saying. Even naked and bio-searched, Philip Anderson could be a carrier, witting or unwitting, of some new biowarfare pathogen. Martinez was doing what he could to minimize the risk, although risk remained. But Martinez had his orders.

"Yes, sir," DiCaria said.

Anderson didn't refuse. The Polyglot vessel carried no weapons at all. After Anderson boarded the *Skyhawk*, the small Polyglot ship was allowed to hover by the gate. If it moved too close to the gate, the *Skyhawk* would shoot it down. If a Landry warship came through, maybe a Polyglot vessel would confuse them. Certainly it had confused Martinez.

An hour after Anderson arrived on the *Skyhawk*, when Martinez had learned his story, Anderson left again. A *Skyhawk* scout carried him, clothed in a bulky s-suit of the kind used for research on inhospitable moons, for his insane trip downstairs. Martinez was not trusting the Polyglot ship to go down to the surface of the planet that Martinez had orders to guard.

The cloud cover was as dense as Martinez had ever seen it; he would know only what the scout and Anderson showed him. The s-suit held ten hours of air-conversion microbes. Anderson would have to return to the shuttle before that. If he lived so long.

"What if I need more time?" Anderson said.

"You don't get it." Odd—the man didn't seem crazy. But, then, Martinez had never experienced so much as an abrupt mood swing. He knew himself unequipped to judge less steady temperaments, let alone delusional ones.

"But if—"

"Those are my orders,

Martinez watched the madman descend to the thick clouds.

25

THE ELEVENTH GATE

In the *Skyhawk* scout, seated beside the pilot, Philip finally remembered the Eddington quote he had tried to recall for Julie, months ago. Arthur Eddington, brilliant maverick, physicist and mathematician and philosopher of science: *"Consciousness is not sharply defined, but fades into subconsciousness; and beyond that we must postulate something indefinite but yet continuous with our mental nature . . . the stuff of the world is mind-stuff."* A position ridiculed on several planets, starting with old Earth.

As the small craft pierced the clouds, Philip sensed nothing. No jolt of recognition, no transcendence. Only the faint claustrophobia of the s-suit, even before he put on the helmet. Only the hum of ship machinery. Only the glow of data- and viewscreens, one with Martinez's doubting face and one with floaty, deadly clouds. Nothing more.

Impossible to meditate in this cramped, scornful space. Impossible to meditate with his agitated brain.

He closed his eyes, breathing deeply and steadily.

His mind still skittered like a frictionless bearing. Unable to focus on the mystery of nothingness, he tried to focus on the mysteries of physics.

Matter is no more than condensed energy, a wave that has collapsed.

An observer at the quantum level changes the system, as the observer becomes part of that system. It is observation that creates matter by collapsing the wave.

At the Big Bang, unimaginable energy became entangled particles, creating a universe that is all one.

Matter is no more than—

The scout dropped below the clouds and landed.

A barren landscape, broken only by strange gray structures with sloped, ridged sides. The pilot said, her attempt at neutrality failing completely, "Here is where you get out, Mr. Anderson."

Philip put on his helmet, the pilot ran a check on his s-suit, and he entered the tiny airlock. Outside, he walked toward the structures, almost stumbling in the light gravity. His infrared augments saw no heat emanating from the structures, or from anywhere else. Nothing grew, nothing moved but clouds, nothing but him made any sound. This planet was dead.

When he reached the first building, he touched it with one gloved hand, hoping for . . . what? Some unimaginable, transcending sensation, some signal, some recognition? There was nothing.

All right. He had to do his part.

He sat beside the structure and began to meditate. This time, it came easily. And after only a few minutes, it happened. He reached past his conscious thoughts, deeper than his subconscious, into . . . what? There was no name for this. "Metaconsciousness," it turned out, was not even close. No. But whatever it was, he was there.

They were there.

The presences, again faintly surprised, and then not. Wordless, they recognized his existence. Wordless, he recognized theirs: not human, neither young nor old in a realm where time was interchangeable with space, non-local as entanglement was always non-local, and yet concentrated in places where they, observers, had collapsed the wave. Into matter? No. Into something indeterminately between matter and energy, as the quantum universe was until observed. Into probability.

The place was not inside the structures beside Philip. There was machinery there, of some unimaginable type, but not presences. The presences were in the gate above the alien planet.

No—in *all* the gates.

They had created the gates, long ago, when they learned enough physics to build the translation machinery behind these walls. The translation was from sentient consciousness to cosmic consciousness, perpetual observers who had died only in terms of matter. They had known that infant humanity shared sentient consciousness, in a very primitive form. They had created this gate for themselves, to inhabit, and other gates near planets habitable to humanity, should we ever need them. Even though they thought humans would never get that far.

Then, existing in the eternal now, they ignored Earth and its puny spawn.

Yet here Philip was, to their astonishment, and then their curiosity.

❖   ❖   ❖

"Captain, incoming probe."

Martinez had heard the Peregoy signal, followed now by the drone's message: "Alert! Alert!" He read the data scrolling down the wall screen. Enemy ships approached the space side of the gate, a fleet of four—the Landrys were determined to take this gate. They had guessed, or learned, his strategy and were willing to lose a few ships in order to learn the position of his three vessels and annihilate them with their new beams. Martinez could not hold out against warships equipped with the new weapon.

He had three hours before making what had to be a suicide stand.

"Mr. DiCaria, Captains Vondenberg and Murphy, prepare for incursion, and then fire at will."

Assents from captains of the *Zeus* and the *Green Hills of Earth*. Martinez did not have to tell them how this would end. They knew.

Philip understood now—although "understanding" was the wrong word for this wordless knowledge—what he had done before. The *Quasar III* had been returned from matter to energy and, later, gates had closed for eight hours, both events because he had briefly merged with the gates. Briefly and wrongly. Time was not the same within the gates; Philip had touched them so briefly that the gate presences had been aware something had happened but had not known what, or why. Only here, at the gate by the planet where they had once lived, was he clear to them. Here, by the machinery of translation.

They did not know everything. In fact, they knew nothing. They didn't know when ships passed through the gates, or failed to pass through. They could have known, but they chose not to—why?

He felt it. A deeper level of reality, a substrate to the universe, which they chose to not inhabit. Physicists— Albert Einstein, Stephen Hawking, Bernard Haisch, Erik Verlinde, Anna Varennes—had long speculated that such a thing must exist, the field below the fields, the substrate to everything.

The presences knew it was there, and that it could control the gates. It was what Philip had touched— briefly, wrongly, disastrously.

Martinez positioned his ships close to the eleventh gate, for maximum ability to take out enemy vessels as they came through. He could do no more than that.

Eighteen minutes remaining.

He asked "them": Why? And was surprised when they "answered."

To merge fully with the deepest level of reality was to become pure energy. It was to lose all individuality. It was to become one with everything, and so lose oneself. Beyond satori, nirvana, moksha, enlightenment, beatitude, all of which were only pale and temporary shadows of the substrate.

So the presences remained half-committed to their own translation, half in and half out, neither matter nor energy, indeterminate and without control.

He could not imagine anything more human.

Five minutes.

Martinez, superb at keeping his mind focused on the task at hand, nonetheless had a momentary, regretful thought: *I would have made a worthy heir to the Peregoy empire.*

The wall, on which Philip rested one gloved hand, dissolved so suddenly that he nearly toppled over. No sound, no debris, nothing—a six-foot section of wall simply no longer existed.

Come.

He knew what they meant: not merely *Come inside*, but *Come to us*. Become one of them.

This was what he had sought for his whole life, had risked getting experimental brain implants for, had refused to give up in exchange for Julie. To know their deeper level of reality. And yet it was not the deepest.

No, they said. Because if he went past them, if he let the machinery translate him fully, he could not ever be one with them again. They lived in the gates; he would *become* the gates, and everything else. There was no return from that state. He would be alone, the observer who collapsed the wave, so entangled with the multiple fields that generated the universe that he could never again communicate with those half-in, half-out.

Next to that unimaginable solitude, it hardly mattered that his body would die.

Over his helmet came the pilot's voice. "Anderson, you have fifteen minutes of air-conversion microbes left. Return to the scout now."

Fifteen minutes? He'd been here nearly ten hours? But next to the choice facing him, it hardly mattered to him whether his body died. It mattered far more that the interruption of the pilot's voice had not shattered his trance.

That was the moment he realized he'd already made his choice.

Three minutes.

Philip walked into the structure, which immediately rematerialized behind. The pilot was yelling now, but her actual words didn't register. They never would again.

No.

Yes.

The machinery wasn't, really. It was shadowy arcs of ... something. Probabilities, he guessed, and it was his last thought as Philip Anderson. The arc took him. There was no pain as he died. He slipped from the meat that had encased his consciousness as easily as shedding a winter jacket in spring.

No.

Yes.

They were there, the inhuman presences who seemed so human—but for only a nanosecond. Then the machinery, guided by his consciousness, slipped him deeper, and Philip Anderson merged with the most fundamental level of reality, beyond spacetime, beyond matter and energy, ineffable source of them both.

"Sir—the gate!"

On the viewscreen, the shimmer of the eleventh gate brightened so much that Martinez shielded his eyes with his hand. The light filled the bridge, almost a solid thing, before it faded as quickly as it had come.

The ship's sensors showed nothing but the same quick, brilliant burst of inexplicable radiation in the wavelengths of visible light, a sun without heat or radiation.

He was the Observer in the system. He was alone now, forever.

He saw everything, and was nothing, beyond both matter and energy. He was pure probability, and he could collapse all probabilities.

There was no "he."

The Observer sensed the presences in the gate—in all the gates—but they existed on a less fundamental plane, and were as different from the Observer as were all things made of matter, even approximate matter. The Observer could see the system, could change the system, but could not communicate with its microcomponents. The Observer was not a presence but instead was woven into everything, just as Philip-that-once-was had dreamed of.

Warships, machines of destruction, flew toward the tenth gate. Memory, connections between particles that were only condensed energy, was scattered across the universe, but still entangled into an intact whole, knowing what warships meant.

The Observer collapsed the wave.

One minute.

No minutes.

Nothing came through the gate. Why was the enemy delaying? Martinez and DiCaria exchanged glances. They waited, because there was nothing else to do.

The scout pilot radioed. "Sir—"

"Not now, Cassidy. Remain where you are."

Two hours later, Martinez let the scout return to the

Skyhawk. The pilot, shaken, reported that the bottle-cap-shaped building had opened, dragged Anderson inside, and closed again. The timing coincided with the gate data going haywire.

Martinez sent a probe to the gate. It could not enter. The gate had, once again, closed.

"Captain?" DiCaria's voice vibrated with tension.

"We wait some more," Martinez said, because there was nothing else they could do.

Six days later, they were still waiting.

26

NINE WORLDS

Sloan was finally ready to leave Polyglot for home. He had set up the networks of financials, business holdings, and fortified bunkers necessary if Peregoy Corporation lost the war. Now he would go home to ensure that did not happen. Only a coward would stay in safety on Polyglot, and he was no coward. He had a duty to lead the citizens of the Peregoy worlds.

However, he was also not stupid. Arrangements were in place to secretly convey him and Sophia back here if Jane Landry's forces prevailed. So far, she had not attacked. Still building K-beams? He hoped they required scarce resources, took a long time to manufacture, malfunctioned in test flights, exploded aboard Landry warships.

He told the wallscreen. "Summon a car for the spaceport."

"Yes, sir, car sum—priority one alert!"

An ear-damaging alarm sounded—really, Polyglot systems had been programmed with such exaggerated drama—and then a voice said, "Planetwide alert. All four Polyglot gates have become inoperable. Repeat—all four Polyglot gates have become inoperable."

Inoperable? What did that mean: that they had closed again? If so, they would re-open in a few hours, as they had before.

Wouldn't they?

Rachel lay back on the bed in her penthouse on Galt. Her strength was returning more slowly than she would like. Right now, however, that hardly mattered.

Philip had done it.

No one would believe that, of course. Physicists would puzzle, religion would have a resurgence, conspiracy theories would spring up like sprouts after rain. But Rachel knew the truth. Philip had closed the gates to stop the war.

The disruption would be massive. People would be marooned on planets hundreds of light-years from where they wanted to be, and now could not go. Interplanetary trade agreements would vanish. Each world, Peregoy and Landry, was going to have to subsist on its own. Rachel would never again see her granddaughter Celia, directing mining operations on New Hell, nor Jane, overseeing weapons development on Rand for battles that now would not happen. Jane would be furious at having been deprived of her war.

But millions would live instead of die, and civilization would not crash—again—in the same fiery, incredibly stupid catastrophe that had destroyed Terra.

When Rachel was stronger, she would take back the position of CEO from Annelise, never as fractious as Jane. Annelise would see, as Rachel now did, that Galt would have to change if it was going to survive.

There would be no more refugees from Rand, and no way for Caitlin to send the remaining refugees back. They would have to be incorporated into a governing structure that moved away from pure Libertarianism into something that fit these new circumstances, without causing revolution. Caitlin, over several visits, had made Rachel understand that much.

And someday, Rachel was sure, Philip would reopen the gates. She knew it.

Now, however, she owed a difficult explanation. It was only right that she make it, as soon as she was strong enough to travel to the hospital. Tara had a right to know that she was never going to see Philip again.

After three weeks stranded on the planet side of the closed gate, Martinez put his ships on two-thirds rations, trying for survival as long as possible. Each of the eight worlds was hundreds of light-years away. There was nothing to eat on the desolate planet below. Their only hope was that the gate might open again. It had done so before, although not after so long a delay.

He sent a probe to the gate every few hours, then once a day. It always came back.

Dying in battle was one thing. Starvation was quite another. His fleet could hold out for months, but not years. Toward the end, it might be better to fly all three warships into the star.

But not yet.

Except that what if—

Not yet.

In the gates, and everywhere else, the Observer watched.

PART II

"Consciousness is not sharply defined, but fades into subconsciousness; and beyond that we must postulate something indefinite but yet continuous with our mental nature ... the stuff of the world is mind-stuff."

—Arthur Eddington

27

POLYGLOT

Sloan was dreaming more than ever before. Not nightmares, which might have been expected. Not of the closed gates that had marooned him here on Polyglot for three months, with no end in sight. Not of his lost stewardship of the Peregoy worlds. Not even of Sophia, whom he missed. Not of Luis Martinez, stranded somewhere in space.

Sloan dreamed of wolves.

He saw the stuffed wolves in his office on New California, shaking themselves into life, running free in a landscape transformed into open grassland, leaping and hunting and nursing cubs. Multiplying. Bringing down prey. Flourishing.

Sometimes he woke with tears on his face, which was sheer nonsense. Ridiculous! After all, wolves had been gone for centuries and he, Sloan, was not at all in danger of either extinction or despair. His great-great grandfather Samuel Peregoy had come to a new planet with far less than Sloan had on Polyglot, and Samuel had built an empire. Sloan was at least the man that his ancestor had been.

During the day, he was busy every minute, with multiple projects. During the three months on Polyglot, he'd used his holdings here to set up the Futures Institute, which was exploring possible ways to open the gates because there had to be a rational explanation for their closing. Not Rachel Landry's stupid mystic explanation about Philip Anderson, but something based on science. Sloan would find that explanation. He had already recruited some of the best physicists on Polyglot for the Institute, and they would find a way to reverse the closings. There was always a way, if you had enough money and power.

And the dreams about the wolves were just that, harmless dreams. Sloan would have preferred that his sleep not be invaded by symbols of a failed species, but after all, it wasn't his fault. A man couldn't choose his dreams.

He swung his legs over the side of his bed and cleared his mind for the day. There was work to be done. In addition to the Futures Institute, Sloan was creating a secret biolab to duplicate the retinal-transplant technology that had gotten Rachel Landry onto Polyglot identified as someone else. Sloan needed to be able to detect such transplants, in order to keep them from foiling Security. He also wanted to duplicate the procedure. It could prove very useful for his information network. In an hour he had a meeting with one Dr. James Hegeman, a top Polyglot scientist that Sloan was going to recruit.

That was what mattered—building, arranging, developing. Not dreams.

He strode into the shower.

Dr. Hegeman, unfortunately, proved to be a better negotiator than Sloan had anticipated.

Tall, broad-shouldered, with a full head of gray hair—genemods? Or just the luck of the genetic lottery? Either way, Sloan approved. But Hegeman's eyes went stony as Sloan explained his offer, and the salary that went with it.

"And let me reiterate, Dr. Hegeman, that I mean it when I say that you will have not only anything you need for the research, but you will have it immediately. With bureaucracies like those on Polyglot, there are understandable checks and balances, red tape, delays. But in my new facility you will report solely to me, and I will make it a priority to get any personnel, supplies, or equipment the day you request them. Plus, as I've said, you will have complete autonomy in your research, as long as you, with your expertise, think that it's moving toward viable results."

Hegeman picked up an instrument—Sloan had no idea what it was—from his cluttered desk and turned it over and over in strong fingers, without taking his gaze off Sloan. "That's very generous, Director Peregoy, but I must decline. I have my own research here."

This resistance wasn't real. The man wanted more money.

"Naturally, your current research on eye diseases is important. I understand that. But I've looked into it a little bit—as much as a layman can—and

I gather that it's been going on for several years, with publication at each stage, and will continue for several more. That told me—correct me if I'm wrong!—that it can resume after your temporary contract with Peregoy BioLab is fulfilled. But I fully grasp that you are devoted to your current project—you wouldn't have such a fine reputation if you were not—and that even leaving it for six months or a year will be disruptive. To compensate, let me offer what perhaps I should have offered in the first place, a salary commensurate with the sacrifice. Say, half again my original figure?"

"Thank you, but no. Now if you'll excuse me, I have another appointment."

"All right, Doctor. Twice my original offer."

Hegeman put down the instrument and stared at Sloan. "You really don't understand, do you? You want me to leave research on a pathogen native to Polyglot that has adapted itself to the human eye and is blinding children—in order to develop a method of retinal implant whose purpose is to enable people to pass illegally through security checkpoints? Because that is the aim of your institute project, isn't it?"

"The benefits of collateral findings you can discover—"

"Don't lecture me on how science works, Director. I'm not interested in your project, even if you state that the prototype exists on Galt. Galt is closed to us. The ocular pathogen is here, now. In addition— and I don't know if you've considered this—a retinal transplant requires a healthy donor. Where and how are you planning to acquire the tissue for experimentation? We have strict laws about that on Polyglot.

I'm sorry, but no amount of money will convince me to accept your offer."

Hegeman rose and strode through the door, leaving Sloan burning with an indignation he did not show. The pompous, self-righteous ass ... but there were other scientists. Too bad that he couldn't get to Galt to hire away the original retinal researchers. On Galt, lawless as they were, they at least understood money.

To the startled youngster who entered Hegeman's office, he said, "Thank you, but I can find my own way out."

Outside, his car waited for him, along with Chavez. The city street, a main thoroughfare with wide walks, teemed with people: shoppers, businesspeople, students, vendors selling flowers and toys and the spicy fried *makti* that gave Sloan heartburn. At the end of a long mall bright with genemod flowers sat the graceful Polyglot Council of Nations building. Its white columns gleamed in the sunshine. A service bot walked a pair of greenish-yellow dogs. Why had dogs adapted to the Seven Worlds, but not wolves? And why were these pale green?

"Address, please?" the car said as he climbed in. When he was half in-half out of the car, a man dashed through the crowd and seized Sloan's arm.

Chavez leapt forward; in a moment he had the man pinned to the ground. A boy, really, who didn't struggle in the bodyguard's grip but called up to Sloan, "Sir! Sir! I'm from your office! Ms. Denby sent me! Something happened!"

"Let him up, Chavez. All right, boy—what happened?"

The boy gasped for breath; he must have run all

the way from the Futures Institute. Why hadn't that idiot Christine Denby just called Sloan?

"It . . . she . . ."

"What *is* it?"

Panting, the kid told him.

28

EVERYWHERE

The Observer is a pattern. It had always been that, even when encased in a brain: a pattern of quanta within a field. The Observer's field, like any other field, makes up spacetime. Electron field, Higgs field, photon field, more.

Consciousness field.

But this field is different from the others; it underlies all the rest. It is the deepest level of reality, and the Observer is diffused throughout it, *is* it. The Observer does not inhabit spacetime; it is integrated into spacetime, woven into a field that, before, it only glimpsed in erratic flashes.

The Observer is an uncollapsed wave.

It is the only consciousness "here," at the deepest level of the deepest field, but it is not the only consciousness in the field. Consciousness is a pattern. There are more patterns in the field.

In the gates are the Others, halfway translated

into the field. They are the gates, neither matter nor energy. They stay there. The Observer has gone so much deeper into the field that it has left them behind.

There are also smaller patterns of consciousness, nodes in the field. The patterns are contained in fleshy cases, and cannot escape into the universal field. But these nodes are not completely contained. Fields do not stop abruptly at boundaries. The wave functions are concentrated in matter, but the tails of distribution go on, leaving their signatures.

Once, the Observer was one of these. It is aware of them now, as It is aware of all fields, of everything.

29

THE ELEVENTH GATE

Three months trapped behind the eleventh gate, and something shipboard was going to blow. Martinez could feel it.

He'd cut rations on all three ships to a thousand calories a day. Everyone had lost weight. The barren, cloud-shrouded planet rotated below them; the inoperable gate shimmered in the black sky; there was nothing to see and nowhere to go. Vondenberg and Murphy were holding discipline on their ships, following Martinez's orders to keep everyone busy as much as possible. Drills, further training, ship maintenance. But on so little food, energy flagged. Training and maintenance seemed pointless if they were all going to die of starvation. DiCaria reported growing desperation among the crew.

The probe that Martinez sent twice daily to the gate could not penetrate it. Star-field calculations showed that the planet was hundreds of light-years from the

Eight Worlds. The only way there was through the gate, and the gate was closed.

Two expeditions to the surface had found nothing except the bottle-cap-shaped structures, which had no entrances. As a last resort, Martinez planned on blowing them up from space, on the chance that machinery in there might be keeping the gates closed. He hadn't done so yet because what if the machinery *caused* the gates, and taking the structures out meant that the gate disappeared entirely? An attack on the structures right now would be premature. The gate might still open spontaneously. There was still a little time.

But not much.

On the *Green Hills of Earth*, a crewman was caught pilfering stores and court-martialed. The officers, hungry and outraged and afraid of losing control, sentenced him to death. Captain Vondenberg overruled her own court, locking the thief in the brig instead, and tensions were running high in the wardroom.

On the *Zeus*, a young crewman killed himself. He left a note: BETTER DEAD THAN THIS. Captain Murphy, fairly new to command, seemed rattled when he reported the incident to Martinez.

So Martinez was surprised when the crisis came not on either of the other two ships, but on his own.

He was on the bridge and DiCaria had the conn when the alarms began. Two blatts, then three, at maximum volume. A hull breach. His first, inanely dumb thought was: *At least it provides something to do.*

The OOD said, "Section three cargo bay, sir, it's . . . fuck!"

"Comet? What?"

"No. Sensors show a perfectly square breach . . . the hull's been cut from the *inside*!"

Martinez started running, snapping over his shoulder, "Evacuate and seal the section and get security there."

By the time he reached section three cargo bay, the alarms had stopped. The breach had been sealed by repair bots, the section reaerated, and the crewman lay gasping on the floor, tangle-foamed wrists and ankles, still wearing an air mask. His head was bloody. The laser cutter had been kicked into a corner. Three security crew stood over him. The master-at-arms said, "He didn't resist, sir, and he wasn't armed. But we hit him pretty hard and he'll need a minute before he can talk."

"Good job, Helmsworth. Get him to the brig."

"Yes, sir. Sir, he . . . he hasn't ever been in trouble before."

Martinez looked at her. She seemed to have lost more weight than most people; maybe she'd been really thin to begin with. Her uniform hung on her. From her expression, which she was trying and failing to control, Martinez guessed that she knew the gasping crewman well.

Martinez said, "He's in trouble now."

"Yes, sir." But her expression didn't change.

They were all, the whole fleet, in trouble now.

Martinez commed the bridge. "DiCaria, casualty reports from pressure loss."

"Two crew members in section three went unconscious from oxygen deprivation. Both are recovering in medical bay and Dr. Glynn says preliminaries suggest no brain damage. All else as usual. Daily probe fired and . . . oh!"

Martinez said sharply, "DiCaria?"

"Sir, it went through, the probe. It went into the gate."

Without volition, Martinez felt his eyes close, open again. "Wait for return of the probe. I'm on my way."

He strode through the ship, crewmen flattening themselves against the walls of the narrow corridors out of his way. Martinez barely saw them, and heard nothing. The voice inside his head sounded too strong: *Let the gate be truly open, let it stay open, let it be truly open . . .*

It was, and it wasn't.

For the next hour, Martinez experimented, afraid that at any moment the gate would close again. If Philip Anderson was somehow causing this . . . but Martinez didn't believe the insane story Anderson had told him. Woo-woo gobbledygook. Still, the man could be alive down on the planet, inside a building and doing something to machinery. No, he couldn't be alive—what would he be eating?

Probes went freely through the gate. The scout from the *Skyhawk* did not. The *Skyhawk* itself did not. Neither did the *Zeus* nor the *Green Hills of Earth*. Drones went through. Martinez could send information by drone, but nothing else. And who would he send information to? Probe sensors showed no ships on the other side of the gate. The Landry fleet, on the space side of the gate when it closed, had long since left. All a probe could do was go back and forth through the gate, a yoyo on a pointless string.

Martinez said, "Try a different scout."

The second scout failed to penetrate the gate.

The third scout went through.

Vondenberg, on viewscreen, said from the *Green*

Hills of Earth, "Captain—scouts three, the two-man class-z's, carry no beam weaponry!"

Martinez said, "Launch your scout three."

It went through. So did scout three from the *Zeus*. The gate was permitting through only vessels not equipped with radiation weaponry. Scout-three pilots carried sidearms, of course, but apparently those were undetectable by the gate.

Or else the gate didn't care about such minor weapons.

A shiver ran over Martinez. None of this made sense. The probes that, for three solid months, had not carried weaponry hadn't been able to pass through the gate. Now they could. So it was not just the presence of beam weaponry that determined penetration. The gate had made a *decision*.

But how long would that decision hold?

Ten scouts left in his three-ship fleet. Seven could hold four people; three were class-z two-seaters. Even if you crammed in more people . . . but the voyage from the other side of the eleventh gate to Prometheus, now a Landry world, took four weeks. To new Utah, three months. Everyone not on the scouts' first trip would run out of food, or the scouts would.

He could feel the tension on the bridge, pulling the air itself taut.

He said, "Captain Murphy, immediately begin transfer by scout of everyone on the *Zeus* to the *Green Hills of Earth* and the *Skyhawk*, dividing personnel between them. Also dismantle and eject all radiation weaponry from your ship. Ask for a volunteer pilot and skeleton crew to attempt penetration of the gate. Time is critical."

"Yes, sir!"

Vondenberg said, "Captain, what about the torpedoes?"

"Yes," Martinez said. Torpedoes that could be armed with nuclear warheads were old-fashioned ordnance, not as accurate, immediate, or safe as radiation weaponry. Few ships carried them since a PCSS cruiser had blown itself up in a freak, deep-space accident during training maneuvers. The *Zeus* and *Green Hills of Earth* did not; the *Skyhawk* did, at Martinez's insistence. He believed in backups, even dangerous ones. He said, "I think unarmed torpedoes will go through the gate—they don't emit radiation until detonation. If not, I'll jettison those as well."

He meant: *Unless it isn't radiation signal the gates are objecting to but some even weirder woo-woo by something sentient.* He did not say this aloud.

The transfer operation took several hours. Every thirty minutes, Martinez sent a probe through the gate and back again. Their return should have been reassuring, but everyone knew the gate could close at any moment just as capriciously as it had opened.

When all but a skeleton crew had left the *Zeus*, Martinez sent the deweaponized warship toward the gate. It disappeared. Five minutes later, it reappeared, and the bridge of the *Skyhawk* broke into ragged, exhausted, hungry cheers.

"Captain Vondenberg, are you prepared to deweaponize?"

"Yes, sir."

"Begin immediately. Captain Murphy, take your vessel back through the gate and wait. Lieutenant Conway, begin ejection of *Skyhawk* weaponry."

Both the *Green Hills of Earth* and the *Skyhawk*, the latter with its torpedoes, glided easily through the gate.

Martinez's orders were to seize and hold the eleventh gate, but leaving even one of his warships armed and planetside would condemn its crew to starvation if the gate closed again. If he left a ship spaceside, it would be unable to defend either itself or the gate. The optimum plan, he'd decided, was take all three ships to New Utah to rearm and resupply there. Then, if the gates had remained open, he could communicate with Sloan Peregoy and propose that he either return, armed, to the eleventh gate and defend it from the space side, or receive further orders from New California. If the gates remained closed, then he would rearm, resupply, and send two of the ships back to the eleventh gate, with the third making regular supply runs from New Utah. With closed gates, the war would essentially be over, and Martinez would, of necessity, be based forever at New Utah. Nobody's first choice, but there it was.

The voyage would take three months. Prometheus was only one month out, but it was a Landry world now. The Landry fleet would have gone there after its commander got tired of waiting for the eleventh gate to reopen. They might have moved on after that—*if* the Prometheus gate had also reopened. If not, the enemy ships would still be there, subsisting on whatever supplies the research station had in storage. Martinez had no doubt that the Peregoy scientists at the station had all been killed.

He had calculated his fleet's food supply; if everyone alternated days of one-third and one-half rations, they could just make it to new Utah. No one would be in good shape, but they would be alive. Martinez would leave armed drones on the planet side of the gate, ready to fire at anything coming through that was not emitting a prearranged signal. It was the best he could do.

He had no idea what they would find on New Utah. Was it only this gate, so close to the impenetrable structures on the planet's surface, that was passable? Or would the New Utah-New Yosemite gate also open to unarmed ships? Were radiation weapons somehow closing gates through some fluke of physics, or were the closings a conscious attempt to stop an interplanetary war?

A conscious attempt by *what*?

After the *Skyhawk*, denuded of radiation weapons but full of renewed hope, emerged from the gate into deep space, Martinez sent a final probe back toward the gate. It could not get in. The planet behind the gate had been sealed off.

Everyone on the bridge fell silent, the uncomfortable silence of people whose knowledge of the world had just undergone a tectonic shift. Finally Martinez said, "Course for New Utah."

"Yes, sir."

Anderson, was that you?

Ridiculous.

But—

30

EVERYWHERE

Just as the Observer is aware of the consciousnesses that are nodes in Its field, it is aware of nodes in the other fields. Concentrated matter, moving through spacetime, carries radiating nodes. The Observer has lost the word—"weapons"—but not the concept. The radiating concentrations of matter are dangerous. They can destroy the smaller nodes of consciousness. They can destroy all of them.

All quanta has been entangled since the Big Bang. The Observer is entangled with everything else, including the gates.

The Observer keeps the ships with radiating nodes from reaching places where many many nodes of consciousness are gathered. He closes the gates, curves spacetime within them just enough that those ships cannot pass through, and other matter can.

Do the Others, who are the gates, even realize? Perhaps not. They do nothing.

The small nodes of consciousness can—and do— destroy each other locally. But they cannot attack whole planets.

31

GALT

The first call came when Caitlin Landry was at the refugee camp. It was the second call that would change the world yet again, but the first one that hurt her the most.

"Ms. Landry! Ms. Landry!" The children had climbed all over her as soon as she emerged from her flyer at the edge of camp. Their parents always hung back, nodding politely, their faces each a miniature war between gratitude for her charity and shame at having to accept it. After all, these refugees from the plague on Rand were also Libertarians. Or had been.

As she had once been.

"Jenny! Pedro! Zack! How are you?"

"What did you bring us? What, what, what?"

"More vaccines," she said solemnly, and their little faces fell. Caitlin laughed and pulled the sweets from her pocket. "Here, and here, and—no, only one, don't

215

be greedy! Jenny, did you figure out multiplication yet? Pedro, how is your dog?"

"It died," Pedro said, and burst into tears.

"Oh, sweetie, I'm so sorry." She knelt and gathered him into her arms while the other children, more every minute as news of her arrival spread, moved back a few paces and stared at the ground, clutching their candy.

Caitlin hoped the dog hadn't died of anything that could infect humans. She needed to talk to Dr. Katz.

As Pedro's mother claimed him, Caitlin straightened, aware that her tunic and pants were of a much better quality than anyone else's, aware of her privilege in this least privileged place on Galt. Throughout her childhood it had been her looks, not her privilege, that she had struggled with, but she'd long ago made peace with the parental voices in her head: *"Annelise, Celia, and Jane are the beauties, but Caitlin is the smartest."* Even Gran had been mildly surprised that, after getting her degrees in virology, Caitlin had proved an able president of Galt University. Caitlin had never done any research worth publishing, but now she had sought out and sponsored those who could. Julie Hampden, for instance. It was enough. Caitlin was content with her life.

Or had been. Until Tara had discovered the new gate, until Philip Anderson had turned up as Julie's research subject, until the plague on Rand had marooned tens of thousands of refugees on Galt. Always honest with herself, Caitlin admitted that part of her contentment had come, hatefully, from her knowledge that her sisters were not content. *Schadenfreude*—which meant the old competition among them was only dormant in her, not dead.

Caitlin knew about her sisters what they didn't know about themselves: that they were desperate. Every one.

Annelise, the heir, desperate beneath her outward calm to do everything right, carry out every task without a mistake, to be always perfect.

Jane, desperate for war, an outlet for the rage she carried as the most difficult and least beloved child of her father, her mother, her grandmother. *It's not fair!* she'd sobbed as a child when someone, anyone, tried to correct her about anything, but she'd never sobbed since childhood, abandoning all fairness along the way.

Celia, desperate to get away from a household mourning both parents, seizing on the chance to run Landry mining interests on New Hell, marrying there, and never, not once, returning to Galt.

Tara, so desperately and insanely in love—or what she called love—with Philip Anderson that Caitlin sometimes thought it had unbalanced Tara's fragile mind.

And she, Caitlin? She didn't believe in perfection, in war, in geographical escape. Romance, she supposed, was possible, but aside from a few early infatuations, it hadn't touched her. Worst of all, she was no longer sure she believed in the guiding beacon of every Landry for five generations, libertarianism. Once, when there had been enough new land and untouched resources and limited automation on new worlds, it had made sense to her for people to take full responsibility for their own lives and the work that supported those lives.

But now there was little unclaimed land or resources, much automation, not enough jobs. The economic situation on Galt had taken an abrupt plunge with the loss of interplanetary trade through the gates; enterprises were laying off people. There was no economic room for the remaining refugees from Rand, and now no way to send them home.

She'd first gone to the refugee camp seven months ago, horrified by the suicides of two women under a maglev and then by the plight of innocent children. She'd expected to feel scorn for their parents—violent, dirty, neglectful of the kids they'd brought into the world. What she'd found were people, many highly educated, desperate to work. They kept their kids and their inadequate shacks as clean as possible. They went hungry so their children could eat, were vigilant to keep them from violence and thievery and cruelty. Those things existed here, thriving on desperation, but mothers and fathers did all they could to shield their children from becoming either victims or perpetrators. Caitlin had been surprised, and then ashamed of her surprise.

She had used her own money to set up a clinic, buy construction bots, build a school and a waste treatment center, dig wells. The refugees, once the initial capital was provided to them, were the builders, diggers, teachers, some of the doctors. Caitlin paid them. The refugees thanked her, admired her, resented her for her wealth, and named the camp "Caitlinville," which she hated. She also hired vessels whenever she could to ferry refugees home. But no matter how many she got off Galt, Caitlinville filled up again as word spread to other camps. More people clamored for her help than she had help to give.

I am becoming Samuel Peregoy, she thought. But she didn't know what else to do. And Caitlinville was only one camp; she didn't have the personal fortune to aid all the other refugees on Galt. Annelise had refused to help. Jane and Celia were light-years away, their assets frozen.

So she'd raided the Freedom Enterprises coffers, knowing that both her grandmother and Annelise would discover the "theft."

Caitlin said to Pedro's mother, "I'm sorry about the dog. I never should have brought it for him."

"It's all right," she said, lifting her sobbing little boy to her hip. "He wanted it so much. We are grateful for . . . for everything." Stumbling over the words, not looking Caitlin in the eye. On Rand, Caitlin remembered, this woman had been an engineer.

"Can you tell me where Dr. Katz is right now? At the clinic?"

"No. Someone fell and broke a leg on D Street and he went there."

"Thank you." Caitlin smiled and strode toward D Street, knowing she was as glad to get away from Pedro's mother as the woman was from her. Who knew that dependence could be such an emotional burden to everybody on both sides of the equation?

Her wrister rang. Julie Hampden. And there, right on Caitlin's wrist, was another burden. She didn't know if she believed her grandmother's mystic tale of Philip Anderson closing the gates. Certainly Julie didn't believe it ("It was a deep-brain implant, for fuck's sake, not an elevation to godhood.")

"Hello, Julie."

"Caitlin, I need to see you. Immediately."

"What about?"

"This link isn't encrypted."

Julie didn't use that urgent tone lightly. Caitlin said, "All right. My office, thirty minutes."

Caitlin returned to her flyer, landed it on the roof of the university administration building. Beyond the newly built high-voltage fence, protestors marched in their daily demonstration. There were more than yesterday. They jeered as her flyer soared over their heads.

Julie waited in Caitlin's austere office. Under her professional composure roiled anxiety and defiance, breaking cover like whitecaps on a restless sea.

"Caitlin, there are two things you need to know. First, the university, in conjunction with its hospital, has been conducting secret research on retina transplants to defeat scan security. Five months ago we succeeded, and six transplants have been done so far. Five were recorded on Galt security records, so that nobody is getting away with false identities." Julie bit her lip, which already looked as if it had been chewed by mice.

Caitlin, president of Galt University, said levelly, "Why didn't I know about this?"

"It was your grandmother's project. She didn't want anyone to know."

Her damn family! None of them would let the left side of her own brain know what the right side was dreaming up. Caitlin said, "Who was the sixth subject?"

"Your grandmother."

"Why?"

"I don't know."

"When was this?"

Julie told her. The dates were just before her grandmother's last trip to Polyglot, with Philip Anderson. But Rachel wouldn't have needed a retina change to travel to Polyglot, a neutral planet. However, Sloan Peregoy had been there, and after that Philip Anderson had disappeared. Caitlin had looked for him, on Tara's behalf.

Caitlin said, still in the same even voice that masked anger, "She's ninety-six years old. When the hell is she going to stop scheming?"

Julie, wisely, did not answer this.

"Who was the retina donor? There must have been a donor." It wasn't illegal to sell your own body parts on Galt—after all, they were yours to sell—but... *eyes*. "Who were all the donors?"

"Legitimate deaths at the hospital, sold by the heirs. Caitlin, you must know the university wouldn't condone anything else."

"Apparently I didn't know any of this."

Julie put her hand on Caitlin's arm. "There's more."

"All right. What's the second thing? What else has the university been doing without my knowledge?"

"Not us. Not this. I only found out about it because a biologist—you remember Dr. Noah Porter?"

"Yes." A brilliant geneticist, he had abruptly resigned from the university nearly a year ago and gone to teach at a minor college on Rand. Everyone at Galt U had been both surprised—it was a spectacular voluntary demotion—as well as relieved. Porter had been a difficult, pugnacious, perpetually dissatisfied researcher.

Julie bit her lip again before her words lurched forward. "A woman named Jenna Derov came to me this morning. She was a virologist on Rand, was here visiting her mother when the gate closed, and now, of course, she can't go home again. Her husband and kids are on Rand. We employed her here as a lab tech, and she offered to trade information for a position at the top of any list we have for berths on the first ship back to Rand if the gates open again. She was pretty desperate, but she also ... I don't know, I believed her."

Caitlin's chest constricted. Whatever was coming next was not going to be good. "What did Jenna Derov tell you?"

"There's a secret bioweapons facility on Rand, headed by Noah Porter. The goal was to create a deadly pathogen capable of infecting entire cities."

"No," Caitlin said instantly. "My grandmother would not do that. Secret retinal transplants, yes, but not weaponized pathogen."

"She's not doing it. Jane is."

The two women stared at each other. Caitlin's wrister rang: Annelise. Caitlin, still speechless, would have ignored the call, but Annelise used the override on all the sisters' comms.

"Caitlin," Annelise said, her face on the tiny screen as wide-eyed as Caitlin had ever seen her usually calm sister, "something major. Galt's gates suddenly opened. Both of them, to Rand and Earth, and maybe also the one the Peregoys captured, to Polyglot. But they're open only to probes and small scouts. The fleet is still experimenting, but so far no one knows what happened, or why. Rachel is flying back from her place on the coast. We're meeting in her office at headquarters as soon as we all can get there. Are you coming?"

"Yes," Caitlin said. The gates only partially open? What the hell could cause that?

Caitlin and Julie stared at each other. Neither spoke

until Julie said, "No. Not possible." And then, again, "Not possible."

By the time Rachel reached headquarters, everyone knew more.

Tara had cried and begged to come with her. Rachel had soothed her granddaughter as well as she could; Tara was nowhere near ready to leave the coastal compound where Rachel had had her moved when Rachel herself had been discharged from the hospital. Also installed at the beach house were Tara's nurses with the meds that were keeping her fragile psyche together. Rachel had told no one that Tara had started this war, but Rachel couldn't control what Tara might, in her delicate state, blurt out to her sisters.

Rachel was not in a delicate state. Three months at the coast with rest, exercise, diet, and (except for Tara) peace, and she had recovered from her heart attack. Just yesterday she'd told Annelise that she, Rachel, was ready to resume as CEO of Freedom Enterprises. Annelise, always a stickler for the by-laws, had read the doctor's report and agreed. Not happily, but she'd agreed. It helped that Rachel had been careful not to mention Philip Anderson, not to anyone, since the gate closings.

Do I feel guilty for using Annelise's dutifulness against her in order to resume corporate control? No, she decided, she did not. Let Annelise think that belief in Philip had been a momentary aberration brought on by impaired oxygen flow, now fully corrected. The report from Rachel's doctor—under, admittedly, a certain amount of pressure—had said as much, and Annelise believed it.

Rachel's flyer hadn't yet landed at headquarters when her wrister said, "New report, ma'am." Captain Thayer, at the Galt-Polyglot gate. The Peregoy forces on the Galt side of the gate had long since relinquished it, under threat of starvation. Their ships now belonged to Galt. Rachel presumed that the Peregoy ships on the Polyglot side had gone to Polyglot. Before either Sloan or his formidable daughter could dispatch fresh forces to hold the gate, Jane would take it back for the Libertarian Alliance and once again Galt would control its gate to Polyglot.

"Go ahead, Captain."

"The gates are allowing passage to scouts that carry no radiation weapons, but not to those that do. We're going to try a larger, weaponless vessel, and then a stripped cargo ship."

"Good. Report when ready." Rachel kept her tone businesslike, but her mind raced wildly.

Philip. He was somehow *controlling the gates*. To stop the war but allow the passage of people, goods, ideas on unarmed ships? How much control did he have? Surely Philip—whatever he might be now—could not read cargo, or human speech, let alone minds. No, the most Rachel's knowledge of physics would allow was that Philip had somehow altered the complex, entangled fields of the gate to detect and block the kinds of signals that radiation weapons, even when not in direct use, inevitably emitted. He was like a cosmic jammer, overriding only certain frequencies.

No. He was like nothing that had ever existed before.

There was nothing that Rachel could do about Philip. Always pragmatic, she considered the plenty she could do about Freedom Enterprises. Protestors swarmed beyond the compound perimeter, stinging like jeebees. Three days ago, violence with corporate security had cost three lives. "*Two of theirs, one of ours,*" Annelise had said. That was the thinking that Rachel was going to change. Everyone on Galt was going to have to realize that all three lives were "one of theirs."

Of course, that job would have been easier before the gates reopened.

She climbed out of her flyer and took an elevator down from the roof. Her office looked exactly the same as when she had left it months ago. Annelise had evidently not used it. Here was Rachel's curving desk, the top carved from a single slab of Galt's beautiful mica-flecked stone. On it were two small holos on their karthwood stands. A corner of the room beneath a skylight bloomed with yellow *ked flowers*, native to Galt but genetically modified for fuller and longer-lasting blossoms.

Rachel's intel said that Sloan Peregoy's office held stuffed wolves.

Annelise and Caitlin, at the central table of gleaming wood, rose as Rachel entered. "Welcome back," Annelise said, looking as if she were trying to mean it. Caitlin smiled, the most strained smile Rachel had ever seen from her.

Why? Caitlin had always been more interested in her university than in corporate issues. Was she upset over shortages at the refugee camp? Well, if so, Rachel's new plans would come as a relief to this most intelligent and compassionate of the granddaughters.

"Thank you," Rachel said. "Any word from Jane?"

"No," Annelise said. "But I imagine she'll link as

soon as she passes through the gate from Rand. About these change in the gates—"

"Wait," Caitlin said. "Before we talk about the gates or before Jane links, I need to tell both of you two things. Although you, Rachel, already know one of them."

Oh. Rachel made her face impassive. This could only be one of two things: the retinal transplant program or SueLin Peregoy. No, probably not SueLin; Caitlin had never cultivated an intel network like the other girls, or like Rachel herself.

"Rachel—" no *Gran* now "—you've been running a secret off-campus facility—in connection with my university—that has developed retinal transplant to evade security scanners."

Annelise said, "*What*?"

"And you had the surgery yourself."

Rachel said calmly, "Yes. For very good reasons. I suppose Julie Hampden told you."

Annelise said, "Wait. You didn't tell *me*?"

Caitlin said, "She didn't tell anyone. When Jane discovers this . . . You think you can control it, but that's not how science works. Word will spread, and others will exploit it. Peregoy scientists, rogue doctors, protestors, anyone with either expertise or money to hire expertise. The genie never goes back into the bottle, and no one's security system will be safe, just as happened when fingerprint transplants took hold."

"I know," Rachel said. "That's why I have people working on new security systems involving brain scans. Hard to transplant brains."

Annelise was still stuck on grandmotherly betrayal. "You didn't tell *me*?"

"I would have, dear heart. Soon. I had a heart

attack, you know, just as the research was coming to full fruition. But, Caitlin, what is the second thing you need to tell us?" Diversion—always a good tactic.

Caitlin said, anger emerging as a brutal bluntness, "Jane is running a biowarfare lab on Rand."

Rachel felt her mouth open to an involuntary O. "No. She wouldn't. Not even Jane. How do you know?"

"From Julie Hampden, who was told by a desperate virologist named Jenna Derov. It's been in the works a while. They're engineering one of the Rand plagues to be airborne through changes to both its RNA and cell envelope. Plus other changes."

Annelise said to the wallscreen, "On. Jenna Derov, virologist, all information. Visual only. Caitlin... you can't be sure."

"No. But I don't think it's beyond what Jane might do if the war goes against us."

Annelise said, "There is no war anymore! The gates..." She realized, and let out a soft whimper.

The gates were open again. Not to armed warships, but you didn't need a warship to carry bioweapons to a Peregoy world. *Philip can't read minds*, Rachel had told herself. He had stopped the weapons using— this must be true, it was the only explanation that fit—manipulation of the laws of physics, not biology. Biology was, as always throughout history, a wild card.

She said, forcing herself to calm, "Where is the biowarfare facility on Rand?"

"Julie didn't know. Jenna Derov wasn't going to give her that piece of intel until she got proof she was at the top of all lists for passage home to Rand. Now, Derov will probably withhold the location until she arrives there."

Annelise, reading information on her screen, said, "She has a family. Two kids and a husband."

Rachel said, "Forget lists. Annelise, send a flyer with Security to pick up this Derov person—where is she, Caitlin?"

"I'll take care of it. I'll bring her and Julie here."

Rachel said, "Yes, bring Julie Hampden here as well. I definitely want to talk to her."

Caitlin turned to face her grandmother. "Rachel, Julie is my employee, and my concern. You will not bully or threaten her in any way for telling me about the retinal transplants. Yes, I know you're CEO again and that's fine, but the university and its research are my concerns and I will run them. You've already erred in keeping the retinal project from me. Do we understand each other?"

"Yes." Caitlin would never believe it, but Rachel's heart sang with pride. She had at least one granddaughter who had both steel *and* the knowledge of when rules applied and when they did not. Unlike tradition-shackled Annelise, broken Tara, not to mention—

"The gates are open!" Jane cried as her face appeared on their wristers. Damn override. "Did you know? I just cleared the Rand-Galt gate. I'll be there tomorrow. The war will resume now, and I know how we can win it."

32

NEW CALIFORNIA

The moment his ship cleared the Polyglot-New California gate, Sloan called Sophia. When her beautiful, austere face appeared on his wrister, Sloan's eyes went salty. He blinked hard; not only would Sophia not have appreciated tears from her father, but the small vessel was so crowded that there was no privacy.

Sloan had done it. He'd found on Polyglot an accomplished neurologist who'd once worked on the retinal transplant project, and he'd persuaded Dr. Antonin to work for him. The persuasion had included not only an enormous salary but complete control over labs and personnel. Now Sloan was transporting the fledgling effort to New California; Antonin had brought a team with him. The ship, meant to seat ten, held sixteen, including Sloan and Chavez. Sloan could have waited for a larger ship to be stripped of radiation weaponry, but he hadn't wanted to wait. He wanted to resume control of the Peregoy worlds, to see Sophia, to tell her about this success.

Partial success. Sloan had recruited retina-transplant scientists, but not any physicists who knew anything more about the gates than physicists already on New California. In fact, Sloan hadn't been able to discover if such physicists even existed. All his network had turned up was nonsense about Julie Hampden's deep-brain implants and Philip Anderson. That people could actually believe in that coincidence—Anderson dying on the new planet and the gates closing—was beyond Sloan.

"Sophia," he said to her image on his wrist.

"Welcome home, Father."

Impossible to say much, personal or professional, in the crowded, listening craft. "All is well?"

"Yes," she said, but her face on his wrister said there was more. SueLin? When Rachel Landry had traded SueLin for Anderson's ridiculous trip to the eleventh gate, Sloan had had SueLin sent, under guard, back to New California. She should still be under guard, safely protected—and isolated—in a mountain cabin. Was she? Sloan would have to wait to ask Sophia.

As the small ship landed at Peregoy Corporation Headquarters, Sloan was shocked to see how many protestors massed outside the compound walls. Why hadn't Sophia had them arrested? More important, what were they protesting about in the first place? He provided everyone in his care with jobs, housing, medical, education . . . and with the closing of the gates, Sophia would have ended extended conscription—hadn't she? What more could his people want?

Outrage filled him. This was personal. They were kicking him in the face—he, who gave them everything.

He just glimpsed some of the holosigns before the ship dipped below the compound walls:

ELECTIONS NOW
STRIKE FOR FREEDOM
REMEMBER SUELIN—AND ACT!

What?

Sophia had sent people to escort the scientists to their quarters. Sloan rushed to meet her in his office, brushing past the faithful Morris, who stood waiting by the door with a tablet in his hand. "Welcome home, sir. This is a—"

"Sophia!"

"I'm so glad you're home, Father."

"Yes. Those protestors—are they actually striking? Why haven't you arrested them?" Everyone on New California was, in theory anyway, an employee of a licensed sub-business of Peregoy Corporation, and striking was illegal. If someone didn't like his or her job, transfers were readily available, or quitting. But nothing interfered with production.

"I did arrest them. More came. I arrested those. More came. The jails wouldn't hold them all. It's not just a protest, Father. It's a rebellion."

"They want *elections*? A corporation's CEO is not elected by the employees!"

"You spoiled them. You gave them so much that they think they're entitled to everything now, including what's ours. Including control."

Something in her face chilled him. He took the tablet from the trailing Morris, dismissed him, and closed the door. He kept his tone quiet. "What did you do when the jails became full?"

"I found out who the leaders were and sent them to a labor camp on Horton Island."

"We have no labor camp on Horton Island. Or anywhere else."

"We do now. The owners of the island were paid handsomely and resettled."

"Sophia . . ."

"Don't, Father. This was necessary. You don't know, you weren't here. Besides the strikes disrupting everything, the protests turned violent. Property was destroyed. A factory owner who defended you publicly was beaten by his own workers. He nearly died. I'm restoring order to New California before the situation grows worse."

"We're stewards of this planet, Sophia. Not dictators."

Her face cracked into emotion. When had he seen anger from Sophia? Never.

She said, "Stewards? Really? Look at your wolves, Father. Do you know what happened on Terra when they were eliminated from the top of the food chain? Their prey proliferated, grew too numerous, and starved, but not before they'd overgrazed all the plant life and wrecked whole ecologies. An ecology—including New California—needs dominant beings at the top of the food chain, or the whole system crashes. I'm doing what is necessary for all our people."

Sloan heard the unspoken coda: *So don't try to stop me.* Vertigo swooped through him; the bottom was falling out of his world. But only for a moment.

From long experience in handling people, he said quietly, "We can talk about this later, when I'm more rested."

"Of course." Her face resumed its usual calm. "Tell me about these scientists you've brought. What project are they intended for?"

"In a minute. First tell me about SueLin."

"She's safe in the cabin where you put her. But she's turned into a sort of symbol. Half the protestors think you killed her, the other half that you've imprisoned her. The whole propaganda program is being driven by one Scott Berman, who was an engineer at the Carrington bot factory. He's clever, manipulative, and dangerous. I have infiltrators in the Movement—that's the pretentious name they're calling it—but so far he's eluded me. They seem to have a very sophisticated communication system. Berman has no family that I could work through."

Work through. She meant threaten. How had things gotten this bad in the three months since Sloan had been gone? Or had Sophia set up some of her control systems as soon as the war began, without telling Sloan? Maybe even before the war? Sophia had always been more ruthless than he—but how ruthless was she?

He looked at this beloved, competent daughter, his heir, and realized that he needed to go slow. Before challenging her directly, he needed more information. Then he could plan.

He said, "You asked about the scientists I've brought with me. This is potentially very valuable, Sophia. I want them to get to work immediately. At Galt University, researchers have developed..."

As he talked, Sloan gazed past Sophia's shoulder at his stuffed wolves. How had she learned all that about wolves' place in the food chain? It wasn't the kind of thing that usually interested her. Luis Martinez must have told her, during the brief time that Sloan had thrown them together, hoping for a marriage. Where was Luis now? If his fleet had survived Landry attacks plus the three months of gate closure, he could be on his way now to New California. Sloan could use Luis. The world was collapsing, and Sloan needed help in shoring up the beams.

The wolves' yellow glass eyes shone back at him, unblinking.

33

DEEP SPACE

One month into the three-month voyage to New Utah, the *Skyhawk* braced for attack.

Martinez had the conn, with a pilot-in-training at the helm—what could be dangerous in this vast stretch of empty space? Then two Landry ships appeared as distant, distinctive blips on his scanner. The OOD said, "Captain—"

"I see them," Martinez said, at the same time that messages came in from the *Zeus* and the *Green Hills of Earth*. Martinez put all three ships on battle alert.

These two Landry warships must have been caught on the Prometheus side of the Prometheus-Polyglot gate when the gates closed. The rest of the Landry fleet defending the Prometheus-Polyglot gate had probably mostly been on the Polyglot side, able to voyage back to Polyglot. But these two vessels must have waited a while to see if the gate would reopen and then, when it did not, had done the only thing they could do to avoid starvation, the same thing that Martinez was doing: set a course for the Peregoy planet of New Utah.

The two Landry ships had therefore not gone through any gates. Unlike Martinez, they were armed. With the Landry meta-beams? If so, they could destroy as much of New Utah as they chose.

And they could destroy Martinez's small fleet.

The Landry ships were between him and New Utah; Martinez couldn't get there first. He could, however, warn planetary defense. He did that, knowing the Landry ships would intercept the signal. But if he knew the Landrys were here, then the reverse was true. At least the inhabitants of New Utah had ample time—two months—to prepare. The message was sent to New Utah.

Martinez said, "Send this message to the Landry fleet on all frequencies: 'This is the Peregoy Corporation Space Service ship *Skyhawk*, Luis Martinez commanding. The war ended with the closing of the gates. Are you attempting to negotiate safe orbit and resupply on New Utah for your ships?'"

The OOD's shoulders tensed. He sent the message.

There were three possibilities. One: the Landry ships had the meta-beam and would use its greater range to destroy the *Skyhawk*, *Zeus* and *Green Hills of Earth*, before using it to take New Utah. Two: the Landry ships did not have the meta-beam and would fight a conventional space battle, which Martinez's fleet would lose as soon as the enemy realized Martinez's ships were not armed. Three: the Landry ships did not have the meta-beam and were willing to peacefully negotiate for food on New Utah, either because they believed hostilities had ended or because they thought they could not win against the New Utah planetary defense. Or even against Martinez, who had three armed (they thought) ships against their two. Thus, they might even surrender to him. If so, Martinez thought wryly, then they were all back in the Napoleonic Wars, taking enemy ships as prizes.

None of those things actually happened.

Neither Landry vessel replied to the *Skyhawk's* hail. Were they maneuvering for position to fire?

"Lieutenant, send the message again. Are you on all frequencies?"

"Yes, sir."

No reply.

No reply to four more attempts, spaced over half an hour.

The OOD said, "Sir . . . there's something odd about those ships' motions."

"They're on course for New Utah," Martinez said.

"Yes, sir. But they're not maintaining constant distance between them. They're drifting apart. It's like—I can't be sure about this, but it's like something knocked one of them askew and nobody has corrected for it."

"Comet? A hull breach?"

"Unknown."

Martinez considered. His ships were outside what he estimated to be meta-beam range, and if they circled around the Landry vessels and toward New Utah, the enemy would be expected to match course and initiate battle. He said, "Get Captains Vondenberg and Murphy on the encrypted frequency."

"Yes, sir."

"Captain?" Murphy said from the *Zeus*.

"Take the *Zeus* on a wide evasive maneuver around

the Landry ships, toward New Utah, staying well out of what we know to be K-beam range. If they match course, retreat. Maintain contact with me. Vondenberg, maintain position."

"Yes, sir."

"Yes, sir."

The data blip that was the *Zeus* began to move. Distance widened between her and the two Landry vessels, neither of which changed course. Now Martinez could get a clear visual on the distance widening between the Landry ships.

It could be a trick.

But after several hours, it seemed less of one. The *Zeus* had made a wide semi-circle around both Landry ships and was now positioned between them and New Utah. There was no pursuit, and no attack.

Murphy said, "Out of presumed meta-beam range."

"Proceed to New Utah."

"Yes, sir!"

Martinez heard the jubilation in the young captain's voice; his ship was on the way to food.

The two Landry ships flew on, the distance between them ever growing, their comm frequencies silent. Martinez trailed them, out of meta-beam range although he was increasingly sure that they were not equipped with the long-range weapon.

What was the Landry fleet captain doing?

"Move slowly within firing range."

"Yes, sir."

Cautiously the *Skyhawk* crept toward the closer of the Landry ships, the one drifting off the course for New Utah. The ship did not fire. Its image grew on the viewscreen. The *Skyhawk* circled the enemy ship.

"Captain, the hull is breached, starboard side, just behind the bridge."

"I see it." A big gaping hole. Why hadn't the repair bots fixed it? By now there would be nobody left alive on that ship. Had the crew evacuated to the other vessel? Or—

"Move closer. Keep their hull between us and the other Landry ship."

No reaction from either ship. At a few klicks apart, the name of the ship was visible: the *Dagny Taggart*. Martinez grimaced. He doubted that anyone aboard his ship even knew who that was; few people read propagandist novels nearly three hundred years old. The second ship, the *Galaxy*, showed sensor data just as inert as the first.

Martinez, having exhausted the simple possibilities in his mind, ran through the more fanciful ones. Deliberate mass suicide—it had happened before, on Terra. A crazy captain that had released poison gas to kill everyone on his ship. But—*two* crazy captains? Or maybe a hull breach that had knocked out all bot repair capability on the *Dagny Taggart*, the survivors had transferred to the *Galaxy*, and—then what? A comet-borne spore-borne disease that had killed everyone? Aliens?

The only alien structures he'd ever seen or heard of were on the planet sealed behind the eleventh gate, and those had been as dead as the *Dagny Taggart*.

DiCaria said. "We could board her, sir, and investigate."

"No." Some instinct, deeper than reason, warned Martinez. "We'll board the intact ship, if possible."

"Yes, sir."

For the better part of a day they moved toward

the *Galaxy*, keeping the hull of the drifting and dead *Dagny Taggart* between them. The *Skyhawk* was not fired on. The *Galaxy* had no visible hull damage. It did not answer hailing messages. It flew on, serenely silent, toward New Utah.

Martinez grew increasingly sure that it was traveling under inertia, not command.

He fired an old-fashioned torpedo, of which the *Skyhawk* still carried a few, to miss the ship. No reaction. Nothing.

Martinez said, "Prepare to board. Standard boarding party. No, belay that—two crew members only. Volunteers. Full EVA gear."

The OOD glanced at him. EVA gear would inhibit the boarders' movements, including the use of sidearms. "Yes, sir."

Three hours later, Lieutenant Carol Gonzalez and specialist Jordan Wilson left the *Skyhawk*, now close to and matching the trajectory of the *Galaxy*. They rode a vacuum sled to the Landry ship, docked, and laser-cut the airlock door. Martinez had spent a long time with both, explaining hazards and their possible consequences. They were the eighth and ninth volunteers he'd talked to; the others had all backed out after hearing Martinez's theory.

Gonzalez said, "We're in, sir."

"Proceed with caution."

Both wore recorders. Martinez watched the inner airlock door open, releasing the ship's breathable air. "Alarms sounding, sir, but no other response. We're in a suit-storage area with benches and cabinets— ship design is similar to ours. Moving through a far door...okay. Yes."

Her voice had become strained. Two bodies lay on the floor, dressed in military uniforms with Freedom Enterprises badges. Their faces were a mass of purplish pustules; their hands had partly rotted. Impossible to tell their gender, how long they'd been there, or anything else. When the ship had been pressurized, the smell must have been terrible.

Gonzalez said, "Sending images for database matching . . . proceeding through the next corridor."

Wilson said nothing. He knew. They both knew.

Most of the corpses lay in their bunks. Some had undressed, perhaps preferring to die out of uniform. The captain had died in her chair on the bridge. It took Wilson, the software specialist, nearly two hours to get into the ship's computer. All files were heavily encrypted, but Wilson sent them to the *Skyhawk* anyway, everything that he could find. Everything physical was photographed.

Gonzalez said, "Sir, I can't see any way to discover the source of the infection."

"We'll probably never know," Martinez said. His own voice sounded thick. "I don't think it was on this ship. I know this isn't what you expected, Lieutenant."

"I knew it was a possibility. You were clear on that, sir."

A possibility, yes—but not a probability. The *Dagny Taggart* had clearly been disabled by the comet breach, and then survivors transferred to the *Galaxy*, which now carried more corpses than beds. But the comet was not what had killed both Landry ships. The disease had been carried by a transfer of something—food, personnel, hardware—from one ship to the other. The pathogen had gone along with the transfer.

The blood and tissue sample analyses that Gonzalez had sent back from her hand-held lab, the photographs of the purple pustules, what had to be a very fast incubation period since one or the other ship had all been infected before the captain knew enough to not contaminate the other vessel—all of it was given to Dr. Mary Glynn, ship's physician. She informed Martinez that none of it matched known diseases in the *Skyhawk's* medical data base. "This pathogen may have been genetically engineered, sir."

It wasn't natural, and it hadn't been created aboard either ship. Gonzalez and Jordan found no biolabs, nor any record of one, on either the *Dagny Taggart* or the *Galaxy*. The Landry ships had been transporting the pathogen from somewhere else, to somewhere else.

How had it gotten loose? An accident, or a deliberate act by the same sort of crazed, half-starved spacer that had tried to cut a hole in the *Skyhawk*? Or—the most chilling idea—had the Landry captain known that he didn't have enough supplies to make it to New Utah and so he infected both ships in hopes that a Peregoy vessel would investigate, and then carry the pathogen to the Peregoy worlds?

The Landrys, not satisfied with the meta-beam, were planning biowarfare. And pathogens, unlike radiation weapons, could pass through newly opened gates.

Gonzalez said, "Anything else we can do here, Captain?"

"No," Martinez said. "Lieutenant, if there were any other way..."

"I know there is not, sir."

"I'll personally deliver both of your Distinguished Space Service Medals to your parents."

"Thank you, sir."

Specialist Wilson said nothing. Martinez heard a soft sound, but the boy—God, he couldn't be more than twenty-one standard—straightened his spine. On the bridge of the *Skyhawk*, all heads bowed. Everyone understood that Martinez had no choice. Nothing was known about this vile weapon—not if it could cling to the EVA suits, not if it could survive the decon procedures built into Peregoy airlocks. Martinez had no choice.

The *Skyhawk* and *Green Hills of Earth* moved away from the two Landry vessels. At a great enough distance, Martinez said, "Fire." A second later, the torpedo with a nuclear warhead fired, and both the *Dagny Taggart* and the *Galaxy* were vaporized.

Sometimes these archaic weapons, which most ships no longer carried, had their uses.

Martinez turned to the data files from the Landry ship, blinking to clear his eyes enough to see them.

34

EVERYWHERE

Fields interact, ceaselessly, ceaselessly. Quanta changes from matter to energy, energy to matter. Particles appear, exist for the briefest of moments, disappear. Out of the quantum interaction of fields comes time, which both does and does not exist at the quantum level. "Slower" near large concentrations of matter, "faster" away from them, time has no objective meaning in the quantum flux. Time becomes space, space becomes time, and neither is local.

Except to the Observer.

Millennia pass. A minute passes. No time at all passes; the equations governing quantum fields can run in either temporal direction.

Except in the field of consciousness. Because it is consciousness that creates time, even when It cannot measure it.

Something is happening to the Observer.

Interacting fields change each other, even the field

of consciousness. The Observer is not as It was. Quanta have been affected, changed, destroyed. The Observer is more diffuse. It is weaker.

Fields can decay.

35

TWO LANDRY WORLDS

As soon as she landed on Galt, Jane came to Rachel's office, sweeping in with gale force. Despite her commander-in-chief uniform, Jane seemed a wild woman inexplicably dressed in an overly elaborate military uniform. She had lost more weight during her enforced stay on Rand and now looked like an erotic drawing from some artist's fevered imagination: tiny waist, full breasts, black curls foaming above glowing green eyes. Too glowing, too green.

Jane said, "Where's Caitlin? She should be at this meeting, too. I might need research support from the university."

Rachel said smoothly, "She's on Polyglot. I sent her there to try to hire some key scientists away from the Berlin Medical Institute. Neuroscientists. Caitlin hasn't come back yet, but of course she will now that the gates are open. These neuroscientists—"

"All right, we'll go ahead without her," Jane said.

Jane was not interested in neuroscientists—as Rachel had known.

Annelise said, "Go ahead with what, Jane? You said you think the war will resume now and you think we can win it."

"I don't *think* so, I *know* so. Fuck, Annelise, you're always so cautious!"

Annelise didn't take the old, old bait, for which Rachel gave her credit. God, these granddaughters of hers!

Rachel forced herself to say calmly, "So tell us what's on your mind."

"No radiation weapons can go through gates, right? But those aren't the only kinds of weapons. Now, Grandma, don't protest before you hear me out. These are desperate times, and that calls for desperate tactics. We *must* win the war or Freedom Enterprises is finished, and I don't intend to be finished. Samuel Fucking Peregoy is not going to annex Galt to his private dictatorship."

"I asked," Rachel said, "what you plan to do, not your motives for doing it."

"I'm going to threaten New California until Peregoy surrenders. Threaten him with biowarfare."

Annelise gasped. She was a poor actress. If Jane had not been concentrating so hard on Rachel, she wouldn't have believed her sister's pretense of shocked ignorance. Rachel said quickly, "Biowarfare? With what?"

"Joravirus. Genetically altered for both increased virulence and airborne transmission."

Rachel said, "No."

"Yes," Jane said, and in the calmness of that denial,

a calmness so at odds with Jane's hectic expression and clenched fists, Rachel saw how completely she had lost her. "Grandma, I know you're CEO again. Fine. But I run the space and security division, and my captains are behind me. I can do this."

The eternal strategy of palace coups—whoever controls the army can seize the throne. Rachel didn't think Jane wanted the throne. Ruling wasn't her goal; conquest was.

Annelise, her shocked ignorance now genuine, said, "But...but where did you alter the joravirus? How? And how would you threaten New California with it? *Jane*—"

"You don't need to know that." Jane said brutally. "Don't worry, Annelise, Galt won't be in any danger, and neither are you as heir. You're just going to have more worlds to administer, is all. Soon."

"How soon?"

"Not sure. But you'll know. Tell Caitlin when she returns from Polyglot. Send a scout message to Celia, if you like. But now I have to go. People are waiting for me."

Jane turned to leave. Rachel thought: *I could have my own security grab her right now. I could shoot her down. I could beg and plead and cry. I could threaten something she cares about.*

None of those would work. Jane was not stupid. Viruses were not massively engineered overnight. Jane had planned carefully, and for a long time, to alter the pathogen that had caused one of Rand's periodic plagues. If Jane were imprisoned, her military would storm Freedom Enterprises and rescue her. If she were dead, others would carry out her biowar. Emotion would not sway her, nor threats to something she cared about. This was what she cared about, with the same singleminded obsession that Tara had brought to her pursuit of Philip.

Philip—who, whatever he was now, would neither know about nor stop viruses.

Jane strode out. Into the suddenly dead air of Rachel's office, Annelise quavered, "Rachel, even if we destroy her lab, what if she's moved virus samples elsewhere..."

"One issue at a time," Rachel said.

One part of her mind registered irony: Of all her granddaughters, now only Jane, the dangerous warmonger, still called her by the childish and affectionate name "Grandma."

Julie Hampden's rogue virologist had lied about Jane's biowarfare facility.

Caitlin left Galt with the virologist, Jenna Derov, for Rand. Caitlin hadn't wanted to go, but her grandmother said there was no one else. Rachel, resuming the leadership of Freedom Enterprises, couldn't leave Galt, and anyway Caitlin didn't want Gran jaunting around the galaxy, not after her heart attack. The woman was ninety-six standard! Annelise had been running Galt since the gate closings, and Rachel needed her information and advice. And Caitlin was the only one who could understand the science anyway.

"I don't think you have to understand science to destroy a lab," Caitlin said grimly. All of this still felt unreal to her—an engineered bioweapon? Would even Jane do that? "Gran, I wouldn't have the first idea how to go about it."

"You don't have to know," her grandmother said. "I'm sending someone with you who will contact the right people to do it."

"Then why do you need me?"

Her grandmother made a little moue of impatience. Caitlin had seen that mouth twitch since she'd been a child, and she'd flinched at it for two decades. It meant that Caitlin was not grasping some essential point, was being naïve about how the world worked.

"I need you because you and Annelise are the only people I know who are always honest. Most people can be bought, Caitlin, and most people will lie if it's to their advantage. You need to learn that. I've worked with the man I'm sending with you, Eric Veatch, for a long time. But that doesn't mean I can ever fully trust him. It's your job to make sure that Jane doesn't learn from Veatch—or anyone else—that we're going to destroy her monstrous lab."

What a bleak way to live! But Caitlin said only, "Then how do you know you can trust Jenna Derov to be telling you the truth? Maybe there isn't even any bioweapons lab on Rand."

Her grandmother smiled. "Very good, Caitlin. You're learning. I don't know for sure that the Derov woman is telling the truth. That's another reason you're going, in order to find out. You know, dear heart, you and I are not as far apart in thinking as you believe. I know Galt has to change, that pure Libertarianism isn't going to work anymore."

"Is that a trustworthy statement, given everything you just said?"

Rachel laughed, suddenly seeming much younger. "Even better. You *are* learning. But, yes, I mean it.

We're going to face insurrection otherwise. One of the things I'm going to do while you're gone is meet with Ian Glazer, if he's still a leader of this rebellion."

"If you can find him."

"I can find anything, including the lab on Rand. Or at least Eric Veatch can. It will take me a few weeks to arrange this and—"

"Why?"

"There are arrangements to be made," her grandmother said evasively. "And I'm sure you will have things to tie up at the university, too. But this takes priority over everything else, Caitlin—I know you can see that. I'm just sorry that your traveling companions aren't more pleasant."

They were two of the most unpleasant people Caitlin had ever met.

The ship was a luxurious personal craft, newly stripped of weaponry so it could pass through the Galt-Rand gate. The *Princess Ida* had four small staterooms, a common area, crew quarters, and a bridge. Eric Veatch and Jenna Derov didn't seem to sleep; whenever Caitlin went into the common area, one or both were there. Veatch worked at a computer, humming constantly, loudly, and off-key. When asked to stop, he snarled, "No." Derov paced around the perimeter of the room, nervous and twitchy as a cornered *bukcat*. Occasionally she stopped to hurl a bitter statement at Caitlin: "It's different for you rich," or "People like my family have no control over our lives so fuck Libertarianism." Caitlin spent the two days of the voyage, one on each side of the gate, in her room.

Until a few hours before they landed on Rand. Then Veatch took over.

"Okay, Jenna, we're going to talk. Ms. Landry, you need to hear this."

Caitlin, on her way after lunch back to the sanctuary of her cabin, stopped. The common room was suspiciously empty, and the door to the bridge, which usually stood open, was closed. "Hear what?"

"What's going to happen on Rand. And how this bitch has been lying to you."

Jenna Derov whimpered and bolted for her stateroom. Veatch caught her, shoved her into a chair, and stood over her, three hundred pounds of bully.

Caitlin said, "Stop that immediately."

"No. Rachel's orders override yours. I've been contacting people on Rand ever since we passed the gate. People who know you, know Rand, know what goes on. There's no secret bioweapons facility on Rand. Is there, Jenna?"

"Yes! There is!"

"Tell me the truth," Veatch said, and hit her.

"Stop!" Caitlin cried. Veatch ignored her. Caitlin dashed to the door to the bridge and yanked on it. Locked. They were all in there—pilot, copilot, engineer, steward—and of course they could hear over the intercom. They knew. Rachel had ordered this, or at least had told the crew to not interfere with Veatch.

Caitlin strode over to Veatch. "If you hit her again, you'll regret it for the rest of your life. I'll see to that."

Veatch hit Jenna again. Caitlin picked up a chair and raised it. Before she could smash it over Veatch's head, Jenna sobbed, "Okay, yes! The facility isn't on Rand. But it exists! It does!"

Veatch's voice abruptly went soft. "Now we're getting somewhere. Ms. Landry, *don't*. I'm not going to hurt her anymore. Jenna, where is it? Tell me and you can go. We land in a few hours and you can go home to your kids and we won't bother you anymore. But if you don't tell me, and tell me the truth, you're going back to Galt and I guarantee you'll never see your family again. They won't even know what happened to you."

"Okay! The lab is on Prometheus!"

"And you know this how? Be very, very specific."

Jenna babbled between sobs. At times Caitlin could hardly understand her, but Veatch seemed to have no difficulty. Jenna's tale was long and convoluted, with names unfamiliar to Caitlin, but one part she understood. Jenna had lied in saying the facility was on Rand because if she'd said that it was on Prometheus, Jenna would have had nothing to hold over the Landrys so that she could go home. Prometheus, cold and rocky, had only one human habitation, a bleak research station that had been leased to the Peregoys until Landry warships captured it.

Caitlin listened numbly. So this was why Jane had tested her K-beam so far from Galt. She'd wanted Prometheus for her bioweapon development. What had she done with the Peregoy scientists there?

Jenna finished blubbering. Veatch sent her to her stateroom. Caitlin faced him. "How do you know she's telling the truth now?"

Veatch threw her a look of contempt. "You think I can't tell? This is what I do. Why your grammy hires me."

"Why didn't you just use a truth drug on her?"

"This is better. Now she knows to tell no one, ever. And she won't." He returned to his computer.

Caitlin heard the bridge door unlock from the other side.

She said, with as much authority as she could muster, "You're going to let her go, Veatch."

"Yeah, sure. As soon as we land."

"And then what?"

"You and I are going to load cargo and supplies and go on to Prometheus."

"What? No. I'm going home."

"Not my orders."

"Damn your orders! I'm not going to Prometheus!"

Veatch didn't even answer.

Caitlin thought of a dozen things to yell at him. *This is kidnapping*: But on her grandmother's order, and did she want to indict Gran on that? *I'll scream*: But it was clear the crew would not aid her. *I'll escape*: But that was clearly impossible, in space or on the ground. She raised her wrister to call Security on Rand. Her wrister had been disabled.

She wanted to believe that her grandmother wouldn't have allowed Jenna to be more than bruised. She wanted to believe that Gran had instructed Veatch to take Caitlin with him, if that proved necessary, only because Caitlin was so vital to stopping Jane. She wanted to believe that Veatch knew what he was doing, that it wouldn't be hard to destroy the facility, that she would be home in a few weeks. But could she really trust those beliefs? Or anything else?

I'm learning, Rachel.

Rachel worked through the evening, reviewing with Annelise everything that had happened on Galt while Rachel had been recuperating at the beach compound. Rachel also received scout-delivered administrative reports from newly accessible Rand and New Hell.

The one report they both waited for, from Caitlin, did not come. But at nearly midnight, she received an encrypted link from Eric Veatch, conveyed by a scout pilot as soon as the scout had passed the Rand-Galt gate.

Annelise waited, completely still, as Rachel decrypted and read it.

"The lab isn't on Rand, after all," Rachel said. "My people and Caitlin are going to Prometheus. Veatch says he has strong reason to believe it's there."

Annelise said, "I'm going home now. I haven't seen David or my kids in two days."

"Annelise—"

"I'm going home now."

Rachel saw that Annelise had reached the bottom of her well. It would fill again overnight, but for now she was dry. "Yes, dear heart, go home." And then, belatedly—and why hadn't she thought to ask before? These were her great-grandchildren—"How are the kids? And David?"

"All fine. Come with me, stay the night, visit with the children."

"I will soon," Rachel said, knowing she wouldn't, knowing she had no time, knowing that she wasn't great-grandmotherly enough. Well, she hadn't really been maternal enough, either. Not really.

After Annelise left, Rachel stared for a long time at the twin holos on her desk. Her husband and son, both named Paul. Paul Senior, not she, had been the nurturer. She had been too busy running the corporation bequeathed by her own father. Paul Junior had inherited his father's gentle character, plus something else, closer to depression. Or maybe his wife, Maria, had depressed him; unlike Rachel's, theirs hadn't been a happy marriage. So maybe Rachel's five granddaughters' aberrations came from their genes, or their difficult childhoods, or—who knew?—from curses by ancient and neglected gods. It didn't matter. They were what they were. You had to go on from there.

Midnight. Rachel wasn't sleepy. She had been thinking a lot about what Caitlin had told her, and now Rachel was working on her own plan to send the remaining Rand refugees back home. But it wouldn't do any good to just send them back. Rand's economy had been devastated by this last, most virulent plague, and now that it was over, Rand would need financial help in rebuilding. Caity was right—the days of pure Libertarian self-reliance were finished. But whereas Caitlin's motives were what she considered humanitarian, Rachel's were practical. In order for the Landry Libertarian Alliance to survive at all in changed times, it was going to have to become less libertarian. Freedom Enterprises would have to subsidize both refugees and their businesses.

Annelise, that bastion of tradition and rules, wasn't going to like it. But this was not a democracy, and Rachel was CEO. Still, there must be a way of presenting it to Annelise so that charity didn't look too much like . . . well, charity. Rachel would need to find that persuasion, need to build it into her plan. Which might also assuage Ian Glazer's protest movement. Glazer—she would have to try for a meeting with him.

She got down to work.

36

DEEP SPACE

Martinez was puzzled. At first, the data that his dead crew, Gonzalez and Wilson, had sent from the two Landry ships made sense. And then, as more of the data was unencrypted, it didn't.

The *Dagny Taggart* and the *Galaxy* had indeed been carrying a deadly bioweapon, which killed everyone on board both vessels.

They had been headed toward New Utah.

Martinez's original assumption had been that the Landry ships had been caught on the Prometheus side of the closed Prometheus-Polyglot gate. The tiny research station could not indefinitely furnish food for two warships without resupply from Polyglot. The station could not, in fact, have fed itself for more than a few months, assuming that the Landry takeover of Prometheus nine months ago had left any of the original Peregoy scientists alive. So the *Dagny Taggart* and the *Galaxy* had first plundered the station

Nancy Kress

for what it could scavenge, and then waited for the Prometheus-Polyglot gate to open, as the eleventh gate had opened to allow Martinez's ships through. But might that have been a special opening, to remove humans from access to the alien planet? That idea seemed confirmed by the alien gate's closing as soon as the *Skyhawk* and the *Green Hills of Earth* had cleared it, but Martinez didn't really know.

Either way, the two Landry ships had been marooned around Prometheus for at least three months. So they'd started the long trek to New Utah to surrender, their best option for survival.

Or so Martinez had assumed.

However, ships' records had been sent to the *Skyhawk* by data specialist Jordan Wilson before he died. (*Before you vaporized him, Martinez. Call it what it was.*) The records revealed an entirely different scenario. Both Landry ships carried much more food than usual, and a much lighter crew list. They could have reached New Utah, turned around, and gone back before they ran short of provisions. However, as far as they knew, the Prometheus-Polyglot gate still would have been closed. The ships had not been deweaponized. That suggested that they had left Prometheus before its gate reopened—if it had—and didn't realize they were able to return to Polyglot. Or that they did know the gates were open, planned to attack New Utah, and would return to Prometheus afterward, stripping their radiation weapons only just before they passed through to Polyglot.

But an attack on New Utah would have been fatal to the Landry ships. Although sparsely settled, New Utah did have a military station and planetary-defense weapons. Sloan believed in securing his own. The *Dagny Taggart* and the *Galaxy* would have been shot down—unless they'd been equipped with long-range meta-beams. That's what Martinez had expected to find in the ships' installation records, and he did. Both Landry ships carried the new weapons, which the Landrys called "K-beams." How many more did the enemy have? There was no intel on this critical question.

"Sir," said DiCaria, waking Martinez from a nap in his quarters, the first he'd taken in thirty hours, "the data team found something else."

"What?" Martinez sat up, instantly alert. Or as alert as possible, anyway. DiCaria's expression brought him the rest of the way.

"I think you should see the unencrypted data for yourself."

Martinez did. The specialists, looking exhausted and tense, were jammed into a small cabin off the wardroom. It smelled of stale food and bodies that had not showered in too long. The lead specialist, Tiana Stevenson, was a very young woman with such dazzling encryption skills that Martinez had had to fight to get her for the *Skyhawk*. Stevenson neither stood nor saluted. Nor did the others. Martinez had long ago decided that these specialists' lack of military polish was irrelevant.

"Sir, they had missiles," Stevenson blurted. "Adapted. They could be fired from pretty far out and aimed at the planet."

"Nuclear?" Those could be tracked and shot down long before they reached a planetary surface. It was what he'd expected the *Dagny Taggart* or *Galaxy* to do to his torpedoes.

"No, sir, that's just it. What we were trying to figure out. These are basically big rocks. They have no guidance machinery, no warheads. They're big enough to survive atmospheric entry, but small enough to escape probe detection or to do much impact damage. They'd either explode over random areas or just blow a smallish hole in the ground and break apart."

"Go on," Martinez said, but he already knew.

"The design allows for a hollow center. To be stocked with pathogens, sir. And the continent on New Utah is a windy place."

"Yes," Martinez said. And then, a beat too late, "Good work, Stevenson, all of you. Is there more?"

"No, sir. I mean yes, there's evidence that the pathogens were indeed brought up to the *Dagny Taggart* from Prometheus. The rest seems routine ship data, but we're still digging."

"All right. Get some sleep, all of you."

On the bridge, he briefed Vondenberg and Murphy. Elizabeth Vondenberg, her face thin from half rations, frowned.

"Did the data contain any information about what planetary defenses the Landrys installed on Prometheus? In addition to what we had there before?"

"No information. But there wasn't much there when it was a Peregoy research station. Virtually nothing." Nobody had wanted the barren, cold little world until the discovery of the eleventh gate.

From the *Zeus*, a few days ahead on the voyage toward New Utah, Murphy said, "They had time to install K-beams before the gates closed."

"Yes, if they had more of them. And there might be more Landry ships on the way to Prometheus now, if the Polyglot-Prometheus gate is open. Either way, the primary objective is now to destroy that bioweapons facility."

"Yes, sir."

"Murphy, the *Zeus* will continue on to New Utah. Vondenberg, the *Skyhawk* and *Green Hills of Earth* will set course for Prometheus, maximum speed."

With the gates supposedly closed for good, the Landrys might have assumed they would never be able to contact their bioweapons facility again. If the gates had all reopened, they might still assume that since they controlled—or had controlled—the Polyglot-Prometheus gate, and since the Peregoys did not know about the bioweapons, there was no need to rush warships to Prometheus.

Or right now they might be sending K-beam-equipped ships to defend the dwarf planet and its lethal facility.

Martinez did not have enough information. He would have to proceed without it. The bioweapon and its diabolical delivery system posed the single greatest threat to the Peregoy worlds that he could imagine. Old Earth had a long, rich history of wars in which disease killed more people, combatants and civilians alike, than died in battle. Including, of course, the final biowars that had ended up killing Earth itself.

As the *Skyhawk* and *Green Hills of Earth* changed course and strained their engines, one additional thing continued to puzzle Martinez. He'd scoured the intel data on Rachel Landry. She seemed intelligent. Under her long leadership of the Landry Libertarian Alliance, its crazy brand of libertarianism had allowed much suffering on Galt and Rand, unrelieved by government regulation or aid. Everyone for themselves, pull yourself up by your bootstraps, self-reliance as king, all that essentially heartless non-governing. However, she'd seemed, in his opinion, callous but not murderous. And as far as he could discover, she hadn't welcomed this war. Even if she read as little Earth history as Sloan Peregoy, she of course knew about the disease-heightened death throes of Terran civilization. Scorched-earth biowarfare didn't seem her style.

So why was it happening?

Six days later, the *Skyhawk* and the *Green Hills of Earth* reached Prometheus.

Martinez had been fortunate in one respect. Prometheus and New Utah shared a star, with New Utah in the Goldilocks zone and Prometheus orbiting very far out. Their current orbits brought Prometheus much closer to Martinez's position than might have been the case. The tiny planet would one day slip the star's gravity and wander off into the black depths of space, but right now it was here in all its frozen bleakness, requiring only a slight detour off his course for New Utah.

Prometheus suddenly looked to Martinez very like the planet behind the eleventh gate. Was its only reason for having a gate to enable humanity to eventually find the new gate beyond it?

Fanciful speculation.

The research station, located near the equator, lay mostly underground. The *Skyhawk's* database held the station blueprints. The Landrys might have dug additional tunnels after they wrested Prometheus away from Peregoy Corporation, but a nuclear bomb could devastate the entire area. First, however, Martinez had to get a scout close enough to fire it.

As they approached the dwarf planet, both the *Skyhawk* and the *Green Hills of Earth* searched for Landry ships. They found none. Apparently the *Dagny Taggart* and *Galaxy* had been the only vessels caught on the Prometheus side of the Prometheus-Polyglot gate, and the Landrys had not yet sent new warships. Was that because it took time to retrofit them with K-beams?

That left planetary and orbital defenses. The *Skyhawk's* sensors had picked up automatic signals from orbital probes. The station knew he was there.

He sent Vondenberg's ship to the far side of the planet. With both ships out of even K-beam range, Martinez signaled. "This is the PCSS ship *Skyhawk*, Captain Luis Martinez commanding. Research station, identify yourself."

Silence.

And what would he have done if station personnel had claimed to be the original Peregoy scientists, who had somehow overpowered and disposed of both the Landry conquerors and the bioweapon facility? Even if Martinez verified their identities, he still would have no choice of action. The biological pathogen came from here, and no potential carriers could be allowed to survive. But his mission would feel easier if the men and women downstairs were wartime enemies who had already murdered the Peregoy scientists. Then there were no innocents on Prometheus.

Are you sure? No one has their families with them? Their children?

He pushed the thought away. "This is the PCSS ship *Skyhawk*, Captain Luis Martinez commanding. Research station, identify yourself. Repeat, research station, identify yourself."

Silence.

"One more iteration and only one: Captain Luis Martinez of the *Skyhawk*, Peregoy Corporation Space Service. Research station, identify yourself."

Nothing. Was everybody down there already dead? Or completely defenseless? Not likely. The facility was just playing dead, waiting for him to get within firing range. That's what he would have done in their place. There was no way to fire a nuclear weapon accurately without getting within radiation-weapon range.

Martinez waited. The planet's six-hour rotation had to bring the station into exactly the right position.

Seventy-two minutes later, as the gate disappeared behind the curve of the planet, still no response from Prometheus. Martinez closed the hailing frequency and switched to an encrypted link. "Scout bay, are you prepared to launch?"

"Yes, sir. Prepared."

"Launch scout one. Lieutenant Adebayo, good luck. *Green Hills of Earth*, commencing operation."

"Yes, sir," Vondenberg said, simultaneously with Lieutenant Tad Adebayo's affirmative.

Scout one streaked out of the *Skyhawk* toward Prometheus. Its trajectory had been carefully calculated; it would reach firing range at the same time that scout one from the *Green Hills of Earth* would break above the horizon 180 degrees away. But before either of those things could happen, Vondenberg said from her ship, "Abort! Abort!"

A beam shot up from the research station, but too late. Adebayo had already banked sharply to return to the *Skyhawk*. He escaped: young reflexes, plus radiation beams that could not bend. Martinez said sharply, "Vondenberg?" She would never have aborted without good cause.

"Sir, a ship coming through the Polyglot gate!"

It couldn't have radiation weapons, but Vondenberg was wisely taking no chances. A moment later, she said, "Not a warship. Looks like a class 6A...a personal vessel. Move to block its return through the gate?"

"Yes. And recommence operation. Adebayo?"

"Yes, sir."

"Launch."

Vondenberg would be giving the same order on her side. Scout one from the *Skyhawk* flew at maximum speed toward Prometheus. Adebayo ejected. The ship continued on automatic pilot. A brilliant flash, and the beam from the planet vaporized the scout.

But before the beam artillery could swing around to take out the scout from the *Green Hills of Earth*, the small craft was within range and fired its missile. The beam vaporized the second scout; its pilot had not ejected in time. But the missile hit and the station went up in a mushroom cloud of methane, nitrogen, rock, and death. If anyone or anything survived in tunnels deeper than the blueprints showed, they were never coming up.

Martinez said, "Maneuver to retrieve ejected pilot. Vondenberg?"

"Ship is a Landry vessel, registered on Polyglot as the *Princess Ida*. Awaiting orders, captain."

He wanted to blow up the Landry craft. Adebayo was alive, but he'd taken radiation. The other scout pilot had just died. And although the bioweapons facility had been destroyed, that didn't mean that samples of the pathogen had not already been taken elsewhere, as they had been on the *Dagny Taggart* and *Galaxy*. That was probably what this personal craft was here to do—export even more of the bioweapon. Damn all the Landrys to hell forever and beyond.

He said to Vondenberg, "Force the vessel to surrender and board it. Use a scout and keep the *Green Hills of Earth* out of detonation range in case they try a suicide attack. Recruit volunteers for the boarding party, who are authorized to use whatever force is necessary to take everyone on board prisoner. The vessel was flying toward the facility, not away from it, so it isn't yet transporting the disease, but take all possible precautions anyway. When you've secured the *Princess Ida*, contact me. The *Skyhawk* will move away from the gate and you'll follow as soon as feasible."

"Yes, sir."

"As soon as we know it's safe, I want the prisoners aboard the *Green Hills of Earth*. Interrogation to follow. They *are* going to tell us everything they know about this fucking operation."

If his uncharacteristic cursing startled Vondenberg, she didn't show it. "Yes, sir. We'll get them aboard."

The *Skyhawk* flew back toward New Utah. Martinez didn't dare risk using the Prometheus-Polyglot gate, although that had been his original plan. The gate was open and Polyglot might still be neutral, but depending on how the war was going, there might be Landry warships waiting on the Polyglot side. After all, a Landry *pleasure craft* had just gone through the gate. The detour to Prometheus had cost Martinez time, but if he cut everyone's rations again, they could make it to New Utah. Barely.

And maybe the *Princess Ida* was well-stocked. If so, the prisoners weren't getting the food. Let them starve.

He was experienced enough to know that his anger was dangerous to clear thinking.

Tad Adebayo exposed to a too-high radiation count and Fiona Haller, the other scout pilot, dead. Both excellent officers. A deadly engineered pathogen possibly loose in the Eight Worlds. Had the Landrys learned nothing from Earth's horrors? Did Rachel Landry never read any history? At least Sloan Peregoy, who also was too ignorant about the human past, was not a monster. Sloan would never have created a bioweapon.

When the *Green Hills of Earth* joined the *Skyhawk*, the ships slowed to match speeds and trajectories. Vondenberg had reported a successful capture.

The Landry pleasure craft, the *Princess Ida*, contained fourteen people. Four small staterooms, a common area, crew quarters, and a bridge. The ship had surrendered immediately, which surprised Martinez a little, even though it was true that unless the *Princess Ida* self-destructed, she had no battle advantage. She couldn't outrun the *Green Hills of Earth*. She didn't know if the warship still carried radiation weapons to vaporize her. Her crew was far outnumbered. Still, a boarding party was always at a tactical disadvantage, and the Landry crew must have carried sidearms. In their position, Martinez would have fought. But they had not, which suggested they had no valuable information they could be forced to give up. Either that or cowardice: better to be prisoners than molecular rubble.

Vondenberg finished her report with, "They could have blown themselves up, and us, too. The boarding party found a lot of plastic explosives."

"Retinal identifications of the prisoners?"

"In process...here comes the data. Querying data banks...okay. Thirteen matches with Polyglot records. One male without any scan data whatsoever. IDing everyone else now."

Martinez waited. Neutral Polyglot shared security data with the Eight Worlds. If the fourteenth person was not in the databanks but the ship had come from Polyglot, that suggested a very high-level altering of records. Someone with major influence.

Vondenberg said, "Four crew members: two pilots, one engineer, one steward. Two lab techs, trained at Bernhoff College on Polyglot, employed by Formano Biotech, a Landry-owned company on Polyglot...okay, one of the lab techs was fired for criminal activity, charges pending. Six Galt citizens, registered on Polyglot as security guards, all ex-military. Those are the six that the boarding party said looked really unhappy about surrendering their weapons."

So why had they, instead of putting up a fight? Someone had given firm orders.

Vondenberg said, "Still nothing on the undocumented male. The fourteenth passenger ID coming up now...*whoa.*"

Martinez said, "Who is it?"

"Caitlin Susan Landry."

One of Rachel Landry's granddaughters. What was she doing way out here, and carrying large amounts of plastic explosives?

Vondenberg said, "She's president of Galt University. Degrees in biology."

Martinez said, "Strip search everyone. Take tissue and blood samples and analyze for matches with the d-base information we already have about the pathogen. If the prisoners come up clean, transfer them naked to the *Green Hills of Earth*. We don't want any spores or whatever coming aboard in clothing. When you have them aboard and they've gone through enhanced decon, isolate and guard the Landry woman and the unidentified male, separately. Lock the others in a secure cabin. Notify me when medical analysis and transfer are complete.

"I'll be coming aboard."

37

PROMETHEUS

Caitlin stood naked in her cabin on the *Princess Ida* while a woman in a Peregoy military uniform probed every cavity of her body, taking samples. She kept her head high and her face stony, or tried to. The pain was minimal, the humiliation enormous. Was Veatch undergoing this procedure, too? She hoped so,

He'd wanted to fight the soldiers boarding the *Princess Ida*. So did his mercenaries, the six thugs that Veatch had hired. Not for the first time, Caitlin wondered just what Veatch would have done if they had reached the biowarfare facility on Prometheus—killed everyone there as well as blowing it up? Were those Rachel's orders? No, surely not. Her grandmother was trying to stop Jane's monstrous plan, not murder the scientists carrying it out. Rachel hadn't even known the facility wasn't on Rand.

It was Caitlin who'd made the decision to surrender to the *Green Hills of Earth*—dumb name for a warship. The Peregoy fetish for old Earth was pathetic. And so was she, for ending up in this degrading position. When she'd insisted, wielding threats in the Landry name, that there be no attempt to battle the boarding party, Veatch's six mercenaries had looked uncertainly from her to Veatch and back again, trying to decide whom to obey. They'd chosen Caitlin. She was a Landry. Or maybe they just wanted to survive.

What would the Peregoy fleet do to her, to them all? She hoped for a ransom bid. Rachel would pay it, if it was just money. But what if these Peregoys wanted some sort of war concession that Rachel wouldn't make?

The soldier finished with Caitlin's body and threw at her a flimsy 3-D-printed robe. "Put this on."

Caitlin did. "Now what?"

"Wait."

To analyze the tissue samples, of course. Did they think Caitlin was carrying the deadly pathogen? Maybe. But if so, they didn't think it very seriously, since by now she would have transmitted it to this impassive soldier.

Their medical analysis was quick. Caitlin was herded into the *Princess Ida* airlock and then into a vacuum sled. "Where are the others?"

Her guard didn't answer. She sealed the sled and it shot through its escape slot. Were they jettisoning her into space to die? No, they wouldn't waste the sled. In less than a minute, it jerked to a halt. Another few minutes and the sled opened. Caitlin climbed out.

She stood on the deck of a large vehicle bay, surrounded by Peregoy uniforms. She demanded of the closest soldier, "The others on my ship? Are they safe?"

No one answered. A female soldier who looked as if she could lift mountains grabbed Caitlin's arm and led her through a door. The flimsy robe tore. The guard deposited her in a small room empty of everything but a table bolted to the deck and three chairs. Another soldier dumped clothing onto the table. Without a word, both soldiers left, locking the door behind her.

Caitlin replaced the torn robe with the actual clothes: pants, boots, a tunic a bit too tight for her. Somebody's old civvies. The boots pinched. This time, the wait was longer. Caitlin felt the slight acceleration when the vessel started to move. She was aboard a Peregoy warship, a prisoner, and she had no good course of action. Well, she could try to smash a chair onto whoever came through the door next, but that wouldn't really get her anywhere. Her best choice was to try to negotiate.

Caitlin knew she was not a good negotiator, not like Annelise or Rachel. Science didn't negotiate truth; it tried to discover and prove it. But negotiation was all she had. If the Peregoys would not bargain and she was going to die, she wanted to do it calmly. If she was going to be tortured for information she didn't have, calm probably wasn't possible, but she would try.

After what seemed like hours but was probably not, the door opened and a single man came through and stared at her. Tall, dressed in a Peregoy uniform of high rank—she didn't know what rank the insignia indicated—he had the coldest face she had ever seen. Under the ice, he was suppressing fury and doing it well, but fear swept through her anyway. She stood, chin lifted, saying nothing. This was the person in charge.

"Caitlin Susan Landry." It wasn't a question.

"Yes. And you are . . ."

He ignored the question. "Sit."

She ignored the command. "What have you done with my crew?"

"I'm asking the questions, Ms. Landry. Who is the man without ID?"

"His name is Eric Veatch." It probably wasn't, but maybe it would be good to appear to cooperate. "What have you done with him?"

"Why were you, Veatch, and the others traveling to Prometheus?"

Caitlin stayed mute.

He watched her closely. "There was a research station on Prometheus. It had been converted to manufacture a deadly pathogen for biowarfare. We've destroyed that facility."

Caitlin felt her chin drop—too late to hide surprise. "You did?"

"Yes."

"Are you sure? Completely destroyed?"

"Yes. You don't seem distressed."

"I'm not. It's what we went there to do."

"You can't expect me to believe that."

"I don't care what you believe," she said. Her mind raced. If he wasn't lying, then Jane's horrific genocide wouldn't happen. Unless— "Do you know if there are more facilities elsewhere? Or if any of the pathogen had been stored anyplace?"

"You tell me."

"I don't know." She took a step toward him and locked gazes. "Look, I don't know anything at all, except that the biowarfare facility existed. If you know my name, you know that I am the president of Galt University. I'm not involved in my family's war plans. There is nothing useful I can tell you."

"You have degrees in biology. You run a research university. Do you really expect me to believe that you had no part in developing the bioweapon and are completely ignorant of its intended uses?"

"Well...yes. I learned only recently that the bioweapon even existed. Then I was sent to destroy the facility, because I'm a Landry and we wouldn't be shot out of the sky. We were supposedly bringing two new lab assistants—if you IDed everyone but Veatch, you know that's true. You also know we had explosives to destroy the station once we were inside. You must have found them on the *Princess Ida*."

"And how were you going to 'destroy' the station from within without also blowing up your own people?"

"I don't know." Veatch had refused to tell her. The data library on the *Princess Ida* had been locked down. Caitlin had been virtually a prisoner on the ship, although she was not going to reveal that.

"I see. You were leading a mission that you had no idea how to carry out."

"I wasn't leading it. I was just...just a name. A key to unlock the station. But yes, before you ask—I wanted it destroyed, too. What it was doing was a monstrous human abomination."

A long silence. Then he said, "I will give you this, Ms. Landry. You're among the best liars I've ever seen."

"I'm not lying!"

"Let's assume for just a moment that you're not. Your mission was to destroy the research station. You were just an innocent lamb, sent along—"

"I didn't say—"

"—to create enough credibility to gain entrance for the mysterious Mr. Veatch. Who sent both you and him?"

Should she answer that? If this war ended, there might be a war crimes court, as there had often been on old Earth. Caitlin had to protect Rachel. And—yes—even Jane. They were family. Although maybe it was a protection to Rachel to say that her grandmother had wanted to forestall biowarfare. But on the other hand—

"I'll ask you again. Who ordered your supposed mission to destroy the biowarfare facility?"

"My grandmother, Rachel Landry."

Clearly he didn't believe her. Caitlin plunged on. "No, it's true. My grandmother doesn't want biowarfare any more than you do—" true? Maybe he did want it, for his side "—or anyone sane. I've studied what engineered pathogens did over decades of escalating war on Terra. Rachel Landry doesn't want that for the Eight Worlds—she's not genocidal. She didn't even want this war, it somehow got started by accident, and she went to Polyglot to try to reason with the Council of Nations and with your dictator. Her heart attack interfered and things only got worse. But this isn't what Rachel wants."

"If that's true," he said, not looking as if he believed it, "then someone else ordered biowarfare, developed the pathogen on Prometheus, and was carrying it on two of your warships toward New Utah when I destroyed the ships. I lost two good soldiers there and a pilot on Prometheus. Someone on Galt caused that. If not you or your grandmother, then it must be the Landry commanding your fleet. Your sister."

"No," she said, heard her own lie, and knew that he heard it too. She couldn't risk him not believing the rest of what she'd said. He'd just voiced the terror that had kept her awake every night on the *Princess Ida*, that made her chest tighten unbearably now: *carrying the pathogen on two of your warships . . .* The disease was out.

She managed to say, "Or rather, yes . . . it was Jane. Not my grandmother. The rest of us didn't know and don't want biowarfare. That's why Rachel wanted the research station bombed. You did it thoroughly enough to sterilize the entire area? Are you sure?"

"Yes."

"Thank the gods." She closed her eyes briefly, involuntarily. Although if Jane had sent more samples out from Prometheus on more ships . . .

When she opened her eyes again, he was studying her. Abruptly he said, "You're going under truth drugs."

"Yes. All right. Although—you do know those are not reliable for all personality types under all circumstances? People with—"

"I know."

"Veatch, for instance, is—"

"Don't lecture me on brain function, Ms. Landry," he said, with the first irritability she'd seen from him. "Not even if you're a biologist."

"Sorry. But please—tell me you haven't killed my crew."

His face hardened again. "You killed mine," he said, and left her alone.

Martinez regretted that parting shot. Not professional. But she was not what he'd anticipated. Either she was the Landry Libertarian Alliance's champion actress, or the situation on Galt was disintegrating. Intrafamily schisms, rogue military, no discipline or overall strategy. But what could you expect from libertarians, who believed every person's only duty was to themselves?

No. That, too, was a cheap shot. Martinez had read enough to know that libertarianism was more nuanced and complicated—although that didn't mean it was suited for wartime. Much better to have a single, sane commander-in-chief who considered his duty to all his people, military and civilian both. Martinez would be glad to reach New California and plan again with Sloan Peregoy.

Meanwhile, his small fleet, the *Zeus* ahead of the other two vessels, continued on to New Utah.

38

NEW CALIFORNIA

Sloan's four-person flyer landed in a tiny upland meadow, beside a large cabin built of rough karthwood logs. In the passenger seat, beside the pilot, Chavez awaited orders. Sloan glanced at his longtime bodyguard—did Chavez now receive his orders from Sophia?

She'd approved this flight, of course, with that silky approval that looked deceptively like mere interest. Sloan was under no illusions. If Sophia hadn't approved this trip to see SueLin, Sloan would not be here. During his three months on Polyglot, what had been shared control of Peregoy Corporation had radically altered.

Not officially, of course. Sloan was still CEO. But so skillfully had Sophia promoted or replaced key executives, shunted funding to various divisions, built political and financial alliances, threatened and bribed, that she now had more control than he did. Sloan was still uncovering all of her changes; he could not yet undo them.

The secrecy hurt him most. She was not telling him everything, not anywhere close. He believed her reasons to be unselfish; Sophia honestly thought that she was doing what was best for the Peregoy worlds, and that if Sloan knew of all her draconian measures, he would try to reverse them.

She was right. He didn't, and he would, as soon as feasible. Sloan knew more than Sophia guessed.

About SueLin, however, they were in agreement. Their heir must not come anywhere near the protest movement that had made her its unlikely symbol of Peregoy "oppression." It both angered and shamed Sloan that he felt it necessary to check on SueLin's treatment at Sophia's hands.

If only he had some word of Luis Martinez! Was he still alive and on his way home? Or had he been trapped on the wrong side of the eleventh gate and died there of starvation? Sloan couldn't bear to think that. If Sloan's son Jonathan had lived, he might now be just as desirable an ally as Martinez would have been. Might yet be. An ally against both the Landrys and against—

No. Don't even think that.

Appalled at himself, Sloan flung open the flyer door and climbed out. Chavez followed close behind. The meadow, the only flat place on the tiny Jabina Island, was filled with bright flowers. Beyond, the sea sparkled in sunlight. It was beautiful, remote, impossible to leave except by air.

Security advanced to meet them. The entire meadow was shielded; Sloan's wrister gave a small bleep of protest as it died. SueLin was not allowed electronics of any kind and neither were her guards, lest she figure out a way to steal one. There was a transmitter hidden somewhere on the mountain that filled most of the island, but SueLin never went outside alone.

The cabin looked comfortable, with one large common room, a dorm for the guards, a room for SueLin, storage and kitchen. Shelves held books, games, a holo player and hundreds of film cubes.

Sloan said, "My granddaughter?"

"Out hiking, sir, with two guards. She should be back soon. Assistant Director Peregoy transmitted only half an hour ago that you were arriving."

"And you have no way to tell SueLin's guards that I've arrived?"

"No, sir. Sorry, sir. But Ms. Peregoy is never gone long."

Not a hiker. Not a reader. No birds to breed. She must be so bored.

Sloan filled in the time by inspecting everything, asking questions, learning what he already expected: SueLin was being treated well and behaving badly. The security guard had a purpling bruise on the side of his face; probably SueLin had hit him with something. Sloan didn't ask.

She erupted through the cabin door and, to Sloan's dismay, flung herself at his feet and clasped his knees. "Grandfather, please, please get me out of here! I won't do anything, I promise, I won't even talk to anyone! Just take me home!"

"Get up, SueLin. Have some dignity."

It sounded colder than he intended, but distaste overrode compassion. No Peregoy should act so craven, not ever. He was embarrassed for her, and for himself, in front of the guards.

His coldness, or her own fury, sent her leaping to her feet. "Dignity! How am I supposed to have any fucking dignity when I'm a prisoner in this fucking place? Are you going to take me home or not?"

"No. I'm sorry, but I can't. The—"

"You mean you won't! You and that cunt Sophia!" She beat on him with her fists. A guard pulled her away and carefully pinned her arms. SueLin flailed, spat at Sloan, and started to cry.

Horrified, Sloan wiped the spittle off his tunic and spoke as calmly as he could. "SueLin, the protestors have made you a symbol of their so-called 'oppression.' They would use you to whip up violence for their illegal demands, might even kidnap you for ransom. They seek to harm all the Peregoys, including you. Don't you understand? Control of New California is at stake here."

"I don't care! I want to go home! Take me home!"

She was a child. She was a danger to Peregoy Corporation. She was a completely unfit heir to everything generations of Peregoys had built.

"I can't," he said gently and he left, more shaken than he wanted to admit, followed out the door by her shouted and foul curses.

In the flyer, he sat for a long moment before saying to the pilot, "Take off now."

Five minutes in the air, Chavez said, "We're headed the wrong way, sir."

"No, we're not. We're flying to Horton Island. To the labor camp."

The bodyguard's face hardened, which answered one of Sloan's questions. Sloan watched Chavez weigh his choices. He was Sophia's man, and Sophia had told him to bring Sloan home. But Sloan had substituted his own pilot for Sophia's; the flyer was in the air and attacking the pilot would be dangerous; Sloan was still CEO. Chavez scowled but said nothing.

Sloan said quietly, "Contact my daughter, if you like. Record anything you choose. But don't interfere with me."

Horton Island, the top of a volcano that had erupted seventy years ago—Sloan remembered the eruption— consisted of rock and hardy scrub around a lake-filled caldera, isolated in the vast ocean. All food and supplies had to come in by air or boat. As they approached the island, a cargo drone flew low and parachutes floated down several large, canvas-wrapped bundles.

Smart. Sophia hadn't needed guards for this place. There was no way to attack the drones, no wood to build rafts, no possibility of escape. Low, crude shelters dotted the island, built of parachute cloth and scrub wood. Sloan watched figures run toward the new drops. God, it must be constant warfare down there. Unregulated competition for food, women, control.

It was not.

"Unknown flyer, come in," said a woman's voice over the flyer dashboard, startling Sloan.

"They have a transmitter down there?"

"No, sir. That was a wrister transmission . . . we'll be out of range in a minute."

"Circle back and keep circling, as low as is safe. Open a response channel. I want to talk to her."

Chavez shifted uneasily beside Sloan. Sloan ignored him. The pilot said, "Horton Island, this is the flyer above you. Are you receiving?"

"Yes. Who are you?"

Sloan leaned forward, speaking loudly from the back seat. "This is a representative of Peregoy Corporation. Are you—"

"I recognize your voice. Sloan Peregoy." And then, "So the gates are open again."

She was quick. Sloan said, "Who are you?"

"Hannah Kruer, United Citizens for Responsible Government, sentenced here two months ago by your thugs, Sloan. What do you want now? Aren't starvation rations punishment enough, or do you intend on taunting us while you starve us?"

Sloan said nothing, waiting to hear more. The figures far below opened the parachute bundles and began carrying the contents to the largest of the makeshift shelters.

"I know what you want," Hannah said. "You want us to kill each other over what you send. That's why you include one special thing in each shipment, isn't it? To tempt us to fight over it. Well, it's not working. We share and share alike, Sloan. We've set up fair ways of distributing food, supplies, and labor. We govern ourselves, with free speech and equal votes, free from conscription and oppression from you and your daughter's dictatorship. Free from Peregoy surveillance and control and punishment. No matter what you do to us!"

Sloan said to the pilot, "Leave now."

He had given his people everything, protected them, cared for them. And now this.

Yet ... starvation rations? Sophia should not have done that. He would change the order. Sophia would have to give way. He was still CEO.

❖   ❖   ❖

Some days, Sloan felt his age, but not as he'd imagined. He'd always thought that very old age would bring arthritis, failing organs, fatigue. None of that had happened, perhaps thanks to the rejuv treatments and excellent, continuous medical care. Except for some stiffness when he woke in the morning, his body went on as usual. Not as when he was thirty, of course, but without staging any major rebellions. Nor did his mind seem less agile or less involved with Peregoy Corporation.

No, what age was giving him was a strange, irritating sense of speculation. He pondered things he'd never thought about before. What if there really existed life after death? What did a human life mean? Was it only a personal narrative, ending with death, or did it mean something more?

Such thoughts annoyed him. They were irrelevant. Yet they intruded anyway, and at strange moments: in the shower, as his dinner arrived from the kitchens, as he gazed out the window of his office at the garden bots trimming genemod flowers beside the Peregoy Corporation walls.

There were no protestors out beyond the walls, not anymore. Sophia had seen to that. And yet Sloan knew they were still there, planning and waiting. His private intel network hadn't been able to locate their leader, one Scott Berman. Had Sophia found him? And done—what?

"Background research," he said to the wallscreen. "Most recent photo and voice, compact text. Hannah Kruer, citizen of New California."

There were three Hannah Kruers, but one was a child and one almost as old as Sloan. When he'd chosen the third woman, the screen displayed her most recent photo. Pale skin and dark, very intense eyes. Unsmiling; this was a police photo. The wall said, "Hannah Marie Kruer, twenty-eight, born in Capital City, maintenance engineer at Tennessee Province Water Facility, no recorded marriage, no children. Arrested three months ago for treason and conspiracy to murder. Sent to Horton's Island. More?"

"No. Records of all persons sent to Horton Island, photos and police charges only."

Cameron Struppa, treason and conspiracy to murder and treason.

Jean Antoinette Palmquist, treason and conspiracy to murder.

Aliya Mosolf, treason and conspiracy to murder.

John Stephen Hughes, treason and conspiracy to murder.

Sherica Ann Miller, treason and conspiracy to murder.

Christopher Daniel Larsson, treason and conspiracy to murder.

Jackson Victor—

The door opened and Sophia entered. "Father?"

Sloan didn't blank the wallscreen. She would know what he'd been doing, anyway.

"Come in, Sophia. Do you have the reports from the New Yosemite mines?"

"No, not yet. This is about something else."

She was quietly, definitively, furious. Nothing showed on her beautiful, impassive face, but Sloan knew. He had a sudden memory of Sophia at four, guilty of some childish infraction, feeling she'd been unjustly accused, facing her mother with her little face still and her thin body quivering with anger.

This, too, came with old age—the past was so much more vivid in memory than it had seemed when it occurred.

"What is it, Sophia?" Sloan said, although he already knew.

Her pretty voice was calm, reasonable. "You countermanded my rations order for the political prisoners on Horton Island."

"I did. You've removed them from society and they can do no further harm. There's no point in further punishment, which can't even act as a general deterrent since the prisoners have no chance for outside communications."

"The point is the punishment. But more important, by overriding my orders, you eroded my authority with our employees."

"I think, my dear, that you've gone a long way toward eroding mine."

They stared at each other, neither blinking. Sloan spoke first. "Sophia, have every one—all hundred and two—of your prisoners really committed both treason and conspiracy to murder? Murder whom?"

"You. Me. Peregoy Corporation."

"I can't find trial records."

"There are no trials in wartime, Father. Treason is punishable by death. The prisoners are lucky I didn't have them executed."

"We have no protocol for wartime."

"Precisely why I had to pull from the database for old Earth. But you're evading my point. By overriding my orders, you're creating confusion in the reporting chain. You and I can't issue separate orders, and you've always left security to me."

Which was why Sophia now controlled the police. Sloan didn't say that aloud. "You yourself just said that wartime is different. Didn't Terra invest wartime control in a single commander-in-chief?"

"Of the military, yes, and of course that's you."

"Sophia," he said abruptly, "Let's not fence like this. Not you and me. Strikes are illegal and I understand your arresting those who lead them, especially with the factories working so feverishly to produce more ships. But illegality is not treason, and I'm having trouble believing that every single one of your prisoners planned to murder me. Peregoy Corporation cannot be 'murdered.' I won't free the Horton Island prisoners because you're right, that would undermine your authority. But they will receive enough food, the basic necessities of life, and a volunteer medical team if I can find one willing to be marooned there. Are we agreed?"

"Yes," she said, "and now I'll try to get those reports for you."

She left. But Sloan had seen that one tiny quiver of her rigid body.

He returned to the list of Horton Island "traitors." The name he looked for, Scott Berman, still wasn't there. He didn't search for it in the entire d-base. Sophia would know.

He sat a long time at his desk, his face in his wrinkled hands. How had it come to this? How?

39

GALT

Rachel dreamed of Philip Anderson, which was odd because she never had before. In her dream, Philip stood before her, a handsome young man on the blue sand of her beach compound. He smiled and then began to melt, oozing into the sand until only his lips remained, still smiling in horrible disembodiment, until they also dissolved to become just more grains of sand. Rachel tried to scream but couldn't, no sound would come and—

"Rachel, wake up, we're here," Annelise said. Gently she shook her grandmother's shoulder. Rachel pulled herself upright in the back seat of the flyer. Her bodyguard and pilot sat in the front. Below the flyer, the refugee camp sprawled in pearly dawn light.

Caitlinville, they called it, although Caitlin herself hated the name. Rachel had received word from Veatch that "the antique you seek" was not on Rand and "when you receive this, I'll already be on my way."

That was worrisome. But, then, what was not? Rachel shook sleep from her eyes, and both Veatch and Philip from her brain. She and Annelise had a job to do.

Annelise said, "Are you sure you're all right?"

"I'm fine Annelise. I'm just old. The old often nap. Now let's get on with it. And be grateful Jane isn't here."

They could not have undertaken to send the refugees home to Rand without Jane's cooperation. She controlled the fleet. Rachel knew that the only reason Jane had consented was that the major shipyards were on Rand, closer to vital mining operations on New Hell. Nobody except miners lived on New Hell, of course, but the rare ore found there were critical to building spaceships. Jane's massive program of ship-building was stabilizing Rand's economy, shattered by plague and the people fleeing plague. Jane needed the refugees back to work on her new fleet of warships, and she needed them badly enough to temporarily divert six cruisers and six huge cargo ships to ferry them all home.

"No protestors," Annelise said with satisfaction.

"Nothing to protest about," Rachel said. *The uses of war*, she thought, cynically, regretfully, with acceptance. She climbed out of the flyer.

The refugees of Caitlinville were ready. The plan was to ferry them in batches up to the ships in orbit, using every smaller craft that could be mustered. Hadn't there been some wartime operation on old Earth when small boats had carried thousands of soldiers to safety somewhere? Caitlin would know. She read Terran history.

The refugees had organized themselves into groups.

As Caitlinville emptied, refugees from less-favored camps arrived to await their turn at re-emigration, or whatever the term was. Some had credit enough to arrive by maglev; the poorest trudged along with their possessions on their backs, in hand carts, or—for a lucky few—on carrybots. The refugees looked ragged, thin, exhausted. Some had walked astonishing distances for days, families sticking together. In some ways, Rand was even more fiercely Libertarian than Galt, and families replaced government in caring for the old, the young, the sick and disabled. Nothing was more important than family.

"Here come the transfer vessels," Annelise said.

At least a hundred small craft began arriving, their landings directed by a robocontroller. The vessels ringed the camp. Groups of refugees moved toward each for retinal scans. It was all orderly, measured, a perfect reflection of Annelise's orderly mind, even though Annelise hadn't wanted to do this at all. But Rachel was CEO, and to Annelise, an organization reporting chart trumped all.

Rachel said, "You've done a wonderful job, dear heart."

"Thank you. I—uh oh. Here she comes."

A flyer plummeted from the sky, landing not in Annelise's careful ring but meters from Rachel's own flyer. Her bodyguard tensed and drew his weapon, sheathing it when only Jane leapt from the flyer, her elaborate uniform spotless, her beautiful face maroon with rage.

Rachel said to Annelise, "Let me."

Rachel had expected this. She hadn't exactly told Jane that this operation was not being paid for by loans to the refugees, at a good rate of interest that would have enriched Jane's war chest and strapped the refugees for years. Nor had Rachel *not* told Jane that. She'd let Jane assume it, knowing that sooner or later her granddaughter would learn the truth. Obviously she had. Now there would be screaming about robbing the Freedom Enterprises coffers, hobbling the war effort, betraying the principles of Libertarianism by unearned handouts, setting horrific precedents that only fed the baseless grabbings of the protest movement, etc.

Rachel was wrong.

"They did it," she said through teeth that barely parted to speak. "The fucking shithole bastards did it."

Annelise, who never liked rough language, winced. Before she could say anything, Rachel laid a warning hand on Annelise's arm. A long shiver ran down Rachel's spine. Jane was not screaming or even shouting. Her face had purpled, but her voice was steady and deep-space cold, her body so still that the insignia on her chest didn't even rise and fall with her breathing.

Rachel said, "Who did what, Jane?"

"The Peregoys destroyed my biowarfare facility on Prometheus."

On Prometheus? But . . . "How do you know?"

"I sent supply ships there, of course, as soon as the gates reopened. They retrieved a recording from an orbital probe. Two Peregoy warships bombed the site. It's nuclear rubble. Everyone dead and the Peregoy ships have gone."

Rachel felt vertigo swoop over her; she fought it off. Caitlin? Annelise put an arm around her and said, "What else did the recordings show?"

"Isn't that enough? The fuckers won't get away with this." The mottled red was draining slowly from her face, leaving it pale as white stone. "Grandmother, I need these warships. Your refugees will have to wait."

Rachel said, "We need to confer before you—"

"No, we don't. I run the military. The ships are leaving."

Annelise said, "Jane, let them take at least the first load of refugees to Rand. This camp. We'll postpone the rest."

"No," Jane said.

"Yes," Rachel said.

"No. I control the fleet and army."

Their eyes met. So it had come, the battle she'd known was coming, known ever since the war began. This was what war did—gave the military, any military, power to topple civilian control. Had that happened often on Terra? Caitlin would know.

Where was Caitlin? Had she died in the bombing of Prometheus?

Rachel said, "Listen, Jane. I'm not going to go head-to-head with you on this, or anything else. But if you're going to attack Peregoy gates, you need at least a day to plan with your commanders. I don't know military strategy like you do, but I know at least that much. During that day, the ships can reach Rand, offload refugees, and return to you at Galt. Your commanders aren't on board today, or at least not most of them, not for this safe run between two Landry worlds. Please, let's do it this way. It's just one day."

Jane was silent so long that Rachel feared her refusal, even though she'd just been presented with a course of action to her own advantage. How consumed was Jane by her desire for revenge? As consumed as Tara had been by her desire for Philip?

Finally Jane said, "All right. One refugee run to Rand."

"Yes," Rachel said. "Good." She would not thank this granddaughter for usurping control.

Jane turned toward her flyer. It was Annelise who asked the question Rachel should have asked.

"Wait a minute, Jane. Are you going to attack the Peregoy gates?"

Jane turned, studying her sister, and Rachel's heart split along its seam.

No no no . . .

"Or," Annelise continued—but then, Rachel had never doubted Annelise's bravery—"are you going to attack the surface of New California? And Jane . . ." Annelise couldn't get the words out.

Rachel did. "Did you have samples of your biowarfare pathogens stored someplace else besides Prometheus?"

Jane climbed into her flyer without answering, which was all the answer necessary.

Annelise whispered, "She can't."

Rachel knew Jane could, and would.

"Rachel—"

"We don't know where the pathogens are. How many places. How close to Peregoy gates. We don't know the incubation period or transmission vector or anything about the disease. And I don't see any way to stop Jane. She'll have given orders for her commanders to carry this out if she herself can't."

"But—"

"There's only one thing we can do, Annelise."

"What? I don't see—"

"We can warn Sloan Peregoy."

❖   ❖   ❖

Sloan, Rachel knew, had returned to New California as soon as the gates reopened. Neither Rachel nor Annelise could travel to New California; they would become prisoners of war. Rachel's emissary to Sloan would have to be a Polyglot citizen. It would have to be someone important enough for Sloan to see personally. Someone who would agree to carry an encrypted message plus the memorized encryption, without reading the message themselves.

Who?

She sat in the flyer, watching refugees methodically loaded onto small craft for ferrying up to the waiting fleet. Annelise, her bodyguards staying between her and the refugees, directed efficiently. Rachel leaned back against the seat, closed her eyes, and let her mind drift. Sometimes that worked.

Fifteen minutes later, a name wafted into her mind: Dr. David Darter.

He'd been the physician who'd attended her during her heart attack on Polyglot. Head of cardiology at Edward Jenner Hospital, he had nonetheless altered his schedule to visit her twice a day—she was, after all, Rachel Landry, CEO of Freedom Enterprises and head of the Landry Libertarian Alliance. They'd talked. He'd been ambitious, yes, a clear climber up the medical-status mountain, but he'd also struck her as an ethical man. Just before her discharge, he'd interrupted his own advice on diet and rest to say abruptly, "You could end this stupidity between Landrys and Peregoys, you know, before it escalates into outright war."

She'd resented his presumptuousness. "Really? You do understand that was why I came to Polyglot, don't you?"

He'd ignored her sarcastic tone. "Yes. It was the right action. Do it again. When you're strong enough, go to New California and bargain with the Peregoys." He'd hesitated a moment and then added, "With the director, not his daughter."

That had caught Rachel's interest; it implied he knew something about Sophia Peregoy, maybe something new. But before she could carefully pursue this, he stood and said sharply, "Follow my directions on rest, diet, and medication, Ms. Landry," and left. Later that day, Rachel had begun the arduous trip home.

Sloan Peregoy might see the doctor who'd saved Rachel Landry's life and now said he had important information for New California. Dr. Darter would probably not be in danger; Sloan would vet the hell out of him and conclude that this man was not in a position to be of further use. Still, there would be some risk. Would Darter do it?

She would have to trust him to not use the encryption key, which he would have to memorize in order to read the encrypted message himself. A Polyglot doctor who knew that a deadly pathogen might be loose in the Eight Worlds...his first response would be to notify the Council of Nations, who would prohibit all ships, cargo, and people from entering Polyglot. Not that Polyglot had anything like the warships or military to enforce a sweeping, all-out embargo, but people would die trying. So would Rachel just be escalating the war?

She couldn't use Dr. Darter for this mission. Too many unknowns.

But she had no one else.

Back and forth she went, her mind plodding from

yes to *no*, until she had exhausted herself without moving a single muscle, and Annelise had crammed all the refugees she could into ships that would return them to Rand. As the last trip finished, far into the evening, a cry went up from those left behind, most of them arrivals from the other camps. Fights broke out. These were not people to whom Caitlin had brought her charity, and they were desperate. Desperate people didn't behave rationally.

How desperate am I? Desperate enough to risk using Darter?

She still hadn't answered the question when Annelise's bodyguards hustled her into the flyer, away from the chaos in the camp. The flyer lifted.

"Rachel?" Annelise said. "Are you all right?"

"Yes," Rachel said. She shifted on the seat and her body, stiff from sitting, protested. "There's an idea I want to discuss with you, but not here."

40

DEEP SPACE

Martinez watched Dr. LaShawn Parsage, ship physician on the *Green Hills of Earth*, administer a truth drug to Eric Veatch. Veatch lay strapped down on a gurneybot in a bare cabin. The small room seemed crowded even though it held only Martinez, Parsage, and the intel officer, Lieutenant-Commander Joanne Stiles. Well past middle age, experienced and unshakeable, Stiles had a mind like a Link browser. If there was anything findable in the memory of this weasely mercenary, Stiles would find it.

The doctor slid a syringe into Veatch. In a few moments Veatch's expression smoothed from a glare into semi-vacancy.

Narcosynthesis, like much medicine and its less savory offshoots, had not advanced very far while humanity had been occupied with first destroying and then fleeing Terra. Most medical research had concentrated on controlling the depredations of alien microbes against which humans had no natural immunity. With Parsage's drug, a witch-brew of depressant, barbiturate, and ataraxic, timing mattered. The subject fell into sleep, and then partially aroused from it. Questioning needed to happen during the brief period of twilight consciousness, when inhibitions were lowered and the cortex no longer functioned as inhibitory control over what was said. Maintaining that state required frequent, carefully balanced doses of the drug. Even so, what resulted was often a mishmash of fact, fantasy, and gibberish, although much depended on the individual personality being interrogated. Susceptibility varied widely.

The doctor nodded and Stiles said, "What is your name?"

"Eric Veatch."

"What are your other names?"

"Er . . . Eric Veatch Veatch Veatch."

"What is your name?"

"Eric Veatch."

Was that the shadow of a smile on Veatch's ugly face? Martinez wasn't sure.

"Tell me your name."

"StarStud. I banged her from the front and I banged her from the back and I—"

"Where were you born?"

"Polyglot. Cunts are juicy and I—"

It went on and on like that. Veatch had had extensive training in engaging the sex drive at will, so that it became powerful enough to override everything else. He had a strong erection.

"Increase the dose," Stiles said. The doctor did, and Veatch fell asleep.

They kept at him for another half hour, but got nothing useful, unless it counted as useful that this was no usual mercenary. Stiles said, "Sorry, sir. His resistance training is superb. There must be formidable advances on Galt."

Martinez said, "Is it worthwhile to continue?"

"I don't think so, sir."

The pilot was next. Young, with a minor criminal record for smuggling, she answered questions readily but didn't know much. Mr. Veatch had engaged her to take Caitlin Landry and the others to Rand. She'd filed the flight manifest on Galt. On Rand, one passenger, Jenna Derov, had been sent planetside. Mr. Veatch had re-engaged the pilot, at three times the usual fee, to take the ship to Prometheus, via first the Rand-Polyglot gate and then the Polyglot-Prometheus gate. She didn't know why they were going to Prometheus. Mr. Veatch told her he'd filed the necessary flight plans. She never looked too closely at why she'd been hired, what paperwork was done, or what was brought aboard on Galt—maybe it was smuggling? No, smuggling didn't worry her.

They had not landed on either Rand or Polyglot, and nothing had come aboard from either planet. The ship had emerged from the Polyglot-Prometheus gate and been captured by the *Green Hills of Earth*. Ms. Landry had told Mr. Veatch and his men to not resist when they were boarded. She had not overheard any conversations between Mr. Veatch and Ms. Landry.

And, Martinez thought, she had no idea that she might have ended up dead in an explosion of a bioweapons lab. Venal, criminal, she was also criminally stupid.

More questions, up to the limit of how much drug the doctor said was probably safe, elicited the major events of the war while Martinez had been trapped behind the eleventh gate and then traveling out of communication range to Prometheus.

Finally Stiles said, "I think that's all we're going to learn from her."

Martinez had the pilot removed to sleep it off, and Caitlin Landry was brought in.

She came without a struggle, except in her eyes. She was frightened, of course, but had it under control. Just before the first syringe pierced her, she looked directly at Martinez. "Don't stop until you verify my entire story, including that my grandmother did not plan biowarfare. Or war."

Martinez had never before had an interrogation subject give him directions about the interrogation. He doubted that Stiles had, either.

"What is your name?" Stiles began.

Landry's face had relaxed, looking almost peaceful, not fighting the drug. An ideal subject—or the product of the same training as Veatch.

"Caitlin Landry."

As Stiles continued with the baseline questions, the woman's answers were clear and concise, a perfect match to the information Martinez already had. The first piece of intel came when Stiles was drawing out background information about the Landrys.

"Who ordered the biowarfare facility built in the Peregoy research station on Prometheus?"

"My sister Jane."

"Did Rachel Landry know that biowarfare was being developed there?"

"No."

"Did Rachel Landry know that biowarfare was being developed anywhere in any Landry holding?"

"No."

"Did you know that?"

"No."

"Who else knew about the facility?"

"I don't know."

"Are there more biowarfare facilities elsewhere on the Eight Worlds?"

"I don't know."

Martinez had already studied the available data and photos of Jane Landry. In charge of Freedom Enterprises security, she'd become commander-in-chief of a military organization that must have been building for quite a while. Not very much was known of her personal history. Abruptly she reminded Martinez of Sophia Peregoy, even though they looked nothing alike. Both were beautiful, as Caitlin was not, but Sophia was all smooth control and Jane Landry's bright green eyes held fierce recklessness. She might be an uncertain commander, acting too impulsively, making mistakes. Or, of course, she might not be. Looks could deceive.

Stiles took Caitlin through the same sequence of events as the pilot, gaining essentially the same story except that Caitlin claimed Veatch had brought her to Prometheus on his own initiative, not hers. Had her grandmother authorized him to do that?

"I don't know." And then, "Probably."

Dr. Parsage said, "She's drifting off again."

"Increase the dose. There's more I want to know."

The doctor said, "Too much is dangerous, sir. Perhaps another session tomorrow would—"

"Now."

He injected the syringe. Martinez said to Stiles, "I'm going to question her."

"Yes, sir."

The doctor said, "Quickly, then, sir, before we lose her again."

Martinez said, "Caitlin."

Her face contorted. "Uh...uh...uh..."

"*What was Jane Landry going to do with the biowarfare pathogen?*"

"Uh...ah...ttack New California." Tears sprang onto her cheeks.

The doctor made a strangled sound. Martinez was silent; it was the answer he'd expected.

"When?"

"I...don't...don't...know..."

They were losing her. Martinez asked one more sharp question, surprising even himself. "Who was Philip Anderson?"

"Tara's...in love...him," she got out before lapsing into sleep profound as death.

The rest of the interrogations confirmed what had been learned about the general course of the war and the specific mission to Prometheus, although not how that mission was supposed to be carried out. Martinez suspected that only Veatch knew, and that it would have involved saving himself, Caitlin Landry, and the pilot, and turning most of the others into unwitting suicide bombers, through remote detonation. For that, you needed stupid thugs, and Veatch's six, all subjected to truth drugs, qualified.

The *Princess Ida's* surprisingly extensive stores had

helped extend rations on the *Skyhawk* and *Green Hills of Earth*. The *Zeus*, ahead of the other two ships, reported that New Utah would be able to resupply Martinez's fleet—welcome news. Meanwhile, however, everyone still went hungry. When Martinez dressed, his pants gaped at the waist.

Caitlin Landry asked to see him. He could have had her brought to him, but chose not to have her moved throughout the ship. She sat in her bare, isolated cabin, dressed in what looked like cast-off civvies: pants too large for her, a top too small, no shoes. Boots rested in the corner—ill fitting? Someone must have donated a comb; her shoulder-length hair was wet from the shower but not tangled. Martinez had given orders that the prisoners were not to be mistreated. They were bargaining tools, especially Landry.

She rose when he entered. "Could we talk alone?"

He dismissed her female guard, Spacer First Class Henderson, an augmented giantess who could possibly have defeated Martinez in hand-to-hand. Henderson was probably overkill, considering Caitlin Landry's slight build, but Henderson was silent to the point of catatonia. No subversive friendship would develop with the prisoner.

"Captain," she said, "I don't know what I told you under truth drugs, but I want to make sure it was the truth. Will you tell me what I said?"

"No."

She didn't seem surprised. "Are Veatch's crew all right?"

Previously she'd referred to them as "her" crew. Now she was distancing herself from them. Deliberate or unconscious?

He said, "No one has been harmed."

"Are they still on this ship or on your other one?"

"Not relevant."

"Where are you taking me?"

"Ms. Landry, I granted your request to see me in case you have additional information to tell me. If you do not, this interview is over."

"Yes. All right. I do have something to add. I am a virologist, or at least I was trained as one. The pathogen my sister developed is probably based on an existing disease—it's too hard to start from scratch to build a virus that can be weaponized. She probably used one of the plagues we've had on Rand. I don't know if you know this, but Rand was—is—home to more microbes adaptable to colonizing humans than any of the other Eight Worlds. The luck of the draw."

Martinez did know it. He said, "Go on."

"I worked with epidemics on Rand, before I took over as president of Galt University. I'm familiar with most of them, at least in the forms they had five years ago—microbes evolve really quickly—and I've kept up with the literature. You said you'd lost soldiers to this bioweapon. Did you take tissue samples? Or at least have information about symptoms, incubation period, kill rate, anything? I might be able to identify it. If you have samples and a gene sequencer, I might even be able to tell how it's been altered."

"To what end?"

"I don't know until I see it. But surely the more information you know about the plague, the better you can prepare for it."

"And why would you be interested in helping us, the enemy, do that?"

All at once her calm cracked, so completely that only now did Martinez become aware of how much energy she'd needed to keep it in place. Her voice erupted into fury. "Because it's a bioweapon, you idiot, an *epidemic*! Epidemics are only containable with large-scale and timely efforts, and sometimes they're not containable at all! This thing could spread through an entire world, or more. Even if it doesn't spread and Jane wipes out just New California, do you think I don't know that you Peregoys will retaliate? This war will end up doing what biowarfare helped do to Terra! Don't any of you people read any history? This is evil! Evil!"

She was sincere. He said, "*Lex talionis.*"

Surprise replaced fury, at least momentarily.

"You think," he said. "that no one besides you reads Terran history? The ancient law of retaliation . . . I've already thought of everything you said, Ms. Landry. And don't ever call me an idiot again."

"I'm sorry," she said, and it was his turn to be surprised. She looked as if she meant it. "Will you tell me what you know about the pathogen? It's not like I can do anything harmful with it—I'm your prisoner. And if Jane has her way, none of it will matter anyway."

"Is your sister insane?"

She looked him straight in the eyes. Her chest still rose and fell with emotion. The small top was too tight across her breasts.

"Yes," she said finally, "I think she is, if vengeance and ambition are insane. But my grandmother is not. Can I see your information on the pathogen?"

He made a sudden decision. His anger at the deaths of Gonzalez, Wilson, and Haller was not gone; it would never be gone. But this person was not the target, and someday he would settle scores with Jane Landry. Meanwhile, even if Caitlin Landry lied to him about the results of her examination of the pathogen data, Peregoy scientists on New Utah would have the samples soon. Whatever she told him could be proven or disproven— but he didn't think she was lying. At least, not yet.

"Yes, you can see the pathogen data."

Her eyes brightened. "What have you got? Tissue samples?"

"Yes, but you won't have access to those. You can talk to Dr. Glynn, ship physician, the closest thing aboard to a virologist. She can tell you what equipment we have. The only thing I can tell you about the pathogen is the kill rate."

She waited.

"One hundred percent, Ms. Landry. Everybody."

41

THE ELEVENTH GATE

The Observer is more diffuse. Its field, all fields, undergoes change. For the Observer, change is decay of its pattern.

It no longer has the coherence and energy it once did.

Energy is needed to affect the gates. The Observer has been using its energy to counteract that of the Others and keep sixteen gates closed to dangerous ships. It can no longer do this.

The Others do not decay. Now the Observer understands why the Others did not translate completely into the base level of reality, proto-consciousness. The Others do not leave the gates, which are neither matter nor energy but something else, something made of— maybe—sheer probability. Within the gates, the Others do not interact with other fields. They stay intact.

The Observer contracts itself into a single gate, the one closest to the point where it was translated. Before it does so, it expends a single huge burst of energy to alter the gates once again. Now they cannot stop matter from passing through. But they can still stop dangerous radiation, including the quantum signatures of matter that emits dangerous radiation.

It is all that the Observer can do to protect the tiny nodes of consciousness, the beings it once resembled.

The Observer contracts itself into the gate closest to the translation machinery. Within the boundaries of perpetual probability, where only the basic field of observational consciousness fully exists, the Observer does not decay. Here, it is safe.

42

DEEP SPACE

Caitlin hadn't expected Captain Martinez to agree to let her see the pathogen data. But then, nothing about her capture, or him, was expected. Rachel had feared torture—if not for her, who could be held for ransom, then for everyone else. Before her transfer to the other Peregoy ship, the *Skyhawk*, she'd been allowed to see the others for a few minutes. They were crammed into a room with too few bunks, all except Veatch, who must be housed elsewhere. They were unhurt, being fed the same meagre diet as the ship's crew, dressed in castoff Peregoy clothing. Veatch's six security guards had loosely bound wrists and ankles; the pilot and *Princess Ida* crew were free.

For the ship-to-ship transfer, she put on the boots given to her. They were too small and pinched her toes. Her mother had, alas, developed bunions early in life, and it looked to Caitlin like she might do the same. Nonetheless, she crammed her feet into the boots, under the watchful eyes of her guard, Henderson. Caitlin wouldn't have known Henderson's name if she hadn't heard Martinez use it; the guard did not respond to conversation.

Caitlin didn't even try to talk to Martinez on the short trip to the *Skyhawk*. Immediately afterward he strode off, and Henderson led her, silently, to a tiny cabin as bare as the one she'd had on the *Green Hills of Earth*. Caitlin pulled off her boots and inspected her sore feet. A few moments later a woman entered. Middle-aged and short, she had a long braid of graying hair and sharply intelligent eyes.

"I'm Dr. Glynn," she said, without warmth. "I am under orders to tell you what we know about your bioweapon and the tissue samples it destroyed. This tablet contains the available data on the engineered pathogen, plus the usual viral-analysis tools. The captain has also had it loaded with recreational reading. That is absolutely all that is on the tablet, and it won't reach ship's library or any other data base or comm device. If you have anything to report or any questions, Spacer Henderson will send someone for me. Do you understand, Ms. Landry?"

"Yes."

Dr. Glynn left, and Caitlin brought up the data. She recognized the pathogen almost immediately from the electron microscope images: a version of joravirus. The original had killed her father on Rand. What went on in Jane's twisted mind that she would weaponize this particular microbe? The accompanying data from a Landry ship called the *Galaxy* had been carefully collected. The photos of the victims' faces, covered with purple pustules, sickened her. The pathogen was airborne, which the original *Joravirus randi*, had not been; that suggested changes to the cell walls, among other alterations. Dr. Glynn had estimated the incubation period at three days, and an *r naught* of 5.1, which accounted for its rapid spread on the *Falcon*. Each infected person infected 5.1 others.

She studied all the data, which seemed incomplete. When she was sure she'd learned all she could, she had Henderson send someone for Dr. Glynn.

"It's a poxviridae," Caitlin said.

"I know it's a poxviridae," the doctor snapped. "Your identification is correct—it's *Joravirus randi*. It first turned up on Rand twenty-two years ago, a spillover from mullins, small mammals native to Rand. We eradicated it there within a few years, since then it wasn't airborne and mullins are the size of small dogs and could be locally contained and eliminated. The pathogen never even made it to Galt, let alone the Peregoy worlds. The incubation period was short, the same two days that you recorded, but back then the kill rate was about thirty percent. Before the epidemic ended, only a few hundred people died." *Including my father.*

Dr. Glynn nodded brusquely, as if she'd already known some, maybe even most, of this. There were scientific journals, after all.

"How was it weaponized?" Captain Martinez said.

Caitlin hadn't heard him enter. He stood by the cabin door, behind Dr. Glynn. Caitlin said, "Without a gene sequencer, I can't tell that. I'd also need the genome of the original, which isn't here and I don't remember in detail. Still, even without a sequencer I might be able to figure out some things."

"Such as what?" he said.

"Since it's airborne, the cell wall was probably altered. I don't know what else was done."

"Sir," Dr. Glynn said, "there are complete genescans in the data taken and decrypted from the infected Landry ship. I didn't include them on the mobile because—"

"Show them to her," Martinez said.

The little doctor had a big stubborn streak. "Sir, with all respect, this could be construed as giving wartime intel to the enemy."

Martinez said coldly, "The responsibility is mine, Doctor."

Caitlin said, "Do you have genescans of various unaltered forms of the virus?"

Glynn said, "Yes."

"Did you run a comparison?"

"Yes. There are differences, but I'm not a geneticist."

Caitlin said, "I need everything you have. Plus time to study this."

Martinez said, "Take her tablet and put everything on it. Everything, Doctor, this time." There was no mistaking the finality in his voice.

"Yes, sir," Glynn said unhappily.

They left with her tablet. When it was returned to her, Caitlin sat cross-legged and barefoot on her bunk, working on the data. Streams of base pairs—UGGCCU on and on—poxviridae were large viruses. The additional algorithms she needed had been loaded onto the device.

Henderson stood stiffly by the door. Caitlin worked for hours, stopping only to eat the few mouthfuls of food that were brought to her. Her back grew stiff and her head began to ache, but she kept at it, making careful notes, looking for certain patterns. Everything she had not done in years came back to her, all the pattern seeking and biodata manipulation she had once loved, before her grandmother had insisted she take over her share of familial duties by running Galt University. Family first. Libertarian freedom only for each granddaughter to run her own division without interference.

A belief that had brought the family to Jane's monstrous actions.

How could Jane—no, don't think of it. Concentrate on the data.

There was something here. She could feel it, almost smell it. Jane's virologists had worked in haste once the war began, and they had not been top-tier scientists to begin with. Caitlin knew where all the most eminent researchers were posted, and that none of them had left recently for Prometheus. Nor would any of them have created a bioweapon. Only—one of them had.

She slept, woke, went back to work. More than once? Maybe.

There was something here.

There was—

Yes.

She'd forgotten the sense of lightness, of something close to joy, when you discovered something significant. Not joy, because nothing about this abomination was joyful. But a sense of triumph, of possibility.

"Henderson," she said to her impassive guard, "please send someone for Dr. Glynn. No, for the captain. No—for both."

❖   ❖   ❖

On the bridge, Martinez had Captains Vondenberg and Murphy on viewscreens. The *Green Hills of Earth* was only a few hundred klicks away, the *Zeus* days ahead. Murphy's young, beardless face looked puzzled.

Martinez said, "What is it about communications with New Utah that seems to you somehow off?"

"I'm not sure, sir. The station had all the right codes and they said they can resupply our ships, but I haven't been able to raise them since I spoke to the OOD. Even before then . . . I don't know. Something."

"Could be equipment breakdown and shortage. They were cut off for three months, too."

"Yes, sir."

"Who was the OOD you spoke to?"

"Lieutenant Stock."

"I'll make contact," Martinez said. "I know the station commander; we've served together. She's competent. Anything else, Murphy? Vondenberg?"

"No, sir."

"No, sir."

"Stand by."

The *Skyhawk* tried to raise New Utah Planetary Defense. For an hour he received no answer, and then a recorded message, no visual: "*Skyhawk*, New Utah is able to resupply you. Proceed. Lieutenant Commander Naomi Halstead is incapacitated; Lieutenant James Herndon in temporary command. We are having commlink failures. Apologies."

Murphy was right. There was something "off" here. What was happening on New Utah?

When Martinez finally came to Caitlin's cabin, she was asleep. For twenty-four hours she'd been studying data, performing virtual holographic experiments on it, waiting for the captain or Dr. Glynn. Eventually she fell asleep without even knowing it, her head on her arms at the cold metal table. Someone shook Caitlin's shoulder, and it took her a long, fuzzy moment to realize it was Henderson, grim as ever. Behind her loomed Martinez, who didn't look any happier.

He said, "You wanted to speak to me? About what?"

Caitlin tried to clear her head. It was hard to think, after such a long session of doing so much of it.

"Ms. Landry? What did you learn about the pathogen?"

She sat up. Every muscle felt stiff, and her mouth tasted like something had died in there. "It does have changes in the cell wall to make it airborne. Its virulence has been amplified, which means it produces more toxin, faster. You do that by engineering the cell to create more toxin-producing organelles. I think I've also identified the surface protein that unlocks entry into cells. Viruses can only reproduce inside other cells, you know, hijacking their reproductive machinery."

"Yes, I know. What else?"

"Nothing else, yet." What else she'd discovered, at least tentatively, she would keep to herself. Could he tell she was withholding information?

Evidently not. He said, "You will explain all this to Dr. Glynn. When we reach New Yosemite, there'll be scientists and doctors with more and better equipment. You'll work with them, under strict guard."

"What will these scientists and doctors be doing?"

"Looking for a cure, or a vaccine."

Caitlin gaped at him. "But . . . that isn't possible.

Developing a vaccine takes a long time. The researchers on Rand never succeeded in doing so."

"Nonetheless, that's what you'll do."

"Why aren't you taking the samples and data to New California? Your best research facilities are there."

"I'm not risking contaminating the Peregoy homeworld."

It was an inadequate answer. Caitlin studied Martinez. She saw a man under tremendous strain, who was nonetheless in control. Abruptly he said, "Did you know Philip Anderson?"

Caitlin blinked. "No."

"You merely received reports from Dr. Hampden? You didn't know him personally?"

"No. Did you? How did you even know to ask me about him?"

Martinez didn't answer, asking instead, "Did he ever tell you, through Dr. Hampden, what he was looking for?"

"Only a few people know about Anderson's delusions. How do you?"

"Are you positive they were delusions?"

"'Were'? What happened to Philip Anderson, Captain Martinez?"

"I don't know."

She sensed his puzzlement. There was something here, some connection, and it was clear he wasn't going to tell her what. Anderson had been a Polyglot citizen; Martinez might have met him there. But that didn't explain why he knew about Anderson's quixotic "quest," or why he was asking Caitlin about it now.

After a few moments, she worked it out. "You learned about Anderson from Sloan Peregoy. The deal that he and my grandmother made to get Anderson to the eleventh gate."

"You're quick," he said, neither confirming or denying.

"Were you at the gate? What happened to Anderson?"

"I don't know."

"But you must have some idea of—"

"That subject is closed, Ms. Landry. I'm here only to learn what you discovered and tell you on what, and how, you'll be working on New Yosemite. Let me reiterate: You will touch nothing. Only advise."

Caitlin snapped, "I don't think I'm up to much sabotage as a prisoner under heavy guard."

"Oh, I don't know—you strike me as a pretty resourceful woman."

She was astonished to find that his praise warmed her. Confused, she attacked. "You said two Freedom Enterprises ships were carrying the bioweapon toward New Utah when you destroyed the ships. That's how you got the pathogen data, isn't it? And the soldiers you said you lost on the ships and on Prometheus—they died of it, didn't they? What were the names of the ships?"

"Why? I thought you knew nothing about Landry fleet activities."

"I don't. But I have a good friend who's captain of a warship...a childhood friend...what harm can there be in telling me the ships' names?"

"The *Dagny Taggart* and the *Galaxy*."

"Thank you."

"Was your friend commanding either?"

She was surprised that he'd asked. "No."

"You people," he said bitterly, "name your ships after selfish and discredited heroes."

"Dagny Taggart wasn't exactly a hero. She was—"

"I know who she was. I read that novel."

More, and greater surprise. "You did?"

"We on Peregoy can read, Ms. Landry."

She retorted, "I know that, or you wouldn't have known what *lex talionis* was."

His eyes narrowed. "Do you remember every single thing I've said to you?"

"Yes. I remember everything anyone says to me."

"Then remember this: You will advise the vaccine team, nothing more."

"Captain, I'm telling you that's *futile*. You don't have time to develop a vaccine before Jane lets loose her pathogen, if she has more of it. Which I'm sure she does, somewhere. A vaccine would take years. Listen to me!"

He smiled, not pleasantly. "I am. And why are you giving me information about this pathogen in the first place? Do you realize that everything you just said is treasonous to your own side?"

"Do you realize that there are no sides when we're talking about wiping out the human race on one or more worlds? I told you—my grandmother and I didn't want this war to start, we don't want it to go on, and we don't want idiots like you and my sister Jane to ramp it up! How can you be such a jackass?"

His smile disappeared. "Watch yourself, Ms. Landry."

"Or what? Go ahead, murder me! Torture me for information I don't have! Kill thousands of innocent people, destroy whole economies, wipe out individual freedom! That's what war is, isn't it? Don't you read any history, Captain Martinez?"

He turned toward the door. Caitlin hated herself for losing control like that. But she'd meant every word.

He was a warmonger and she was not.... Only if she was not, if she truly believed what she'd shouted at him, why had she withheld—

"Captain," she called as Henderson moved aside to let him pass, "Captain, wait!"

He turned.

Now or never. "There's one more piece of data about the pathogen. Something...something I didn't tell you yet."

Martinez walked back to the bridge of the *Skyhawk*, checked on everything there, and went to his cabin. He needed to think.

There were too many questions without answers.

One question: Could he trust what Caitlin Landry had just told him about the bioweapon? She'd said it could be verified by other researchers, which Martinez would damn well do. He didn't trust her. And yet...

Another question: Why hadn't Martinez received orders from Sloan? Weeks ago, Martinez had transmitted reports about the *Dagny Taggart* and the *Galaxy* to New Utah, to be relayed by scout to New California. By now, he should have received status reports and orders. If Sloan was ill or had died, Martinez should have heard from Sophia. Why hadn't he?

Why wasn't New Utah answering hails?

And the largest questions of all: Jane Landry's bioweapon. Did she have more of it? Where? And what would she do with it next?

Caitlin Landry had said the target was New California. But it made more sense to first test the pandemic on New Utah. Easier to approach, less defended. People fleeing the plague would then carry it to New

Yosemite and New California, without the Landrys having to risk a single ship.

And then to Polyglot and the Landry worlds... on one point, at least, Caitlin had been telling the truth. Jane Landry was insane. Unless, of course, the Landrys already had a vaccine.

Or, if not a vaccine, then what Caitlin had just suggested to him.

Would that work?

There was only one question to which Martinez did have a good answer. The Landry warships that had come through the Polyglot-Prometheus gate, just after Vondenberg captured the *Princess Ida*, had not pursued Martinez and Vondenberg. He guessed why. Jane Landry must have installed additional defense weapons on Prometheus, away from the station that Martinez had bombed. Now the Landry ships were digging up and installing those weapons aboard, to replace the ones they couldn't bring through the gate. They would be armed—possibly with a K-beam—and he was not.

He hoped the weapons retrieval from frozen, inhospitable Prometheus took a long time.

Martinez returned to the bridge to try again to raise New Utah.

43

NEW CALIFORNIA

"Sir," said Morris, Sloan's human assistant, "A Dr. David Darter to see you."

"Who?"

Morris stood in the office with his back pointed at the stuffed wolves. He didn't like them, although he had never said so, but Sloan knew. Morris was not much to look at: short, skinny, pot-bellied, with the broad flat face and wide eyes of a kitten with a scraggly beard. But he was efficient and hard-working, especially necessary since Sophia was now so often gone, usually to the shipyards on New Yosemite. Also, Sloan could count completely on Morris's loyalty, unlike Chavez's. His private intel network had unearthed Chavez's reports to Sophia.

Morris said, "I vetted Dr. Darter myself, sir. A Polyglot citizen, Chief of cardiology at Edward Jenner Hospital, sterling record. Only known political activity is with environmental organizations. He was the doctor who treated Rachel Landry when she had that heart attack at the Polyglot Council of Nations, and he says he has important information, for your ears only, about Rachel Landry. He passed every scan-and-search. I thought it best to check whether you want to see him."

Information about Rachel Landry? What intel useful to Sloan could a Polyglot doctor have, and why would he give it to Sloan? Unless...

"Is this about research into the physics of the gate closings? They're pursuing that on Galt." And it still rankled that Sloan had been unable to lure any of those researchers to New California.

Morris said, "I don't know, sir. Although it doesn't seem likely, given that Darter is a cardiologist."

Sloan made a sudden decision. "Bring him in."

Darter was everything that Morris was not: tall, handsome, commanding. Briefly he reminded Sloan of Luis Martinez, who still had not arrived at New California. Where was Martinez, and why hadn't he sent more information?

Darter's voice was deep. "Director Peregoy, thank you for seeing me. I know how busy you must be."

"I am, yes. So please come to the point."

"Not here," Darter said, and now Sloan picked up on what Darter's appearance and bearing had masked: This man was frightened. Of what? Not of being on a Peregoy world; Morris's vetting revealed that before the war, Darter had been on New California half a dozen times for medical conferences. "Can we talk somewhere else?"

Sloan stood. Darter was, of course, only trying to avoid routine recording, but maybe it was a good idea to also evade the hidden cameras that Sloan was increasingly sure Sophia had installed. "Follow me."

He took Darter to the roof, where Sloan's flyer waited. He signaled to Chavez to wait by the flyer and led Darter to the high parapet, looking out over the city, where wind made it necessary to lean close to hear another person. Sloan had recently had his implant removed, telling everyone that it had begun to irritate his ear. Implant communications could be intercepted by someone who knew what they were doing.

Darter gazed at the protestors massed behind the compound walls, shouting and raising their fists. A three-story-tall holo sign flared, held for twenty seconds, subsided: FREE SUELIN!

Sloan said brusquely, "Be brief, doctor. I understand you have information about Rachel Landry."

"Not about—from. There was a data cube, but your people took it away from me. I suppose they think they can break the encryption."

Chances weren't good, but the procedure was standard. He said, "So tell me what was on the cube. You must know or you wouldn't still be here."

"I do know. I'm not supposed to, but I do. I read her message. I think Ms. Landry wanted your people to break it, but she didn't want me to learn what it said."

Stranger and stranger. Sloan said, "Then how did you learn it? And what is the message?"

"She told me the encryption key, trusting me not to use it. I did anyway, because I wasn't going to carry a message unless I knew it wouldn't hurt people. My responsibility to cause no harm overrode my promise to her."

A prig. Unless this was an act to whip up Sloan's curiosity, in which case Darter was succeeding. The realization annoyed Sloan; he didn't like being manipulated.

"The *message*, doctor. Please don't waste my time."

Darter turned from gazing over the parapet to look directly at Sloan. Wind whipped his thick gray hair across his forehead. Anguish contorted his face.

He said. "Rachel Landry wants to warn you that her granddaughter, Commander-in-Chief Jane Landry, has genetically engineered a deadly disease and plans on setting it loose on New California."

"No," Sloan said instantly. "Who do you think you're scamming, doctor? If that were true, why would Rachel Landry *warn* me? Also, we have an extensive profile on her. Biowarfare does not fit it."

"I just told you—it isn't Rachel, it's Jane Landry."

The two men, both angry, faced each other. The protestors below finally caught sight of Sloan's head above the high parapet and the shouting increased threefold. Holo signs flared.

Sloan said, "I don't believe you. Once a plague is out, it can't be controlled. The Landrys would be putting their own people at risk."

"Do you think I don't realize that? But surely Rachel Landry is in a better position than you or I to know what her granddaughter will or will not do."

"But this makes no sense. No. You're lying to me, or Rachel Landry is."

Darter said coldly, "I hope so."

"You can tell Rachel Landry that her disinformation campaign is not working."

Darter strode away without answering. Sloan said into his wrister, "Morris, have Dr. Darter escorted out," and cut off the link without waiting for a reply.

He stayed on the roof a few minutes longer, watching the protestors, breathing deeply enough to tamp down his anger, wondering how the world had changed so much, so fast.

The Peregoy security experts easily broke the data cube encryption. "Too easily, sir. It's like they wanted it broken."

"They did," Sloan said. It just confirmed what he knew: This was disinformation from the Landrys, designed to panic him. He would share it with Sophia when she returned from New Yosemite.

He conducted a half dozen meetings with good outcomes. Just as he prepared to leave the office for dinner, Morris reappeared, his morose face even more morose than usual. "Someone else to see you, sir. Karen Healy. You told me to always allow her immediate access."

"Yes," Sloan said, although he'd hoped that Healy would never request access. She was the pilot who made cargo drops of food and supplies every week onto Horton Island. When Sloan had taken over the supply program from Sophia, part of their uneasy compromise about the "prison camp," he'd replaced Sophia's choice of pilot with his own. Since then, Horton Island had been receiving adequate food and other supplies. Sloan had even found a doctor willing to take a posting there. Healy sent him weekly reports, but she had never asked to see him.

"Bring her in," Sloan said.

Karen Healy had the stern, unflappable air you wanted of a pilot during a crisis. Nonetheless, at the first sight of her face, Sloan's stomach tightened.

"Sir, when I initiated radio contact with Horton Island during last week's drop, there was no answer. I went today with this week's drop, and I could see that the parcels were untouched—they come down by parachute, you know, and they—"

"I know," Sloan said. "Continue."

"I flew lower. No radio contact. I circled, and when I had a close view, I took photos. Of the bodies, sir. Most of them are probably in the shelters, but some were lying on the beach or out in the open. They're dead, sir. Everybody on the island.

"All dead."

Sloan sat at his desk, head in his hands, trying both to think and not think. Reason it through, but the conclusion...

The prisoners on Horton Island had not died of the Landry biowarfare that Dr. Darter had described. New California was ringed with orbitals, warships, surveillance probes. If the Landrys had developed some way to get the weaponized pathogen to the surface, it would have been detected even if it couldn't be stopped. But not so much as a meteor had struck Horton Island in the last two weeks.

It might have been a naturally developing plague. New California had had a few of those in the early years, although nothing like Rand, where microbial evolution showed more similarities to Terra and so adapted more easily to human hosts. If this was a natural disease, it was deadly. But why Horton Island and only Horton Island? Had the disease jumped species? There weren't any mammalian species on the island, which was one reason Sophia had put her political prisoners there. Still, Sloan had a hazy idea that diseases could spill over from birds to humans. Horton Island had seabirds.

The birds came and went. The plague had killed everyone within one week. If birds carried it, it would have turned up elsewhere by now, on other islands or ships or even the continent. But there was nothing; Sloan had checked.

So Horton Island had been targeted with a deadly pathogen. Genemod? And by whom?

His first thought had been the protestors. They had turned SueLin into an unlikely symbol—perhaps they wanted to do the same to an islandful of martyrs. But Sloan rejected this idea. The protestors were young, idealistic, on fire with stupid righteousness. They might accept martyrs created by Peregoy Corporation's "oppression," but they would not kill a hundred eighteen of their own. That just didn't fit his intel.

So the labor camp prisoners had been murdered by someone on New California, someone with the resources to weaponize a genetically modified pathogen and keep its development from Sloan's information network, someone who wanted the protestors gone. Someone ruthless enough to isolate the prisoners so no one would know when they were gone.

No.

There was no other conclusion.

He felt a surge of anger so strong it frightened him. What was wrong with her? What was wrong with Jane Landry as well? Because now he had to believe what Dr. Darter had told him: Rachel Landry had, genuinely if incredibly, been trying to warn Sloan about how far her granddaughter would go to win this war. And not only Jane Landry.

What should Sloan do next? He had no idea whatsoever.

44

GALT

Getting people to do what you want required that you know what they want. This wasn't the first time Rachel had had this thought, but it was the most urgent.

She wanted Annelise to be less meticulous and more far-seeing. Annelise wanted to not have to face the fact that meticulousness did not work in the midst of chaos. You could go on applying orderly protocols forever and only make the situation worse.

Rachel said, "Linear equations will not describe chaotic systems."

"What?" Annelise said.

"Never mind, dear heart. I'm just exhausted."

They were both exhausted. For twelve long hours they had worked in Rachel's office, preparing three worlds for war, trying to think of ways to stop the war, and wondering when the war would actually resume. Nothing had been attacked. Not by beam weapons, which could no longer travel through gates.

Not by Jane's bioweapons, or Rachel would have had word via Polyglot. Was a war really a war if no one was fighting?

Yes.

Jane commanded bioweapons.

Caitlin and Veatch, along with the *Princess Ida*, had gone missing. Had they died while destroying the Prometheus biolab?

Armed ships were massed beside the Landry gates and, she was sure, the Peregoy gates as well. Even neutral Polyglot had its inadequate fleet dispersed thinly on the Polyglot sides of its four gates. Scouts were still freely allowed through, which was how Dr. Darter had returned safely from his interview with Sloan Peregoy.

"He didn't believe me," Darter had said flatly, and Rachel saw that under his concern was the quiet outrage of an eminent specialist who was accustomed to being not only believed but obeyed. "And, Ms. Landry, I read your message to Director Peregoy."

"I half expected that you would."

"You must stop this bioweapon immediately."

Christ, didn't he think she was trying? Rachel could not just snap her arthritic fingers and recall a granddaughter-turned-fleet-commander-turned-raging-war hawk. Jane had delusions of being a conquering military hero, defending the Landry worlds' way of life. Didn't Darter know that such people were willing to sacrifice long-term perspective for short-term gain, usually without even realizing they'd made a sacrifice? How could a man so intelligent be so stupid?

She'd said, with restraint, "I am trying, Dr. Darter. Thank you for your service."

"I have a duty to warn my colleagues that this pathogen has been weaponized and may be let loose on the Eight Worlds."

"I'm sorry, but you can't do that. You'll create panic here and I can't deal with panic right now, on top of all else."

"It's in the nature of epidemics to spread," he'd said, with enormous condescension but even more concern. "It's my duty to warn people."

"But not just yet," she'd said, and had called Security to take him away and lock him up.

No choice. But she didn't tell Annelise. Libertarianism did not sponsor a police state, even though that's what Jane was well on her way to creating. Annelise would have said, with great earnestness, that there was neither cause nor precedent for jailing Dr. Darter. She would be right.

Linear equations did not describe chaotic systems.

Annelise accessed the Freedom Enterprises intel reports. "Jane cleared the Galt-Polyglot and Polyglot-Prometheus gates, so she's in deep space somewhere, on her way to—where? She didn't attack New California, after all, but—"

"Annelise, you've said all that before. We both said all that before. Jane is going to verify for herself that her biofacility really has been all destroyed, or else she's got a cache of bioweapons somewhere in space or hidden elsewhere on New Prometheus, or she's going the long way around to attack New Utah, or . . . *oh my gods.*"

"What? What, Rachel?"

Why hadn't Rachel thought of this before? Jane was going to Prometheus, yes. She may or may not have stored more pathogen there, or elsewhere. But Veatch and Caitlin had expected to destroy a biological facility on Rand, not Prometheus. They had the explosives to destroy the facility on Prometheus, but the *Princess Ida* was not equipped to also take out buried surface-to-space weaponry, dispersed across the dwarf planet. In fact, Jane may have installed more of those after the Landry fleet captured Prometheus from the Peregoys and before the gates had closed for three months. She couldn't take beam weapons through gates, but she could equip her ships with those scavenged from Prometheus, a detour on her way to New Utah.

"I know where Jane is," Rachel said. "And what she's going to do." Rapidly she explained to Annelise, who would have turned pale if she hadn't already been gray with fatigue.

Annelise whispered, "What can we do?"

"I don't know. Unless . . ."

"Unless what?" Annelise looked like a woman grasping at a twig as rough currents swept her to a steep waterfall.

And Rachel's idea *was* a twig. Less than that—a leaf, a bud. But it was all she had.

"Listen, dear heart, I can't explain it to you. You wouldn't believe it anyway. But I need to go to Polyglot, now, myself."

"That's not safe!"

"It's safe enough. I have to go." To Polyglot and beyond, but Annelise would never accept that.

"Why? For gods' sake, what's so necessary that you have to travel, in wartime and in your state?"

"There's nothing wrong with my state," Rachel

said crossly. "I had a heart attack, not a burial. I'm recovered now. I have to do this."

"The doctor said that at any time you could have another—"

"I'm going, Annelise."

Annelise gave a soft moan. Resignation—a good sign. "How long will you be gone?"

"Only a few days." A second lie: one of omission and one of commission. *Hit all the bases, Rachel.* "You can handle things here just fine."

"Of course. But—"

"There is no but," Rachel said. "I have to go."

"Alone?"

"Well, with a pilot and crew, of course."

"I can't let—"

"Annelise, my dear, there's no 'let' involved here. I need to do this, Jane is not going to attack New California in the next few days, not while she's on the other side of the Polyglot-Prometheus gate, and I'll be perfectly safe on Polyglot."

Lie number three.

Plus the one she hadn't been forced into telling, or at least not yet: All this wasn't based on "necessity" but on daring, desperate conjecture. Stupid conjecture? Possibly. Probably.

But Rachel didn't see any other path through the morass the Eight Worlds had become since the discovery of the eleventh gate. This idea was all Rachel had.

This incredible, and incredibly bizarre, idea that had sprung open her mind like a complicated e-lock responding to the right code.

"One more thing, Annelise," she said, in her don't-argue-with-me voice. "I'm taking Tara with me. She's so much better now, and she's restless cooped up in my beach compound."

"Tara? She's restless so you're taking her off-planet during a *war*?"

No possible way to tell Annelise the real reason for taking Tara. Rachel said, "Polyglot is neutral, and no one wants to upset that neutrality. Not Sloan Peregoy, not even Jane."

"But...Tara? Don't you think that—"

"No, I don't," Rachel said firmly, even though she had no idea which, of a million possible objections, Annelise had been going to raise. "I don't, not at all."

The ship belonged to Annelise. Jane controlled nearly everything else in the Freedom Corporation fleet except this class 6A ten-passenger personal vessel, the *Kezia Landry*. A name so typical of Annelise—bland, unimaginative, honoring tradition.

It had taken precious weeks to equip the *Kezia Landry* with the specialized equipment Rachel wanted aboard, some of which had to be manufactured, and the necessary personnel. The ship carried three techs and the doctor that Annelise insisted accompany Rachel and Tara. No security personnel. If Rachel needed a bodyguard where she was going, the plan had already failed.

They passed through the Galt-Polyglot gate and began the week-long voyage to the Polyglot-Prometheus gate. Soon Rachel's techs could begin their tests.

Late at "night," when the lights had dimmed everywhere but on the bridge, she roamed the ship's one corridor. Unable to sleep, unable to do anything but go over and over the reasoning that had brought her on this preposterous mission. Twenty steps down the corridor, past the closed cabin doors, twenty steps back to the commons area. Twenty steps to circle that. Repeat, unless she wanted to duck into the tiny galley and add seven more steps. The galley was well-equipped, despite the great haste with which the trip had been assembled.

Despite the haste, she might be too late.

Twenty steps down the corridor, past the closed cabin doors, twenty steps back to the commons area. Twenty steps to circle that. Repeat.

The art on the corridor walls, shadowy in the dimness, were holos of mountains, a waterfall, a flock of young *prikabi* at play—art as unimaginative and solidly grounded as Annelise. Rachel had switched off the sound on the softly splashing waterfall, unwilling to be distracted. Although maybe distraction should be welcomed, considering her thoughts.

She only hoped the *Kezia Landry* would succeed in this insane mission.

45

NEW UTAH

When the *Zeus* reached New Utah, it was attacked.

Martinez scrambled from his bunk as "Captain to the bridge, Code 1" sounded throughout the ship, simultaneously with his wrister. The OOD's face appeared. "Captain, the *Zeus* reports being fired on by New Utah Planetary Defense. Captain Murphy awaits orders."

"On my way."

He yanked on his uniform. The *Zeus* fired on at New Utah—by whom? Had the Landrys taken the planet? How?

They had not. Edward Murphy was on viewscreen. "Captain, at 0200 hours the *Zeus* was fired on by New Utah Planetary Defense, after giving me go-ahead to make orbit. Two R-beams fired, both missing the ship. No casualties or damage. I have retreated beyond firing range. No follow-up communication from New Utah, and they do not answer my hail."

"R-beams? Not a K-beam?"

"No, sir."

"Anything else?"

"No, sir."

"Maintain position, Captain. Do not approach either the planet or the stargate to New Yosemite—it'll be defended."

"Yes, sir."

"Signalman, open contact with New Utah."

"Opening contact."

If Planetary Defense wanted to attack, how the hell had they missed hitting the *Zeus*? That argued that whoever was in charge down there either wanted to miss or was massively inept.

"Contact open."

"New Utah, this is the Peregoy Corporation Space Service ship *Skyhawk*, Luis Martinez commanding. Who fired on the PCSS ship *Zeus* and why?"

No response.

"Repeat: this is the Peregoy Corporation Space Service ship *Skyhawk*, Luis Martinez commanding. Who fired on the PCSS ship *Zeus* and why? Answer, or I will assume that Planetary Defense is held by the enemy and I will proceed accordingly. The *Zeus* was not armed; I am." Martinez was days away, but whoever held the planet might not know that, nor that the *Skyhawk* and *Green Hills of Earth* were without beam weapons.

Silence.

"This is the Peregoy Corporation Space Service vessel *Skyhawk*, Captain Luis Martinez commanding. Who fired on the *Zeus* and why? Answer or I will assume that planetary defenses are held by the enemy and will proceed accordingly."

Silence.

"Lieutenant, arm weapons," Martinez said, even though his ships had been stripped of their radiation weapons. But New Utah did not know that. He gave the order clearly and loudly. Something weird was happening here. If the Landrys had taken New Utah, they would not have miscalculated the attack on Martinez's ships.

"Weapons armed, sir."

"Prepare to fire," Martinez said, without specifying what was to be fired on.

"Wait!" a woman's voice shrilled, without visual. "Don't fire! You'll kill innocent people!"

"Identify yourself."

"This is Compatriot Christine Hoffman of the Movement. Compatriot Berman will be here in a few minutes. He'll talk to you. Don't fire at anyone!"

Martinez blinked. Compatriot? And the woman sounded completely unmilitary. What had been happening on New Utah during the months that Martinez had been out of communication?

New Utah had never been an important planet. Nearly all Peregoy Corporation commercial activity occurred on much richer New Yosemite and New California. When the New Yosemite-New Utah gate had been discovered, the corporation had claimed it mostly because it was there, was reachable by the long voyage from Prometheus, and was another world to add to the Peregoy empire. Habitable by humans but just barely, New Utah had one city, Cascade, which consisted mostly of spaceport activity. Farms spread out from Cascade to supply it, but the land wasn't rich and would grow only the sturdiest crops.

Farmers who'd chosen to emigrate there in the last
hundred fifty years were independent, survivalist sorts
who liked to be as far from government as possible.
Military postings were by short rotation, since the
place was so boring.

Boring but defended, as Sloan Peregoy defended
everything that belonged to him. When Martinez had
last resupplied at New Utah, it had been guarded by
two warships, unmanned defense orbitals, and surface-
to-air weapons. Commander Naomi Halstead, an able
soldier, had been in charge.

"I want to talk to Commander Halstead."

"She's under arrest," Hoffman said. "Please wait.
Don't fire, and we won't, either."

"I demand to know why you fired on the *Zeus*."

"Please just wait, for fucking sake."

A few moments later came a male voice, considerably
more assured, still without visual. "This is Compatriot
Scott Berman. Captain Martinez, the *Zeus* was in
violation of Movement airspace. We—"

"You gave permission to make orbit!"

"—intended to warn the ship, only that. Permission to make orbit was sent by mistake. You and the
Zeus both now have permission to approach the New
Utah–New Yosemite gate and pass through without
interference. If you do anything else, we will fire on
you both, and it won't be a warning."

Martinez said coldly, "You are defying warships
of the Peregoy Corporation Space Service. Identify
yourself fully."

"I have identified myself."

Martinez said, "Commence firing."

"No!" Hoffman cried, simultaneously with Berman's

saying, "You're not in range. Surveillance has not picked you up anywhere near us. And you are probably not armed, like the *Zeus* wasn't."

So they knew that much. But... permission was sent "by mistake"? Who were these clowns? Martinez said, "Delay firing. Mr. Berman, you have no idea what weapons we are carrying."

Which was true enough.

Silence on the other end. Was Berman, whoever he was, reconsidering? Martinez said, "I demand to know who you are, and why you gave no warning before firing on the *Zeus*."

"I told you, it was a mistake. Anyway, don't you warn your enemies before you attack?"

"I just did."

Silence.

Finally Berman said, "All right, our fire was to determine if the *Zeus* was armed. If it could have returned fire, it would have. We never intended to hit it. But if you attack us now, we will retaliate. Meanwhile, since the *Zeus* isn't armed, it's free to pass through the gate to New Yosemite. And so are you."

What? Berman didn't care if New Yosemite Command learned that a New Utah military base had been taken?

Martinez said, "Who are you?"

"I told you—we are the Movement. New Utah now belongs to us."

Martinez said, "New Utah is Peregoy Corporation property."

"Since when?"

"Four months ago."

And in four months, New Yosemite hadn't already

tried to retake New Utah? Even without radiation beams, which couldn't pass the gate, there had been time to equip warships with older weapons. If Sloan hadn't done that, why not? What was going on here?

"I repeat, New Utah is Peregoy Corporation property."

"*Was* their property. Now this is a free state. All we ask is that you leave us alone and go through the gate to verify our story on New Yosemite. If Sloan Peregoy wanted to reclaim us, he would."

Martinez considered. Retaking a rebel planet was not included in Martinez's orders, especially since he didn't have the weapons to do so. But there was more involved here, and he saw Berman's trap.

"Mr. Berman, I can't go through a gate without stripping my ship of all radiation weapons, as you well know. I am not going to do that. Recently—" he would not say just when "—I sent a scout to this gate to proceed through it. What happened to the scout?"

"It was shot down, with a warning. The pilot ejected, and we have her here."

"I want to talk to Commander Halstead. If you've murdered the entire planetary defense deployment, I will annihilate you."

Hoffman cried, "We aren't murderers, unlike Peregoy Corporation!" In her cry, Martinez realized for the first time how young she must be. Had Sloan's military been defeated by an army of children? And for gods' sake, *how*?

Berman said, "I can get Commander Halstead. It will take about half an hour." Contact broke.

Martinez said, "Vondenberg?"

"No additional intel, sir."

"Captains Murphy and Vondenberg, stand by."

DiCaria, who had arrived on the bridge as hastily as Martinez, said, "Sir, the d-base has three Scott Bermans. Most likely match is a New California citizen, twenty-eight years old standard, engineer at a water-treatment plant in Capital City, no criminal record. Of course, this is months out of date. Here is his file, sir."

Martinez read it. The half hour passed. When the link reopened, it included visual.

Martinez recognized Naomi Halstead even out of uniform. She wore the same loose dun pants and tunic as Scott Berman, who stood beside her. He had a thatch of ungroomed brown hair, a beard, and the fevered eyes of a fanatic. The eyes didn't match his cool voice: a dangerous combination. Halstead's wrists were bound with tanglefoam.

"Captain Martinez, Commander Naomi Halstead reporting."

"Are you allowed to speak freely, Commander?" There was a code for this: If she answered, "I'm allowed to speak freely," it meant she was not. Anything else meant she could tell him the truth until she used the code phrase.

"Yes, I can tell you what happened."

"Proceed."

"Space Command ordered the two planetary-defense cruisers home as soon as the gates reopened. No one wanted to risk not having them on New California if the war resumed. New Utah Planetary Defense was left with orbital and ground-to-space weapons. There was already some unrest here, sir, fanned by the Movement based on New California. We—"

"What Movement? What sort of unrest? I have

been out of communication for nearly a year standard, Commander."

"Understood. Even before the gates closed for three months, dissidents arrived as settlers on New Utah in fairly large numbers. Taxes had been raised to finance the war effort, and a greater percentage of crops redirected to the military."

"Stolen, you mean!" Hoffman said. Her face appeared on screen before Berman pushed her gently away. She was indeed young, maybe no more than eighteen.

"Dissent spread," Halstead continued, as if Hoffman did not exist. "It corrupted some of the military here. There was a mutiny. Soldiers—too many—joined the rebels. Officers were captured, as were loyal soldiers. Most of them were sent on a deweaponized ship to New Yosemite. Some of us have been held prisoner as, I presume, bargaining chips. There has been no extraction effort from New Yosemite that I am aware of."

Martinez heard her resentment over this. It didn't sound like Sloan, whose stewardship of his people would have precluded leaving officers to some unknown imprisonment, torture, or death. On the other hand, Sloan couldn't get warships through the New Yosemite-New Utah gate without deweaponizing them. Martinez phrased his next question carefully. "Has any message come through to you from the director?"

"Not that I'm aware of."

Hoffman cried, "Because to him people are just expendable possessions!"

The creak of a door, followed by its closing. Martinez guessed that she'd been removed from the room. That she'd been there in the first place spoke gigawatts about discipline in this ragtag Movement.

He said, "Have you or your troops been mistreated, Commander?"

"No."

"How many of you are being held prisoner?"

"Thirty-eight, sir, including a captured scout pilot."

More than he'd expected. "Do you have any information about the course of the war?"

"No."

"I do," Berman said, unexpectedly. "We are in communication with New Yosemite compatriots. Your Director Peregoy was stuck on Polyglot for the three months that the gates were closed. Sophia Peregoy is the one who's crippling working people with taxes, forcibly conscripting young men and women to die, and sending anyone who speaks out against the Corporation to the labor camp on Horton Island, where they'll die of starvation to save her executing them publicly."

Martinez kept his face carefully rigid. Sophia? Did he believe she was capable of all that? New California had never had labor camps for political dissent.

"Commander Halstead, can you confirm or deny those allegations about Ms. Peregoy?"

"No, even though I'm allowed to speak freely."

Martinez understood. Berman would not have minded if she'd agreed that yes, Sophia was responsible for everything Berman said she was. But Halstead, loyal to the Peregoys, would not speak out against Sophia. This was the best Halstead could do to agree with Berman without disloyalty.

Berman said, "That's enough, Captain Martinez. Commander Halstead doesn't know any more than she's told you. Kowalski, take her back."

Kowalski, another young man with intense eyes, appeared on screen and grasped Halstead's arm. She shook him off. Kowalski took a second to glare at the screen and say, "Free SueLin!"

SueLin Peregoy? What the hell did she have to do with this?

Berman said, "You don't really have options, Captain. If you approach the planet, we'll fire on you again and this time it won't be a deliberate miss. The *Zeus* can proceed through the gate, but you can't, not with beam weapons. You'll have to strip yourself of radiation weapons, and then you can't attack us."

"Unless, of course, I'm carrying weapons you don't know about. Such as a version of the Landry K-beam, which could hit you before you could hit me."

"You would have used it already."

"No. Real military officers assess the situation before attack. The *Skyhawk*, unlike the *Zeus*, is a fleet flagship. Are you positive that I'm not equipped with a K-beam and won't use it when the *Skyhawk* arrives at New Utah? And are you sure that trying to push around an armed warship is in your best interest?"

Berman's face didn't waver—he was too good for that—but Martinez felt the young man's hesitation. If the *Skyhawk* had been armed, Martinez knew a half dozen ways to attack planetary defense. But he wasn't armed, and he wasn't going meekly through the gate to New Yosemite. Nor was he sending the *Zeus* through; he didn't trust Berman not to fire on her. Martinez was going to extract the captured PCSS officers. He was also going to act on what Caitlin Landry had told him.

Berman said, "Where would you have gotten a Landry K-beam?"

"From Landry defenses installed on Prometheus. We've retaken it." Too bad that wasn't true.

Scott Berman said nothing.

"Mr. Berman, neither of us wants to fire. You don't want your rebellious movement destroyed, and I don't want to kill as collateral casualties the thirty-eight loyal Space Service soldiers that you've illegally imprisoned. Nor am I going to just go away and leave you in illegal control of Peregoy property. I suggest instead that we negotiate. I have information you want to know."

Silence, except for intense, indecipherable whispers in the background.

Martinez waited.

Finally Berman said, "There is nothing to negotiate. The offer of safe passage through the gate is withdrawn. Approach New Utah or the gate to New Yosemite, and we will shoot you out of the sky. That's if you have no beam weapons. If you do, then attack us, and your thirty-eight officers die with us. But you may lose your ships, and at least some of us in the countryside will survive."

Berman broke the link.

46

NEW CALIFORNIA

"Father, what are you doing here so late?"

Sloan looked up from his desk. "What are you doing back from New Yosemite? Weren't you supposed to return tomorrow?"

"Yes, but something has developed and I wanted to discuss it with you."

Sophia looked just the same, and this struck Sloan as the most monstrous thing of all. Composed, beautiful, her hair in its usual smooth chignon, her tunic expensively cut to her slender figure. She didn't look like his idea of a mass murderer, although he now knew that all his ideas needed revision. Nothing was as he'd supposed. He was lost in a dark wood, and right now, at this moment, the most important thing was to keep Sophia from seeing that.

He had not told her that he knew about the murders on Horton Island.

Long, long habit helped. His face stayed calm, his

manner decisive. "What has developed? Do you mean on New Yosemite?"

"No. New Utah. Several weeks ago, I was on New Yosemite when one of our warships, the *Leonardo da Vinci*, came through the gate from New Utah. Stripped of her weapons, of course, and carrying planetary defense troops from New Utah, all but thirty-eight officers. New Utah has been taken by the rebels. Scott Berman is there, in charge. He's been joined by many—too many—of the Peregoy soldiers, who've joined his treasonous 'Movement.'"

Sloan digested this. *Several weeks ago*—He had been cut off from major intel for several weeks. Nothing could have made it clearer how much power he had lost to Sophia. Finally he said carefully, "The entire planet is in rebellion?"

"There weren't actually that many people left. I moved most of the population to New Yosemite to work in the shipyards."

"Did you know Scott Berman was on New Utah?"

"Yes, of course. But I thought he'd fled there to avoid arrest here."

"Why didn't you have him arrested there?" *And why didn't you tell me*?

"I would have, but then this happened."

"And now—" He didn't finish the sentence.

"And now," she said, putting her hands on the far edge of his desk and leaning forward earnestly, "I don't think it's worthwhile just now to try to retake New Utah. Any warships we send through the gate will have to be deweaponized, and the rebels are in possession of both orbital and surface-to-space weapons. The planet is pretty worthless except as a gateway to

New Yosemite, and we're better off guarding that from invasion by stationing warships on the New Yosemite side of the gate and shooting at anything, Landry or rebel, that comes through. Berman's pathetic band can be dealt with later, and meanwhile he's removed from New California. Maybe that will weaken his ridiculous rebellion. What do you think?"

She was so convincing. That kind of conviction sprang only from genuine belief. She believed everything she'd just said, believed it was as much of the truth as he needed to know, believed she was doing the right things for Peregoy Corporation. Believed that New Utah was worthless, inhabited only by expendable rebels. And the thirty-eight space fleet officers the rebels held—did Sophia believe they, too, were expendable for the good of the greater cause?

Did she believe her biowarfare needed additional testing?

Sloan couldn't look at her. He gazed down at his folded hands, as if in deep thought. When he could manage it, he said the only thing he could.

"Yes, my dear, I think you're right. That's how we should proceed."

"Good." She straightened and smiled at him. "My ship for New Yosemite is waiting for me. It's better if I personally oversee shipyard production. This time I'll be gone quite a while. You go to bed, Father. It's late."

"Yes. I will."

He watched her leave: her graceful walk, her tiny wave to him at the doorway, her mind that he had not understood, not ever, not at all.

How had it happened? How had Sophia, this beloved daughter, come to this? Had Sloan done too good a job of emphasizing the supremacy of Peregoy Corporation's interests as being for the good of all? Had Sophia inherited the same strain of selfishness that animated Sloan's other daughter, Candace, and Candace's daughter SueLin—and kept it hidden all these years? Was it Sloan's parenting or his genes that were responsible for Sophia's horrific beliefs?

In the darkness, Sloan clung to the one of Sophia's beliefs that she had not even mentioned. She must believe that Martinez's fleet had been lost, either in a space battle or behind the eleventh gate. She must believe that Luis was dead.

Was he?

No. Sloan needed Martinez too badly for that to happen. And Martinez, the child that Sloan should have sired, was too competent to let it happen.

So why wasn't he here yet?

But Luis would come home. He had to.

47

DEEP SPACE

During the long nights while the *Kezia Landry* traveled through space between stargates, Rachel paced. A quotation sat solidly as a huge boulder in her mind: *"What we observe is not nature itself, but nature exposed to our method of questioning."* Werner Heisenberg, that old-time Terran physicist who had known quite a bit about war, having lost one. She couldn't remember just which Terran war it was—Caitlin would have known—but it had been a big one. It was his physics, not his history, that had interested Rachel, all those decades ago when she'd been a student.

But Heisenberg had been right about history, too. Everyone on both sides of this war had been using wrong methods of questioning. The key was not K-beams, nor biowarfare, nor military strategy. The key was the gates.

Rachel had thought obsessively about Philip since the gates closed, then opened again. She, nor anyone else, hadn't been able to find any explanation for those phenomena. The timing of gate changes coordinated with Philip's vague descriptions of having "touched something"—but why? Rachel had combed through journals, followed on-link debates, talked to the most important physicists on Galt. There were theories, but none of the theories stood up to the facts.

When only one explanation did, then you went with that, at least provisionally, no matter how weird. The only thing Rachel had that fitted everything was Philip. It didn't get any weirder than that. Still—Occam's razor.

She went over and over the ideas behind an ultimate substrate of reality made of a field of consciousness, or something like consciousness, or something not like consciousness but able to be controlled by consciousness. After all, the knowledge of an observer affecting quantum events had been known for two hundred fifty years. Terran physicists had dipped at least one toe in the waters that Rachel was now drowning in.

John Wheeler with his "participatory anthropic principle," citing human beings as "participator in bringing into being not only the near and here but the long ago and far away."

Roger Penrose, linking quantum events in the human brain with quantum events in space.

Bernard Haisch, Gregory Matloff, Anna Varennes. Had Philip read all of these same theories? Of course he had.

Rachel couldn't stop Jane's monstrous pathogen if it had already gotten loose in the Eight Worlds. It seemed that biology, not mechanical engineering, would be humanity's undoing. But Philip, if she was right about him, no longer had any biology. She would have to reach him some other way. And she needed to reach Philip before Jane reached New Utah.

Because that's where Jane was going, yes, after first traveling to Prometheus. She may or may not have more stored pathogen there, or elsewhere. But Veatch and Caitlin had expected to destroy a biological facility on Rand, not on Prometheus. They had the ordnance to destroy the facility on Prometheus, but not to also take out all the surface-to-space weaponry that Jane had undoubtedly installed there. Perhaps even including a K-beam. After all, Prometheus was the only place she'd used a K-beam so far, when she'd taken the dwarf planet from the Peregoys.

Then, armed with weapons scavenged from Prometheus, her ship could set out across deep space for New Utah. She wouldn't need to pass through a gate to reach that Peregoy planet, which meant she could take the scavenged radiation weapons with her. With a K-beam, she could take out any Peregoy warships and planetary defenses, and then either obliterate New Utah or easily infect it with her pathogen. Probably the latter. The inhabitants of New Utah would be her expendable lab rats.

Rachel couldn't overtake Jane before she reached Prometheus, and wouldn't have been able to do anything useful if she had. That wasn't her plan. Instead she had what was perhaps the most desperate, and possibly stupid, plan in a time of desperation and stupidity.

Heisenberg, Wheeler, Penrose, Haisch, Matloff, Anna Varennes—

"Gran, what are you doing?"

Tara, emerging sleepy and wild-haired from her cabin. Since Rachel had told her where they were going, Tara's hopeless indifference had been replaced by some of her old wire-taut animation. Some, but not all. This was a Tara not quite so obsessive, not quite so unbalanced. Some of that was the drugs. Doctors had installed deep in Tara's skin, where she couldn't easily remove it, a med-drip that calmed her down. She hadn't wanted it, but Rachel had insisted.

"I won't take you with me otherwise," Rachel had said. She'd been lying. She needed Tara. Tara knew this area of space, as Rachel's crew did not. The crew and techs were people Rachel trusted, paid an exorbitant amount for this trip, and Rachel had told them they couldn't access any flight records or navigational charts. Annelise would have discovered what they'd scanned or downloaded. And, given her spy network, so might Jane's people.

"Tara, go back to bed. I'm just walking myself tired. Old people have a much harder time sleeping than you youngsters, you know."

Tara nodded but didn't move. She slept in a flimsy short top with nothing underneath, her lovely young body on full display, and Rachel was glad it hadn't been any of the crew prowling the corridors. Tara and modesty had always been strangers.

Tara said, "Gran, do you think he'll answer us?"

No doubt whom she meant. Rachel said gently, "It won't work like that. I explained it to you, dear heart."

"I know. But maybe..."

"No." Best to be firm about this, and to go on being firm.

"Then do you think he's okay?"

"Tara, there is no 'he' anymore. It's not a human being."

"But he closed the gates and then opened them. You said so. You're the only one who said so."

"I said I *think* that's what happened. It's incredible, I know, but—"

Tara was not interested in the incredibleness of Philip's injection into the field of cosmic consciousness. She was recovering from her psychotic episode, but she was still Tara, interested only in what concerned her directly.

"I just want to know he's okay. You explained about the decay."

"It's not decay, exactly, the . . . Tara, it's the middle of the night. Go to bed."

"Just one more thing." Tara grimaced, looking in that quick moment uncannily like her father. It never went away, that lance of pain over the lost child.

"Well, then, what?"

Then Tara surprised her. "Gran, I didn't just come with you because I'm hoping for . . . something from Philip. I came because I know I'm responsible for this war with the Peregoys. It wouldn't have started at all if I hadn't tried to create an alliance against aliens that maybe aren't even there. It's my fault. I want to do whatever I can to help you end the war."

Rachel put her arms around her granddaughter. If this new maturity was the end result of a psychotic break, too bad Jane didn't have one, too.

"I know, dear heart. Now go to bed. I will, too. We both need our sleep."

Tara went into her cabin and closed the door. Rachel switched on the waterfall holo in the corridor, which ordinarily annoyed her, and raised the volume high enough to mask the sound of her footsteps. She paced the twenty steps down the corridor, past closed cabin doors, twenty steps back to the commons area. Twenty steps to circle that. Repeat.

All her tests on Galt had failed. After running the equations, she'd half expected that, which was why she'd already been equipping the ship and bribing the crew. Tomorrow they would repeat those tests, here in deep space. If those, too, failed, then she would have no choice but to try the test again at their final destination.

She had to reach Philip before Jane reached New Utah.

48

NEW UTAH

As the *Skyhawk* and *Green Hills of Earth* traveled closer to New Utah, the rebels on the planet ignored all attempts to communicate. Scott Berman had stated his position, calling Martinez's bluff: Martinez's ships could not approach the gate. They could engage in a battle with the planet or not. If Martinez possessed beam weapons and fired on New Utah, the planet would return fire. Cascade might be vaporized, but so might Martinez's ships. He had no doubt that even now Berman was dispersing his people away from the city. The Movement would go on.

If Martinez possessed no beam weapons—which was in fact the case—Berman would wait until everyone aboard the PCSS fleet starved.

Berman's big gamble was that Martinez did not possess a K-beam. Martinez's only ace was that Berman couldn't be sure one way or the other.

The *Skyhawk* and *Green Hills of Earth* voyaged

on toward New Utah. The *Zeus* had been ordered to hold position out of weapon range. On all three ships, DiCaria reported, the mood was grim. The lowest-ranked spacer knew what was at stake.

Caitlin Landry did not. Martinez went to her cabin, taking Dr. Glynn with him. He wanted to learn as much about the weaponized Landry pathogen, *Joravirus randi*, as he could.

"I don't think there's anything more I can tell you," Caitlin said.

"I want to be sure I understand what you're proposing be done to the virus on New Yosemite, and make sure Dr. Glynn understands as well."

"Are we still going to New Yosemite?"

What had she heard, and from whom, for chrissake? He said, "Yes."

Her eyes, brown-flecked green, bored into his. "Is that the truth? It doesn't...doesn't seem like it. Or at least, not all of the truth."

He felt, rather than saw, Mary Glynn's surprise: How does a prisoner know enough about the captain to know when he's lying? The doctor studied them both intently.

Abruptly, Martinez ended the interview.

A day out from New Utah, Martinez sat on the bridge when the OOD said, "Sir, contact with—"

Scott Berman's face burst onto the viewscreen, tears of fury unabashedly on his young cheeks. "They're all dead!"

Martinez said, "Who's dead?"

"All of the freedom fighters on Horton Island! We just got word from New Yosemite!"

Horton Island—the labor camp on New California that Berman had mentioned before. "Dead? A Landry air attack?" But how had a Landry warship got itself—and its beam weapons—through the Polyglot-New California gate and then close enough to the planet to fire?

"No!" Berman shouted, all his previous poise dissolved in rage. "A plague! They died of a disease, and you can't tell me it was natural! Sloan Peregoy murdered them!"

"How do you know they're dead?"

"How do you think? We have intel going back and forth through the gates, you idiot! We surveilled the island by drone. You people—"

Martinez put into his voice all the authority he had. This intense young fanatic commanded a lot of people, and if word got to New California that Berman believed Sloan had killed his prisoners on Horton Island, Berman would gain a million more followers. Berman was dangerous.

"Listen to me. It wasn't Sloan Peregoy. It was the Landrys."

"I don't believe that!"

"It's the truth, Berman. I'm going to tell you what's going on, all of it. Just listen before you decide." Carefully, Martinez went through the entire story, from finding the *Dagny Taggart* and the *Falcon* through to the destruction of the biolab on Prometheus. He left out only three pieces of intel: his ships' lack of radiation weapons, Caitlin Landry's presence on the *Skyhawk*, and her last revelation about the genemod pathogen.

As Berman listened, his anger turned from volcano to glacier. "Why should I believe you? I don't believe you. How could Landrys have gotten a bioweapon onto Horton Island? New California is too well defended."

"Yes, it is. I don't know how the Landrys did it. But I'm sending you a data packet with pictures of the bodies on *Galaxy*. You can see that they're dead. You can see the horrible way they died. If you have images from Horton Island, you can see if they match."

"You might have killed those Landry spacers, testing a Peregoy bioweapon on their ships before you used it on us at Horton Island."

"And how could I get the bioweapon aboard Landry ships?"

"How did the Landrys get it onto Horton Island?"

They were at an impasse. Martinez, playing for time, said, "Look at the holoimages. Listen to the last recording by the captain of the *Galaxy*. The data should reach you any moment."

It did. Martinez saw Berman turn to another screen somewhere in his command room, out of Martinez's line of sight. Berman's profile faced Martinez, a curve of bearded cheek and one eye. Enough to see the eye narrow, brow crinkle, lips part in shock. Berman glanced at his wrister, up at the unseen screen, back to his wrister.

He said, "Martinez, the images from Horton Island don't look like that. No pus-filled things on the face, no purple swelling—not at all like that."

Martinez waited, hoping.

Finally Berman said, "It's a different bioweapon entirely."

"No," Caitlin Landry said, awkwardly holding the tablet close to her face to study the images, "that's not the same disease."

"What is it?" Martinez demanded.

"I don't know. Do you have any information about it? Anything at all?"

"No. And the doctors on New Utah don't recognize it, either." Berman had said as much, just before Martinez's difficulty persuading him to stay in contact, to wait for just five minutes while Martinez researched something.

The "research" was proving futile.

She said, "If New Utah doctors don't recognize the disease, then I'm certainly not going to. I'm not a physician, Captain."

He demanded, "Is your sister weaponizing two pathogens? Is that possible?"

"Possible but unlikely. Where are these . . . these deaths occurring?"

"Is there anything else you can tell me from these images?"

"No." She looked up at him, without fear. "Are the dead people your citizens? I'm sorry."

He let out a blistering oath and left.

Berman had not broken contact, although now there were three or four people filling the screen behind him, all whispering and pulling at him, all with faces contorted by rage. None of Martinez's bridge crew looked at him directly.

He said, "Berman, I don't know where this disease came from, but I don't believe it's from Director Peregoy. He would know that letting a weaponized pathogen loose anywhere on New California would be incredibly stupid. It could spread to—"

Berman said, "That's not what Dr. Belinski thinks."

One of the people in the background stepped forward, a middle-aged man with bright red hair. He said, "I know Horton Island. If this pathogen can only be transmitted person-to-person, and if no one goes to that isolated island, the disease can be contained."

Berman aid, "Contained enough to kill only Movement prisoners. Sloan Peregoy did this, Martinez."

"I know you believe that, but I do not. I believe it was the Landrys. But since we can't prove it either way, Berman, let's stick to facts. Landry ships are on their way from Polyglot via the Prometheus gate, carrying biowarfare to New Utah. My sources say it's possible to deliver pathogens inside canisters that can be aimed at a planet from pretty far away, burn up partially in the atmosphere, explode over land, and release viruses, at least some of which might survive. Are you—"

"Stop," Berman said, and turned away, consulting with the others. When he turned back, his face had gone gray. "Go on."

Martinez pushed his point. "Are you confident that you can shoot down every single meteor, day and night, indefinitely?" Of course he wasn't.

Berman said nothing.

Martinez continued, "Here is what we can do. I'm staying at New Utah to stop the Landrys from taking Peregoy property, but I need to resupply. I can send a deweaponized scout through the gate to New Yosemite and it will send back a cargo ship with—"

"No cargo ships. Nothing that big."

"All right, then, a class 6A vessel." They would have to pack it to the ceilings with food. "You're convinced this is a Peregoy pathogen, so I'll send orders to New Yosemite Command that nothing else is to come through the gate to New Utah except that one class 6A vessel.

You don't let anything from anywhere land—not even your own scouts or more of your rebels. You don't know what they're unwittingly carrying. If anything tries to land anyway, shoot it down. Even your own."

A boy behind Berman cried, "He's just trying to get us to turn on each other!"

Martinez ignored him. "If I learn from New Yosemite anything about either bioweapon, I'll tell you. New Yosemite already knows that you've seized New Utah—you told me as much. So you won't be risking anything. Agreed?"

"Except being infected by Landrys and/or Peregoys. Some choice."

Martinez kept his face blank. Berman's choice would come later, if Martinez could exploit what Caitlin Landry had told him. If.

Berman said, "All right, Martinez. One scout, with one class 6A vessel to return."

Instantly an angry clamor broke out behind Berman. People shoved forward, waving their arms and shouting at each other.

Civilians.

So this was how the war was going to be fought. Not with beam weapons, not with guns, not with defined targets. With microbes causing the indiscriminate mass murder of civilian populations. With the same terrible and stupid tactics that had killed civilization on Terra.

Nobody learned anything.

"Gate approaching, sir," said the scout pilot.

"Proceed through gate."

"Proceeding through gate."

The old familiar shimmer, and then the scout was

through. Martinez had not told Berman that he himself was going to New Yosemite, nor that he was bringing Caitlin Landry with him. Nor the second reason for this "supply run." During his absence, DiCaria was acting captain, Vondenberg acting fleet commander.

Martinez gazed at the planet below, not as close a match to old Earth as was New California, but close enough. Blue seas, white clouds, a single large land mass plus islands flung like green crillberries onto the ocean. His wife Amy was buried here; she'd died in a flier accident while he'd been stationed with New Yosemite planetary defense.

A sudden image of Amy flashed into his mind, but not accompanied by any pain. It was so long ago, and they'd been married such a short time. But, he realized unpleasantly and for the first time, Amy resembled Caitlin Landry.

She sat behind him in the scout, motionless and, for once, asking no questions. He'd already told her why he needed her here.

On the New Yosemite side of the gate, he said, "Request encrypted personal contact with Vice Admiral Mueller, Planetary Defense."

The scout pilot aid, "Yes, sir."

Martinez and Sean Mueller had been at Military Academy together. Mueller was unconventional and honest, which was why Martinez trusted him. Mueller would tell him whatever he knew about events on New California, not only with the war but with Sloan Peregoy, with the so-called Movement, with any large-scale outbreaks of disease. Mueller would also aid him with the tissue samples of what Caitlin Landry called *Joravirus randi*. New Yosemite, like

New California, had a military hospital in orbit to service sick or injured spacers. Martinez needed it, immediately.

Mueller might also have additional information about the pathogen on Horton Island. Or not, if Scott Berman had indeed obtained this information through some Movement channel and the deaths weren't generally known even on New California, let alone on New Yosemite.

Most important, Mueller would understand why Martinez's mission had to be kept unofficial. Or, if he didn't understand, he would still respect Martinez's judgment.

What Mueller probably couldn't tell him was something that Martinez desperately wanted to know. Mueller read history, but not literature, especially literature almost three thousand years old. He probably hadn't ever heard of the House of Atreus and its familial struggles for power, its utter ruthlessness, its murderous offspring.

Even the daughters.

49

DEEP SPACE

Nothing in the universe is static.

Rachel stared at a wallscreen on the bridge of the *Kezia Landry*. The screen displayed data confirming her failure. Hallie Dunn, the tech who'd operated the expensive, newly installed equipment, said, "Try again, ma'am?"

"No. Not here. Mr. Mahjoub, continue on course with all possible speed."

"Yes, ma'am," the pilot said.

Tara said, "I don't understand! What did you do? What just happened?"

Weariness took Rachel all at once, like a perigean tide. She'd been awake most of the night running and rerunning equations, and she was too old for this. Saving civilization should be the province of younger people.

"Gran? What just happened!"

"Tara, come to my cabin while I rest for a bit. Hallie, you rest, too. We'll try again tomorrow."

"Yes. ma'am."

In her luxurious cabin—Annelise's master's cabin—Rachel stretched out on the bed and pulled the fur coverlet to her chin. She felt cold. She needed to sleep.

"Gran?"

No sleep until she'd satisfied Tara, who paced around the tiny cabin—luxury on a personal spacecraft didn't include much room—like a caged Polyglot lion. Rachel envied the girl her energy, if not its source. Philip Anderson shone in her eyes, pulsed in her pacing.

The beginnings of romances, even one-sided romances, were all the same: flutters in the belly, light in the eyes, hope in the heart. It was the endings that differed. But never before had a romantic ending been as different as this one.

"Tara, are you—"

"No, Gran, I'm fine. The meds work. I'm just... curious."

A world-smashing understatement. Rachel accepted it, because what choice did she have? And Tara was no longer unbalanced, if you defined "balanced" as giving up the belief that she and Philip Anderson could be together.

By any definition other than that, of course, this entire expedition was unbalanced.

"Nothing in the universe stays the same," Rachel began. This had all been explained to Tara before, but it was difficult to know how much the girl retained. Tara had never been the brightest of the granddaughters. That had been Caitlin.

Before heartache over Caity could consume her, Rachel plunged back into her explanation. "At the quantum level, the universe is made up of fields, and those fields all exist sort of on top of each other. In each other. They interact and change constantly. I believe—" unlike anyone else in the Eight Worlds "—that Philip has put himself into a field nobody had yet discovered, the field of consciousness. There are theories that it must exist, because of the way that observation can create change in other fields. There are even theories that it is the substrate of reality."

"I know all that," Tara said impatiently, although Rachel had no idea what "knowing" consisted of when you couldn't follow the math. And didn't even want to. Tara's "knowing" was mostly desire. She wanted Philip to somehow still exist, so in her mind he did.

Was the rest of humanity really that different?

"If Philip did somehow get himself injected into the field of consciousness—" and how in the name of all deceased gods could that have happened? "—then it was—"

"He did," Tara said, "because he closed the gates! And then opened them again to let through only ships without radiation weapons! To stop the war!"

"That's what we hope, dear heart."

"What else could have done it?"

Out of the mouths of babes. Rachel was staking everything on that very question. But she didn't feel up to explaining Occam's Razor to Tara. Gods, she was tired. How could she make this as brief and intelligible as possible? Only with gross oversimplification.

"Philip is a field, or in a field—there isn't any difference, really. We're trying to get his attention. We can't enter the field of consciousness directly, since we have no idea how Philip did so. But all fields interact. Their interaction is what produces both space and time. No, Tara, don't ask—I really can't explain that to you without the math. We're trying to get Philip's attention by sending a signal through a quantum field we do understand and can manipulate a little. The same field that drives starship engines outside of gates. It involves manipulating particles that—"

"But Philip isn't getting the signal," Tara said, going straight to what she cared about.

"Isn't perceiving it, whatever 'perceiving' means to him now—Tara, I've told you, over and over. He isn't Philip anymore."

"But you don't know what he is."

"No. It's unimaginable to us. And either he isn't 'perceiving' my signal or doesn't understand it or doesn't choose to do anything about it or is no longer the sort of...of entity that can choose anything, or—"

"But you said you sort of expected he wouldn't get the signal here. In deep space."

"I knew it was a possibility. A strong possibility. All fields change."

"So he died again." Tara stopped pacing and loomed over the bed. Her eyes glinted with tears.

Rachel held onto patience. "He isn't dead because he wasn't alive. Isn't alive. Isn't even 'he.' Tara, I need to sleep."

"But you'll try again."

Right now, Rachel would have tried anything to get Tara out of the cabin, including grand-filicide, or whatever the word would be. She said, "I'll try again, closer to a gate. If a field decays, it can be preserved longer by concentrating it. Sort of."

Not true, but how to explain to Tara the Second Law of Thermodynamics, entropy, and open versus closed systems?

"And," she added for good measure, "I'll boost the signal. It sustains interference over distance, you know. It would be different if we could have brought radiation-beam weapons, but then we couldn't have gotten through the Polyglot gale... I mean, gate..."

"You know what, Gran? You should sleep now. You look a little tired."

Tara crept out, closing the cabin door and turning off the light.

Days later, the *Kezia Landry* reached the Polyglot-Prometheus gate. Rachel had made one more signal attempt during the flight from Polyglot to the gate. Nothing had happened. Now she tried again, on the Polyglot side of the gate. Tara hadn't been told when the signal would be sent; Rachel didn't want her on the bridge. It wasn't yet "dawn" on the ship.

"Go," she said to Hallie.

The tech activated the signal. Rachel had thought hard about this signal—what might get the attention of an unimaginable entity "inhabiting" a field for which physics had theoretical equations but no messenger particle, no integration with either relativity or the standard model, no experiments? Philip was the only experiment, and it had not been verified or replicated. It wasn't even "Philip" anymore.

But whatever it was that had closed the gates, it had once been human, an intense, handsome young man on a quasi-mystical quest. And that posthuman entity *had* altered the gates to forbid the passage of ships equipped with weapons of mass destruction. That argued not only consciousness but also some sort of caring what happened to the humanity that the young man had transcended. Rachel was staking everything on that.

Which didn't answer the question about what sort of signal to send to Philip-that-had-been. How did you contact a god, a meta-capital-letter Observer who could collapse wave functions in quantum-gravitational fields?

She'd rejected prime numbers; the Observer might notice them, but they conveyed no urgency. The same with a Fibonacci sequence or a numerical constant. She considered Morse code, that ancient Terran method of signaling disaster. But Morse code wasn't used on Philip's native Polyglot.

In the end, she'd settled on disturbing the quantum flux by using the *Kezia Landry's* drive. Philip, she'd discovered from library research, had done some marine research as part of his graduate work in biology. When all else failed, oceangoing ships on Polyglot signaled distress by another ancient Terran method: a high intensity white light flashing at regular intervals from fifty to seventy times per minute. Rachel used the ship's drive and the equipment she'd had installed to create regular bursts of brief-lived subatomic particles at the rate of sixty a minute. Would the Observer recognize that? Rachel had no answers.

But, then, the greatest mystery had always been human consciousness. Even in actual humans.

On the viewscreen the gate shimmered, silver against the black of space. So beautiful, so mysterious, so fraught.

"Sending signal," Hallie said, and Rachel held her breath. The very air on the bridge seemed to suspend not only movement but time.

Nothing happened. No response.

They tried a few more times, with no result.

"We'll try inside the gate," Rachel said.

The pilot glanced at her, said nothing, and returned to his console.

"Gran," Tara's voice said from Rachel's wrister, "where are you? What are you doing?"

"I'm on the bridge," Rachel said in as normal a voice as she could manage, "but I'm about to go have breakfast. Are you hungry?"

For the next trial, Rachel wasn't able to keep Tara off the bridge. The signal was sent inside the Polyglot-Prometheus gate—or at least, Rachel hoped it had been. The *Kezia Landry* passed through so fast and the composition of the gate—if "composition" was even the right word for something that seemed to be neither wholly matter nor wholly energy—was so unknown, that it was impossible to tell what happened with the sixty bursts fired by the ship. But the bursts seemed to make no difference to anything.

Rachel had feared passing through to the Prometheus side of the gate: What if Peregoy warships had reclaimed the dwarf planet? They had not. There was no one here, not even defense probes. And there was no Philip-response to her message, although she had no idea what such a response would look like. How did a demi-god respond to rhythmic disturbances in a quantum Mount Olympus?

So it would have to be the eleventh gate, after all, A month-long further voyage. Tara's eyes glittered; she'd convinced herself that Philip was on the planet behind the gate she'd discovered. Rachel, convinced of nothing, was losing hope.

But the eleventh gate was all she had left.

50

NEW CALIFORNIA

Sloan was in a corporate meeting when the building exploded.

He and six executives sat around a polished karthwood table in a conference room at corporate headquarters. One moment the table holoscreen glowed with data, the coffee urn gleamed on a side table, Donna Charmchi expounded on her division's budget. The next moment the ceiling buckled, the urn sprayed coffee, the holo dissolved, and all the noise in the world filled the room with dust and debris. Sloan, knocked from his chair, crawled under the table.

A second explosion, more distant.

Charmchi gasped, "Not this wing..."

None of them were hurt. They staggered to their feet, glancing wildly at each other. Sloan stood, covered with dust and coffee. Alarms blatted. Security rushed in, including Sloan's bodyguard, Chavez. "Sir—"

"I'm fine. What...what happened?"

"Surface-to-surface missile, sir. Hit the east wing."

More explosions, far more distant. Sloan said, "We're retaliating?"

"Yes, sir. Please follow me to the basement, all of you."

"Wait . . . who? You said surface-to-surface . . ."

"The protestors, sir." The man actually bared his teeth. "Somehow they got military weapons. Please come with me."

"No," Sloan said. "The rest of you, go."

He thought rapidly. Sophia's office was in the east wing but she was on New Yosemite. If the protestors had military weapons, that suggested either the existence of a serious black market, which Sloan would have known about, or a recent defection of a critical cadre of soldiers to the protestors' cause. How many soldiers? Armed with what else?

His bodyguard echoed his thoughts. "It's not safe here, sir. We don't know what else the fuckers got."

"Accompany me to my office. The rest of you—go to the bunker. Now."

Chavez led Sloan through corridors thick with foamcast dust and partially blocked by falling debris. The closer they came to Sloan's office, the less the damage. He had not been the target; Sophia was.

Did the protestors know about Horton Island? He guessed yes.

His office looked untouched. The wallscreen worked. Sloan issued orders even as he studied images streaming from the east side of the building. They came from drones; the recording and imaging equipment on that side of the building had all been destroyed.

He saw no protestors, no holosigns, nothing in the streets beyond the compound walls. But at the edge of Capital City, another explosion. The protestors had fired from there, and Sophia's army—whatever part of it had stayed loyal to Peregoy Corporation—was obliterating them.

Sixteen people had died in the east wing. Among them, on some corporate errand that Sloan would now never know about, was Sloan's personal assistant, Morris.

He stayed in his office all night, receiving reports and issuing orders. Assessing, repairing, planning. The protestors did not have control of any of the warships in orbit or massed by the New California stargates, at least not yet. Word had gone to New Yosemite, and Sophia sent word back that she was safe but could not yet return to New California. She didn't say why not—some new crisis at the shipyards? Were workers in rebellion there, too? How much rebellion?

The world had gone insane.

At dawn, Sloan sat writing a message to Morris's brother, his only family. The words would not come. Sloan's very bones ached; he felt limp with fatigue. With fatigue, with heartsickness, with anger that he could not get to rise higher than dull embers.

Morris, that supremely faithful little man.

Fifteen others, people under his stewardship, his care.

A city descending into civil war, this violence grown in the foul soil of what had happened on Horton Island—he was sure of that—and fertilized by seething discontent that Sloan still did not understand. Yes, he had controlled his people, but always, always for their own good. True, Sophia had gone too far in stifling dissent and increasing conscription, but did that wipe out decades of—

Then a hand was shaking his shoulder and he was lifting his head from the desk, where it had fallen in sleep. "Sir, sir..."

Chavez, whom for a brief disoriented moment, Sloan thought had come to kill him. But Chavez only said, "Are you all right, sir?"

"Fine." He could barely move, cramped from sitting so long, still gray with fatigue.

"Sir, there's a messenger with priority one clearance and... and news from the rebellion."

Sophia? Sloan dragged himself to his feet. "Go on."

"There were more attacks by the protestors, sir, on a circuits factory just outside the city and on the branch headquarters in Washington City. The factory was empty because it had gone on strike. The headquarters didn't have too many people there this early in the morning, but there were... the news channels have it all, sir."

His bodyguard giving him intel... but Sloan had no time for this anomaly. He said, "Where is the messenger?"

"Downstairs, sir. It's a scout pilot. She claims to come from Captain Martinez. I didn't bring her right to you, sir, because she hasn't been vetted and no one is here who can do—"

"Bring her in. Disarm her first, but bring her in."

Still Gomez hesitated. "I can do that, but if she's a suicide bomber with any sort of new body-planted—"

"Bring her in now."

The pilot was young, wide-eyed at the destruction, not the sort that Sloan would have expected Luis to send. She saluted—something that always annoyed Sloan, he was a corporate director, not a dictator—and said, "Lieutenant Maria Stebens, sir, with a message from Captain Luis Martinez."

Sloan took the tiny data cube. "Where is Captain Martinez?"

"When he sent me here, he was on his way to New Yosemite, sir."

"Wait outside, Lieutenant."

"Yes, sir." Another salute.

Sloan put the tiny cube into his wrister, which broke the encryption and scrolled the text, without either audio or holo. "To Director Peregoy from Captain Luis Martinez. Am carrying out a vital mission on New Yosemite and will continue until it's complete."

That was it. Sloan concentrated on what Luis had not said.

He hadn't named the mission. Highly unusual. Did he expect that this message might be intercepted? Had it been, and if so, by whom?

Luis hadn't said how long the mission would take.

He had not reported on where he'd been these long months, or what he'd been doing.

Most of all, he had not asked even *pro forma* permission to continue on New Yosemite instead of returning to New California, which was what he was expected to do.

Meticulously, Sloan destroyed the data cube. Sophia had told him that she was on New Yosemite. Technically, Luis should report in to her. Had he? Sloan had no idea what they would tell each other.

He would question the pilot further—and why was Luis using such young and presumably untried pilots? Had he had major decreases in force? That, at least, she should be able to tell Sloan. After he interviewed her, he would return to yesterday's damage. If the—

Another explosion. It was somewhere in the distance, but through his window Sloan saw the smoke and debris rise above the city. Also, the protestors were returning. Very stupid—didn't they know they'd be arrested? Or did they know, through collusion with elements within corporate security, that they wouldn't be?

Everything was unraveling.

Holosigns leapt higher than the compound walls: FREE SPEECH NOW and AVENGE HORTON ISLAND and—still!—FREE SUELIN.

Force, which Sloan had never wanted to use in the first place, had failed. That left negotiation.

"Chavez," he said to the bodyguard, "Bring that pilot back in. And equip her scout with whatever weapons it lacks, for a trip to Jabina Island." If Lieutenant Stebens came from Luis, he could trust her.

Chavez, who was his bodyguard but Sophia's agent, looked uncertain.

"Don't just stand there, man," Sloan said. "Do it now."

51

NEW YOSEMITE

Sometimes luck was on your side.

It seemed an odd thought for someone who was a wartime prisoner, someone who was possibly committing treason, which used to be a nonexistent crime on Libertarian worlds without state government. Someone who was praising the purported enemy. Yet Caitlin had the thought anyway: *We just got lucky.*

She stood outside a Biohazard Level 3 lab on a research hospital orbital around New Yosemite. Through the unbreakable plastic window, she watched Peregoy lab techs creating batches of the virus *J. randi mansueti.* The scientists who had modified Jane's version of the virus were all asleep after arduous days of day-and-night effort. Caitlin didn't need to sleep; she hadn't been working on the genemod. All she had done was share the initial insight, and the research team that Luis Martinez had assembled had done the modification in ten days.

They were superbly trained, these scientists. On

Peregoy worlds, university was free to the qualified, part of the extensive government social programs that on Galt were thought of as "enfeebling handouts." At Galt University, students had rich parents, or worked their way through advanced education for decades, or never attended at all. Innovation was unfettered by regulation, but much talent went untapped.

This orbital, too, was owned by the state. Peregoy Corporation *was* a state, no matter what it called itself. It taxed, conscripted, controlled. No one kept much of the money they earned, except corporate owners like Sloan Peregoy. But the orbital was beautifully equipped, and whatever the team needed that hadn't been here already, including personnel, Captain Martinez had commandeered from the planet almost instantly. He—

"Ms. Landry," he said, behind her.

She turned. Her guard, Henderson of the Perpetual Silence, stepped back respectfully. Caitlin was aware yet again how tall Martinez was. "Captain."

"I want to talk to you. Come with me, please."

She followed him to somebody's office, which he must also have commandeered. The room abutted the outer edge of the cylindrical orbital; a window displayed a rotating panorama of stars. The desk held no clutter, just a dirty coffee cup. Martinez frowned and tossed it into the recycler.

A detail she hadn't known about him: he was a neat freak.

He said, "Have you been treated well?"

"Yes. About my imprisoned crew on the *Green Hills of*—"

"Assume they're fine. Please explain to me exactly what this genemod version of the Landry virus will do."

Caitlin's brow wrinkled. "Haven't your own scientists explained it?"

"Yes. I want you to do so as well. It was, after all, your idea."

Not that she had a choice; she was his prisoner. His manner, however, had changed from its former suppressed rage. Behind his eyes lay—not fear, but anxiety. Well, given the situation, who wouldn't be anxious?

No, this was something more.

"Ms. Landry," he prompted, not patiently.

"The researchers were lucky," she said. "Usually it takes a long series of trials to modify a virus in exactly the way desired, because altered genes affect other genes, turning them on or off, creating methyl groups that . . . never mind, you don't want that level of detail. They were lucky because this time it took just a few weeks. Only one simple gene change was involved to turn *J. randi* into a less virulent version of itself. I suspect that Jane's virologists were working with a mild form of *J. randi* to begin with, much milder than the outbreak twenty-two years ago—viruses mutate on their own, you know. Whoever altered it to greater virulence did so really hastily. Sloppy work."

"How mild is what these scientists just created? How sick will it make people who get this version of the disease?"

Caitlin shifted in her chair. Below the window, New Yosemite came into view, cloudless blue ocean. "We won't know until the pathogen is tested. My guess is that severity of the disease will vary from person to person. The very old or those with compromised immune systems might become very ill, and so might some others. But for most people, *J. randi mansueti* will feel like a bad cold, or slight flu. A few days of feeling oinky."

"Oinky?"

Caitlin felt herself blush. "In mild discomfort."

"Where did 'oinky' come from?"

"A made-up word from when my sisters and I were small and we got sick."

Almost he smiled, but only briefly. "You christened this form of the virus, didn't you? 'Mansueti'—the Latin for 'mild.'"

"Yes. Why did you study Latin?"

He ignored this to return to the main issue. "And anyone contracting the mild form becomes immune to the virulent form of *J. randi*? Like with smallpox and Jenner's milkmaids who'd had cowpox?"

He was always surprising her with how much he knew about things not military, especially Terran things. Or was he, in his austere way, showing off, with both Jenner and Latin? Why?

She said, "In theory they'll be immune, yes. Of course, the virus will have to be tested on human subjects."

They stared at each other. All at once the air in the small office prickled like needles. The orbital rotated on its axis, and stars replaced the view of New Yosemite.

She said, "You're going to test it on my crew and me."

"Yes." He watched her closely.

"Well," she said, "I suppose if I were you, I'd do the same thing."

Surprise widened his eyes.

Caitlin said, "Did you think I didn't suspect that?

But your own scientists must have told you that it probably won't harm us."

"They did. What I want from you is your estimate of how probable 'probably' is. What are the chances of not falling dangerously ill?"

"I estimate around ninety-five percent. It's only an estimate, of course."

He nodded; the research team must have given him the same rough odds.

She said, "So we're going back to New Utah?"

"Yes."

"And then what?"

"Then, if the 'cowpox option' works, we infect New Utah. That's where I think Landry ships will attack."

"Jane will be there soon," Caitlin said, and wondered if that, too, was "treason." But of course he'd already figured that out.

She thought the interview was over, but Martinez asked something else. "How likely is it that a second, different pathogen could be made into a milder version, like this one was? Quickly?"

"A second pathogen? Do you have reason to think that Jane made *two*?"

"Just answer the question."

"Unlikely. Really, really unlikely. We were lucky here, as I just told you. And if you have no data or samples of the second pathogen—do you? You haven't shown me anything!"

He stood. "Henderson will take you to your quarters, Ms. Landry. We leave within the hour."

She stood, too, so quickly that she bumped her elbow on the desk. It hurt. Without even thinking, she grasped his sleeve with her other hand. "Please, just tell me—is there a second pathogen?"

He removed her hand from his sleeve; his fingers were warm. He didn't answer her.

In the corridor, Caitlin watched Martinez stride away, and then she stepped forward to peer again through the window to the biolab. Hazard-suited techs worked busily, creating a disease to save a planet from Caitlin's sister's agents of death.

Henderson loaded Caitlin—that's how it felt, like she was just one more crate of food—onto a class 6A vessel that reminded her of the *Princess Ida*. Caitlin was crammed into a central corridor loaded to the ceiling with crates. Martinez was resupplying three ships. For how long? The trip to the gate took half a day, they passed through, and no one fired on them. She'd half expected they might—not that she would have known before she was vaporized. She'd prefer not to die jammed hip-to-hip with Henderson.

Caitlin waited for transfer to the *Green Hills of Earth*, to become a lab rat along with Veatch and his recruits. To her surprise, she was taken by vacuum sled to the *Skyhawk*. Did that mean Veatch and the others were there, too? Why?

No use asking Henderson, or anyone else. She could only wait to see what happened next.

52

DEEP SPACE

It began as a flutter.

If Rachel had been asleep, she might not have even felt it. But she lay awake in her bunk on the *Princess Ida*, staring at the dimly lit ceiling, her unquiet mind churning most of the night. The same ideas, over and over: Philip Anderson. Panconsciousness. Jane. Caitlin. The eleventh gate.

Another flutter.

Panicked, Rachel reached for the plastibox beside the bed. "Open," she said, and was shocked when her words came out so strangled and quavery that the box didn't even recognize her voice. She tried again. "Open."

The lid sprang upwards and she took out a patch, her fingers trembling. She pushed the patch into the bend of her elbow and waited. If this were more than flutters...

It was. Before the patch could do its work, Rachel's

chest constricted, as sudden and painful as if an iron band squeezed her. She couldn't breathe, couldn't move, couldn't cry out, couldn't most of all breathe...

Philip Anderson.

Panconsciousness.

Jane.

Caitlin.

The eleventh gate...

Then everything vanished.

She woke with tubes in her nose, patches on her body, Tara sitting beside the bed. Rachel tried to speak, but all that came out was an animal noise. It horrified her.

Tara jumped up. "Gran?"

Another animal noise. Tears sprang to Rachel's eyes. She was here, inside this body, she was Rachel, and she couldn't communicate.

"Lie still, Gran, Dr. Wexler's here. Just lie still."

Wexler entered the cabin. He took Rachel through a series of idiotic tests: Raise your left hand. Blink your eyes. Idiotic, but Rachel couldn't do any of them except blink. Her body would not obey.

Finally Wexler said—to Tara, not to her—"Your grandmother has had a stroke. She may recover some physical functioning, and for that we'll just need to wait and see. We can make her comfortable, and—"

Rachel stopped listening. She blinked rapidly at Tara, trying to tell her, to make her understand, it was vital! The most vital thing in the universe...

Philip Anderson.

Panconsciousness.

Jane.

The eleventh gate . . .

Wexler finally left. Tara took Rachel's hand. The tears flowed heavier now, dripping over Rachel's cheeks, soaking into the sheets. All gone, all over, the last chance . . . and they were only a few weeks out from the eleventh gate . . . Had she told Annelise to contact Ian Glazer, leader of the protests on Galt, and tell him . . . arrange with him . . .

Tara said firmly, "Listen to me, Gran—you can hear me, can't you? I know you can. I can do this. I'll get us to the eleventh gate and I'll have Hallie send the signal, just as you programmed it, to Philip. I'll tell him. It will be all right. You just rest.

"I'm the one who started this whole fucking mess, and I'll finish it."

Rachel could stay awake for only short periods before sleep took her—*invaded* her, like an unwelcome army. Sometimes she couldn't even tell if she was asleep or awake, drifting into a twilight country where thoughts and dreams merged, becoming two sides of the same thin disk of waning life. She was a small girl at the beach on Galt, only the sands were blue, as they had not yet been during her childhood, and she played with the child Tara. She made love with her husband, only he was Philip Anderson, handsome as a god. She flew through space on a ship . . . yes, she *was* on a ship—wasn't she?

Yes. She'd managed to communicate enough with Tara, through eyeblinks and, once, feeble pointing, to convey that she wanted to be on the bridge. So a crewman had carried her there, where a makeshift pallet filled half the tiny space, and Tara attended her. Rachel tried desperately to study Tara. Was her granddaughter balanced enough, steady enough, *sane* ...

"Don't worry, Gran," Tara said tenderly. "We're almost there. Less than a week to the eleventh gate."

Tara's face glowed. Did the girl still believe that she could contact Philip, that Philip would acknowledge her? That he was actually Philip? He was not. Could Tara do this?

"Soon," Tara said, just before twilight sleep took Rachel again and she dreamed that she floated among the stars, disembodied, while around her weapons detonated in blinding bursts of deadly light.

53

NEW UTAH

Martinez watched the shimmer of the New Yosemite-
New Utah gate grow larger, until it filled the whole
screen. Then the brief moment of disorientation, and
they were through. Different stars, different planet
turning in the distance. Different problems. But no
one had fired on them—not Landrys, not Berman.

"Arriving at New Utah," the pilot said, unnecessarily.

"Open encrypted communication with *Zeus* and
Green Hills of Earth."

"Communications open."

Elizabeth Vondenberg's face filled the screen. Didn't
she ever leave the bridge? The most conscientious officer he'd ever commanded: alert, tireless, and—thank
the gods—not wearing her immediate-crisis expression
of straight-line brows. On the *Zeus*, the exec's face
appeared. "Captain Vondenberg, Lieutenant Boyle."

"Welcome back, sir."

"Thank you. Report."

"All quiet. No communication from the planet, no vessels detected approaching from space."

"Good," he said, although of course it wasn't. There had been only two possibilities: that the Landry fleet from Prometheus had been detected or that it hadn't. The first meant that battle was imminent, a battle for which he had no weapons, plus no time to carry out what he now thought of as the "cowpox option." The second possibility meant that Jane Landry was still delayed on Prometheus to dig up, adapt, and install on ship the surface-to-space weaponry she'd put in place to protect the biofacility that Martinez had destroyed. There were no good possibilities.

Still, Martinez knew he'd been lucky. On New Yosemite, Sean Mueller had cooperated fully with Martinez's requests. Mueller had not sent reports of Martinez's presence on the hospital orbital to Planetary Defense, an omission for which he could be court-martialed. He had put the entire orbital hospital at Mueller's disposal, brought up scientists from the planet, and enforced stringent security around the project.

"Why?" Martinez had asked his old friend.

"You have no idea what's been going on here, Luis. It's Sophia Peregoy. There's a lot of military defiance against her. You don't know what she's done."

"I do," Martinez said grimly, and told Mueller about Horton Island.

"I knew there were political prisoners there," Mueller said slowly. "I even knew they'd been killed. I wouldn't be helping you otherwise, not without orders from the director. But I didn't know there was a second biowarfare plague. Christ!"

"Why hasn't Sloan stopped her?"

"Nobody knows for sure. Best guess is that he can't. He was trapped on Polyglot those three months the gates were closed, and she effected a sort of covert coup. He's still CEO, nominally, and word is he's trying to undo some of what she's done. The old man hasn't been corrupted. But New California is practically in a state of civil war, and too much of Security—now the 'army'—are deserting and joining the protestors."

"Where's Sophia now?"

"No one knows."

A station in deep space, Martinez guessed, overseeing manufacture of whatever weaponized virus had killed everyone on Horton Island.

Sophia. Whom Luis had once, briefly, considered marrying.

Mueller had said, "Have another drink, Luis. A toast to survival."

He sent Vondenberg and Boyle his encrypted OpOrd, and then he transferred himself by vacuum sled to the *Skyhawk*. He put an officer in charge of distributing supplies among the three ships. Vondenberg would begin testing *J. randi mansueti* on the Peregoy prisoners, who would be kept in isolation until they recovered. If they did. If this version of the disease really did behave like cowpox and not its more deadly cousin.

On the bridge of the *Skyhawk*, Martinez tried to raise New Utah. No response.

There were a lot of preparations to oversee and it was evening before he could leave the bridge for Caitlin Landry's cabin. The cabin was still bare; she had no personal items to warm its metal deck or bulkheads. Narrow bunk, made up neatly. Tiny table and two chairs. On the table lay the tablet he'd given her, with its very limited access to ship library. She was, as he expected, both baffled and angry.

"Why aren't I rejoining my crew on the *Green Hills of Earth* for the cowpox-option trial? Are they all right?"

"Henderson, dismissed."

"Yes, sir."

"I asked you a question!"

He said, "Your crew is fine. The answer to your other question, if you think about it for half a second, will be clear to a woman of your intelligence."

"It's not clear. I'm not getting infected with my crew. Why not? Are they all right?"

Intelligent, but she didn't think like a soldier. And why should she? However, a moment later she saw it.

"I'm a bargaining chip. With Jane."

"Yes."

"It won't work."

"Why not? You're her sister."

"Jane is obsessed. She'd sacrifice all of her sisters, and my grandmother too, to win this war. She's no longer mentally balanced. Power can do that to a person. And—"

"It doesn't always unbalance people." Sloan, for instance. Otherwise, he would have backed Sophia.

"No. But my family is given to obsession."

Immediately she looked as if she regretted saying that, which interested Martinez. "How so?"

She shook her head, lips set in a straight line.

"How is your family obsessive?"

"Why are you here, Captain? You don't need me to tell you anything you don't know about the genemod pathogen."

He didn't. Two-day incubation period, two or three days of mild sickness, and immunity to the virulent virus that Jane Landry had developed. At least, if everything went well. If the projections for incubation and infection were accurate. If the Landry fleet didn't show up armed with K-beams and destroy both Martinez's warships and everyone on New Utah. If.

He said, "Tell me about Philip Anderson."

He'd surprised her. She said, "How do you know about Anderson?"

"You mentioned him under truth drugs. But only about him and your other sister, the youngest one."

"Tara. But you already know what happened to him, don't you? In fact, you know more than I do. My grandmother brokered a deal with Sloan Peregoy to get Philip as far as the eleventh gate, but the gate would have been guarded by Peregoy ships. That was you, wasn't it? Otherwise you'd have no interest in Anderson."

Once again he'd underestimated her. He said, "Sit down, Caitlin."

It had just slipped out. He realized he'd been thinking of her by her first name for days.

She sat in one of the two chairs at the tiny table. Martinez took the other one. She said, deliberately, "Go ahead, Luis."

He scowled, then regretted it. The room was too warm. "Ms. Landry, I asked you to tell me what you know about Philip Anderson. I have the story he told me at the eleventh gate. I want your version."

"In exchange for what?"

"No exchange. You're a prisoner of war, remember."

"I remember."

They stared at each other across the metal table, and

across a gulf that was not as wide as he needed it to be. But Martinez had decades of disciplining his body. Peregoy Corporation Space Service had many attractive female officers, and Sophia had been—still was—beautiful. He was neither surprised nor dismayed by his physical reaction to Caitlin Landry as she sat there, defiant and intelligent and his prisoner. His reaction meant nothing except that it had been too long since he'd had sex.

That's all it was.

She blushed, and immediately began to cover confusion with disjointed talk. "Anderson believed he could access some deeper level of reality, some cosmic consciousness, and he . . . you know this already, right?"

"Yes. Did you believe he could?" They were on safe ground again.

"I did not."

"Did Rachel Landry?"

"No."

"Does she believe it now?"

"No."

Caitlin was lying, but Martinez let it go. He waited.

She said, "The sensible view is that Anderson doesn't matter, because he was delusional. But I would like to know what happened to him because one of the researchers at the university, a friend, was . . . was also in love with him. If I ever get home, I'd like to be able to tell her for sure what happened to him."

Martinez couldn't see any reason not to tell her. "He died on the planet behind the eleventh gate."

"*On* the planet? You know what's there? *What*?"

"The planet was deserted, the air unbreathable. No one will ever go there again. That's the one gate that has not reopened."

"Are you sure?"

"Of course I'm not sure—I haven't been there in months. But that was the state when I left."

"I see. Thank you for the information, Captain. Tell me, do you know the origin of the word 'heresy'?"

He shook his head.

"It goes back through French and Latin to ancient Greek, to the word *haireistha*. It means 'choose.'"

He didn't show that he was impressed. "And you think I'm choosing my battles."

"No. I think Philip Anderson did the choosing. He picked belief over doubt. Are you . . . this will sound insane, I know . . . are you positive he's dead?"

"I choose to think so. *Haireistha*."

She smiled, a sudden wide, whole-faced smile full of unexpected and mischievous light. "So—good news and bad news. The gates fortuitously reopened, but the way the entire universe works might have to be rethought."

When had he started smiling back at her? He made himself frown, and she sobered, too. She said, "Let me ask you one more thing. Why did you allow me access to the ship's library of literature and history? Because you thought I'd be bored otherwise?"

"Yes."

"I see." She leaned back in her chair and studied him. "You don't torture or kill your prisoners. You're trying to save the lives of a planet of rebels against your government, who—"

"They hold as prisoners thirty-eight fleet officers."

"—who would blast you out of the sky if you got close enough. You recognized the term *lex talionis*—you read history yourself, don't you?"

He said nothing.

"You do. So answer me this: Why do you serve a dictator like Sloan Peregoy who denies freedom of choice to everyone he controls as if they were pets instead of people?"

Martinez stood. "You understand nothing about Director Peregoy."

"I know that," she said with sudden, unexpected humility. "Only what I read on Galt, and I'm sure that was highly biased. But here's one thing I do know, Captain. Even if Sloan Peregoy is a benevolent dictator, the best kind of ruler in terms of taking care of his people, even if he's fair and just and all those other wonderful virtues, even if all his subjects adore him, even then...do you know the history of Edward IV and his brother Richard?"

Martinez opened the cabin door. Henderson snapped to attention. "Henderson, return to duty."

"Yes, sir."

But Caitlin's raised voice followed him through the open door. "The weakness in any benevolent dictatorship. The ruler can be fair and just, but that doesn't mean his heir will be."

Martinez closed the door and went to the bridge.

Two days later, Jane Landry's ships still had not appeared. Martinez had not seen Caitlin Landry again, and was annoyed with himself that he was so aware of that. DiCaria came to his cabin as Martinez was eating a solitary meal he didn't actually want.

"Captain, routine report from the *Green Hills of Earth*."

"Thank you. Why are you telling me this in person?"

"Because I want to ask you something." His exec hesitated.

"Wait, then."

Martinez accessed the report on his wrister. It was not routine, but the fleet had no report status for "welcome but completely expected information." The first of the captured *Princess Ida* crew had fallen ill in the hastily constructed isolation ward. Low-grade fever, headache, body aches, no loss of mental or physical function. If the illness didn't worsen, the cowpox option was a success.

"Report received," Martinez sent to Vondenberg. "Provide hourly status bulletins." He closed the link. "Now, DiCaria, what is it?"

"Sir, I know I'm overstepping here, but I'd like to make a request. If you're going to try to convince Scott Berman to allow infection of New Utah with this cowpox thing, and he agrees, I'd like to go downstairs with the medical team."

"Why?"

"One of the fleet officers he's holding prisoner is my half-sister. Lieutenant JG Serena Drucker. Berman is going to insist that you infect his prisoners first, isn't he? To see if it's a trick."

"Probably, yes."

"Serena had *J. randi* as a child. The original kind. It was long before the war, of course. She was at school on Polyglot and she made a friend from Rand, and her mother let her visit Karila on Rand the year the plague struck. Serena was very sick but she survived, and now she's immune. Or at least that's what the Rand doctor told us when the planet came out of quarantine and she was allowed to go home. If

Berman lets me see her, I could maybe obtain some of her blood with antibodies in it, and it might be useful to our researchers in making some sort of... of..." DiCaria floundered, having reached the border of his medical knowledge. "Some sort of medical thing. For long-term, I mean. With antibodies."

Martinez said, "I'll take your request under advisement."

"Thank you, sir."

"Dismissed."

Caitlin Landry would know if smuggled antibodies would be useful.

No—the Peregoy doctors on New Yosemite would know, and that's who Martinez would ask, damn it. Not Caitlin. And not the director.

Richard III had been a disastrous, power-hungry, murderous heir to Edward IV.

Every one of the *Princess Ida* crew came down with *J. randi mansueti*, and two days later most of them recovered, some more completely than others. Martinez linked with the captured pilot, whom Vondenberg said seemed like the least resentful of the prisoners. This proved true. Her face conveyed mostly bewilderment: at how a simple mission carrying passengers to Rand had resulted in capture by Peregoy forces, at why she'd been made sick, at the good care she'd gotten to aid recovery, at what this enemy commander wanted from her.

Martinez wanted assurance that the "cowpox option" didn't cause mental impairment. He got it; the pilot was perfectly lucid. Martinez was ready to contact Scott Berman.

"New Utah, this is Captain Martinez aboard the *Skyhawk*. I have an important update for you. Please respond."

Nothing.

"New Utah, this is Captain Martinez aboard the *Skyhawk*. I have an important update for you. Please respond."

Nothing.

"Mr. Berman, if you don't respond, you will be destroyed. The Landry fleet has been detected on its way to New Utah."

Berman responded to the lie. His image flashed onto a viewscreen, face stony, shoulders twitching with emotion that had nowhere else to go. A crowd of Movement "compatriots" stood behind him, partially visible to Martinez. A hand, a face, half a torso.

Berman demanded, "How far away?"

"Before we discuss that, I have something equally critical to tell you. On New Yosemite we created a mild version of the Landry virus. Very mild. It's been tested on thirteen people who became slightly ill but recovered rapidly. We can infect your entire planet with this altered pathogen, *J. randi mansueti*, and it will protect you against the virulent version of the disease that Landry ships are on the way right now to spew over your planet. This *will* protect you."

Berman already knew all this; all the data had been in a report Martinez had beamed at New Utah, to no response.

Berman said, "Doctor?" and a middle-aged woman with cropped hair and dark skin stepped forward.

She said, "I'm Dr. Whitney O'Brien. I've read all your reports, Captain, and gone over the genemod data.

But it's impossible to tell two things: first, whether the reports are false and you're lying about all of it."

"He is!" shrilled a voice out of the link field. Martinez recognized Christine Hoffman, the hysterical young woman who'd berated him before. In whatever way Berman's Movement was structured, it lacked discipline. Apparently anyone could say anything at any time, even during a critical military conference. No way to run a planet.

Hoffman cried, "He lied about how long he'd be on New Yosemite! He's probably lying about this, too!"

Dr. O'Brien ignored the interruption. "Second, even if you're telling the truth and this genemod virus causes no lasting harm, there's no guarantee that it will create partial or complete immunity against the virulent form of *P. randi*. You haven't tested it. To do that, you'd have to now expose your test subjects to the original virus and see if they fall ill."

"I know that," Martinez said. "And we have tissue samples of the original virus. But I'm not letting a pathogen with a one hundred percent kill rate loose on my ship when my crew has not been exposed to the cowpox-option version. And there's *not enough time*. The Landry fleet will be here very soon."

Berman said, "Our orbitals haven't detected approaching ships. What proof can you offer?"

"Sensor data from a distant drone—"

"Send it to me."

He couldn't; there was no sensor data.

"So you are lying. Then why shouldn't we believe that your so-called medical data is also false? Yes, I know your report said we can link directly with your test subjects—but they're all Landry prisoners, aren't they? You could have tortured them into saying whatever you choose. They're not credible."

"Mr. Berman—"

"You're not credible. And you're not infecting New Utah with a Peregoy virus under the guise of 'helping' us."

"Then everyone on New Utah will die. You'll either be annihilated by the Landry attack or else die horribly of the coming epidemic. And it *will* be horrible. You've seen images of the corpses."

Silence. Berman's shoulders gave a massive, involuntary twitch. The young man was pierced by responsibility. But he said steadily, "I still have no reason to believe you."

"Berman—"

"That's all, Martinez." The link broke.

From her ship Vondenberg said quietly, "He might have come around, but his people are pressuring him."

"Decentralized authority in action," Martinez said, more bitterly than he intended. His authority here was not decentralized, but that didn't mean he wanted to do what came next. He would be risking the lives of the thirty-eight officers held hostage by Berman's lunatics.

Officers who would die anyway.

He said to Vondenberg, "Prepare to launch."

54

NEW CALIFORNIA

SueLin said, "What?"

She stood in the middle of her mountain cabin on Jabina Island, facing Sloan. She hadn't run out to meet his flyer, hadn't launched herself at him in fury when he entered. Her voice, flat, barely rose above a whisper. Her hair, once red-gold as sunrise, lay tangled and unwashed on the shoulders of her food-smeared tunic. She stank.

Tears prickled Sloan's eyes. Horrified, he banished them with brusqueness. "I told you, SueLin. You're to come back to Capital City with me now."

"Why?" That same flat, lifeless tone.

"I told you that, too. Bathe first. Do that now."

SueLin didn't move. And then the unthinkable happened: Sloan's pilot, who'd inexplicably followed Sloan into the cabin, stepped forward and presumed to take charge. "Ms. Peregoy, I'm Karen Healy, your grandfather's pilot. We've come to take you home, because Capital City needs you. There's been rioting, striking, burning down buildings, attacks and counter-attacks. People are dying. The rioters are calling your name. 'Free SueLin' they say. They want you home."

The same dull voice, but a brief quirk of eyebrows that might have been interest. "They do?"

"Yes. They don't want to think of you being a prisoner here. You should be free."

Sloan made a choking noise. Karen—Karen!—sounded like a protestor herself, a member of the Movement. But then deep instinct told Sloan that she was not. She was merely handling SueLin, and far better than he had.

SueLin said, "Free."

"Yes. To live as you choose. You breed birds, don't you? And compete with them?"

SueLin grimaced, but her tone grew more normal. "Are my birds okay?"

Karen looked at Sloan, who had no idea what had happened to the birds. He almost said, "Of course," but the same instinct for negotiation that let him trust Karen made him say honestly, "I don't know."

Karen said, "You need to come home to check on the birds. They're your birds, after all—you bred them. But we need you to do something, too, SueLin. We need you to talk to the protestors, to tell them to stop the violence. They trust you. Will you do that?"

"No."

Sloan felt one fist clench, and made it uncurl. He couldn't even tell if the anger was against SueLin, or against himself. He had done this. SueLin was his granddaughter, and if she was completely selfish, it was his fault.

Karen said reasonably, "Why not?"

"Why should I? I don't care what happens to the protestors or to your stinking corporation. I only want to do what you said, live my life and show my birds!"

"Yes," Karen said, "but your birds are in the city, and the city is being destroyed. The protestors have military weapons because part of Planetary Defense has joined them, and the rest of Planetary Defense is retaliating. If you don't address everybody, there'll be no city left, no birds, no anything."

SueLin chewed on her bottom lip. Finally she said, "I don't know what to say."

"Director Peregoy will write out the speech for you."

"And record it? Not here, or you might not take me back!"

Sloan said, more harshly than he'd intended, "Not a recording. They might believe it's faked. You, in person."

"What if I get shot? No, I won't do it, it's too dangerous."

Before Sloan could answer, Karen said quickly, "You'll have shields and high security. The birds, SueLin. Your birds."

More lip-chewing. Finally SueLin said, "Okay."

"Bathe first," Sloan said.

He wrote the speech in the flyer. At corporate headquarters, plasticlear shields were put up on the roof and soldiers stationed everywhere possible. Sloan didn't tell SueLin that the shields could stop side-arm bullets but not artillery and certainly not beam weapons. Loudspeakers blared; radios transmitted; commercial wallscreen programs were interrupted; cheap wristers without encryption programs suddenly spoke at top volume: "SueLin Peregoy will address the city in twenty minutes. SueLin Peregoy in person, from the roof of Peregoy Corporation Headquarters. SueLin Peregoy will address the city—"

"I'm scared," SueLin said. She refused to let go of Karen's hand. SueLin had not once asked for her actual mother, Sloan's daughter Candace, who in any case had fled the war to New Yosemite.

Karen said, without cloying emotion but just as a statement of fact, "You're braver than you think."

SueLin nodded.

Sloan hoped Karen was right. SueLin, clean now and dressed simply in pale blue tunic and pants, held a tablet with her speech. However, she could say anything at all once she was in front of an audience—who might believe anything. After all, they'd believed that they were not free, even before Sophia had tightened controls so much that, in fact, they were not. Public broadcasts censored, dissenters sent to Horton Island and murdered, military divided and destroying itself.

A huge crowd advanced toward Headquarters. They marched down the broad main boulevard of Capital City, joined by tributaries from side streets, from buildings, from, it seemed, the very air. So many! For this spoiled girl who didn't care what happened to any of them. If Sloan's intel network had been able to find the Movement leader, this kid Scott Berman, would they still have made SueLin into such a powerful and ridiculous symbol?

Where was Berman? Did Sophia know?

What was Luis Martinez doing on New Utah?

"Now," Karen said, freeing her hand from SueLin's grasp. "No, I can't come with you. You can do it."

SueLin didn't move. Sloan drew in a deep breath and closed his eyes. All those people massed out there, and if she didn't appear they would rush the building, or fire on it from the weapons that were of course concealed in the crowd, and then soldiers on all the rooftops or at the ready in fliers would fire back, and the slaughter would be—

"Look," Karen said. "There's a bird. A good sign."

Sloan opened his eyes. A common jibird circled over the rooftop, calling stridently. SueLin watched it intently, squinting into the light. Then she stepped out onto the rooftop, walked to the low railing, and raised her hand. The crowd was silent for a moment as long as eternity, and then roars and cheers drowned out the bird.

SueLin's voice, amplified and transmitted, rang out more strongly than Sloan had dared hope.

"People of New California! This is SueLin Peregoy. I'm free, because you demanded that I be free. Thank you."

A wall of noise rising from the crowd. SueLin looked startled, but Sloan knew they weren't cheering her but themselves. They had done this. They had, in their view, brought Peregoy Corporation to its knees.

SueLin said, departing from her speech, "Oh thank you! Thank you!"

Because she was sincere, and because she was pretty and young, and because the crowd believed it had won more than it had, they went wild with cheering and waving. And again Sloan closed his eyes, in chagrin and grief. For just a moment, he saw the loveless little girl that SueLin had been, and shame scalded him.

But only for a moment. What if all this unearned adulation made SueLin decide she wanted even more of it? What if she decided she wanted Peregoy Corporation?

"I have to ask you something," SueLin said, and Sloan's heart began a slow, painful hammer. This was not what he'd written for her to say.

"I have to ask you to stop blowing up buildings and burning them down and shooting each other. My grandfather told me you want a lot of things, like . . . like the things you asked for. To not be so much under his control. And I know what that's like! So if I promise to make him talk to you about those things, will you stop destroying things until after the talking?"

A babble of angry voices. SueLin was losing them. A holosign flared high: REMEMBER HORTON ISLAND.

SueLin said, "I don't know what Horton Island is." Her bewilderment, in her slight frame and on the hugely magnified wall screens on the sides of building, was so genuine that at least part of the mob quieted.

"Look, I just want to go back to my birds. But nobody wants your husbands and wives and friends killed, right? If you won't talk to Sloan Peregoy, will you talk to my Aunt Sophia? No? Then to who?"

The babble resolved itself into a single, incredibly irrational cry, "SueLin! SueLin!"

She turned, fearful now, to look at Sloan. No, at Karen. SueLin didn't know what to do, and she was afraid.

Karen said, "Tell them you're the heir to the corporation."

A flash of the old SueLin: "I don't want the stinking corporation!"

"You don't have to have it. Just tell them that for now."

SueLin hesitated, and Sloan saw his entire life, his entire world, tremble on her quivering lower lip.

She turned back. "I am the heir to Peregoy Corporation," she said simply.

The cheers resumed. They felt vindicated. She'd said 'heir,' but Sloan knew that many of them heard 'director.' Those people, worked up to the point where mobs lose rationality, thought they had won. Sloan Peregoy was out.

And they were right. He would not be able to resume control of Peregoy Corporation again, at least not publicly. Nor would Sophia. SueLin didn't want the Peregoy worlds and was incapable of running them. But she had done the important thing: She had stopped, even if momentarily, the slaughter. Planetary Defense already had Sloan's order to suspend all solitary, lone-wolf retaliation against protestors.

Sophia would not take any of this well. When she returned from New Yosemite, Sloan would need to protect not only his city from the forces tearing it apart, but his granddaughter from his daughter. The prospect sickened him. He wasn't even sure he was capable of doing it.

Why wasn't Luis here?

55

NEW UTAH

"Launch," Martinez said.

The missiles had been prepared even before his last, disastrous link with Scott Berman. They were modified probes of the kind used to sample the surfaces of asteroids and moons. Small, remotely controlled, heat-resistant enough to not burn up during atmospheric entry, they were designed to retrieve payloads. This time, each one would make a one-way journey. They'd been altered on New Yosemite to explode on impact and spray viruses into the air of New Utah's one city, Cascade.

It was a windy day down there.

Planetary-defense orbitals and ground trackers would, of course, shoot at the missiles. They might vaporize a few, but they wouldn't hit them all. *J. randi mansueti* was highly infectious. In two days, most of New Utah would be mildly ill and—Martinez hoped—majorly protected. The *Skyhawk, Zeus,* and *Green Hills of Earth* would stay beyond weapons range.

"Keep the link to Berman open," he said to DiCaria.

"Yes, sir." The exec's face looked strained; Martinez had not forgotten that DiCaria's sister was among the captured PCSS officers.

It was half an hour before Christine Hoffman's face appeared on the screen. "You cocksucker!"

"I'm trying to save your life. All your lives."

Berman pushed her aside. His hair was wet, as if he'd been pulled from a shower with the news of Martinez's missiles. Facing Berman's icy, controlled fury, Martinez thought, *He'd have made a good fleet officer.*

Berman opened his mouth. Before he could speak, an arm snaked around his throat from behind and yanked him backward, out of the field of vision. Yelling, struggling, and another face appeared.

Martinez said sharply, "Berman?"

"Gone," the man said. Older than Scott Berman, he had the hot, twisted face of a thug beyond reason. "We don't need his fucking weak leadership. You deal with us now, fucker."

An internal coup. DiCaria raised his head to look at Martinez, who said, "What is your name?"

"Fuck my name! You think you can manipulate us, kill us, do anything you want the way your fucking boss Sloan Peregoy does—no more, Martinez! You hit us, we hit you!" He threw out one arm.

Two men dragged Naomi Halstead into Martinez's sight and held her. The thug drew back his fist and slammed it into her face. Her head whipped back so violently that Martinez thought her neck had broken. Blood streamed from her nose. She slumped in the men's grip.

Martinez clenched one hand into a fist, behind his

back. They would kill her, possibly kill all thirty-eight Peregoy officers. Torture as well? For him to watch?

But Christine Hoffman, to his surprise, suddenly reappeared, screaming. "No, John! We don't do that! We have to be better than they are or what's the point? Stop!"

"John" turned his head and growled something that Martinez couldn't hear. All at once the screen was full of people fighting each other, yelling, until someone must have thought to break the link and the screen blanked.

"Can't restore communication, Captain."

"Understood. Keep trying."

But no one restored the link on the other end. Martinez didn't know who'd won, who was now in charge of the Movement, who controlled New Utah's defense weapons, or what was happening to the thirty-eight Peregoy Space Fleet officers held hostage. He'd been counting on Berman's idealism and innate decency, and now he had no idea what was occurring on the planet.

For two days, nothing happened. The *Skyhawk* could not raise the planet.

The Landry fleet had not appeared. Martinez still had the option of retreating through the New Utah-New Yosemite gate, leaving New Utah at the mercy of the Landrys. He would be forced to do that unless Scott Berman had regained control of Cascade City, realized that what Martinez had said about the infection was true, and was willing to allow Martinez's troops to land and take planetary-defense weaponry to defend New Utah. Even that would fail if Jane Landry had K-beams. Martinez suspected that she did; otherwise it would not have taken her so long to retrofit her ships at Prometheus. Unless, of course, she'd been slowed down somewhere by battle with Sophia's fleet.

By now, everyone on New Utah should be sick with *J. randi mansueti*.

Were Naomi Halstead and the other Peregoy officers still alive? If they'd been killed, wouldn't the new Movement leadership have sent grisly images of their deaths?

Martinez lacked sufficient information on every front.

His conferences with Vondenberg and Murphy were short and brusque, the communication of captains with nothing to share except a terrible tension that didn't need utterance. Vondenberg, like Martinez, haunted the bridge of her ship, looking haggard. Nothing wrecked sleep like empty waiting.

At evening of the second day, Martinez went to Caitlin Landry's cabin.

Henderson straightened as Martinez entered. He said, "Dismissed until I call you." Henderson left, with a brief and uncharacteristic look of gratitude.

Caitlin lay on the bunk in her ill-fitting, cast-off clothes, feet bare, reading on her tablet. She rose and said, "What's happened? Oh, please tell me!"

No reason not to. "We infected the planet two days ago. They've broken off communication, so we don't know how your disease is taking."

To his surprise, she smiled faintly. "It's 'my disease' now?"

He couldn't smile back, not even faintly. So much was going on inside of him that his order came out more harshly than he'd intended. "Tell me about your sister Jane."

Caitlin tipped her head to one side. "I imagine you've found out all about her already, from your databases."

"The basic information, yes. Now I want to know what she's like as a person. Her childhood, her interactions with the rest of your family, with other people."

"Looking for a psychological advantage, Captain?"

She was always so acute. He said, "Yes. For negotiation."

"There's no negotiating with Jane. There never was."

They stared at each other, separated by the width of the table. Martinez saw her breath quicken. He knew, then, that she was feeling the same attraction he did, and that she, too, thought it monstrous.

She said softly, "Damn evolutionary biology."

He was astonished that she should name it, astonished enough that he blurted, "Why aren't you afraid of me?"

"I am. Of course I am," and then it hit him that she might be interpreting his words differently than he'd meant them. Only...how had he meant them?

He hadn't seen that kind of fearless openness since Amy had died. The women he worked with were often fearless but seldom open; he was their commander. The women he dallied with were...well, not like Caitlin Landry.

He looked away from her face. "Jane Landry. Why do you say negotiation with her isn't possible?"

"Is Jane here?"

"Not yet."

"Why not? She's had time."

He ignored this. "Tell me about her."

"All right. Sit down, Captain."

He waited until she sat first, laying her tablet on

the tiny table. Martinez glanced at it and was again surprised. She'd been reading Sun Tzu's *Art of War*. He said, "'Know your enemy and know yourself and in a hundred battles, you will never be in peril.'"

Now her smile wasn't faint at all, a wide unpremeditated grin that brought light to her hazel eyes. "Apropos. Score one for you. Jane is one of those people capable of tremendous singlemindedness. When she wants something, she becomes completely obsessed. Actually," she added thoughtfully, "I think we Landrys all do."

He suppressed the desire to ask Caitlin what obsessed her. "Give me an example of Jane's obsessiveness, something from long before this war."

She thought a while before answering. He watched her. The hazel eyes had flecks of green around the edges. Her hair, tucked back, sprang out from behind her ears in short, unruly curls. The ears were small, more delicate than her features. Long, firm neck like a column—

Stop.

"When Jane was thirteen," Caitlin said, "our father died. It was . . . difficult for all of us, but especially for my grandmother. She lost her son, and my mother was in the middle of a difficult pregnancy, so Gran had five daughters to raise. Well, Annelise was finishing university and Celia had already moved to New Hell, but Jane and I were teenagers, and then a few months later my mother died giving birth to Tara. She was—anyway, on Galt we cremate. I know you don't do that on New California."

"No," said Martinez.

"Jane got it into her head that our father's ashes should be scattered from orbit, even though his will said that he wanted them stored in the family vault. For a hundred thirty years, since Kezia Landry settled Galt, nearly all Landry ashes are there. He wanted his there, too."

Memory shadows passed over Caitlin's eyes.

"My grandmother tried to reason with Jane. That didn't work. So Gran said no, absolutely not, and considered the matter closed."

Martinez nodded, unexpectedly fascinated by this glimpse into the enemy's ruling family.

"Jane went silent. But she recruited a bunch of jobless no-goods and broke into the vault. It was stone—they used explosives in the middle of the night. She stole the ashes. She had a ship ready to take her to orbit, but—"

"A ship? At thirteen years old?"

"She wasn't supposed to have authority to command a ship, but she managed. Then an accidental witness alerted the police, so—"

"Wait," Martinez said, "I didn't think you had a police force on Galt."

"The family security force, of course. We just called them 'police.'" Caitlin looked at him with sudden dislike. "I can see what you're thinking, Captain. Libertarian planet, only the rich who can afford it get police protection and the hell with everyone else, spoiled kids without rules or discipline because everyone is supposed to be Libertarian free."

That was exactly what Martinez had been thinking.

"It wasn't like that. The point I'm trying to make is that Jane always defied rules to get what she wanted. She was devious, self-willed, single-minded, and oblivious to either reason or other people's feelings. She still is. She's also brilliant at devising strategies to succeed. That's what you wanted to know, isn't it?"

"Yes." He rose to go.

"Wait. I answered your question. Now you answer mine. Why hasn't Jane's fleet arrived here yet? There's been time."

He said nothing.

Her face changed. "Luis . . . please."

If he'd thought that the use of his first name was a deliberate strategy, he wouldn't have answered. But he didn't think that. Caitlin Landry desperately wanted to know what might happen to her, to her sister, to all of them. This open pleading hadn't been planned; he could see that from her face. And, after all, there was no way she could interfere with his plans.

"I think Jane stayed at Prometheus to dig up and arm herself with the surface-to-space weapons she probably had installed around the research station. She's retrofitting them for her ships. She'll be here when that's done."

She understood instantly. "And we have no radiation weapons because you had to pass from the new planet where you left Philip Anderson through the eleventh gate."

"Correct," he said, and then he did leave the cabin, summoning Henderson via to return to duty.

"We" have no radiation weapons. Not *"you."*
Luis.

He was halfway to the bridge when his wrister sounded again. DiCaria's face sprang into holo image.

"Captain, we've detected the Landry fleet coming from Prometheus. They're about thirty hours out."

56

NEW CALIFORNIA

Sloan, an old man who hadn't ever slept much, had now given up sleep almost completely. He knew he needed that restorative, that his health was suffering, but he didn't sleep. Not introspective, he didn't realize that he was punishing himself for what he saw as his failure. His admitted reason, just as true, was that he was learning.

SueLin's speech a week ago had calmed the city. She hadn't appeared in public again, which was probably a good thing, although now and again the Link aired short, bland speeches Sloan had written for her. She'd recorded these without much interest. Small protests still broke out on New California, but mostly people believed that the Movement had brought Peregoy Corporation to its knees, that SueLin was now CEO, that she was the reason the arrests and fighting and conscription had eased. The actual reason, Sloan knew, was Sophia's continued absence.

For the last week, he'd given general orders and then let each corporate division run on routine. When routine wasn't sufficient, he let his bewildered division heads do what they thought best. In defeat, Sloan had found a new, infinitely painful purpose.

During the day, he had people brought to his office, one by one. He'd wanted to talk to Scott Berman, but Berman could not be found. Sloan sat across a table—not his desk—from the people brought into him. He kept Chavez with him because he had no choice, but no other security was allowed in the room. Of each person brought to him, Sloan asked what he or she thought about the riots in the city, the Peregoy Corporation, their lives. Some refused to say anything but what they thought he wanted to hear. Some refused to talk to him at all. But some spoke passionately.

"The so-called 'protestors' captured a transport on Keeler Street, at the edge of the city," said a Planetary Defense soldier, his face creased in disgust. "They disarmed the four of us inside and made us watch while they set the transport on fire, shouting slogans and other stupid shit. Then an army flyer came over and burned 'em all, vaporized 'em to ashes. They got what they deserved, treasonous bastards."

Sloan said nothing. The soldier wore gear Sloan didn't recognize and hadn't authorized, added to a Peregoy Corporation Security uniform dating from before either "treason" or "army flyers" existed.

A woman, plucked from the protestors and dragged into Sloan's office, refused to sit down. She glared at him, hands clasped tightly in front of her. "You think you 'took care' of us so well, Director. Gave us work, housing, education, medical care. Well, you did. But you didn't give us freedom, and that's more important than anything else. My daughter wanted to become a doctor. The testing people said no, she's better suited to be an engineer, we need engineers, blah blah blah. No way for her to even take the tests for medical school—'Not on the approved list.' She hates engineering school. Cries every night. Sometimes I'm afraid she'll kill herself. *You* did that."

Sloan didn't say *A girl who might kill herself wouldn't have made a good doctor.* He said nothing. He listened.

A Link journalist told Sloan how news that was "treasonous" had been suppressed on public Links, underground news channels closed, reporters jailed, the Link monitored for dissent. Sloan knew about the monitoring but had paid little attention to it; Sophia had controlled Public Relations. The new controls had been put into place, with astonishing swiftness, during the months Sloan had been marooned on Polyglot.

"Now," the journalist finished, "you'll put me in jail, too. Before you do, tell me what happened on Horton Island!"

None of Sloan's sources had been able to tell him where the deadly Horton Island pathogen had been created, stored, disseminated. That argued that it was not on New California or New Yosemite. Where?

He listened to more protestors, to low-level Corporation employees, to Link experts, to people brought up from prison. Peregoy security looked at each other quizzically as they escorted each person past the stuffed wolves at the entrance to Sloan's office. Sloan realized that he had never really listened before, except to Sophia. Now he made himself pay attention to the stories brought to him—often brought by force, yes, but no less true for that. His listening was more than intel. It was education, accusation, and atonement.

He'd begun right after he learned that the retinal transplant research, for which he'd so proudly recruited scientists on Peregoy, was using executed political prisoners as a source of fresh eyes.

At night, instead of sleeping, he read. So much of what he'd heard during the day held echoes of things Luis had said to him over the years, as if what was happening on New California was no more than echoes of things that had happened on Terra, no more than variations on a theme. Sloan read the histories Luis had once urged on him, and which he'd dismissed as irrelevant.

"The plain truth of events which happened and will according to human nature happen again. It was written not for the moment but for all time." Someone very ancient called Thucydides, but that history was too convoluted and the book too difficult, and Sloan abandoned it.

Samuel Peregoy, the Terran founder of Peregoy Corporation who had claimed and colonized New California, came from the United States. Sloan accessed a book of United States history, written for youngsters. Much easier to read than Thucydides. He'd already known a great deal about the state of the country in Samuel's time: the terrible climate changes, the biowarfare, the government's arduous efforts to ensure that business could continue so that food and energy could reach the people. To do that, of course, the government had had to allocate itself considerable power. That only made sense.

However, the book written for children described much earlier history, when the United States had rebelled against power. Colonies, lawful subjects of someplace called England, had decided they didn't want that. They'd wrecked everything with war—a war they had no right to wage. People died, businesses were ruined, plantations burned. Shameful.

Only... the book maintained that England had misused its power. The book for children ended with an unchildish quote, from what seemed to be a journalist: "They that can give up essential liberty to obtain a little temporary safety deserve neither liberty nor safety." Benjamin Franklin. Ridiculous! The safety and well-being of those under his care had always come first with Sloan, and that required control.

Only... journalists were being jailed. Young people were being told what careers they must pursue. The army was vaporizing citizens in the streets, without any trial. And there was another quote, from a book Luis had especially championed: *A Short History of Governmental Forms and Outcomes:*

"Unlimited power is apt to corrupt the minds of those who possess it." William Pitt, a leader of that same England.

Sloan lost weight. The lines on his face deepened into ravines. He walked more slowly, and a headache low at the back of his skull would not leave him no matter what meds he took. He read on. Each night of each day he listened to people describe how the Peregoy worlds were falling apart, each day he wondered where Sophia was, why she had not communicated with him, how things could have come to this with her.

And then a final passage, before he stopped all

reading, from an unknown author: "'We have four boxes with which to defend our freedom: the soap box, the ballot box, the jury box, and the cartridge box.'" Author disputed.

Sloan blanked his tablet. Lying on his bed in the dark, he felt his eyes prickle, and then tears slide through the topographical map of his face. He didn't try to stop them, or wipe them off. Instead, he turned his mind to what he still, despite everything, thought of as a corporate problem. Only problem-solving could offer any consolation at all for his monumental failures.

A Short History of Governmental Forms and Outcomes had made clear what the outcome of this terrible time could *not* be. Sophia could not be Sloan's heir as CEO. Her need for power had done just what William Pitt predicted. Sophia would need to be removed and restrained, and it broke Sloan's heart. She would hate him.

Luis Martinez could not become CEO. He was military, and the protestors would see him as a Peregoy puppet, no matter what Martinez did.

SueLin as heir was out of the question. So was her mother, Candace, who had never wanted anything to do with business, governance, or responsibility for even her own children.

SueLin's brother, Tarik, was five years old.

So—when this war was over, if the Landrys did not win, who would run the Peregoy worlds?

And how?

57

NEW UTAH

Thirty hours. That's how far out the Landry fleet was from New Utah. Martinez had thirty hours to either retreat through the New Utah-New Yosemite gate or try to save the planet, the thirty-eight officers held hostage downstairs, and possibly the rest of the Peregoy worlds. All without radiation weapons.

He needed to force Scott Berman, or whoever had ended up in charge on New Utah, to listen to him. Hourly the *Skyhawk* had been trying to raise the planet, with no response. He needed something new to arouse them.

Unless, of course, the milder version of *J. randi* hadn't been that mild after all, and they were all dead.

"Bring Caitlin Landry to the bridge," he linked to Henderson on his wrister. The guard's face registered brief surprise before saying, "Yes, sir."

Caitlin came blinking sleep out of her eyes. Her gaze swept around the bridge, full of officers and soldiers and data on wallscreens. Under truth drugs, she'd said that she'd never been aboard a Landry warship. The last of sleep left her eyes and she studied everything. Martinez couldn't begin to guess how much she understood.

He had already told her what he wanted her to do. On the viewscreen Elizabeth Vondenberg, linked in from the *Green Hills of Earth*, pressed her lips tightly together and set her brows in a straight-across line. Vondenberg didn't know Caitlin the way Martinez did.

Did he really know her?

"I see," Caitlin said. "All right. Yes. I will."

Martinez opened contact with the planet. "New Utah, this is Captain Luis Martinez on the *Skyhawk*. I have made repeated attempts to contact you and received no response. Here is someone else to explain the gravity of your situation. If you won't listen to me, perhaps you will to her."

Caitlin stepped in front of the screen. "This is Caitlin Landry, Rachel Landry's granddaughter. You probably don't have my retina scan in your database, but I'm going to lean very close, just in case. Otherwise, you'll have to just I.D. me visually. I was captured by this Peregoy warship while on my way to New Prometheus to try to destroy the bioweapons lab built there by my sister, Jane Landry, commander of the Freedom Enterprises fleet. I have an important message for everyone on New Utah. No one is compelling me to say this. I want to say it. I want to help stop this war. New Utah, please respond."

No reply. Vondenberg looked stony.

Caitlin said, "I'm a biologist. I helped create the sickness that has infected you all. I did that because

I believe it's the only way to protect you against the virulent form of the disease, which my sister is bringing to your planet. She will kill you all, as an act of war. I *know* this. I also know that right now you're sick, but not very sick. In another day or so you'll recover. But you won't recover from what Jane is bringing to you. You'll all die, and die horribly. You've seen the images."

Caitlin paused, waiting for a response. Nothing.

"The Landry ships are thirty hours out. Whoever is in charge down there, please act now. Talk to Captain Martinez. Would I, a Landry, be warning you about my sister if I didn't know what she would do and if I didn't want to help stop it? What I'm doing now— what I did in the creation of the milder version of the virus—is against Landry interests. I'm a traitor to the Landry Libertarian Alliance, and because of what I'm doing, I'll never be able to go home again. Why would I do this if not to help stop this horrible and unnecessary war?

"New Utah, please at least talk to us!"

Silence.

And then the screen brightened and Christine Hoffman appeared.

Her young face shone with sweat, her eyes with fever. Her scowl could have killed saplings. But she said shakily, "You *are* Caitlin Landry."

"Yes. Who are you? Are you in charge?"

"Compatriot Scott Berman is in charge. But he's still too sick to talk."

Caitlin nodded. From his position behind her, Martinez watched her short curls bob on the back of her neck. She said, "He'll be better by tomorrow."

"Some of us are better now. But I speak for Compatriot Berman."

Oh, Christ, she and Berman must be romantically involved. Martinez could think of no other reason why a competent leader would leave decisions to someone as hysterical as this woman had proved herself to be. Martinez should have realized it earlier. And what had happened to John, the thug who'd beaten Naomi Halstead?

Caitlin said, "What's your name, please?"

"Compatriot Christine Hoffman."

"Christine, I hope you believe me when I say my sister is thirty hours out with a bioweapon that will not only kill everyone on New Utah but also everyone else on the other Peregoy worlds it's carried to."

"I do believe you," Hoffman said bitterly. "Leaders and owners are capable of anything. Sloan Peregoy used a bioweapon on prisoners on an island on New California. Compatriots of ours."

"I heard that," Caitlin said. "And I'm an owner, too. You know that. But I am telling the truth."

"I know you are because we're not all dead."

"What needs to happen," Caitlin said steadily, "is for Captain Martinez to install your radiation weapons on this ship. He will try to stop my sister. I know you were—"

"Why can't he use his own weapons?"

"I know you were told that the two Peregoy ships have radiation weapons," Caitlin said, and Martinez felt his throat tense. This was the crux. "But they don't. They had to strip the ships of radiation weapons to get through a gate."

"So we were lied to again!" Hoffman shouted,

and Martinez watched her face change from quasi-reasonable to outrage.

"Yes," Caitlin said, "but not by me, Christine—*not by me*. This is the first time I've talked to you, and you know that everything else I've told you is true. You're in charge down there. You want to save all your people. I can't prove to you anything I'm saying, but it is the truth. And it's your only chance against my sister." Caitlin took a deep breath. "Who is crazy. She is."

Hoffman's face had purpled. She was going to accuse Caitlin of being a Peregoy pawn, she was going to cut communications, she was going to shut down her deluded band of idealists' last chance for survival—

Instead Hoffman said, "Your sister is crazy?"

"Yes."

"So are some people here." And then, in almost a whisper, "I want to believe you. Scott...he's very sick. Sicker than the rest. The antivirals don't work."

"No, they wouldn't," Caitlin said, "not against this new pathogen. Are you giving him antibiotics against a secondary infection?"

"We don't have any left."

"I'm sorry," Caitlin said, and in her voice Martinez heard what neither he nor Vondenberg could have given: genuine sympathy for a person afraid that her loved one would die. The little picture, lost for Martinez in gazing at the larger one.

Caitlin added, "Give him a lot of fluids and don't let him get out of bed."

Hoffman said, "I will talk with Captain Martinez."

Before he stepped forward into the holofield, Martinez had a moment of dizzying unreality. His military operation had been made possible by two civilians conferring over a sick lover. His military operation was necessary because a mystic lunatic had closed gates, forcing warships to strip off their weapons. The warships were in play because some Landry had done something "by accident." The war had shifted from standard space battles to biowarfare directed by two women who were both nominally subject to two leaders who had never wanted war in the first place.

The moment passed, and Martinez fastened firmly on the here-and-now. He outlined to Christine Hoffman what he planned to do.

There wasn't enough time, but this was what they had.

Martinez sent DiCaria to New Utah in the class 6A vessel that had brought resupplies from New Yosemite. Twenty-five crew rode downstairs to Cascade City. "Maybe I'll keep this ship," DiCaria said. "Much better quarters than on the *Skyhawk*."

"Don't get too used to luxury," Martinez answered. Both attempts at easing tension fell flat.

Martinez would have preferred to go to New Utah himself, but he had to hold off his exposure to *J. randi mansueti* as long as possible, which would be twenty hours after DiCaria was exposed. The exec had only that long to remove what planetary defense weapons he could, load them onto the *Princess Ida*, and transport them to the *Skyhawk*. Then six hours to install the weapons upstairs, while lead data specialist Tiana Stevenson took software control of orbital defenses. None of it would be much use against K-beams, but Martinez didn't know for sure that Jane Landry had

K-beams. Maybe she had been delayed obtaining more pathogen. At any rate, the New Utah weapons were what he had.

During installation, everyone on the *Skyhawk* would be exposed to the cowpox option. Two days later, people would fall ill from their protection against the more virulent virus—at least, anyone who survived the battle.

Meanwhile, the *Green Hills of Earth* had come alongside the *Skyhawk*. Vondenberg had not liked this part of the OpOrd. Martinez had listened to her reasoning, as he always did, and then overrode it. People were being transferred between ships; Martinez would send all non-necessary personnel through the gate to safety at New Yosemite, along with both the *Zeus* and the *Green Hills of Earth*. The enemy had three warships on the way. Vondenberg's and Murphy's weaponless vessels would be no help. Better to save both for future battles.

Martinez watched DiCaria's vessel descend to New Utah.

If Christine Hoffman had been deceiving him, if she—or any other of the rabid lunatics down there—fired on the ship, then DiCaria was dead. Martinez had a backup plan for that, but he didn't want to use it.

New Utah didn't fire. The small ship landed and its crew were taken to the command area where not only Hoffman but also Scott Berman waited. Following DiCaria's transmitted images, Martinez now saw that it was an underground bunker at the spaceport, equipped for war-room status. Good.

"Berman," Martinez said. "You're better."

"No, he's not," Hoffman snapped. "But he insisted."

Berman looked bad. Raspy breathing, sweat gleaming on his forehead, head shaky when he tried to lift it from the robogurney. But he was here, which Martinez respected.

Martinez said, "Please widen the holofield so I can see the whole room."

Berman whispered, "Do it."

Now Martinez could see DiCaria's crew already at work, disconnecting control mechanisms for the radiation weapons around the continent. Techs had been dispatched to the weapon sites themselves; Hoffman had had all the necessary transport ready. Martinez was reassured. Their cooperation was genuine.

"Compatriots," he said, not allowing himself any distaste at the silly title, "here is what we're going to do."

58

NEW UTAH

Twenty hours after he'd left for the surface of New Utah, DiCaria's team returned to the *Skyhawk*, hauling upstairs a load of planetary defense weapons. Everyone in Cascade City who'd been able to drag themselves from sick beds had helped remove, transport, and load the weaponry.

"Well done," Martinez said to DiCaria. "I'm sorry they wouldn't let you see your sister." Berman had kept the PCSS thirty-eight officers. Trust extended only so far. Martinez understood; if this plan succeeded, the Movement might still have to negotiate with Sloan.

DiCaria said, "At least Serena's still alive. Or so they said."

DiCaria didn't look sick, merely exhausted. But he would be sick, and Martinez had made sure that everyone remaining aboard the *Skyhawk* was exposed to *J. randi mansueti*, including himself.

He sent half of DiCaria's team to the *Green Hills of Earth*, just before Vondenberg took her through the gate to New Yosemite. DiCaria's exhausted crew, who had been awake nearly forty hours, would roam the corridors of the *Green Hills of Earth*, breathing on everybody. Then Sean Mueller would arrange for the cowpox option to be carried downstairs.

Martinez said, "Zack, tell your men to get some sleep. We'll need them eight or nine hours from now. You, too."

"Yes, sir. Sir . . ."

"That's an order."

DiCaria stumbled from the bridge. Martinez checked on the progress of the weapons installation and diagnostics. Then he went to Caitlin's cabin.

It was important that everyone aboard the *Skyhawk* be infected.

Henderson had already been dismissed. Caitlin Landry had played one important part in Martinez's plans, and would play another. She was not going to try to sabotage anything, or to take her own life, or to play any of the other nasty tricks that prisoners were prone to. She was no longer a prisoner. There was a strong chance that neither of them would survive the coming battle, but if they did, she too needed to have the protection of the cowpox option.

She rose from her table as he came into the cabin. When her gaze met his, her eyes widened. Later, he couldn't have said which of them moved first, or faster. Her arms went up around his neck, he crushed her close, and their lips met.

Almost sweet enough to die for.

When the kiss finally ended, she said softly, "Luis." Just that.

"Caitlin . . ."

"Don't say it. Don't say anything. I know the odds,

and I know we can't...even if we survive, we can't. Kiss me again."

He did. She said, "Is there time to..."

"No." He wanted it, wanted her more than any woman since Amy. But he had to return to the bridge; in an emergency he could not be found with his uniform around his ankles, making love to his prisoner-of-war-turned-defector.

She pulled slightly away and smiled up at him. "So that kiss was just your way of infecting me with a plague."

God, he'd never known such gallantry. He tried to meet it. "Yes, no more than that."

She laughed at him. "Uh-huh. Go back to the bridge, Luis."

"Someone will bring you there when it's time."

"All right. We have a saying on Galt...no, never mind, it's stupid."

"Tell me anyway." He wanted everything he could have from her, even if it was a stupid Libertarian saying.

"'Do the profitable thing.' That's supposed to be what's best for everyone. And you know what—it *is*. Only 'profitable' doesn't always mean money. Not here, not now. Profit everyone, Luis."

"Caitlin, I—"

"No, don't say it now. You don't need the complication. I'm sorry. Go now, before we both get too riled up."

The moment he closed her door behind him and started down the corridor, Martinez saw how right she'd been. He needed to be calm, focused. There would be time later.

Or not. In which case, she already knew how he felt about her. Next to that, words hardly mattered.

Words, however, would be his first attack on Jane Landry. Christine Hoffman and Scott Berman were ready, Caitlin was ready, the Peregoy crew was ready. And if words failed, he was once again armed. Or would be when the installation crew finished.

Five hours till battle.

When Martinez opened communication with Jane Landry, she was nearing New Utah. She had not attempted to link with the *Skyhawk*, although of course Peregoy and Landry vessels had recorded and analyzed each other's emission signals. The largest of the Landry fleet was a D-class warship named the *Raptor*. Not subtle, Caitlin's sister. Martinez felt briefly grateful that he'd been an only child.

"*Raptor*, this is the Peregoy Corporation Space Service ship *Skyhawk*, Captain Luis Martinez commanding. Do not approach New Utah. Repeat, do not approach New Utah. We are equipped with weapons that will destroy your entire fleet at greater range than you can reach us. Retreat now."

Martinez had expected a delay, but Jane Landry's face immediately appeared on the viewscreen. She was beautiful, far more beautiful than Caitlin, a face out of legend. Her bright green eyes gleamed with madness.

"Martinez. You're lying. Even if you installed planetary defense weapons from New Utah, you don't have the advanced weaponry I do. You have one ship and I have three. You're dead, Martinez. You have nothing."

"Are you sure of that? And I have at least one thing—your sister."

A crewman thrust Caitlin into the viewfield, her hands bound with tanglefoam, her hair disheveled, a bruise on her cheek. Martinez watched Jane's eyes widen. He said calmly, "I'm willing to negotiate."

All at once Caitlin screamed, "He's lying! The planet wouldn't let him take any weapons they're in rebellion and—"

She was knocked out of the viewfield, falling to the deck.

DiCaria cut the link. A moment later the screen brightened again, this time showing the war room on New Utah. Martinez spared only one glance at Caitlin, rising to her feet and cradling her left arm. Her face distorted in pain. Martinez kept his attention planetside. *Come on, Landry . . .*

Two long minutes later, Jane's voice came from the war-room viewscreen on New Utah. Martinez couldn't see her viewscreen but he could hear her. Jane said, "This is the Freedom Enterprises ship *Raptor*, Commander-in-Chief Jane Landry. Come in, New Utah." And then, almost childishly peeved, "I know that you know we're here."

Scott Berman—not Christine Hoffman—said, "This is Compatriot Berman on New Utah."

Martinez leaned forward, as if that would bring Berman into view. Berman sounded weak, and Martinez hoped to hell that Jane didn't realize how sick Berman still was. It was supposed to be Christine who spoke to the *Raptor*. She would have sounded properly agitated. Although maybe Berman was preferable, after all. Christine wasn't a good liar.

Was Berman?

He said warmly, "Welcome, *Raptor*, from the Libertarian Alliance. We've taken New Utah from the oppressors at Peregoy Corporation. You don't know what it has meant to us to have the Landry worlds as models of freedom, places where people aren't owned by Peregoy Corporation."

Silence. Everything now depended on Jane's response. Berman said, "Commander Landry?"

Nothing.

"Are you there?"

The silence stretched on. Into it, Lieutenant Pettigrew at the space-monitoring console said diffidently, "Sir, I'm getting some strange readings at seventeen degrees."

Martinez said sharply, "Radiation signature?"

"Not weapons. It . . . wait, it's gone."

"Monitor the area and don't report unless it seems dangerous."

Pettigrew said, "Yes, sir."

Jane's voice said, "Prove it, Berman. Prove you've taken the planet away from Peregoy Corporation. You can't, can you? You're lying."

"I'm not lying. And I *can* prove it. Look."

Martinez could see what happened next; both screens faced the door of the underground bunker. The door opened. A man dragged in Naomi Halstead, still in uniform, unable to stand. Martinez felt his jaw tighten. Halstead had been beaten again. Bruises purpled her face, although they were not fresh. Probably left from "John," whom Martinez would settle with one day. But the blood running down her face *was* fresh, although that didn't mean the injury was serious. Head wounds bled a lot.

The PCSS officers following her walked upright, although bound. Five men, three women, all in uniform. At least four of them looked ill: lingering *J. randi mansueti.* From the sudden stiffening of DiCaria's shoulders, Martinez knew that the lieutenant JG was his sister.

Berman said, "This is what's left of the Peregoy Planetary Defense officer corps. We sent the enlisted people, all conscripts by Sophia Peregoy's new laws, through the gate to New Yosemite. They're just as much victims as were the Movement members killed on Horton Island, in the Peregoy labor camp there. You know about Horton Island?"

No answer. Jane Landry was considering. Martinez hoped.

Berman continued. "There were thirty-eight Peregoy officers on New Utah. The rest have been executed. As these will be, in time. For now, they're alive in case Sloan Peregoy sends warships with nuclear weapons through the New Yosemite gate to bomb us."

All at once Berman's voice grew stronger, vibrating with passion. "We don't want New Utah to be a Peregoy world, but we don't want it to be a Landry world, either. We want to be free! You're Libertarian, General—you must understand that! All humans deserve the dignity of making their own choices and, if they must, enduring the consequences of those choices. We will trade with Freedom Enterprises, establishing contracts and cooperation. We compatriots have risked everything for that dignity, which we should have had by *right*. We want to be allies of the Landry Libertarian Alliance. Martinez is as much our enemy as yours. We turned our planetary defense weapons on his two other ships and destroyed them. The *Skyhawk* escaped, out of our range now—but maybe not of yours. Destroy it. The ship is weaponless."

Into the silence on the bridge of the *Skyhawk*, DiCaria said softly, "Scout leaving the *Raptor* for New Utah."

"Understood," Martinez said. The Landry scout had a dual purpose, which everyone on the bridge understood. Jane wanted to see if Martinez would—or could—fire on it. If he didn't, the scout would request permission to land, and then would rain down the deadly version of *J. randi*. More efficient than launching canisters from the *Raptor*.

Martinez waited. The scout streaked past the *Skyhawk*. Jane said, "Berman, I'm sending down an officer to negotiate with you. Lieutenant McAuliffe. You will show him every courtesy."

"Of course," Berman said. To Martinez, his voice sounded weaker.

Minutes passed.

More minutes.

And more.

Waiting—it was always the worst.

59

THE ELEVENTH GATE

Rachel lay on the bridge of the *Kezia Landry*. Her pallet took up half the floor, crowding the other four people: Tara standing tensely on the balls of her bare feet, the pilot and two techs intent at their consoles.

"Prepare to fire," Tara said, even though she was not commanding weaponry. From her low pallet, Rachel gazed up at the viewscreen. The eleventh gate glowed against the blackness of space.

Are you there, Philip Anderson?

No one knew. Certainly Rachel did not. She knew only one thing, and though halting speech had returned to her since her stroke, she had not tried to communicate that one thing to her granddaughter. Tara had a job to do here. A job Rachel had handed her, a job that Tara didn't fully understand, a job both desperate and possibly ludicrous, but a job nonetheless. Tara was doing it. Rachel would not distract her with the irrelevancy of her grandmother's pain, for which Rachel refused to take meds that would further cloud her mind. Nor with the irrelevancy of her dying.

Her mind was intact, although it drifted sometimes, confusing the present and the precious past. Once, she thought that Tara was her dead son Paul, but that only lasted a moment. Between drifts, Rachel's mind could follow the actions that she herself had set in motion.

"Fire," Tara said, and chief tech Hallie Dunn activated the equipment that emitted bursts of particles at sixty per minute, aimed directly at the closed eleventh gate.

Recognize it, Philip. He had boated so often on Polyglot—or was that Paul, sailing his little boat on Mirror Lake on Galt? Rachel had bought him the boat for his fifteenth birthday. But surely Philip, too, had boated...yes, he had. Bigger boats, doing marine research. Boats that used, if necessary, the old Terran distress signal of timed bursts of white light, sixty per minute. SOS...no, that was another code, Paul had learned it as a little boy, in the Galt Ranger troop...

"Repeat," Tara said, and all at once Rachel's mind cleared of the past, of her own spent body, of everything but what was happening at the eleventh gate.

Matloff.

Basich.

Varennes.

The field of consciousness.

The entire gate dimmed, brightened, dimmed again. Three short, three long, three short. So Philip had once, in that unknown boyhood on Polyglot, also played at ancient codes.

"Philip," Tara said, with such naked longing that

Rachel was almost ashamed to hear it. "Hallie, do it again!"

The bursts were repeated, but this time there was no response from the gate.

Tara crumbled. "He's gone!"

"No," Rachel rasped from the floor even though it took all her remaining strength, "he...*it*...is working."

60

NEW UTAH

DiCaria said, "Scout entering the atmosphere...scatter canisters launched."

Somewhere behind Martinez, Caitlin made a small, strangled sound. Perhaps she hadn't really believed Jane would do it. Martinez had never doubted that she would. He'd seen the bodies on the *Dagny Taggart*.

DiCaria said, "Enemy ship heading toward us... the *Eagle*."

"Track with armed weaponry."

"Tracking."

Contempt washed through Martinez; Jane Landry was not even going to fight him with her own ship. A coward as well as an insane murderer.

From his console, Pettigrew said uncertainly, "Space anomaly has reappeared, sir."

"A weapon?"

"No, sir. It...I don't know what it is, sir. Some sort of disturbance in space."

"Ignore it unless danger presents." This was not the time for astronomical speculation. Despite Martinez's not shooting down the enemy scout, Jane Landry might—or might not—believe Caitlin and Berman that the *Skyhawk* was unarmed. Martinez might have surprise on his side, but he didn't have much else. His crew was already at battle stations. Caitlin had been removed from the bridge, her part played, and played well.

Jane Landry reappeared on the open link. "Martinez, I want to negotiate for my sister."

"I'm listening."

"Send a scout to my ship with Caitlin aboard. Once I have her, the *Skyhawk* can go through the gate to New Yosemite. I won't fire on you."

She was lying, and not very well. The *Eagle* was moving toward the stargate. If Jane Landry thought that Martinez possessed radiation weapons, it wouldn't have been necessary to block the gate since the *Skyhawk* couldn't have escaped through it. So she'd believed Scott Berman, or Caitlin, or both, that all planetary defense weaponry remained on New Utah and the *Skyhawk* was helpless. The *Eagle* wasn't moving into firing range of the *Skyhawk*, not by the usual radiation weapons. But in a few minutes it might have the *Skyhawk* in K-beam range, while the *Raptor* was staying well to the rear.

A K-beam was on the *Eagle*. And there might be only one. After all, it didn't make sense for her to have installed more than one on Prometheus to defend her biolab, and she couldn't have gotten K-beams through the gates from Galt.

Martinez signaled DiCaria, at the conn, to move

away from the *Eagle* and toward the *Raptor*. To Jane
Landry he said, "Agreed—Caitlin Landry goes to your
ship and mine goes through to New Yosemite. However, all *Skyhawk* scouts have already been deployed.
We'll move close enough to send Caitlin Landry on
a vacuum sled."

"No," Landry said. She believed that Martinez was
helpless, but no commander, even an insane one, would
let him get that close. Even without radiation weapons,
he could have old-fashioned nuclear torpedoes. "Stay
where you are. I'll send a scout to you."

"Agreed."

She couldn't believe he was that stupid—could she?
Martinez had been in the military all his life; he'd
encountered his share of megalomaniacal officers who
overestimated their own cunning and underestimated
everyone else's. Their careers usually went down in
flames. But Jane Landry, new at this and in sole corporate command, hadn't had any superiors to evaluate
or rein her in. And Caitlin said that once Jane fixed
her mind on an idea, she was obsessive.

Martinez said, "Advancing at half speed to meet
your scout." That would bring the *Skyhawk* within
radiation firing range of the *Raptor*, but not within
reliable torpedo range.

Jane said sharply, "Stay where you are!"

The *Eagle* had stopped moving. It hovered between
Martinez and the gate, out of even K-beam range to
hit the *Skyhawk*. DiCaria, as arranged, suddenly sped
the *Skyhawk* at full speed toward the *Raptor*. At the
farthest possible effective range, Martinez said, "Fire."

The *Raptor* was already in retreat, rather than
returning fire: Jane Landry had panicked. But whoever

had the *Raptor's* conn was good. Martinez's beam caught the *Raptor* only glancingly before it was out of range. He couldn't be sure how much damage he'd inflicted. The *Skyhawk* retreated rapidly. If Martinez was wrong, if the *Raptor* had K-beams, then everyone on the *Skyhawk* was dead.

The *Raptor* fired—conventional beams. The *Skyhawk's* defense program evaded them.

Jane Landry, the nonprofessional, let out a stream of obscenities that made the standby medic blink.

Martinez gave a rapid stream of instructions, to which DiCaria responded instantly. The *Skyhawk* needed to avoid both answering fire from the *Raptor* and the more lethal K-beam from the *Eagle*. The *Eagle* sped toward them, but since both ships were moving at maximum speed, the *Eagle* couldn't get into firing range.

For several minutes he led the *Eagle* away from New Utah, the distance between the two ships not closing. Eventually the *Eagle* gave up chasing him and reversed course, back to New Utah. To do what? Not scourge the planet; Jane Landry wanted its Peregoy rebels to develop the infection she'd seeded there. The inhabitants of New Utah were her lab rats, before she took the infection to the other two Peregoy worlds, and she wanted to watch them die in agony.

Martinez said, "Course to circle wide around New Utah and approach from side opposite to the *Eagle*."

"Yes, sir."

Several more tense minutes. Jane Landry had cut communication, and Martinez had to guess what was happening on the *Raptor*. How badly had he hit it? The third ship had moved closer to the *Raptor*—was the flagship damaged badly enough to need evacuation? If so, it would be Martinez's first lucky break. The *Eagle* sped toward both Landry vessels, undoubtedly to protect them.

"Sir . . ." DiCaria said.

"Hold course. Put the planet between us and the Landry fleet."

"Sir!" Pettigrew said, and at her tone, Martinez turned toward her. If this was another astronomical weather report . . .

Pettigrew and DiCaria said together, as if choreographed, "Ship emerging from the gate!" In any other circumstances, their synchronicity might have been amusing.

These were not other circumstances.

DiCaria said, "It's one of ours. D-class warship." A moment later the viewscreen sprang to life. It wasn't Jane Landry.

It was Sophia Peregoy.

61

THE ELEVENTH GATE

At the Observer's gate, there is a disturbance.

Bursts of radiation, not dangerous but rapid and regular, hit the gate. Pause. Repeat. Pause. Repeat.

The Observer stirs.

Memory, a pattern within consciousness, finds nothing in space to match these bursts.

Rapid and regular bursts. Pause. Repeat. Pause. Repeat.

The quantum patterns of memory make different matches. The Observer has no words but it has the concept: danger. The regular, rapid bursts mean danger.

There is no danger to the Observer in the closed system of the gate.

Rapid and regular bursts. Pause. Repeat. Pause. Repeat.

The Observer extends itself beyond the gate. Instantly, it exists everywhere, entangled with everything. Instantly, the Observer begins to lose coherence and energy. The sub-field begins again to decay. The Observer returns to the gate, but not before it observes all.

The tiny nodes of consciousness, encased in the macro-level matter of a ship, hover just outside.

Elsewhere, ships with dangerous radiation signatures once more approach a planet, even though the Observer closed all gates to those signatures.

Danger to all the small nodes on or near that planet.

62

NEW UTAH

"Martinez," said Sophia Peregoy on the bridge view-screen, her face colder than space itself, "you are hereby relieved of all duty. Court martial to follow. Immediately relinquish your ship to your exec. You are under arrest for treason."

Pettigrew said urgently, "*Sir...*"

Martinez ignored Pettigrew, staring back at Sophia. He kept his voice as icy as hers. "There are three Landry ships here, at least one of them equipped with a K-beam. That ship is the *Eagle* and it can annihilate you. I am sending what is known of firing range and capacity."

He expected Sophia to respond to this. She didn't.

"Relinquish command immediately, Martinez."

"On whose authority?" Was Sloan dead?

"Mine."

"I report only to Director Peregoy."

"He is incapacitated. I am Acting Director."

Was that even true? Martinez said, "The *Eagle* is moving toward you."

Sophia's posture didn't change by a millimeter, but her ship, the *Savannah*, shifted to face the oncoming *Eagle* as if to fire. Fire what? She couldn't have arrived through a gate equipped with radiation weapons, could she? What was she doing?

All at once, Martinez knew what she was doing. The *Savannah* began to move, at maximum speed, toward New Utah. The *Eagle* followed. Martinez ordered, "Get in orbit around New Utah. Keep both ships in sight but prepare to change speed as ordered. Weapons crew, stand by to fire."

The *Savannah* flew toward New Utah, the *Eagle* in pursuit. Martinez dropped into orbit, keeping the planet between the *Skyhawk* and the *Eagle*. He adjusted speed so that he emerged into view of the *Savannah* just as she launched the scout and sped away.

A maximum-speed launch like that was tricky. Whoever was captaining the *Savannah* was good, and so was the pilot on the scout. Martinez hoped it wasn't someone he knew, someone he'd served with, someone he now had to kill.

In another moment, the scout would enter the atmosphere and release its scatter canisters. Sophia, like Jane, wanted to exterminate the rebels on New Utah. Sophia, unlike Jane, didn't need lab rats. She knew her deadly genemod pathogen was effective. She'd tested it on Horton Island.

"Fire," Martinez said.

Just before the scout entered the atmosphere, a beam from the *Skyhawk* vaporized it. Martinez then barely had time to orbit around the curve of the planet before the *Eagle* fired a K-beam at him. It hit the ocean below. The *Eagle* streaked off in pursuit of the *Savannah*.

Martinez said, "Take up position near the gate."

"Yes, sir."

Sophia's face appeared on the viewscreen. "Luis—do you think I don't have more?"

He knew she did. Somewhere on New California or on New Yosemite or—most likely—on a secret station in deep space, a biolab was creating more deadly plague. The only way to stop Sophia's using it was to eliminate Sophia. Unless Sloan had also agreed to... but Martinez didn't believe that. Despite everything, he didn't believe it. If he was that wrong about Sloan, he was wrong about everything in his life.

Sophia cut the comm link. The *Savannah* made a huge circle, leading the *Eagle* back toward the gate. The *Savannah* would reach it first, in time to pass through to New Yosemite. Jane's ship, equipped with radiation weaponry, would not be able to follow. Nor could the *Skyhawk*. Sophia would escape, unless Martinez stopped her.

The *Raptor* and the third Landry ship began moving toward the gate.

Scott Berman appeared on the viewscreen. "Martinez, what the hell—"

"Later," he said, and his comm officer cut the link.

Martinez's world shrank to seven dots on a mental datascreen: three Landry ships. Sophia's ship. His own. The larger dot of New Utah. And the gate, a lacy sliver shimmer in the blackness of space.

The *Savannah* tore through space toward that shimmer. The *Eagle* pursued it, not closing distance,

but not lengthening it either. The other three Landry
ships also moved toward the gate. The *Skyhawk*,
closest, reached the gate first and turned to face the
oncoming vessels.

"Fire on my command," Martinez said.

He was going to vaporize Sophia's ship. Sophia,
Sloan's daughter, whom Sloan had wanted him to
marry. Sophia, who had conceived of and manufactured a monstrous bioweapon and was willing to use
it not only on the Landry worlds but on her own
citizens—*Sloan's* citizens, whom Martinez was required
to protect. He had no choice; he could not let her
escape back through the gate.

And after he vaporized Sophia, the K-weapon aboard
the *Eagle* would vaporize the *Skyhawk*.

DiCaria said steadily, "*Savannah* in five units of
firing range . . . four . . ."

Pettigrew yelled, with none of DiCaria's steadiness,
"Something is happening to space!"

63

THE ELEVENTH GATE

Consciousness consists of the ability to be influenced by its previous state and to influence its next state.

The Observer can act, or not act. If it acts, it may expend so much energy that it loses all coherence and becomes too diffuse to exist.

If it does not act, these tiny nodes will destroy each other, and perhaps many more.

The ships turn to face each other, in order to fire.

Once, the Observer was as they are now.

The Observer collapses a section of its own field of consciousness.

As always, observation changes the quantum fields. A dense concentration of spacetime forms, created of matter and energy, as waves collapse. It evolves, in a nanosecond, into matter and energy, as the Big Bang once did. It is, and is not, a black hole, made not of particles but of proto-consciousness growing ever more dense. Now it is dense enough to affect space around it, which ripples and twists and squashes.

With the last of its energy, the Observer stops all of spacetime from collapsing into the object. The Observer contains the rippling and twisting and squashing in a bubble, a sharply defined event horizon. Within the bubble, around the still forming object, spacetime obeys the laws of physics. As matter increases, time slows.

The Observer loses all energy, all coherence, and ceases to exist.

"He's gone," Tara said. And then, again, "He's gone."

64

NEW UTAH

A shimmer, almost like a gate. But not a gate, because there was the New Utah-New Yosemite gate apart from . . . *this*. The shimmer coalesced, turned dark at its center. Then all around it grew a . . . a what? A nothing that was nonetheless something, felt rather than seen. And all the data screens went crazy.

Gravity. The thing was generating enormous gravity.

"Retreat!" Martinez said. "Now!"

They barely made it. If DiCaria had not been so good at the conn, they would not have. Martinez felt his ship slow, even as the drive delivered maximum power. He felt the pull in his bones, and in the bones of his ship. Pettigrew said something and his words took minutes to emerge, hours, days.

"Sssssssssssiiiiiirrrrrr . . . bbblllaaaccckkkk hhhoooo—"

Then the ship gave a tremendous lurch and they were out of whatever it was. A moment later the data screens cleared. Martinez grabbed at a bulkhead to right himself and stared at the viewscreen.

No one, ever, had seen anything like this. No one. Ever.

The four other ships had been caught in the event horizon of whatever this was, the *Eagle* facing the *Savannah*, the other two farther off. All four were motionless. From the *Eagle*, a bright beam of radiation emerged, truncated and frozen in the act of aiming at the *Skyhawk*. The beam did not move, and neither did anything else within the bubble the new black hole—no, not a black hole, there was no *protective bubble* around a black hole. Something unknown with some of the same properties. Martinez knew enough physics to realize that the four ships were all falling toward the thing, but so slowly it might take years, decades, centuries to reach it. In a four-dimensional universe, compressing space dilated time.

Jane Landry and Sophia Peregoy would face each other in war until both of them were crushed by one of the primal forces of the universe.

Someone on the bridge gasped, "How..."

All at once, Martinez lurched, falling almost off his feet. The ship had not jerked. But for him the universe had just turned upside down, spilling out everything he thought he knew.

"Sir...?"

Martinez regained his footing. But he heard his voice quaver as he said, "Open comm link to New Utah."

The planet was intact. A tsunami hit the continent and the tides were tremendous, swamping several rocky islands. However, Cascade City was far enough inland that it could cope with the backwash coming up the river from the coast. Scott Berman, listening intently to all that Martinez told him, already sounded stronger.

"Send the image," Berman said. "Our orbital probes are gone, or have stopped transmitting."

Martinez sent the eerie image: four ships caught in a bubble, the barely discernible dark thing at its center, everything frozen in space and time. Although to everyone on the ships, time was passing normal-to-them—or was it? Ship's computer said the math did not add up. Not the math for the creation of a black hole, not the math for how much and where it exerted gravity, not the math for the survival of the planet, the gate, and the *Skyhawk* just outside that bubble. This was no normal black hole, no normal cosmic disturbance, no more than the gates themselves were "normal." This was inexplicable.

Philip Anderson?

Everything Martinez believed, everything he was, rejected that idea. But he had no other.

No one on the *Skyhawk* could stop looking at the image. Martinez would be glad when he could finally pass through the gate and leave the image behind.

He said to Berman, "I can't send the planetary-defense weaponry back to you." Cascade City was still a colony in rebellion to Peregoy Corporation.

"I know. But we kept enough to defend ourselves."

To defend themselves against Landry and Peregoys alike.

"Berman, I'll do what I can for you at Capitol City. But I want you to send up to me one of the PCSS officers, Lieutenant JG Serena Drucker. She's the sister of my executive officer."

Berman hesitated before agreeing. "All right. Are

you going to infect the other Peregoy worlds with the cowpox option?"

"I don't have any choice." Even as he spoke to Berman, Martinez was receiving reports of his crew starting to sicken with the epidemic that had been carried upstairs by DiCaria and his team. A few had gone to sick bay, although the others were carrying on: individual immune-system variations. Dr. Glynn would be kept busy.

Berman said, "Good luck, Martinez."

"You, too."

He broke the link, wishing that Scott Berman was not a pseudo-Libertarian rebel but instead an officer serving under Martinez. Although Berman wouldn't have appreciated the thought.

When he'd seen to everything possible on the bridge, Martinez went to Caitlin's cabin.

"You look terrible," she said. "Luis, you're getting sick."

"It's nothing. Just a headache."

"So far. Sit down before you fall down."

"I'm not going to fall down."

"Not if I hold you up. Luis, what happens now?"

"I sit down."

The room spun, and a brief vertigo swept over him, shocking him. He was never ill.

"I'm going to call your exec."

"Don't . . . I'm . . . just . . ."

"Who's next in command?"

But he'd passed out, falling from the chair onto the deck and then into the black hole of his own body. He never knew when the *Skyhawk* passed through the gate to New Yosemite.

❖   ❖   ❖

The luck of the genetic draw.

Martinez was the sickest person on the *Skyhawk*, felled by the cowpox option. He wouldn't die, but his fever was high enough to cause a brief period of delirium before meds took hold. When Dr. Glynn had finished with him, Caitlin sat by his bedside in sick bay, holding his hand, and to hell with anyone in the PCSS who eyed her distrustfully.

She was hardly ill at all, no more than a heavy cold would have caused. That was true of almost everyone else aboard ship and on New Utah. DiCaria, acting captain, didn't seem to have any reaction at all to *J. randi mansueti*. Not that he would have told Caitlin if he had.

"Amy," Martinez mumbled. "Gone."

His dead wife. Listening, watching his face, Caitlin knew she was learning more about Martinez than he would have voluntarily told her, this soon. Or perhaps at all. He'd loved Amy. He accepted that she was in his past.

Henderson, who had morphed from dour guard to dour messenger, stepped into the tiny curtained alcove and said, "Message from Lieutenant-Commander DiCaria. Approaching the gate."

"Thank you," Caitlin said. "Tell Mr. DiCaria there's no change in Captain Martinez."

"Doctor already said." Henderson left.

Unfriendly coldness was something Caitlin had better get used to. If she stayed with Luis, there would be a lot of it.

Did she want to stay with Luis? Did he want her to? Where? They had different lives, on different planets. However, if Peregoy worlds would be unfriendly to her, Landry worlds might be deadly. Caitlin had helped stop one—maybe two—epidemics. But she had also aided and abetted a wartime enemy to imprison the commander-in-chief of the Landry fleet in a time-dilated, slow-motion attack that might never end.

The viewscreen on the sick-bay bulkhead had remained dark. Caitlin couldn't bear to look at that frozen tableau in space, four ships caught in an astronomical anomaly that no one could explain. That should not exist. Jane's—what? You couldn't call it "death," exactly—would haunt Caitlin forever.

But the *Skyhawk*, its radiation weapons now jettisoned, was approaching the New Utah-New Yosemite gate. That would be on the viewscreen now. "On," Caitlin said, and watched the mysterious familiar shimmer grow larger and larger, until it engulfed the *Skyhawk*, the ship emerged, and another Peregoy world spun below her.

65

THE ELEVENTH GATE

It was over now. Rachel had done what she could, everything she could. Whatever had happened, it had occurred far from the eleventh gate, wherever Philip-that-had-been was stopping Jane, or was not stopping Jane. Was stopping Tara's war, or was not stopping Tara's war. Had Rachel ever told anyone else what Tara had done, how all this had started? She couldn't remember.

She was so tired.

But the pain had gone, leaving only the tiredness, and that was not so bad. Tiredness meant sleep, meant restful quiet, and Rachel was ready for that. She was ready to let go. Others must take over now, Annelise and Celia and Caitlin, if Caitlin was alive still...

Caitlin was alive. Caitlin was a little girl, frolicking with Paul in the garden on Galt, kicking a ball to her father and sisters. Annelise shouted, "Here, Daddy, here!" while Jane laughed and dove for the ball into a bed of bright red boli flowers. Paul kicked the recovered ball to Annelise, who missed it, and it went sailing high into the blue sky, so high that it became a speck, a darker blue swoop among the clouds, and then a bird.

"Gran!" someone shouted but it didn't matter because Rachel, smiling, was the bird, soaring high above everything below, strong and free, swooping out into space itself.

Free.

Hallie Dunn put her hand on Tara's arm. "I'm so sorry, Ms. Landry."

Tara shrugged off the hand and turned her head away. Tears streamed from her eyes, snot from her nose.

Dr. Wexler said, "We can bury her here in space, or on Prometheus, if you prefer. The ship doesn't have any facilities for long-term storing of—"

"You must be from Polyglot," Tara said, too harshly. "On Galt, we don't bury. We cremate."

"I—"

"We're taking her back to Galt," Tara said, "and putting her ashes in the family vault, next to my father's and mother's and grandfather's ashes. That's what she would want. That's what we're going to do.

"Anything else would just be wrong."

66

NEW CALIFORNIA

By the time the ship reached New California, Martinez had recovered, or told himself that he had. He woke from a deep sleep to find Caitlin asleep in a chair by his bed. Had she been there before? Dimly, he remembered that she had. Slumped in her chair, head thrown back at a weird angle, snoring faintly, she sent through him a wave of tenderness and desire, strong as a perigean tide.

My life will change.

He linked to the bridge. "Captain Martinez speaking. Status report."

DiCaria's voice came from the wrister. "Sir, we're approaching the New Yosemite-New California gate. Are you resuming command?"

"Yes. Proceeding now to the bridge." Damn all doctors. He'd slept, probably drugged, through the entire New Yosemite passage. But he found that now, perhaps as a result of all that sleep, he could rise from

bed and, shakily, dress himself. As he pulled on his
boots, Caitlin woke.

"Luis?"

"Are you all right? Not ill?"

"I'm fine. But you shouldn't—"

"Yes, I should. I'll come to your cabin when I can."

"Dr. Glynn said—"

"I love you," he said roughly, and left.

DiCaria briefed him. The *Green Hills of Earth*
remained at New Yosemite. The *Zeus*, still uninfected
until ordered to become so, had already departed for
New California. There was nothing Martinez could do
right now about Sophia's biolab, wherever it was, but
at least he and Vondenberg could protect the Peregoy
worlds against the Landry epidemic. He linked with
Sean Mueller and New Yosemite Planetary Defense.

This was not going to be an easy explanation.

And at New California, Martinez would have to
explain to Sloan what had happened to his daughter.

"Director, Captain Martinez reporting."

"Luis?" At the message from his wrister, Sloan rose
from the conference table. Fifteen shocked faces swiv-
eled toward him. Why did everyone look so startled?
Then Sloan realized it must be because his own face,
for the first time in months, looked suffused with joy.

He said brusquely, "Irene, carry on with the rest
of the meeting agenda."

"Yes, sir," said Irene Silva, Peregoy Corporation Chief
Operating Officer, not quite keeping astonishment out
of her voice: The director had only just resumed control
of the corporation after the unexplained absences of
both himself and Sophia, and now, at only his second

Board of Directors meeting, he was relinquishing it
again?

Only temporarily, Sloan thought as he strode from
the room to the privacy of his office. Irene Silva had
done a good job as acting CEO, and that was due,
Sloan knew, to his own good management. He'd chosen and trained his executives well. They'd kept the
corporation's complex businesses operating throughout
Sloan's self-imposed sequestration, throughout the
protests that had now virtually stopped. SueLin had
calmed the city enough for Sloan to ease Security
even as he repealed Sophia's arrests and restrictions
and censorship. Irene had carried on ably throughout
Sloan's grief as he learned what Sophia had—

No. Don't think about it.

"Director?" Martinez said from Sloan's wrister.

"I'm here." He activated the wallscreen in his office
and there was Luis's face, thinner and older, dark
rings around his eyes, but *there*.

Here.

Martinez said, "The *Skyhawk* just cleared the New
Yosemite-New California gate. The *Green Hills of Earth*
is in orbit around New Yosemite. The *Zeus* should have
returned to you by now. Sir, I'll be in Capital City
tomorrow and can make a full report then. But first
I need to tell you about Sophia, and I'm afraid it's—"

"I already know," Sloan said, and now there was no
stopping the pain, so piercing that for a moment he
couldn't breathe. He stared blindly at the yellow eyes
of the stuffed wolves across his office, and the light
glinted off them, back at him. Anguish over Sophia
would claw at him the rest of his life. "I sent a scout
to New Utah, and it beat you back here."

Martinez said, "I'm sorry, sir." His tone was gentle, but Sloan heard, too, the relief that Martinez did not have to be the one to tell Sloan of his daughter's treachery, attack, or weird and endless imprisonment in a frozen moment.

Sloan said, "At New Yosemite, did you pick up my reports of conditions here on New California?"

"Yes, sir, I did. Both military and corporate reports."

Reprieved from open emotion, the two men returned to the world of facts and operations, things that could be understood, data that could be put to use. Much would have to wait until they met in person. Then Sloan could tell Martinez of his co-opting of much of Sophia's intel network and dismantling the rest. Of finding, through bribery and intimidation, the location of her weapons biolab on a station in deep space, and destroying it. Of SueLin, still widely perceived to be the CEO of Peregoy Corporation, a situation that could not be allowed to continue much longer. Of the insulting message that had come back with Sloan's scout, from the so-called Movement on New Utah. Above all, of the plan that was desperately needed to keep Peregoy Corporation intact and profitable, while restoring peace to the Eight Worlds.

Martinez would find such a plan. He might pluck it from the vast Terran history that Sloan was, only now, realizing the value of knowing. Or from somewhere else.

Sloan was feeling so old. But he could trust Martinez. Martinez had never been anything but loyal to Sloan, putting first the best interests of the Peregoy worlds. No action of Martinez's—unlike Sophia's—could remotely be considered treasonous.

"Sir, three things you should know," Martinez said. "First, I have one of Rachel Landry's granddaughters as my ally on board the *Skyhawk*. Second, I think you need to cede New Utah to Scott Berman's Movement. Third, very soon everyone on New California is going to be sick with a new plague that I'm going to spread."

EPILOGUE

POLYGLOT

Near the sparsely settled northern pole of Polyglot, in the village of Adarsh, Luis Martinez walked across the savannah. Caitlin ran toward him from a cluster of jeebee nests, stripping off her protective gear as she came. The woman with her turned to watch but stayed at the nests.

"Caitlin!"

"Oh, you! Finally you!"

Their arms went around each other. Five months since they'd last seen each other, five months of society-shaking events on six planets. Everything had changed.

Not everything. He pressed her closer. She said, "I've missed you so."

"Me too. Can we go somewhere to talk?"

"The temple. It's cooler in there."

Heat didn't bother Martinez, but Tara Landry did, still motionless by the jeebee nests, staring at them steadily. Tara was the reason Caitlin lived in this poor, arid, predator-ridden area of Polyglot. For Caitlin, responsible for infecting three Landry worlds with *J. randi mansueti*, there were worse predators on Galt than on Polyglot. Even so, this tiny village was ringed with surveillance and protection. Tara insisted on staying here—something to do with Philip Anderson. Caitlin was here to share mourning over the death of their grandmother, and to keep Tara from breaking up again.

Martinez did not intend for Caitlin to be here much longer.

The temple was empty, its coolness welcome. Unskillful drawings of various gods ornamented the walls, constructed of cheap and durable foamcast. A carved wooden statue of Shiva sat on a stone altar, flanked by dim, bacteria-generated electric lights. A heavy, pungent odor wafted from a bouquet of yellow flowers that Martinez didn't recognize.

He kissed Caitlin again, until she pulled slightly away and looked up at him. "Tara is much better."

"I'm glad," he said, truthfully. A better Tara meant a freer Caitlin.

"It helps her to think she's carrying on Philip's work. He started the jeebee nests, you know. The jeebees keep away the lions, and the villagers sell their nectar."

Martinez didn't point out that a heavy guard around Adarsh kept away "lions" much better than swarms of pseudo-insects. Caitlin knew that. He respected her concern for Tara, but right now, it was Caitlin's other sister that interested him.

"What does Annelise say about conditions on Galt?"

"It's going well. Annelise is implementing some—not all, but some—of the reforms that Gran wanted. I finally got her to work with Ian Glazer, one of the former leaders of the protesters—I told you all that, when we last linked. Annelise could see that she had no choice, not really. A parliament was elected ten days ago, taxes are being levied, some social programs are being planned—Luis, I think you already know all this. I don't believe that the Peregoy intel system isn't operating at full force."

He smiled.

She said, "We Libertarians are becoming more like a corporate state."

"And the Peregoy worlds are becoming more Libertarian. Well, if not that, at least less controlled. New California, too, is holding parliamentary elections soon."

"Sloan Peregoy is still upset that you won't run for prime minister, or whatever you're going to call it?"

"He's an old man, and a stubborn one. He won't accept that I'm a soldier, not a politician, even though deep down he knows that I couldn't get elected if I tried. But Scott Berman might make a good prime minister. He's stubborn, too, but reasonable."

"He'll win your election?"

"Against two Peregoy Corporation executives nobody ever heard of, who are nonetheless tainted with everything Sophia did? Yes."

A child wandered into the temple, goggled at them, and went away, his bare feet leaving damp footprints on the foamcast floor.

Caitlin said, "What about SueLin?"

"She finally managed to convince her adoring public that she doesn't adore them back, won't administer anything, and wants to spend her life raising and showing birds."

"Well, I suppose there are dumber occupations."

"Not many. Caitlin, will you—"

"If Berman wins, are you going to act as his military advisor?"

"Yes. He and I talked about that."

"The power behind the throne."

She hadn't lost the ability to annoy him. "No," he said tersely, until he saw that she was teasing. "Sure. I'll be Cardinal Richelieu, Flavius Aetius, and Edith Wilson all rolled into one."

"You're testing me. Yes, I know who every one of those advisors were."

"I never doubted it."

They gazed at each other; the bantering had suddenly flared into passion.

A woman came to the temple door, calling softly, "Dev?"

Caitlin said, "He was here but he left, Pari."

Pari tossed them a knowing look and strode out in search of the child. Martinez turned back to Caitlin. He hadn't told her that he'd been named Sloan's heir to Peregoy Corporation. Sloan was old but durable as karthwood, and he could still change his mind. OpOrds always evolved over time. Meanwhile, Martinez would advise Scott Berman, if Berman won the hastily arranged election, striving to keep state and corporation in balance while also keeping a military eye on the Landry worlds. Peace treaties, too, could change over time.

"Enough politics," he said, before anyone else could meander into the temple. "Caitlin, will you finally—"

"Yes," she said.

He blinked. "You will?"

"Yes. I can't go back to the university on Galt, or anywhere on Galt. Tara is doing as well here as she ever will. The war is over. So, yes, I'll marry you."

"Not the most romantic acceptance to a proposal."

"It wasn't the most romantic proposal I ever got."

"How many were there?"

"None of your business." She grinned at him, but he found it hard to smile back. There was a lot that hadn't yet been said.

"Caitlin, it won't be easy for you, even now. A Landry living on New California. And I—"

She interrupted him. "Sometimes I think that all human woe comes from othering."

"From what?"

"Othering. Making other people into simplistic others to battle with. Othering."

"I don't think that's a word."

"It should be."

She was stalling, and he wasn't sure why. He pressed on. "It won't be easy for you on New California, and much of the time I'll be away on duty. What will you do?"

He pulled a little away from him, her body taut. "I won't be living on New California. Last week I received the offer of a teaching post at Zuhause University, here on Polyglot. We'll live here, whenever you have leave and can come. It's only a gate away."

He was silent for a long moment. Even without touching her, he could feel the tension in her body, her determination, her desire for him to accept this, to want her enough to agree to her having both him and her own life.

Amy had always followed him everywhere he was posted. But Caitlin wasn't Amy, and he didn't want her to be. Caitlin was herself, and he loved her.

"Yes," he said. "I accept your very unromantic proposal."

She raised her mouth to his, and neither of them would have heard an invasion of villagers, or lions, or anything else.

"The predators always win," Tara said softly to herself, draining nectar from a jeebee nest into a pail. The creatures beat harmlessly against her helmet and face mask.

Hadn't she once said that to Philip, in this very place? Yes, she had. She remembered. She repeated it now, in a soft, childish sing-song. "The predators always win."

No. Not always.

Startled, Tara nearly dropped her pail. "Who said that?"

Was it just in her head? Sometimes it was hard to tell. Only—it had sounded so clear and loud. "Who said that?"

But no answer came.

∽